The Devil's Playground

Charly Cox

hera

First published in the United Kingdom in 2022 by

Hera Books
Unit 9 (Canelo), 5th Floor
Cargo Works, 1–2 Hatfields
London, SE1 9PG
United Kingdom

A CIP catalogue record for this book is available from the British Library.

Print ISBN 978 1 80032 964 5
Ebook ISBN 978 1 912973 95 8

Look for more great books at www.herabooks.com

Printed and bound in Great Britain by Clays Ltd, Elcograf S.p.A.

1

Dedicated in loving memory to Glacier Blue, the best writer's companion a person could ever have had or wanted.

Chapter One

Thursday, April 22

Huddled inside the cramped, darkened closet with her arms tightly wrapped around the children, London Brecken rocked the two of them back and forth, shushing them as quietly as she dared while urging them to cover their ears with their hands, to tune out the muffled screams coming from their mother's bedroom.

Abigail, who'd recently turned three years old, crawled up into London's lap and pressed her wet face into London's neck. 'I want my mommy.' Hiccups punctuated each word and sliced London's heart into ribbons. Battling to keep her own terror at bay, she squeezed Abigail tighter against her.

How had a fun night in with her two best friends turned into the opening scene of a horror film? Half an hour earlier, both she and her friend, Elena – who'd arrived late to the party, as usual – had been watching on with love and amusement as Abigail and her six-year-old brother Carter wheedled five more minutes out of their mother, and when Skye had finally put her foot down and ushered them off to bed, they'd begged London to read them a story. They'd been giggling at her Tigger and Eeyore voices when they'd heard the knock.

Knowing either Elena or Skye would get it, London had continued reading even when the front door slammed with a deafening boom, chuckling along with Carter and Abigail because they'd all jumped at the sound.

Seconds later, their laughter had cut off as abruptly as Elena's sudden terrified scream. All three of them froze as, slowly, London sat up. Without thinking about what she was doing, she lifted Abigail so she could move her to the other side of the bed, farther away from the door and closer to her brother.

Then three things happened simultaneously. The unoiled patio door off Skye's room screeched open, Skye cried out, 'What do you want?' and thundering footsteps raced from the living room down the hall. Filled with pain, Skye's next scream caused arctic fingers of dread to prickle along London's spine. Something or someone fell outside the room, and the sounds of a scuffle, along with Skye's muffled, terror-filled grunts, reached through the walls. London couldn't be sure, but she'd watched enough scary movies to guess her friend had tried unsuccessfully to escape and was being dragged back into her room.

Behind her the bed squeaked, startling a gasp out of London, and she whirled around, half expecting to see another intruder coming in through the window, only to see something slightly less terrifying – Carter flying across the room toward the door. Barely grasping his arm before he could wrench it open, London willed her heart to slow before dizziness overtook her. Gently but firmly, she placed her hand over Carter's mouth and pulled him back with her until the three of them were flush against the wall, partially hidden by a dresser.

Driven now by only one instinct – to shield and protect the children from whatever was happening outside the room – London found herself operating on autopilot as she lowered herself in front of the kids and placed a finger against her lips. Pointing, she directed them to the closet. Carter's wide eyes darted to the door, over to the closet, and then back to his sister and London, making the full circuit twice before, blessedly, obeying her silent instructions. When Abigail's quaking form seemed unable to move, London picked her up and placed her beside her brother.

Before closing the three of them inside, she hurried back across the room, grabbing the extra blanket off the foot of the bed and snatching up Abigail's favorite stuffed animal, an orange hippo she'd named Mr. Orange, and then she switched off the bedside lamp. Doing her best to tune out Skye's horrified whimpers, London squeezed herself into the cramped space and closed the door. With Abigail under one arm and Carter under the other, she whispered assurances that they would be okay, that she would protect them.

From whom she didn't know. All she knew was she could hear two voices, neither of them belonging to her friends, and neither that she recognized.

Slowly, she removed her arm from around Carter who pressed himself closer to her side at the abandonment. Reaching into her pocket for her phone, she cursed softly when she realized she'd left it out in the living room. Tears that had been steadily building finally spilled over, splattering onto her arm.

Her mind whirling with a kaleidoscope of alternative ideas, London stifled the need to scream when each one presented too high a risk of getting caught. If it had only been her, she might've tried, but with Carter and Abigail's lives at stake, she finally had to concede that without a way to call the police, their best option was to pray she and the kids would remain undetected while they waited for the intruders to get what they came for and leave.

Still, with each tormented sound of torture that worked its way into the room, guilt threatened to consume her. The rational part of her brain insisted that staying put to protect the children was the right thing to do. The other part called her selfish and spineless for cowering in the closet.

Without a watch or phone to tell her how long the nightmare dragged on, each second blurred into one ceaseless stream of muffled cries and hoarse screams. Until silence, swift and sudden, crashed around them. Blood pulsing loudly in her ears, London gathered Carter and Abigail's trembling forms even tighter against her and forced herself to remain still. A near impossibility when footsteps moved from Skye's bedroom and paused outside their room. *Please, please don't come in here.* All she had to protect the three of them were plastic hangars.

A dizzying sense of relief swooshed through her when the footsteps moved on. The vibration of Abigail's frantic heartbeat against London's own chest helped her focus on taking deep, quiet breaths as she waited to see if the stillness would last, if the intruders had left.

When an entire eternity passed without sound, she slowly and carefully scooted Abigail off her lap to sit beside Carter who immediately tucked his little arm protectively around his sister. Leaning in close, London whispered, 'I need you both to stay here while I go grab my phone. Do you understand?'

'No, I don't want you to go.' Carter's small fingers bit into London's wrist. 'Please don't leave us in here.'

The pressure in London's chest felt like it might actually explode outward. 'I know, sweetie, and I don't want to, either, but I have to. I promise I'll hurry.' In the dark, she pressed a finger against his lips to silence his next protest. 'I know you're scared, but I have to get my phone so I can call for help. So, no matter what you hear, I need you and Abigail to stay absolutely quiet and wait for me to come back. Do you understand?'

Two little hands touched either side of London's cheeks as Carter brought her head closer to his mouth so he could whisper into her ear. 'How—how will we know if it's you?'

London closed her damp eyes against the fear and confusion in Carter's voice. 'Do you remember when your mom taught you never to trust strangers who pretended to know you? She said anyone who was

4

supposed to pick you up would know the secret password, "*Are you my mudder?*"' A tight fist squeezed her heart remembering how Skye had thought it so adorable when Carter mispronounced the popular P.D. Eastman title. 'So, how about I whisper that when I come back in the room before I open the closet? That way, you'll know it's me. Okay?'

'Promise you'll hurry.'

Even as the promise slipped past her lips, London's stomach soured at the thought of facing the sobering task in front of her. 'I'll hurry back. Promise.' Before she stood, she planted a kiss on top of both Carter and Abigail's heads. Then, pushing to her feet, she winced when her knee popped loudly. Sweaty hand hovering over the doorknob, she sucked in a deep breath and let it out before opening the closet and stepping into the slightly less dark bedroom. Pressing the heel of her hand into her chest in a feeble attempt to still the pounding inside, she moved over to the door where her breathing hammered in and out so fast, she feared she'd either hyperventilate or pass out.

She counted slowly to ten three times before she finally trusted herself to face whatever awaited her on the other side. At a snail's pace, she twisted the doorknob and edged the door open until the slightest bit of light could be seen through the crack. Inch by inch, she slid it further until she could squeeze through. Closing the door softly behind her, she listened for the faint click as it latched, and then she leaned back against the wall, fighting against the clawing need to return to the closet and the kids.

A strange odor drifted her way and instinct had her turning her head even while her subconscious told her to resist. She covered her mouth against the scream that threatened to burst from her at the sight of a blood trail leading from the hallway into Skye's room.

For a precious second, London vacillated, torn between checking on Skye and going for her phone.

Carter's whispered, "Promise you'll hurry" reminded her she didn't really have a choice. The police would know how to help her friend. And right now, the children were her main priority.

Swallowing against the terror threatening to hold her immobile, she held her breath against the smells as she tiptoed toward the living room. She couldn't stop the small mewling sound that escaped when she spotted a spreading pool of thick blood trailing across the tile floor until it reached the edge of the carpet. London's eyes followed it back up until they landed on her friend lying on the floor, her dead stare locked on nothing, and her mouth frozen open on a terrified 'oh.'

She had to move past Elena to get to her phone. Crying, gagging, she forced her feet forward, reminding herself with each step that Carter and Abigail were alone and waiting on her. Just as her shaking hand reached her phone and snatched it to her chest, a loud thud coming from behind her froze London in place.

Her first thought was Carter, and her head swiveled to the hallway, relieved he hadn't disobeyed and followed her out after all. But that meant someone was still inside somewhere. In her peripheral vision, a shadow moved, and she whirled around.

Cold, murderous eyes stared back at her from beneath a dark, hooded cloak. Even as London's brain screamed at her to run, she stood cemented in place. She opened her mouth to yell for help but snapped it closed for fear that Carter would come running. Her mind screeching at her to get away, to draw the danger away from the children, London took a careful step back and then another. If she could get to the kitchen, she could flee through the back door and scream until someone called for help or came to their rescue. But as she took a third step, she slammed into someone else. A small squeak escaped before her neck was wrenched back and a hand clapped over her mouth. The sharp burning sting of a knife plunging into her

6

side ripped away her ability to breathe. As the intruders propelled her down the hall, one of them tore her phone from her hand.

Desperation clawing at her insides, her lungs bursting for air, London allowed herself to be dragged away, praying Carter wouldn't hear the commotion and come investigating on his own to see what was taking her so long. And then every thought scattered as the knife sank deeply into the soft swell of her stomach, causing her to cry out in unimaginable pain.

Chapter Two

Thursday, April 22

The gruesome odor of death and the overpowering, sickening scent of escaped bodily fluids saturating the heavy air inside the house on Greenwood Avenue stung at Detective Alyssa Wyatt's eyes. Wrinkling her nose and breathing only through her mouth, she stepped to the side to allow the videographer to continue recording the crime scene. From information the first responding officer had obtained, it was believed that a single mother of two lived in the home. A laundry basket of toy cars, trains, blocks, and dolls tucked into a corner of the living area told Alyssa the children were young. A fact that chilled her blood as she studied the butchery surrounding her.

Despite her twenty-plus years in law enforcement, she'd never been able to successfully harden herself against some of the atrocious, heinous things that humans inflicted upon one another. In fact, some of those things still haunted her dreams and had her waking in a cold sweat to check on her family. So, though never an easy task, Alyssa knew that forcing herself to think the way a killer might remained one of the things that made her so effective at her job.

Which was why, at almost eleven o'clock on a Thursday night, she stood just inside the doorway of this home, trying to weave together what had happened. Tuning out the voices of emergency personnel all around her, she concentrated on the initial trail of evidence.

Victim number one's body, a young woman, possibly in her early to mid-twenties, lay in the front foyer between the kitchen and living room, her face forever frozen in a mask of confusion, and her mouth opened in a terrified scream – a sound likely cut off when the woman's throat had been slashed nearly ear to ear. Long, smeared streaks of blood along the floor indicated she'd been dragged away from the door, which showed no signs of a forced entry, and led Alyssa to consider that the woman had known her attacker and allowed him inside before being overpowered. The why and who would be something she and her team would have to unravel.

On the counter dividing the kitchen and the living area, two wineglasses – one drained with just a few drops of what was probably a rosé, if the nearby open bottle was any indicator, and the other tipped over on the beige carpet – joined an apparently untouched glass of an amber-colored liquid. A bottle of Jack Daniels rested next to the glass which contained no lip or finger smudges or any other telltale marks that might indicate the person had had a chance to partake of the poured drink.

Spread out near the wineglasses were an array of chips, salsa, and guacamole, now a grotesque, congealed brown. A green chile dip still in its container, a ruffled chip forgotten in the center, perched precariously close to the edge of the counter and held what Alyssa guessed were most likely drops of blood. A shudder rippled along her shoulders at the sight.

Since the one-story house boasted an open floor plan, Alyssa could see both the kitchen and the living area from where she stood. A television mounted on the wall played Pandora in the background. She let her eyes rove the room, drifting upwards toward the ceiling and down along the floorboards and everywhere in-between. Framed children's drawings, along with a mix of well-worn, contemporary, faux leather furniture and scratched, mismatched end tables laden with DVDs of several children's animated movies provided a mental picture of a home filled with love and joy, not the murderous scene before her.

Though the first responding officers had only discovered two adult victims, Alyssa's spine prickled with a sense of dread as she struggled not to allow her mind to jump to the horrifying conclusion that the children might have witnessed the crime before being taken by a monster capable of such savagery. She tried to remind herself that it was entirely plausible that the children who lived there had not been home at all.

She forced herself to stay focused. Letting her mind wander to what-ifs could potentially cause her to overlook crucial details. Traversing the crime markers dotting the floor, Alyssa continued her perusal of the scene by following the faint bloody shoeprints leading from the living room down the hallway. An open door showed a bedroom with a travel bag on the bed.

Just past the first room was the master bedroom where, from the looks of it, the worst of the carnage had taken place. On the wall, the perpetrator had hastily scrawled what appeared to be three letter Fs, presumably using the blood of the second victim, who lay sprawled on the bed, her body far more brutalized than the one in the foyer. Fragments of hair, blood splatter, and skin tissue painted every surface from the headboard to the ceiling, and even a fake plant sitting in the corner. The utter brutality on display led Alyssa to consider this victim to be the true target with the first victim representing a horrible case of being in the wrong place at the wrong time. If she and her team could confirm that, they'd probably have the motive, which might lead them to the identity of the killer.

Victim number two's skirt had been torn from her body, and the ragged fabric now lay against her neck. From the grooved red lines stretching across her face, or what was left of it, Alyssa guessed the skirt had been used as a gag. In its place now was a black, fabric rose that had been shoved inside the woman's mouth. Along with the violent stab wounds on her face that had clearly ruptured the globe of one of her eyes, the woman's chest was a tattered mess of flesh and cloth. In fact, the only part of her upper body seemingly left 'intact' was her right cheek, presumably so her assailant could carve what appeared to be a crude, dagger-like object into it. Alyssa glanced back to the letters scrawled on the wall, wondering what significance the initials held.

If nothing else, the scene inside this room made one thing abundantly clear – the person she was searching for harbored a brutal amount of no longer bottled-up hatred and rage.

On the nightstand near the door, a framed photograph lay face up, the glass cracked. A smiling woman in her late twenties knelt with one arm secured around a giggling little boy while cradling a toddler on her hip. Alyssa glanced from the picture to the woman on the bed. The victim's hair was longer, but even with the damage to her face, Alyssa was fairly certain the woman in the frame and the victim on the bed were one and the same. Once again, her thoughts raced to the children in the hope and prayer that they had not borne witness to their mother's violent death.

'What the—' Alyssa's partner of seven years, Cord Roberts, came up beside her just as she stepped further inside the room, paying careful attention to where her feet landed to avoid unnecessary contamination of the crime scene. Like her, he'd been subjected to witnessing some of humanity at its worst, so Cord's shocked reaction spoke volumes about the intensity and violence of what had taken place inside this house. She didn't have time to respond because another one of their teammates was not so quietly making his way in their direction.

'Jesus, God, and Mother Mary,' Officer Joseph Roe swore loudly as he maneuvered past evidence techs crowding the area. 'Just so you know, the medical examiner just arrived on scene.' Still standing in the doorway of the bedroom, Joe angled his head back toward the living room. 'Can't someone turn that crap off?' The *crap* he was referring to was the classical melody drifting down the hallway from the Pandora app on the television in the living room. 'That sh—stuff doesn't fit with this bloody-ass scene. It's giving me the f—freaking heebie-jeebies.'

Despite the seriousness of what they were dealing with, Alyssa and Cord shared a quick grin with Officer Tony White, Joe's partner and best friend, who was mere steps behind him. For the past month, Joe had been doing his utmost to clean up his language since his two-year-old daughter, Hailee, had begun gleefully repeating everything he said, taking a special amount of joy in reciting his swear words, over and over, while following him around the house. To-date, no amount of sugar, her current kryptonite, worked as a bribe to get her to stop. Both Joe and his wife were torn between amusement and frustration.

Joe turned what could either be a scowl or a twisted smile on Cord. 'Go ahead, ham it up now. But when it's your turn, guess who'll be the one laughing? And *you'll* have *twice* the trouble.'

He was, of course, referring to Cord and his wife, Sara's, now sixteen-month-old twins, Shelley (named after his sister) and Shane. But ribbing each other would have to wait because right now, Alyssa needed her team and everyone on site to focus on what was right in front of them.

The videographer lifted his hand to grab her attention. 'Done in here, Lys. I'm going to hit that last room, and I should be finished up. I'll download the video and email it to you right away.'

'Thanks, Fernando. I appreciate it.'

And she did. Extremely thorough to the point of fanaticism, Fernando made certain he recorded every square inch of a crime scene from the baseboards to the ceiling and everything in between in case there was something that seemed unimportant in the here and now but might prove to be a crucial piece of evidence down the road. Alyssa had been pleased when she'd arrived tonight to find him already beginning the policy-mandated process. With so many officers traipsing through, it was inevitable they'd inadvertently contribute their own DNA, so a recording of the scene, aside from their lapel cameras, remained a crucial piece of any investigation.

She'd just stepped closer to the bed when Fernando's startled yelp stole her attention. With Cord, Joe, and Tony fast on her heels, she bolted out the door and across the hall. It took her brain a second to catch up to what her eyes were seeing because it simply made no sense. Huddled against the wall inside the open closet door, the dark-haired little boy from the photograph – who couldn't be older than five or six – had his right arm draped protectively around the shoulders of the young girl from the photo and whose red, swollen face, wide eyes, trembling lips, and quaking form threatened to shatter Alyssa's composure. Especially when she spotted the little boy's left hand gripping the end of the *Monsters, Inc.* blanket as he tried to wrap it even tighter around their bodies, as if he could hide them from the adults in the room. The irony of a blanket full of monsters symbolically protecting the children wasn't lost on her.

Acid pooled in her stomach as the coffee she'd gulped down on her way to the scene burned a path back up her esophagus. Filled with dread that the children might've witnessed the massacre that had taken place mere steps outside this room, Alyssa's heart didn't just skip a beat; it nearly stuttered to a stand-still.

At the same time, she was overcome with a sudden, profound sense of relief that the children were alive and that she didn't have to worry that they'd been kidnapped by the murderer. A million questions demanding immediate answers churned as her mind tried to conjure up a killer capable of producing the vast amount of carnage in other parts of the house yet conscientious enough to spare two small children. It didn't quite add up or really even seem likely. Neither did it seem likely or logical that two small children could miraculously hide throughout the entire ordeal. Not even an hour in, and this case had already taken a puzzling and disturbing turn.

Her gaze still trained on the children, Alyssa listened as Fernando, who had never stopped recording, explained what had happened. 'I heard a noise and opened the closet thinking… I don't know what I was thinking. I guess that maybe we had another—'

Alyssa's hand shot out, stopping Fernando from finishing that sentence. Even if the children didn't understand what *victim* meant, she didn't want them hearing the word. For a fraction of a second, her mind flashed to the three glasses in the kitchen, but she pushed that aside as she stepped closer to the children.

When tremors rocked the little boy with such fervor that the blanket fell, she immediately halted. With a rush of fury and sadness sweeping through her, she still somehow managed to speak softly. 'My name is Detective Alyssa Wyatt. I'm a police officer. You're safe now. You're going to be okay. No one here will hurt you. Do you understand?'

The little girl glanced up at her brother, but aside from his blink, he gave no indication as to what kind of fear and confusion had to be swirling through his terrified mind.

She tried again. 'Can you tell me your names?'

Nothing. Without taking her eyes off the terrified children, Alyssa ordered Joe to grab the paramedics. Letting her own maternal instincts sneak through to guide her, she addressed the little boy once again. 'I'm going to have someone come in here and take a look at the two of you, just to make sure you're not hurt, okay? Is that your little sister?'

Still nothing. Perhaps, despite her best efforts, her face still displayed the horror of finding the children inside a house full of violence.

Cord, standing beside her, whispered, 'Let me try.'

Alyssa nodded. Among a trillion other things the man seemed to be gold-medal level at, speaking to children ranked high on his list of attributes. Moving slightly in front of her, he crouched down until he reached eye level with the boy, whose scared eyes darted everywhere around the room at once, almost as if he were searching for an escape.

'I'm Detective Cord Roberts. We need to make sure you and your sister aren't injured, okay? Can you tell me if you're hurt anywhere? All you have to do is nod or shake your head, okay?'

Before the little boy even had a chance to answer, the paramedics crowded into the room with everyone else, and his body stiffened as he drew his sister in even closer to him, as if he could absorb her into his own skin and protect her that way.

His bravery in the face of his obvious terror melted Alyssa's heart into a puddle. Overcome with the urge to gather both children into her arms and hug them tight while promising she'd protect them, she thought of how she'd want someone to do the same if it were her own son and daughter, now sixteen and twenty.

Just inside the doorway, the paramedics waited for instruction.

His posture rigid, the little boy swung his gaze over to Cord. 'I want my mom. Where is she?'

Chapter Three

Thursday, April 22

Knowing someone would eventually have to answer the little boy's question, Alyssa felt like she'd been punched in the gut with a sledgehammer. Anger and an even bigger reason for hunting down the person responsible for the bloodbath inside the house helped her to focus.

'What's your mom's name?' Cord asked, and Alyssa wondered if anyone else detected the emotions running just beneath his surface. When the little boy didn't respond, Cord waved his arm behind him. 'All of us here really want to help. I'm sure your mom would want you to tell us your names so we can keep you safe. That's it. Just your names. Can you do that?'

Over the course of her lifetime, Alyssa had witnessed and experienced her share of distrust in others, but not often in children this young, and certainly not to this extent. Of course, what they might've heard or seen tonight would cause even the most hardened person to lose trust in humanity.

Rubbing a fist against his eyes, the little boy pursed his quivering lips. When he finally spoke, his words made no sense. 'What's the code word?'

Cord cocked his head to the side, the only indication he gave for his confusion. 'What's the code word?' Understanding dawned. 'I'm really sorry. I don't know the code word. But I promise we're all here to make sure you're safe,' he repeated.

Whether she trusted Cord or there was more to it than that, the girl finally answered. 'Mommy's name is Skye Isabewa Fweming.'

Mouth rounded into an angry 'oh,' the boy's head snapped down to his sister.

'Skye Isabella Fleming. That's a pretty name,' Cord said. 'I bet she gave you some cool names, too, didn't she?'

The tears that he'd clearly been fighting so hard to hold back finally spilled down the boy's cheeks in little sheets. 'Do you know where my mom is?'

Twice now, he'd mentioned his mom, which was a normal reaction for most children, but Alyssa couldn't help but notice he'd not asked about his father. Her eyes shifted around the room, searching until they landed on a curio shelf where a smaller version of the same picture in the master bedroom rested next to another, more recent family photograph. She guessed the lack of a male presence in either photo indicated the father might not be involved in their lives. Or their mother simply chose not to display those images. It was a line of inquiry she and her team would have to follow.

'I want my mommy.' This time, it was the little girl who made the claim, emphasizing her point by turning her palms toward the ceiling before tilting her head up and whispering in a shaky voice, 'Cawter, I want Mo— Mommy.'

Both Alyssa and Cord latched onto the name the little girl had inadvertently shared. 'Carter. That's a good, strong name. I know you're scared to trust me, and that's okay. Would you mind telling me your sister's name?'

Alyssa knew her partner well enough to understand why Cord had addressed his question to the boy; he wanted to honor Carter's obvious feeling of responsibility as the protective older brother. She imagined he saw something of himself in the little guy.

Pressing herself tighter against her brother's side, the girl answered the question herself anyway. 'I'm Ab-i-gail

Fweming.' She enunciated each syllable clearly. 'Cawter is six. I'm this many.' She held up two fingers, studying them before pushing up a third and showing them to Cord. Alyssa melted a little on the inside.

'Shh, Abigail,' Carter hissed. 'They have to say the *code word.*' The tears that still fell in dirty streaks down Carter's cheeks produced a cloudy film over his widened eyes.

Cord glanced over his shoulder at Alyssa, arching his brows, silently asking her how she wanted him to proceed.

What had happened in this home was difficult enough for Alyssa to process; for a six and three-year-old child, it had to be unimaginable and impossible. But although she would need to find out what Carter and Abigail had witnessed, at this moment, Alyssa, both as a detective and as a mother herself, needed to know the children were physically unharmed. And in order for that to happen, they needed to be checked out by medical personnel. She tipped her head back toward the doorway where the paramedics stood patiently awaiting instructions. Cord nodded his agreement and turned back.

'I tell you what. You don't have to answer any more questions right now, but we still really need to make sure you're not hurt, okay?'

Carter peeked down at Abigail before he reluctantly nodded, much to Alyssa and Cord's immense relief. Even so, when the paramedics moved in, he refused to release his sister's hand, and like him, she refused to let go. Whether he'd been raised to be wary or if it came about because of the night's tragedy, trust was clearly not something the little boy gave freely.

As the paramedics checked their vitals, Carter observed the activity outside the room with disarming intensity. Twice, Abigail peeked up and whispered, 'Ouch, Cawter' when her brother squeezed her fingers a little too tightly. But even then, she didn't attempt to remove her hand from his.

Only when one of the EMTs twisted around, giving Alyssa the all-clear, did the muscles in her shoulders release some of her pent-up tension. Regardless of what they might've witnessed, the children were physically unharmed, and she had to latch onto that fact in order to keep her mind clear of the anger brewing inside her.

'I'm going to step out and call CYFD,' she announced to everyone and no one in particular. According to protocol set in place for these types of situations, as soon as the Children, Youth and Family Division arrived, the state would take custody until a family member willing to provide care for the kids could be located. If none was found, a temporary foster home would be secured instead. For their sake, Alyssa prayed the children wouldn't have to go to a stranger's house. They'd already endured far more in one night than they ever should have had to over an entire lifetime. Taking her phone out of her pocket, she weaved her way past the master bedroom, glancing in as she did, feeling the heat from a fresh wave of horror burn her from the inside out. Continuing down the hall, she pushed her way through the front door.

Outside, her eyes looked past the officers keeping the neighborhood looky-loos at bay behind the yellow crime scene tape and landed on the illuminated Neighborhood Crime Watch sign planted near a bush. Most watches worked together with law enforcement to ensure a safer neighborhood. More importantly, they had assigned roles in order to meet that goal. She made a note to ask the neighbors about it when they canvassed the area.

Before hitting send on the number on her screen, Alyssa took a moment to suck in a cleansing breath of fresh air, both because she needed to clear the stench of death from her sinuses and because with every step that had taken her farther from the room, her emotions at discovering two small children cowering inside the dark closet threatened to overwhelm her.

After placing the call to CYFD and getting an assurance that someone would be sent as soon as possible, Alyssa decided to take advantage of the fresh air to organize the whirring thoughts competing for attention inside her head. When she'd first arrived on scene, it hadn't taken long for her trained eye to ascertain there'd been no forced entry, which had led her to the assumption that victim number one had opened the door to their attacker. Based solely on the degree of assault on the second victim compared to the first, she pictured the assailant dispensing quickly with the first woman before going after his intended victim, the children's mother.

Once again, the three used glasses in the kitchen demanded her attention since only two bodies had been discovered. Could the assailant have already been inside? If that were the case, finding the children alive seemed like an even bigger miracle. For the time being, she allowed for the possibility that one of their deceased victims had enjoyed some wine and had switched to Jack Daniels. But even aside from that, something else tapped at her subconscious. Since she couldn't place her finger on what exactly troubled her, she envisioned the scene inside, mentally walking through as if she'd just arrived.

Despite the violence evident when first entering the home, the living room and kitchen themselves had largely been undisturbed with few signs of a struggle, telling Alyssa it had been short-lived, if there'd been one at all. The shoeprints leading from the foyer down the hallway weren't a large enough imprint for her to determine whether or not their perpetrator was male or female. And she'd been a detective long enough to know that assuming the level of human destruction inside automatically lent itself to a man being involved was dangerous as well as foolish. Over the decades, she'd encountered and arrested her fair share of deranged, bloodthirsty women. Momentarily distracted from mentally retracing her steps when Cord stepped onto the porch, Alyssa lifted her hand to get his attention and watched as his long strides ate up the distance in half the time it would've taken the average person. A perk of being six-foot-two, she supposed.

'That got a little intense in there. Doing okay? Or is that a stupid question?' he asked when he was within a foot of her.

Just like that, a light bulb went off inside Alyssa's head, and she knew what thing had been prodding its way in, trying to grab her attention. Forgetting he'd asked her a question, Alyssa headed to the side of the house, but she'd only managed a few steps when Cord touched her arm, halting her.

'Something I said?'

Still distracted, Alyssa shook her head and explained. 'Sorry. Something's been making my neck itch, and I think I just figured out what it is. The glass door off the master bedroom wasn't entirely closed, which could mean nothing at all, but I want to check it out before I head back inside.'

'Maybe the assailant didn't come through the front door,' Cord suggested. 'Maybe he entered through the bedroom.'

'Possibly, but I don't think so. Too many issues with the positions and state of the victims' bodies.'

Taking advantage of the floodlights surrounding the scene, Alyssa led the way to the patio, stopping outside the door. One of the blinds was stuck, as if someone had left in a rush. Earlier, when she'd been standing in the room, she'd heard a faint whistling sound, and she realized now it had been the breeze making its way in through the slight opening. Stepping closer, she shined her flashlight up and down, trying to scratch that itch that told her there was something important here she needed to find.

And then she did. On the blinds, about halfway down, a faint but bloody smudge smeared in a descending arc, as if someone had tried to grab onto them as the blinds slipped from her grip. Silent, Alyssa trailed her light along the wooden slats of the deck, but aside from that bloody print, nothing else stood out. Well, the grass was trampled, but that could've been a by-product of all the foot traffic on scene or something else. But the more she studied it, the more it looked as if the grass had been trampled *away* from both the house and the alley, not toward. Regardless, she'd make sure the evidence techs gathered what they could.

'What're you thinking?' Until Cord spoke, she'd actually forgotten for a moment that he'd followed her.

She pointed. 'You tell me.' She wasn't trying to be coy; she just wanted him to share his thoughts and opinions without influencing him with her own.

'I see what looks to be a smudged handprint.' He cocked his head to the side and squatted down for a closer inspection before rising back to his full height. 'Maybe the second victim heard or saw something and tried to escape through here before being caught.'

'The same thought crossed my mind,' Alyssa said. 'However, based on the photographs I spotted, I'm assuming the victim in the bedroom is Carter and Abigail's mother, and to think she'd try to escape that' – she pointed inside – 'while leaving her children at the mercy of a sadistic killer doesn't feel right. Clearly, she was the type of person who taught her children not to speak to strangers unless that person knew the "code word," and that alone opposes the idea she'd abandon her children for the sake of securing her own safety.'

'Unless she knew the kids were safe and she was going for help.'

'Why not call the police instead? I spotted a phone on top of the dresser. If nothing else, she could've grabbed that on the way out,' Alyssa countered.

Cord fell silent as he nodded, agreeing with her assessment, so she decided to fill him in on that other little niggling voice that wouldn't stop nudging her. 'Something else that's bothering me. I noticed three glasses in the kitchen which would suggest three people had been drinking, yet only two victims were discovered. What happened to the third person, and was it the attacker or just someone who left before tragedy struck?'

'I saw that, too. But you know it's possible one of the victims simply switched from wine to whiskey and used a different glass for both.' Cord's explanation felt like he'd plucked it straight from her earlier thoughts. 'Backing up to the topic of Carter and Abigail's safety, I assume you were able to reach someone at CYFD?'

Alyssa rolled her eyes, not in response to her partner's question, but because of the CYFD's reaction to her call. 'Yes. And they said they'd send someone "as soon as they can." Because, you know, there could be something out there more important than getting two small children somewhere safe after a night of terror and trauma.' Frustration mixed with disgust deepened her growl into a less than feminine timbre.

Cord's scowl replaced the look of concern that had been etching deep lines into his forehead. '*When they can? Seriously, what the hell?*' Movement from the side of the yard interrupted his mounting frustration and snagged their attention, and the two of them turned in unison to watch as two paramedics carried Carter and Abigail over to a waiting ambulance that would most likely escort them to the University of New Mexico Hospital where they'd undergo another, more thorough, round of examinations and observations.

Though Carter and Abigail's faces were pressed into the paramedics' shoulders, most likely in an effort to prevent the children from seeing the carnage in the house, both of their hands were still tightly linked together. After being placed inside the ambulance with his sister beside him, Carter leaned forward as his neck jerked back and forth as if he were searching for someone, possibly his mother. When he caught sight of Cord, Alyssa swore the little boy's shoulders relaxed the tiniest bit. But then Carter pulled his sister onto his lap and wrapped his arms around her, and Alyssa turned away so she could swallow around the orange-sized lump lodged in her windpipe.

Cord cleared his throat. 'Hey, listen, maybe I shouldn't have done this, but before I came out, I asked Carter if he'd seen anything tonight. To be honest, I didn't expect him to answer, but he kind of did.'

Alyssa's eyebrows lifted into a vee of confusion. 'What do you mean "kind of"?'

'Well, he shook his head no, but he hesitated just long enough for me to wonder if he was being completely honest.'

Alyssa wanted to delve deeper into Cord's observation, but a red-haired woman she recognized from past cases strolled up the sidewalk, her demeanor indicative of a person used to being in charge and expecting others to fall into line as she saw fit. Rosemary Covington, the CYFD investigator, had taken less time to arrive than Alyssa had predicted.

Covington signaled for the officer closest to her, flashed her credentials, and ducked beneath the yellow crime scene tape as the officer glanced over his shoulder before pointing her in Alyssa and Cord's direction. It took just a few seconds for the woman to traverse the small yard and reach them.

Just as she had the other times they'd encountered each other at crime scenes involving children, Covington offered a nod as greeting and dived right in. 'I saw the children sitting in the ambulance. The call I received claimed no injuries were found.' Rosemary posed the statement with an almost accusing slant to her tone.

'There were no signs of physical abuse in the initial exam,' Cord verified.

'What are their names, and how much of the crime did they witness?' The investigator lifted her head to stare up at Cord before moving her gaze back down to Alyssa. At five-foot-nine – eleven in the platform sandals she wore – she towered over Alyssa's own five-foot-three-inch height.

'Carter and Abigail Fleming are their names, and we don't know what they may have seen or heard.' Cord's attitude, abrupt in a way that was out of character for him, had Alyssa glancing up, but in the shadow of the night, she found it difficult to read his face.

Covington blew out a puff of air. 'Did you *ask*?'

Alyssa couldn't decipher the woman's tone, so she didn't know if the CYFD investigator was annoyed or merely gathering information for her records.

Cord's head jerked down in a quick nod. 'I did ask, but Carter denied witnessing anything. I just finished telling my partner that something about the way he hesitated tells me he may not entirely be telling the truth. We're hoping we'll be able to get a clear-cut answer when we interview them later.'

Rosemary swapped her laser-like stare from Cord over to Alyssa as if she were trying to bore a hole into the center of her forehead. 'I know you've got experience with safe-house interviews, but when was the last one you did?'

While Alyssa herself could be direct and appreciated it in others, she found the woman's mannerisms mildly grating, not to mention a bit cold. Still, she kept her patience in check. She didn't have to harbor warm, fuzzy feelings toward the CYFD investigator. After all, the woman's mannerisms could stem from years of practice separating her emotions from the situations she encountered. On top of that, it was possible Covington was slightly preoccupied with all the necessary legal steps required to make certain the children were safe.

But before Alyssa or Cord could answer, Covington waved her hands in the air to dismiss her own question. 'Never mind that for now.' She peeked at the watch on her wrist. 'I highly doubt you'll get to interview them tonight, anyway. I imagine the children are not only traumatized, but exhausted.' This time, her voice softened, leaving Alyssa feeling better about her. 'Okay, give me a quick rundown on what occurred here, or at least what you can tell me, and then I'll go talk to the paramedics.'

'All we can say for now is that we have two victims, and the children were asking about their mother,' Alyssa began. Then, tag-teaming, she and Cord gave a brief rundown on what had transpired inside the house, being careful not to share certain details with the investigator that she didn't yet need to be privy to. When they finished, Alyssa asked, 'Where will you be taking them after they leave the hospital?'

'Until we find placement, our main center. I assume you're familiar with it?'

'We are,' Alyssa said. 'Both Detective Roberts and I will be present for the interview.' She had a feeling Cord's presence would help put the children at ease, marginally at least.

Rosemary nodded once. 'I have your number, so I'll let you know when we're ready. As is our protocol, Carter and Abigail will be transported to UNMH where they can be checked out more thoroughly. As I mentioned earlier, that will, of course, take precedence over your interview, I'm afraid. I'm sure you can understand that their physical wellbeing needs to be tended to first.'

'Of course,' Alyssa said at the same time Cord responded with, 'Absolutely.'

'I'll contact you as soon as the hospital staff gives the all-clear.' Without offering a goodbye, Rosemary turned and weaved her way back through the officers crowding the lawn until she'd reached the ambulance.

As soon as Covington moved away, Alyssa pointed to one of the neighbor's houses. 'According to Captain Hammond, Mrs. Lillian Holt called 911 at approximately ten tonight to report that she thought something bad might've happened to her neighbor. But all Dispatch could get out of her was that there might be a body in the doorway. I know a couple of officers already spoke to her earlier when they first arrived, but why don't we head on over now and see what else we can find out?'

'Let's get it done. I'll text Joe to let him know what we're doing.' As he fell into step beside her, automatically matching his stride to hers, Cord pulled out his phone and shot off a message. 'Sent,' he said, shoving his phone back into his pants and then patting his jacket to make sure he had his ever-present notebook and pen.

Even as they drew closer to the neighbor's house, Alyssa couldn't get the image of Carter and Abigail asking for their mommy out of her head. Though it wouldn't bring their mother back, she would move heaven and earth to find out what had happened because *that* was something she *could* do.

Chapter Four

In the driver's seat, Draven shifted left then right, his knees bouncing so hard that the van incessantly jerked from the constant acceleration and deceleration. The sweat from his hands coated the now wet steering wheel, making it glisten each time they passed beneath a streetlight. The way his fidgeting fingers continuously strayed to pluck at the loose threads on his clothing annoyed Mara because it was interfering with the high she'd achieved from the magical drug cocktail they'd both taken before they'd killed two people.

Whether his nerves came from the aftermath of what they'd done, the unexpected but exciting glitch to their plan, or the hit of acid they'd done beforehand wreaking havoc with his head, she couldn't say. Regardless, he needed to get it together – and fast – before a police cruiser spotted them weaving all over the road.

Leaning to the side, she twisted around so she could peer into the back where their prisoner lay bound and gagged with strips of an old, discarded velvet dress Mara had found in the corner of the van. After securing the girl's hands and feet, she'd pulled a dirty, wadded-up paper towel from beneath the passenger seat and crammed it into the girl's mouth before securing it with more of the velvet strips. In essence, the currently unconscious girl was trussed up tighter than a Thanksgiving turkey. And she planned on taking her sweet time carving her up. But that couldn't happen if they got stopped by the police first.

The unexpected appearance of others inside the house had taken Mara by surprise, but as her dagger had stabbed the woman in her side, the idea of snatching her instead of killing her had grabbed hold almost instantly. Without vocalizing her intent, Mara had begun dragging the woman down the hall, and Draven, seeming to intuitively understand, had moved to assist. To ensure the woman wouldn't slip free before they could get her to the van, Mara had stabbed her again, stopping herself from plunging her knife all the way to the hilt because killing their prey right away would've defeated the purpose of taking her in the first place.

After securing her inside the van, Draven had moved to throw out the phone he'd snatched from her hands, but Mara had stopped him. The police would search the dumpster and she didn't want them finding the phone and wondering about it. So she'd suggested a slight detour first so they could fling it over the bridge and into the river before taking their prisoner somewhere no one would ever think to search.

Excited that they'd have more time to act out their fantasies, Mara closed her eyes so she could relive what they'd already done. After parking in the dark alleyway outside the house, Draven had curled his lips into a lazy smile. When his glazed eyes drifted over to her, his smile became a full-blown grin.

In a drawl that suggested they were going to brunch rather than killing someone, he said, 'I'm ready to do this. You knock on the front door as a distraction while I sneak in the back.' His fiery gaze danced from her to the house and back again. 'Ready?'

Her neck felt disconnected from her body as her head bobbed up and down. Quietly, they'd climbed from the van, making sure the doors remained unlocked.

While he'd crept around to the back, Mara had checked the neighbors' houses and the street before raising the hood of her cloak and approaching the front door. The charged energy zipping through her bloodstream invigorated her. And then the door opened...

In the back of the van, the woman moaned, wrenching Mara back just as her replay had reached the really good stuff. She swiveled her legs to the side and swung around as their prisoner slowly regained consciousness. Mesmerized by the confusion and terror flittering across her features as she struggled to loosen and dislodge her gags and bindings, Mara giggled. When the woman's wide-eyed, horror-filled gaze darted in her direction, Mara's giggle turned to outright laughter. She had a feeling this one would be more fun than their intended target, Skye Fleming.

While Mara had noticed Skye from the beginning, she herself had been invisible to the other woman. Watching Skye throw her head back in laughter, her straight, dark hair cascading over her shoulder and showcasing that long, sleek neck, Mara had decided in that moment what she wanted – needed – to do. When she'd shared her idea with Draven, the excitement in his eyes triggered her own.

During the days leading up to the event, she found it difficult to keep her mind focused on work or anything else. Though there'd been just a tiny space in her head warning her that killing another human may not live up to the hype she'd created in her own mind, in the end, the reality had been intensely electrifying and far more gratifying than the fantasy. *And* had gotten them an unexpected bonus. At the reminder, her Skye-fueled fantasy tumbled away, and she again turned her attention to the woman now attempting to scream through her gag.

Even more eager to reach the place where she and Draven could take their time and savor every moment, Mara forced herself to turn back around to the front. The combination of adrenaline and drugs amped up her awareness, and she was a little afraid if she continued watching the woman, she'd end up acting in haste. And now that she'd had an actual taste of the real thing, she didn't want to risk it. Still, she lowered the sun visor to a position where the lighted vanity mirror allowed her small glimpses of the terrified woman. Feeling the weight of Draven's stare, Mara caught his eyes as they bounced between the road and their victim, and in that moment, she knew she wasn't alone in her enthusiasm to reach their secret hideaway.

Chapter Five

The Holt house, similar to many of the others in this not-the-best but definitely not-the-worst neighborhood east of South Valley was an older, single-story home most likely built in the late forties or fifties. Despite its age, it had been kept up over the years. All along the porch and the front windows, window-sill planters overflowed with fragrant purple, yellow, and fuchsia pansies.

Disappointed but not necessarily surprised when she noted the absence of security cameras, Alyssa knocked, raising her badge when a teen's face appeared in the rectangular picture window. A few seconds later, the door opened to a woman who appeared far younger than Alyssa had expected, and it took her a second to realize the person in front of her wasn't another teenager.

'What's going on over there? What happened? Are the kids all right? I saw the paramedics carrying them to the ambulance. What about Skye?' As she fired her questions, barely pausing to take a breath in between each one, the woman's eyes drifted to the police activity next door. When she finally dragged her gaze away, she shivered and gathered her navy-blue Air Force hoodie tighter around herself.

'Are you Mrs. Holt?' Alyssa asked.

Her voice unsteady, the woman answered before repeating her earlier question. 'Yes, I'm Lillian Holt. I'm the one who called 911 earlier. What's happening? Two

32

officers stopped by earlier asking who lived over there but said they couldn't tell us anything when I asked.'

Alyssa's first thought was to wonder why Lillian Holt had chosen to remain indoors if she was so eager to find out what had happened. More often than not, she found that the more police activity outside a residence, the larger the crowd, *especially* if there was the possibility of bodies being brought out. Despite – or perhaps because of – the fact Mrs. Holt had been the one to call emergency services, her absence from the other curious onlookers threw up a small red flag for Alyssa. While it wasn't entirely unheard of, it was highly unusual for a close neighbor to ignore the opportunity to grab juicy snippets of inform- ation so they could pass it along like the kid's game of telephone; by the time the information reached the end, it would be entirely skewed, but would still fan the flames of the rumor mill.

'I'm Detective Wyatt,' Alyssa said, 'and this is Detective Roberts with APD. We'd actually like to talk to you about your call. Do you mind if we come in and ask a few questions?'

Mrs. Holt glanced over her shoulder then back at Alyssa and Cord before she finally nodded and stepped back, inviting them in. 'Of course. We'll try to be as helpful as possible, but I'm not sure what… I mean, like I said, I don't even know what happened. We were concerned, so that's why we called in the first place.'

'We appreciate anything you can tell us,' Cord assured her as he followed Alyssa inside.

Mrs. Holt closed the door and twisted around to intro- duce the teen standing rigidly against a wall, his eyes darting from his mother to the detectives to the windows, repeating the circuit almost as if he had a nervous tic. 'This is my son, Kenny.'

Impressed when the young man stepped forward, arm extended to shake their hands with a firm grip, Alyssa smiled.

'Nice to meet you,' he said. 'Or, I mean, not like nice, but…' Kenny's face shifted through a multitude of shades as he stepped back and let his words hang in the air.

Alyssa turned to Mrs. Holt. 'I noticed there's a Neighborhood Watch sign in front of your neighbor's yard. Are you a part of that as well?'

Lillian Holt sighed and rubbed her head. 'No, not anymore. I mean, none of us are, really. The signs are left over from before. The couple in charge of running it moved to Florida about six months ago to be closer to their grandchildren. Some of us tried to keep it going, but fewer and fewer people attended the meetings until it just kind of dissolved on its own. Most of us chose to take our signs down, but Skye liked having hers up. She said it made her feel safer, like it deterred would-be criminals.' With jerky movements, Lillian removed a tissue from her pocket and blew her nose loudly before excusing herself to toss it in the trash.

Alyssa hid her frustration, realizing she'd been subconsciously counting on an active neighborhood watch to provide possible witnesses. 'Is there anyone else home with the two of you tonight? We'd like to make sure we speak to everyone.'

Shaking her head, Mrs. Holt's eyes darted to the left before her wringing hands moved up to clutch the neckline of her sweatshirt. 'No. Um, just Kenny and myself. I'm divorced. My ex-husband lives in Oregon now, and August, my oldest son, no longer lives here – not that he was home much when he did. Even if he *did* still live here, he probably wouldn't have been able to tell you anything because he didn't really know Skye since he preferred to keep to himself. If he wasn't out, he stayed holed up in his room. And anyway, ever since he got together with his girlfriend, we don't even hear from him unless he needs something, usually money.' Her lips tightened into an angry line. 'In fact, the last time I saw him was last month when he came by to ask if I'd cover his share of the rent.

I told him no because I could clearly see he was high on drugs.' Mrs. Holt's eyes suddenly widened as if afraid she'd shared too much. Her back stiffened, and she jutted her chin out. 'But like I said, he hasn't been around for several weeks now, and Skye was simply someone he nodded to on occasion, if they both happened to be outside at the same time.'

If Mrs. Holt's eldest son had a drug habit that forced him to ask for money – that his mother had refused – was he also the kind of person capable of breaking into his ex-neighbor's house and committing murder? Even though Mrs. Holt insisted her son hadn't been around for several weeks, Alyssa decided it might not hurt to speak to him anyway, just to be thorough. She considered asking Mrs. Holt for August's contact information, but something stopped her. She shifted her hand slightly to the left so she could tap Cord's leg, knowing he'd understand she wanted him to write down August's name. From the corner of her eye, she noted his nearly imperceptible nod.

Mrs. Holt, her demeanor still tense but decidedly less defensive, dropped her arms and pressed her clasped hands into her stomach. 'Um, shall we stand here, or do we sit? I guess I'm not familiar with the protocol here.'

'Wherever you're most comfortable, ma'am.'

Mrs. Holt glanced once toward her living room before changing her mind and leading Alyssa and Cord toward the kitchen table and inviting them to sit. As they followed behind the Holts, Alyssa took the opportunity to note their shoe sizes, mentally comparing them to the bloody imprints left in the carpet of their neighbor's house.

As Cord extracted his notebook and flipped to a clean page, noting the date and time at the top, Alyssa began the interview. 'Earlier, you asked about the children and Skye. Those are your neighbors?' Of course, she already knew the answer, but preferred to have it verified anyway.

Kenny nodded. 'Yeah. Skye Fleming and her kids, Carter and Abigail.'

'What about their father?' Cord asked.

Kenny shook his head. 'No dad in the picture. Skye never really talked about him.'

Considering Skye and the children shared the same last name, Alyssa's curiosity was piqued. 'Do you know if Skye was ever married to Carter and Abigail's father?'

Kenny's brows shifted together as he thought about it. 'I didn't think so, but now that you mention it, I guess I don't know.' He looked to his mom, but she shrugged and shook her head.

The scratching sound of Cord's scribbling pen across paper had Alyssa sneaking a quick peek to see that her partner had written *ex-husband*, following it with several question marks.

Even though a multitude of possibilities existed as to why Skye had never discussed the children's father, a scorned lover or an enraged father was just one of several avenues she and her team would have to explore.

'Mrs. Holt, when you called 911 tonight, you said you were concerned that something may have happened to your neighbor. You mentioned there might've been a body lying in the doorway. Tell us what you saw that made you think that.'

Lillian Holt kneaded her fingers together like she was weaving them into a basket. 'Well, that was more Kenny, so I'll let him explain.'

With everyone's attention now entirely focused on him, Kenny wiped his palms up and down his pants until he realized he was doing it. Pink eked its way back into his cheeks as he lifted his hands from his legs to funnel them through his thick hair, tugging on the ends before dropping them back onto his knees only to reach into his pocket and grab his phone, holding onto it as if it were his lifeline.

Though not her strongest trait, Alyssa waited patiently while the teen tried to get his anxiety under control. Admittedly, her patience stemmed more from the fact that his fumbling allowed her the ability to openly scrutinize his hands, but she spotted no obviously recent wounds that might indicate his actions stemmed more from guilt than nerves.

Expelling a deep, raggedy breath, Kenny finally started talking. 'Okay, so well, about eight thirty tonight, I headed over to my girlfriend's house. I was running late because I helped a buddy of mine fix the brakes on his car, and time got away. So, my girlfriend was all kinds of pissed by the time I got there, and I was trying to get her to chill so she wouldn't be ragging on me all night, you know?'

Alyssa nodded even as she watched for any of the normal tells that a person was lying, such as sudden changes in his speech pattern, constantly shifting the direction of his eyes, or excessive fidgeting. Of course, she was fully aware that talking to the police often caused the same nervous habits in both the guilty and innocent.

'Like, I said sorry a dozen times, but she was all like, "Forget it. Why don't you just leave" and stuff like that. So, I did.' When Kenny once again tunneled his hands over and through his hair, Alyssa feared the teen risked acquiring a wide bald spot by the end of this interview. 'When I got home, I was wound pretty tight, so I went for a walk to try to clear my head.' He shot an irritated sideways glance in his mother's direction. 'She doesn't like it when I drive upset. She thinks I'll cause an accident or something.'

Lillian Holt shrugged unapologetically. 'He rammed my truck into the garage once when he was distracted over a girl.'

Like any typical teenager, Kenny rolled his eyes and muttered something about 'once' and 'get over it already' under his breath. 'Anyway, about two blocks into my stroll, the idea of bouncing it off Skye to, you know, get a woman's take on the situation, occurred to me. So, I headed back and knocked on her door. When no one answered, I waited a minute or two, and then left.'

Cord stopped writing. 'And what time was that?'

'Um, maybe between nine thirty, nine forty or so? I don't really know.'

'That's all right,' Cord assured him. 'Do you remember if the lights were on in Skye's house when you knocked?'

Kenny's head bobbed up and down. 'Yes, sir.'

Cord waited a beat before he asked for clarification. 'Yes, as in you remember, or yes, they were on?'

'Both.' Kenny's tone hinted that he'd thought his answer had been obvious and that Cord was a little slow.

'And you didn't think it was odd that the lights were on and no one answered?' Alyssa asked, pulling the teen's attention to her.

The lines in Kenny's face deepened as he stared at her. 'No. She could've been putting the kids to bed or whatever.'

Alyssa nodded. 'Go on with what you were saying. You knocked, no one answered, and then what?'

'Well, I thought about going home, but I was still too coiled, so I figured maybe I should walk around the block one more time. It actually helped, but as soon as I turned on our street, I got a text from my girlfriend saying maybe we should see other people, and so I was distracted and didn't see the van coming from the alleyway until it almost hit me.'

Cord's spine stiffened. 'The alley beside Skye's home?' he clarified.

'Yeah. But, like, loads of people leave their cars there and head over to different parties in the hood, you know. Like, that's chill. Nobody really cares. It's not unusual to see, like, half a dozen or more cars there, but that's usually on the weekends. Skye has Fridays off, so her weekends start on Thursday.'

Though the mention of a possible vehicle leaving the scene raised enough red flags to entice half a dozen bulls, something else Kenny said troubled Alyssa as well. Not only had the teenage boy sought out Skye's advice at an odd hour, he seemed to know her schedule, too. Considering Skye had to be at least close to a decade older than him, that relationship begged further exploration. Years of experience allowed her to pose her question in a non-accusatory tone. 'You and Skye sound like you were quite close. Tell us about your relationship with her.'

Kenny's eyebrows clapped together almost comically. 'What do you mean my relationship? She's my neighbor. Like, that's all. I have – had – have, whatever, a girlfriend.'

'Yet, you felt comfortable enough to, how did you put it' – though she didn't need to, Alyssa peeked at Cord's notes – '*get a woman's take on the situation*, and you chose to go to Skye.'

'Like, what other woman was I going to ask? My mom?' Practically choking on the words, Kenny's face told Alyssa he'd rather eat slugs.

'Did you talk to Skye often about things that troubled you?'

Clearly confused, Kenny nodded slowly. 'Well, yeah. I mean, not often, but yeah, sometimes, sure. Mostly about girl-trouble stuff.'

Alyssa waited.

But it was Lillian Holt who came to her son's rescue with a biting, scathing tone that underscored her displeasure with Alyssa's line of questioning. 'I can assure you, Detective, that my son's *relationship* with Skye was purely innocent and platonic.'

Kenny's face blanched as his mother's growled words flipped on the lightbulb for him.

'He initially got to know her when Kenny and some friends were playing football in the front yard, and Carter came over to watch. Later that afternoon, after Kenny's friends had left, he spotted Carter sitting on the grass, bouncing a soccer ball against the side of the house and asked Carter if he could join him. Apparently, Skye had been watching from the window, saw Kenny approach, and came out. To cut this story and this ridiculous *insinuation* of yours short, Skye appreciated how my son took time out of his teenage life to teach a little boy how to toss a football. When Carter joined a youth league, he asked Kenny to attend his games. Kenny did when he could. And that was *all* there was to it.'

From both the tone of Lillian Holt's voice and the horrified – and somewhat disgusted – expression on Kenny's face, Alyssa believed her. And though her question had clearly upset the two of them, she'd had to ask. Nodding that she was satisfied, she returned to the subject of the van Kenny had seen. 'Tell us about this van you mentioned a few minutes ago. Was it one you'd seen before in the area?'

Kenny shrugged, clearly still embarrassed. 'Naw. I mean, it might've been in the alley when I was heading out to see my girlfriend, but like I said, I don't usually pay attention to the cars parked there.'

'I'd really like you to think back and try to recall if that van was there when you left at eight thirty,' Alyssa said.

The corners of Kenny's mouth turned down as he closed his eyes only to jerk his head from side to side before reopening them. 'I'm sorry. I just don't remember one way or the other.'

Alyssa needed to narrow down the timeline of events, but she decided not to continue pressing the issue right away because she didn't want Kenny claiming he'd seen something that he hadn't. In the spirit of wanting to help, potential witnesses had a habit of claiming things they assumed authorities wanted to hear, which only served to lead them down the wrong path. 'Can you describe the van you saw? Was it cargo or passenger? Did you happen to note the color or a license plate?' Anything might prove to be helpful down the road.

The muscles in Kenny's face relaxed. 'Light-colored cargo van, not white and not quite yellow. At least that's how it looked under the streetlights when it drove away. Anyway, it was an older model and had a few dings and rust spots on it. It was pretty dark out, so I can't really be sure about that. And it never occurred to me, you know, to get a look at the plates. I'm sorry.'

'That's okay, man. Keep going,' Cord said. 'What time was this when the van almost hit you?'

Kenny snapped his phone off the table and performed some kind of one-handed, complicated swipe to unlock it before tapping the screen and turning it so Alyssa and Cord could see the timestamp. 'Nine forty-eight. That's when Breanna—uh, that's my girlfriend's name, Breanna Duncan, in case you need that. I can give you her number and whatever, too, if you need it. Anyway, that's when she sent me the text.' The muscle ticcing wildly in his jaw made it obvious he was still sore about being dumped, especially in such an impersonal way.

As a mom to a teenage boy, Alyssa couldn't help but feel a twinge of sadness for Kenny, but in that moment, she'd never been so grateful for this generation's reliance on phones or for their occasional lack of tact because it helped her compile a crucial timeline of events.

'Her contact info would be great,' Cord said. 'Thanks.'

'Can I ask a question?' Kenny leaned forward.

'Sure, go for it,' Cord said.

'So, if you talk to Breanna, and she full-on craps out that I wasn't with her or something because she's still hell-a-mad, you can verify I'm telling the truth by, like, triangulating my calls or tracking my location by the cell towers or whatever, right?' Kenny jutted his chin toward the living room where a muted television streamed a popular crime show.

Not quite used to the teenage lingo, it took Cord a moment to mentally translate. Alyssa could tell the second it clicked because of the effort it took her partner to hold his amusement at bay. Like so many others, Kenny compared real life policing to the way it played out on television and in the movies. If only it were ever that simplistic.

'We'll be able to verify your whereabouts, for sure,' Cord reassured him. 'So, this van came out from the alley beside Skye's house and almost hit you. Did you get a look at the driver?'

Instead of answering, Kenny's eyes widened suddenly, and Alyssa rotated so she could see what had stolen his attention. Across the room, a window peeked into Skye's yard where paramedics were currently carting out one of the bodies, encased in a body bag. She knew it had to be the victim in the front room because it would take much longer to process the second victim before they were able to move her. Which was a good thing because it would give Alyssa and Cord another chance to look things over when they finished the Holt interview.

In an effort to redirect Kenny's attention, Alyssa repeated Cord's question. 'Kenny, did you get a look at the driver of the van?'

He swallowed and pointed to the window. 'Is that... is that Skye?'

Alyssa knew they'd have to answer the question of what had happened eventually but now wasn't the time because they still needed answers, so she answered truthfully, at least as far as she knew. 'No, it's not.' Again, she repeated the question, this time stressing his name to divert his attention from the window. 'Kenny, did you get a look at the driver?'

Reluctantly, the teen dragged his wide-eyed stare away from the scene next door. 'No, ma'am. I was still pretty distracted.'

His response disappointed but didn't surprise her. 'Okay, at nine forty-eight, the van almost hits you, but you didn't place the call to 911 until ten. What happened between those two times?'

Kenny's throat bobbed up and down as he swallowed. 'So, after the text from Breanna and after the van almost hit me, I realized Skye's lights were still on, so I figured I'd try again to go bend her ears since she's a really good listener.' His eyes darted back to the window. Within seconds his legs began to bounce before the rest of his body, trembling violently, joined in. Scooting back his chair, he pressed his shaking hands down onto his knees, which didn't help in the least.

'Kenneth, please.' Lillian Holt covered her son's hands with her own. 'You're shaking the entire table.' To Alyssa, she said, 'I'm sorry. I only know about how these things work through the television shows I watch, so forgive me for asking, but do I need to call a lawyer?' Her tone suggested she still hadn't let go of her earlier irritation.

Alyssa's eyebrows drew together. 'That's your call, Mrs. Holt. Right now, all we're doing is trying to get an understanding of what occurred tonight, and as you and your son are the ones who called 911, we wanted to speak to you first.'

Five seconds, then ten ticked off before Lillian finally nodded her consent for Kenny to continue. Alyssa breathed a quiet sigh of relief.

'Anyway, I started to knock on Skye's door, and that's when I realized it wasn't latched, but I swear it had been closed earlier – but, like, I couldn't *swear* swear.'

Alyssa interrupted. 'The front door?' she clarified.

'Yeah.' Like he had when he'd answered Cord's question about the lights being on, Kenny drew the word out, making it clear he thought his answer had been obvious. 'Anyway, no one was moving around, and I don't know… Like, I didn't *feel* anyone moving and didn't hear anyone inside, and I don't know, it was just so *still*. I just got this seriously creeped-out vibe.'

'I'm not sure I'm following,' Cord admitted while Alyssa's mind fixated on the knowledge that both the front and bedroom doors were open. It made sense that the perpetrator would enter through the front and exit out the back to more easily avoid detection. She doubted the alleyway would contain any cameras, but she made a note to check it out.

'I don't know how else to explain it, man. I just got a bad vibe. Like you know that slithery sensation you get when you just *know* someone's staring at you? It was kind of like that, but darker, man. So, I kind of tried to peek through the front window, and I thought I saw someone lying on the floor all weird, and I know this probably sounds crazy, but there was a really strong smell I don't even know how to describe.' His nose crinkled as if the stench still remained with him. Sadly, it probably did.

Cord prompted Kenny to continue. 'Go on. You got a bad vibe, saw someone, smelled something…'

Kenny shook his head to clear it. 'Yeah, um, anyway, I thought about how fast the van left, and that's when I kind of freaked out, ran back here, and told my mom to call the police.' The rest of Kenny's words spilled over each other in their rush to get out. At the same time, the teen's shoulders dropped as he released a heavy sigh, as if getting that off his chest had lifted a huge weight.

Alyssa opened her mouth to ask another question, but before she could, Kenny blurted out something so fast, she knew he'd been holding it in for a while. 'Listen, we saw Carter and Abigail being carried to the ambulance, and I just saw a body bag being hauled out Skye's front door, so clearly something bad happened over there, and I don't want to go and point fingers at anyone or anything, but—'

Lillian Holt muttered her son's name in warning. 'Kenny.'

He waved his mother's objections off, shooting her another teenage glare. 'What? You don't think the cops might need to know Skye had her own personal stalker for a while? If he's innocent, they'll' – he jerked his thumb in Alyssa and Cord's direction – 'figure it out or whatever.'

Stalker? Alyssa could hear the sound of her own heart-beat pulsing through the blood in her ears. 'I don't suppose you know this guy's name?'

Still glowering, Kenny nodded. 'Roman Cordova. Dude was, like, obsessed with Skye for a long time. When she kept refusing to go out with him, he became a real a-hole. Period. Full stop. Seriously, just Google "piece of—"' This time, he heeded his mother's growled warning. 'Sorry. I just know Skye was tired of being nice about it and was actually thinking about a restraining order. I mean, the guy left a dozen roses on her doorstep one morning and just randomly showed up one night, pounding on her door. It scared her because of Carter and Abigail, you know? I think she actually filed police reports for those ones.'

'Those ones?'

'Yeah, before that, she had to call the police a couple of times because she spotted him lurking outside across the street. But by the time the police showed up, he'd already bailed, and they said even if he'd been there, since he wasn't lingering, really, all they could've done was talk to him and ask him to move on. Skye hated guns, but she still considered getting one after the roses thing.'

There was something familiar about that name, Cordova, but Alyssa couldn't put her finger on the why. Regardless, she now had a name and a place to start. 'Do you remember how long ago it was when he left the roses or showed up?'

'He showed up a few weeks ago. I think it might've even been April Fool's. And the roses were a little bit before that.'

'And did you personally ever see him?'

'Just the time he showed up. I heard her yelling that she was calling the cops, so I grabbed my baseball bat and headed over, but when I walked outside, he looked at me and took off.' Kenny cleared his throat. 'So, can you, like, tell us what happened over there now?'

Knowing it would be all over the news anyway, she said, 'First, Carter and Abigail are safe, but I'm sorry to inform you that Skye and another woman were murdered tonight.'

Chapter Six

Lungs and throat burning with every wheezing breath that see-sawed in and out of her chest, London struggled to suck in enough air to stay alert and not succumb to the mind-numbing fire raging through her stomach and sides. But the nearly impossible task was made more harrowing as she was jostled about in the back of the cargo van where she'd been tossed two lifetimes ago.

The gritty sensation of sandpaper rubbed against her teeth and pressed into her lips while the rough material of the cloth gagging her scratched tiny lines into her face, making them sting when tears, sweat, and dirt from the floor of the van seeped into them. The bindings at her wrists and ankles bit in just as deeply as the gag and scorched the ripped skin until London almost believed she'd catch fire.

She didn't realize she'd moaned aloud until the passenger, the same person who'd stabbed her, swiveled around to stare at her. A long time ago, she, Skye, and Elena had watched a documentary on Richard Ramirez, the Night Stalker. Witnessing the evil in his eyes even through a television screen had frightened them so much they'd decided to sleep together on the floor of Carter and Abigail's bedroom. While a combination of the cloudless night, the darkened van, and a haze of pain mostly kept the person now staring down at her in shadow, London could sense the cold malevolence that made Ramirez's demeanor appear downright angelic in hindsight.

And the music blasting through the speakers only managed to heighten London's terror. Most of the high-pitched screechy lyrics were indecipherable, yet phrases like the 'devil's blood,' 'rites and rituals,' 'necessary sacrifices,' and 'opening the gates of hell' caused her veins to ice over. Who were these people, and why had they killed Skye and Elena and kidnapped her?

The driver veered suddenly, sending London's body rolling across the floor of the van. Flashes of white-hot agony shot through her skull when her head slammed into the metal paneled wall. The throbbing seemed never-ending, but nothing compared to the searing streaks darting through the gouges in her side and stomach with every single motion.

Trying to breathe through the pain, London fought to stay alert, trying to peek through the windshield in an effort to see where they were, but the long, snaky, and bumpy road they were on made it nearly impossible. When the van finally slowed before coming to an abrupt halt, every thought but one scattered into the abyss. *Please wake me from this nightmare.*

Without looking back at her, both the driver and the passenger unbuckled their seatbelts and climbed out, leaving the headlights on to slice through the darkness stretched out in front of them. With an unexpected, ear-piercing squeal, the side door of the van slid open, and both her attackers latched onto her bound legs, tugging her forward until they could wrench her around and grab her beneath the arms. They dragged her from the vehicle, not slowing their stride in the slightest when her legs slammed into the ground.

Something sharp stabbed through her jeans and gouged a long strip along her flesh. Yanked mercilessly forward, her ankles twisted as she was hauled across rocks, thorny sticks, and other pointy objects until, without warning, she was dropped to the hard ground, where something jagged tore across the knife wound in her side. The gag inside her mouth was the only thing that held her scream inside.

Through eyes clouded with panic and a brain short-circuiting on fear, London tried to focus on figuring out where she was, to see if she would die in a foreign place or somewhere she'd recognize. But from what little she could tell, they were in the middle of nowhere, surrounded by nothing. Even the trees were sparse, which likely ruled out any of the mountains in the area.

Only when one of her attackers roughly hauled her back to her feet did she notice not where she was, but what stood in front of her. An old, abandoned church, the kind she'd seen in movies set in the 1800s or early 1900s, listed so far to the side that the wind generated from an eagle's wings might topple it the rest of the way. At some point, someone had replaced the disintegrated front steps with stacked and chipped cinder blocks. Stained and sagging pieces of cardboard littered with smeared bug guts covered two of the busted-out windows.

Up the steps and through the front door, two lanterns with fake flames lent an eerie light to the darkness and illuminated the thick piles of rodent droppings. Her assailant released her long enough to shove her into a corner where she barely missed hitting her head against a loose board covered with rusted nails as she toppled to the ground. Neither assailant spoke as they scurried about with a frenzied excitement, lighting sconces scattered along what might've once been a sanctuary, or possibly a fellowship hall.

A cold, biting breeze blew down on London, and when she lifted her eyes, she spotted a large hole in the ceiling. Outside, no stars peeked through, as though God and the sky itself were too afraid to expose the pitch-black horror of her situation. As if adding an exclamation point to her thoughts, cracks in the siding emitted a high-pitched whistle that sounded like demons screeching in the night.

Her eyes darted everywhere, searching for a way to escape, though she knew if a miracle dropped down from heaven itself and revealed a path to her, she'd never make it. Even if she managed the impossible and found a way out of this place, where would she hide, and how and who would she summon for help? She had absolutely no idea where she'd been taken… or who she could trust.

At the sound of heavy footsteps drawing closer, thoughts of escape disappeared, and her heart hammered painfully against her ribcage. One of her attackers reappeared and, grabbing her beneath the arms, tugged her toward a staircase. Splinters and old nails scratched across exposed skin as her lower body thumped down the steps until she and her assailants reached the bottom, where she was released once more. Unlike the room above, the basement area was better lit, which made it possible for London to spot the crudely made coffin lying in the corner with its lid leaning nearby against the wall. Groaning deep in her throat, she attempted to wiggle backwards, only to be stopped short when she rammed the top of her head into the stairs.

Her eyes drifted to the space above the doorway and to either side of the walls. Painted in dripping red and black letters were two vulgar phrases that threatened to shatter any remaining sanity she may have been clinging to. Her pulse thudding loudly in her ears, she read the ominous words, *The Devil's Playground* and *Sacrifice Here* - the second message written above an arrow pointing down to where a dark substance coated what appeared to be an altar.

The words and images burned into her brain until a shrill, bleating cry snapped her attention away from them. Her gaze rooted around the space until she found the cause of the noise. If she'd thought for even a second that things couldn't get worse, she'd have been proven wrong.

Inconceivable horror gripped her insides at the sight of a young goat tethered to a wooden pole in the opposite corner of the room. Its terrified, confused cries pierced the air as it tore at its bindings.

As her gaze remained locked on the animal, one of the assailants knelt in front of her and whispered into her ear. 'As Shakespeare once wrote: *Hell's empty. All the devils are here.*'

If her body had been submerged in a frozen lake, London couldn't have been any colder.

Chapter Seven

Friday, April 23

Running on the fumes of less than three hours' sleep, Alyssa and Cord found themselves parked in front of a cute cottage-style house tucked into a quiet little cul-de-sac on Albuquerque's West Side. With the sun barely beginning to kiss the top of the Sandia mountains, the streetlights shone down on a rainbow of rose bushes lining either side of the walkway leading to the front door. Turning off the ignition, Alyssa glanced past Cord and watched as someone inside the house peeked through the blinds.

After speaking to the Holts, Alyssa and Cord had returned to the Fleming home where, from a license one of the crime scene investigators had pulled from the pocket of victim number one, they'd learned her name was Elena Garcia, aged twenty-six. A large red icon located on the front screen of the woman's phone, also discovered on her person, spelled the initials 'ICE.' In Case of Emergency. Curious, Alyssa had tapped it. The name Ash preceded both a number and address. They had put in an extremely early morning phone call to their teammate, Hal Callum, who had quickly dug into Elena's history and discovered *Ash* referred to her older sister Ashlee.

'I hate this part,' Alyssa muttered before sucking in a deep lungful of air in an effort to steel herself as much as possible against the emotional storm they were most likely about to encounter.

'You and me both,' Cord answered.

Exiting the vehicle, they paused on the sidewalk for a second before continuing up the walkway constructed with pavers and sand. But just as Alyssa reached out a fist to knock, the door opened to reveal a tall, willowy woman with cropped black hair, a partially made-up face, and a mascara wand clutched in her hand. Alyssa let her arm drop back to her side.

Keeping the screen as a barrier between them, the woman, suspicion coating her words, asked, 'Can I help you?' The hand not holding the mascara wand hovered above the lock on her door.

Unfortunately, Alyssa remained all too aware of how flimsy that lock would be if someone wanted to get in badly enough. She flashed her credentials. 'Ashlee Garcia?'

Frowning, the woman's eyebrows drew together to form a vee on her forehead. 'Yes. How can I help you?'

'Detectives Wyatt and Roberts with the Albuquerque Police Department. Do you mind if we come inside and talk to you?' It came as no surprise that Alyssa's gently spoken request managed to add to Ashlee's suspicious nervousness. It happened to be part and parcel of being in law enforcement. Her son Isaac had once told her he equated that aspect of her job with waiting to speak to the principal, even when he knew he hadn't done anything wrong.

'Do you mind if I ask what this is about first?' From the slight tremor that suddenly developed in Ashlee's hand as well as her voice, Alyssa knew that Elena's sister sensed that this unexpected visit from the police was about to forever change her life. Alyssa wished she could tell her she was wrong.

'It's about your sister, Elena,' Cord said.

A medley of emotions zigzagged across Ashlee's face. 'Elena? Is she in trouble or something?' She posed the question as if the very idea of it sounded both foreign and ludicrous. Alyssa could tell the moment Ashlee sensed the reason two detectives might appear at dawn on her doorstep. Her head already shaking in denial, she staggered like a person who'd had one too many cocktails.

'Or something, I'm afraid,' Alyssa said softly.

Releasing her grip on the doorknob, Elena's sister stepped to the side and wordlessly invited them in where the scent of cinnamon and orange potpourri lingered in the air and collided with the tantalizing aroma of coffee and toast.

Ashlee, stumbling with each step, shuffled backwards until she bumped into a tall coat rack that wobbled precariously. Her right arm coiled around her center and squeezed. Voice vibrating with anxiety, she asked, 'What's happened to my sister? Is she okay?' As if a blast of frigid air had blown over her, Ashlee's entire body shivered.

Concerned by Ashlee's unsteadiness, Alyssa didn't answer right away, instead urging the woman to sit before she delivered the tragic news. 'Why don't you go ahead and have a seat first,' she suggested.

Not surprisingly, Ashlee resisted. 'Please, just tell me what's happened. Please.'

In all her years of being a detective, Alyssa had learned that it didn't matter how gently the news was delivered; no amount of preparation would alter the impact of hearing that a loved one had died, much less been brutally murdered. So, as delicately as she could, she ripped the rug right out from beneath Ashlee's world. 'I'm so sorry, but Elena was found murdered last night.' For the moment, Alyssa left out any mention of Skye Fleming. First, she needed to determine what, if anything, Ashlee could tell them about who may have wanted her sister and her sister's friend dead, who hated them enough to rationalize that level of slaughter.

Recoiling as if Alyssa had struck her physically, Ashlee stiffened until the only noticeable movement for the next several heartbeats was her rapidly blinking eyes as her mind tried and failed to force the sequence of harsh words to make some sort of logical sense. 'What?' she finally managed to breathe out into the space separating her from the detectives.

Instead of repeating herself, Alyssa simply said, 'I'm sorry,' knowing the words sounded empty, no matter how much she meant them.

Ashlee's hands flew to her mouth, the forgotten mascara wand smudging a line of black along her cheekbone. Instantly, tears flooded her face and streaked what makeup she'd managed to apply before Alyssa and Cord had come along to deliver the devastating news of her sister's death.

In a matter of seconds, Ashlee's shock and disbelief manifested themselves in broken wails that sliced Alyssa's heart into thin ribbons. She'd been quite young when it had happened, but she and her family had once been on the receiving end of similar earth-shattering news, and no matter how often she had to deliver the blow to families, each time she found herself temporarily transported back to that time. After sneaking a peek up at Cord and witnessing the pain flashing in his eyes, she knew he, too, had been thrown into mentally reliving his own family's tragedy.

Cord visibly pushed his memories aside and stepped forward in time to catch Ashlee's crumbling form when her knees buckled and sent her reeling toward the floor. Only when Ashlee remained upright by clutching the counter so tightly that her knuckles paled from the effort, did he release her.

From both personal and professional experience, Alyssa knew that this young woman and her family's lives would forever be changed, so she gave Ashlee Garcia's brain time to assimilate and accept this life-altering news.

While they waited, Cord disappeared into Ashlee's kitchen and returned with a coffee mug full of water; sadness and compassion filled his gaze as he set the cup on the counter beside her. Gently, he asked, 'Is there someone we can call for you, who can come be with you so you're not alone right now?'

Through heart-shattering, tormented cries, Ashlee managed to whisper, 'My brother,' before adding, 'I have to call my parents. They live in Maine.' Finally sinking into the nearest chair, her arms snaked around her middle as she rocked back and forth. 'Oh my God, this is going to kill them. There's no way they'll be able to survive this. Ohmygod, ohmygod, ohmygod. This can't be happening. Please, God, tell me this isn't really happening.'

Alyssa and Cord exchanged shared haunted expressions. Unlike some individuals in law enforcement, neither of them had ever managed to make themselves entirely immune to the pain stemming from the loss of a loved one, be it family or friend. A quick glance down at her watch showed Alyssa that nearly ten minutes had passed since delivering the news of Elena's murder. And as much as she hated to forge forward, her team needed answers so they could capture the person responsible.

Slowly, Ashlee's sobs subsided to agonized whimpers accompanied by the occasional hiccup. Numbly, her gaze cast toward the floor, she asked, 'Is it all right if I call my brother? I need…' Her sentence trailed off, as if those few extra words were more than she could handle.

'Of course.'

When her brother didn't answer, Ashlee left a panicked message. 'Mateo, this is Ash. It's urgent. Call me the second you get this.' With quaking hands, she fumbled her fingers over her keyboard. 'I'll send a text.'

Within seconds Ashlee's phone rang, disturbing the grief-stricken air around them. 'Mat—' Renewed sobs briefly stole her breath. 'Elena's dead. Some—someone killed her… Yes, I'm serious. No, the police are here right now. I need you. Can you come over? Please hurry.' Eyes still glazed over in crushed disbelief, she ended the call and clutched her phone tightly to her chest. 'He's on his way,' she choked out.

'Do you mind if we ask you a few questions while we wait?' Alyssa shifted her eyes from the family photo displayed on the mantel back to Elena's sister.

'Ye-yes. It'll take my brother at least twenty-five minutes to get here anyway.' Ashlee yanked a handful of tissues from a box beside her, blowing her reddened nose on one and pressing a clutched wad of the others beneath her eyes. It wasn't long before the tissues resembled little more than a mushy, ineffective mess. 'I need—can we move into there?' She pointed to her living room.

'Of course,' Alyssa said. She and Cord waited for Ashlee to stumble the few steps into her living room and collapse onto one of the two loveseats before settling themselves across from her. 'I know this is an extremely difficult situation, so take your time answering, okay?'

A fresh wave of tears flooded Ashlee's face as her head tipped forward in what Alyssa took as agreement.

'Do you remember the last time you or anyone in your family spoke to your sister?'

'Yesterday evening. Me. Elena and I speak or text almost every single day.'

'Do you remember what time that was?'

Most people needed a minute to think about the time, but Ashlee answered immediately. 'Six thirty. She was planning on going over to a friend's house for a movie marathon.'

'A movie marathon on a Thursday night?' Alyssa asked.

'Yeah. Elena and her friends have Fridays off. They work for Sales and Marketing over at Intel. In fact, that's how they all met. Anyway, she was planning on calling an Uber to drop her off since she knew it was going to be a late night with drinking involved, and she didn't want to be tempted to drive.' One corner of Ashlee's mouth tilted up even as she shook her head. 'As if Elena would ever do something like that.'

Alyssa was careful to keep her tone even. 'You said, "That's how they *all* met." What did you mean by that?'

'Skye Fleming and London Brecken. The three of them were going to hang out at Skye's like they usually did.' Ashlee's hands flew to her mouth. Between her fingers, she cried out, 'Oh my god. Skye and London. They need to know.' Abandoning the clump of useless tissues in her hands, she wiped her sleeve across her cheeks, staining the cloth with tears and smeared makeup. 'I don't have their numbers, so I don't know how to get ahold of them to tell them.'

Alyssa's mind flashed back to the third glass in the kitchen. 'You're sure Elena's friend, London, had plans to join them?'

Ashlee's efforts to blink tears from her eyes were wasted. 'Oh yeah. Movie marathon nights were something the three of them were practically geeks about, so I can't imagine London would miss it. But then, I also know Elena said London's car was in the shop again, so maybe she decided not to go. Why?'

From the corner of her eye, Alyssa watched Cord's pen scribbling across the page, and she peeked down to see he'd jotted London's name, underlined it three times, and followed it with three exclamation points and a question mark.

For the moment, Alyssa ignored Ashlee's question. 'It sounds like your sister and her friends were quite close.'

Ashlee sniffled, this time opting to grab another tissue from the box to blow her nose. A sad laugh filtered through as she answered. 'Practically inseparable for the past six years. They never even had the occasional bicker some friends have. They all just clicked and would do anything for each other.'

That answered Alyssa's next question, whether Ashlee was aware of any possibly underlying tensions in the girls' relationship. Though she wouldn't normally divulge the name of any other victims until next of kin had been notified, Alyssa decided it was time to deliver the rest of the news. In part, because neither the Holts nor any of the other neighbors they'd talked to had been able to provide names of known family members, including the children's father. Neither had Rosemary Covington nor Hal been successful in that regard.

Inhaling deeply and counting to ten as she exhaled, Alyssa said, 'I'm afraid I have more bad news for you.' She waited for Ashlee to look up from her clasped hands. 'Your sister was found murdered last night at her friend's house. Skye Fleming was also murdered.'

Ashlee's chest heaved with an expulsion of air as if someone had rammed something heavy into her gut. 'What?' Her eyes closed briefly as if preparing herself. 'London?'

'We found no other adults in the home.'

Her head shaking in denial, Ashlee weaved her arms back around her middle and squeezed as if she were hugging herself. 'Carter and Abigail? Skye's children?'

Cord jumped in to reassure her. 'Uninjured. At this time, authorities have been unable to locate any relatives, so they'll remain in CYFD's custody for now.'

'What will happen to them? Did they… were they—' Ashlee's breath sawed in and out so rapidly, Alyssa feared she might be on the verge of hyperventilating.

Still, out of an abundance of caution for the children, Alyssa neither confirmed nor denied Ashlee's fears.

After several seconds of attempting to get her breathing back under control, in a voice numb with disbelief, Ashlee finally said, 'CYFD won't be able to locate any of Skye's relatives because she doesn't have any. Elena told me that her parents and younger sister were killed in some kind of accident when she was a teenager, so her grandparents raised her. In fact, if I remember correctly, that's how Skye and London originally bonded because London was kind of raised by her grandparents, too. Anyway, both of Skye's grandparents have dementia, so they live in a nursing home right now, so I guess she *does* have family, but…'

Alyssa started to ask if Ashlee knew anything about Carter and Abigail's father when a car skidded to a stop outside, and when she turned around and looked through the window, she spotted that a dark sedan had barely missed hitting her bumper. A man and woman who clearly appeared to have been roused from sleep sprinted up the walk and through Ashlee's door without bothering to knock.

In less than a heartbeat, Elena's sister torpedoed across the room where she and her brother collided with a force that jarred Alyssa's teeth. Behind them, a slender young woman remained in the doorway, looking lost and unsure of what she should do.

Cradling his sister to his chest, the man peered over her head and darted his attention between Alyssa and Cord. 'Mateo Garcia, Ashlee and Elena's brother. What happened?' Denial and anger blended together in his tone.

Before responding, Alyssa turned toward the woman still in the doorway. 'Are you Mateo's wife?'

The woman's teary eyes shifted from Mateo and Ashlee over to Alyssa and then back again. 'Girlfriend. Chrissy Madison.'

Still clutching his sister tightly in his arms, Elena's brother, his voice unsteady now, repeated his question. 'What *happened*?'

For the second time that morning, Alyssa delivered the news as gently as she knew how. 'I'm afraid your sister and a friend of hers were found murdered in the friend's home last night. We received a call shortly after ten. We're still trying to piece things together so we can answer that question for you and your family.'

At the mention of his family, Mateo dropped his chin to rest on top of his sister's head before he pulled away to stare down at her. 'Did you already call Mom and Dad?'

Ashlee stumbled as she whipped her head back and forth. 'No! Not yet. I think… I can't… I don't know *how* or even *what* to tell them.' Her voice cracked. 'I'm afraid this will kill them both, Mat.'

Mateo reached out and crushed his sister back to him, so tightly that Alyssa found herself struggling to breathe. His fists clenched and unclenched on Ashlee's back as, once again peering over the top of her head, he asked the questions that were almost always the first ones asked. 'Elena was the baby of our family. *Everyone* loved her. Everyone who ever met her. Who did this? As far as I know, she hasn't even had a boyfriend for at least eighteen months, and the only reason they broke up was because he moved away to Alaska. And how was she killed anyway?'

Alyssa hesitated before settling on, 'The medical examiner will be providing some of those answers after an autopsy is performed.'

Ashlee swayed on her feet, and this time, both Chrissy and Mateo were there to support her from collapsing. 'An autopsy?'

Cord nodded. 'Because of the manner of death.'

Mateo swallowed. 'When can we see her? Or get her body so we can start planning her funeral?'

Cord responded as gently as he could. 'I'm sorry, but we're not sure how long that might be. We know this is a difficult thing for you and your family to process, so if you think of anything or have any questions, we'll leave our cards so you can call us anytime.'

A few minutes later, Alyssa and Cord showed themselves out.

Back in the car, Alyssa buckled herself in and turned the ignition before checking her mirrors and pulling away from the curb. 'Well, it might be a jumbled mess of information, but I think we have a little more to go on than we did a few hours ago. But the first thing I think we need to do is locate London Brecken. If she *was* there last night—' Alyssa didn't finish her thought because there were so many reasons they needed to find Elena and Skye's friend, if for no other purpose than to assure themselves she was safe. She shot a quick glance at Cord. 'What are you thinking?'

Cord scratched his jaw. 'I agree with you about finding London. As far as persons of interest, however, I still think we start with Skye's alleged stalker, this Roman Cordova.'

'I thought the same thing. I'd also like to look into who Carter and Abigail's father is. A furious ex-boyfriend, ex-husband, ex-lover… any one of those three could potentially want to inflict the kind of damage done to Skye Fleming's person.'

'It's like you read my mind.'

'If the father's in the system somewhere, we might be able to determine his identity by getting DNA samples from the kids.' As long as the CYFD maintained custody of them, Alyssa should be able to obtain the swabs needed to provide those answers.

'Also,' Cord said, dragging her mind away from Carter and Abigail's father, 'If Skye, Elena, and this London were as close as Ashlee claimed, she might know who the father is without us having to jump through a bunch of legal hoops.'

Alyssa peeked at the time on her dash. 'We're meeting Liz for that safehouse interview in less than half an hour, so why don't we call Hal on our drive over there and see if he can dig up an address for her?'

Liz Waterson, friend and teammate, happened to be one of the most top-notch forensic artists in the state and several surrounding ones as well. Over the years, she'd conducted many safehouse interviews with children, and Alyssa had high hopes that, if Carter and Abigail had witnessed anything, Liz would be able to pull it out without further traumatizing them. Which was why they'd called her as they left the Fleming residence to request her assistance.

Beside her, Cord was already dialing Hal to get him started on tracking down London Brecken's whereabouts in addition to digging into Roman Cordova's background.

While Cord tried Hal, Alyssa thought about their next interview. Late last night, or rather early this morning, Rosemary Covington had called to inform her that Carter and Abigail had been cleared by a doctor and moved to emergency foster care, but that their little bodies had simply given in to the crushing fatigue, devastation, and confusion of the past few hellish hours, and so the interview would have to wait – not that Alyssa or Cord had been surprised by the news.

And as much as she knew they needed to hear what Carter and Abigail had to say, Alyssa's stomach clenched at the thought of what they might've seen or heard, and she had to admit she was grateful that the drive over meant she had just a little more time to brace herself.

Chapter Eight

Friday, April 23

On the way to meet Liz, Alyssa spotted one of her favorite coffee shops. Without a second's hesitation, she flipped on her blinker, changed lanes, and nearly squealed her tires trying to make the tight turn into the parking lot, earning a 'What the hell, Lys?' growl from Cord, along with an irritated side-eye. When he glanced up and saw where they were, his annoyance turned to an all-out eye-roll. But since beginning their day before five – after working into the wee hours of the morning – and then breaking the emotional news that their sister had been murdered to Ashlee and Mateo Garcia just after six, Alyssa felt like she'd already worked a twenty-hour shift. When she combined that with fighting the morning commute traffic which was clearly conspiring against her, she tended to lean a little on the grumpy side.

She was climbing out of the Tahoe when Cord, who'd just gotten through to Hal, stopped her. 'Leave your phone because Hal's going to call your number when he calls back.' He pointed to the coffee shop. 'Do you—'

Before he could launch into his same, tiring lecture, Alyssa held up her palm to stave him off. 'Zip it. I need coffee. As a full-fledged grown-up capable of making my own decisions, I get to choose when I have it.'

One eyebrow shot up the way it often did whenever she claimed she needed coffee. Lately, Cord's insistent crusade to end her caffeine addiction extended beyond the legendary and now dipped into obnoxious territory, especially since he'd actually won the tug of war that drew her kids Holly and Isaac to side with him, the traitors. Not that it had been a difficult task, considering they'd been hounding her since long before Cord came along.

'Besides, aren't you ready yet to join the dark side? You know you want to, so why continue fighting it?'

'I'm a million percent positive you already know the answer to that.' Cord's cocky smirk acted as a temptation for her to buy two cups just to irk him.

'Suit yourself. It's your loss, as usual. Personally, I don't see how you've managed to survive without it, with Shelley and Shane running around like escaped monkeys half the time.'

Cord snorted out a laugh. 'Exactly. And yet Sara and I have managed. Imagine that.'

So she wouldn't have to hear the rest of the same argument, Alyssa shut the door on his last words. Since the line inside was surprisingly short, she returned in no time, armed with a large cup of strong, black coffee, one orange juice, two bagels, and one cheese Danish. 'The bagels and orange juice are yours. Leave my Danish alone. Grovel at my feet later.'

Cord peeked inside the bag. 'Wouldn't dream of getting between you and your incurable sweet tooth.'

Alyssa backed out of the parking spot and waited for traffic to clear before pulling back onto the road and reaching for her Danish. After taking a huge bite and washing it down with a gulp of hot coffee that burned her throat, she covered her cough, and shot her partner a look. 'One, I know you're salivating, so don't bother denying it, and two, I'll have you know that studies have shown coffee can—'

'Improve one's memory and mental faculties,' Cord interrupted. 'Yeah, I've heard you recite that same story before. I bet I can find one equally as compelling about the many negative effects—'

Saved from the customary back and forth by her phone ringing, Alyssa glanced at her Bluetooth, expecting it to be Hal, but saw it was her husband Brock instead.

'Hey babe. As usual, you're on speaker. How's the conference going?' Wednesday night, he'd flown up to Colorado for work. One benefit of toiling long hours was that she didn't have to focus on missing him so much.

Brock greeted Cord before answering Alyssa. 'Heading over now, but so far, it's been okay, at least as far as endless meetings can go. Been snowing off and on here, so whenever it gets too humdrum in there, I humor myself by staring out the window. Sorry I didn't respond last night. I didn't get the text you sent me until I woke this morning. Double homicide. That's rough.' Alyssa imagined him shaking his head.

A loud beep indicating another call cut off whatever Brock said next. This time it really was Hal. 'Hey honey, I've gotta run. Hal's calling us back. I'll get ahold of you later when I can.'

'All right. Talk soon. Love you, babe.'

'Love you.'

Tapping the green icon, she switched over to Hal. 'Morning.'

'Sorry about earlier. Was on the phone trying to run down whatever info I could on that list of names you gave me last night in the hopes I'll have something to share by the time the team meets this morning. So, what else can I do for you?'

'Carter and Abigail, the children we found hiding in the closet, were placed in emergency, temporary foster care, and Liz agreed to meet us over there this morning, so that's where we're headed right now to see if we can determine what they might've seen or heard. In the mean-time, we've got another person we'd like you to try to track down for us – London Brecken.' Alyssa flashed her lights at the car in front of her when the driver sat staring at his phone after the light they were stopped at had changed to green.

'Anyway, when we broke the news to Ashlee Garcia this morning, she mentioned the name, claiming Brecken is best friends with both our victims.'

'Actually,' Cord cut in, 'the word she used was "inseparable."'

'Right. Anyway, when she learned her sister had been murdered at Skye Fleming's home, she seemed quite surprised to learn London Brecken hadn't also been at the house. We'd like to find out what she might know about this Cordova guy. Plus, there's also the fact that there were three used glasses on the kitchen counter, but only two victims. Could be a simple explanation, but if she did happen to be there at some point, that'll help us narrow down our timeline.'

Alyssa could already hear Hal clacking away on his keyboard. 'You got it. I'll get started right away. Unless she's got some kind of invisible footprint, I should be able to have that for you by the time you and Cord get to the precinct. And if that's all, I'll let you two go and wish you luck with the kids. I suspect no matter what you hear, it's going to be rough.' Hal's voice, usually so jovial, filled with sadness and maybe a little anger.

The weight of Cord's heavy sigh thickened the air in the Tahoe. 'You can say that again.'

—

At seven thirty on the dot, Alyssa and Cord rolled up to Kyra and Milton Sanderson's home where both Liz Waterson and Rosemary Covington were waiting inside their own vehicles. Shifting the Tahoe into park, Alyssa glanced over at Cord. 'Needless to say, asking two traumatized children to relive what will, in all likelihood, be the worst tragedy of their lives leaves a hole in the pit of my stomach.'

'Yeah, my ribcage has been shrinking with each block closer we got.'

In her rearview mirror, Alyssa spotted Liz and Rosemary walking their way, so she removed the key from the ignition and climbed out.

'Morning,' Liz greeted them.

Much as she had last night, Rosemary forewent any type of pleasantries. 'Is everyone ready?'

'As ready as we can be,' Alyssa said, already experiencing the suffocating air of tension. Cord and Liz both responded with sharp nods.

The four of them had taken only a few steps toward the house when Mr. Sanderson stepped outside and tipped his head toward the doorbell. 'Every little noise triggers them, so I figured I'd circumvent this one. Plus, my wife and I wanted to prepare you beforehand. Neither child, as I'm sure you can probably imagine, slept well, so we had a bit of a rough night. Understandable and expected.

'Mostly, Carter insisted on sitting sentinel over Abigail. One of the times we checked on them, we were both surprised and relieved to see he'd finally crashed.' He paused and shook his head. 'Even asleep, he still managed to keep his arm flung over his sister. Since we peeked in on them hourly, just in case, I can tell you his sleep was fitful, and it didn't last long.' Sadness crept into Mr. Sanderson's eyes. 'Twice, he woke screaming, "Mommy" and something else we couldn't decipher.'

If Mr. Sanderson had slammed a hammer into Alyssa's gut, it would've been less of a blow.

'We appreciate you letting us know ahead of time,' Liz said. 'That'll help me figure out where to begin.'

Mr. Sanderson shifted uncomfortably as he cleared his throat. 'Look, I understand that you have to speak to the children, but' – he waved his hand toward the four of them – 'do you *all* have to be present? I'm just a little worried being confronted by six strange adults will be a little hard for them to handle.'

'I understand your concern,' Alyssa said. 'Unfortunately, however, we do all have to be present for various reasons. Of course, we'll do everything we can to make it less frightening for them.'

Mr. Sanderson nodded once before he inhaled deeply, opened the door, and quietly ushered everyone into his warm, inviting home.

Immediately, Alyssa's eyes were drawn to a tight little space between an entertainment center and a wall where Carter and Abigail, engulfed by a thick green blanket, curled together. Clutched in Abigail's arms was the bright orange, stuffed hippo that Alyssa recognized from last night. As soon as she spotted the four of them, Abigail hugged the colorful hippo tighter to her chest and burrowed deeper into her brother's side. Pressing her face into his neck, she popped her thumb into her mouth.

Alyssa thought her heart would sprout wings and take off when Carter gathered himself as if he were preparing to run to Cord. But a few seconds later, his body went so completely still, he could've passed for a statue.

Much like he had last night, Cord moved around the others until he could squat down in front of the children. 'Hey buddy,' he said softly. 'Do you remember me from last night?'

Carter blinked once and nodded, a motion so imperceptible, it managed to be practically invisible. Compassion and sympathy lodged themselves in Alyssa's throat, keeping company with all the other emotions she struggled to choke down. Not every day did she encounter such bravery, especially in children, and definitely not after being witness to murder.

Cord continued speaking softly. 'I hear you had some pretty bad dreams. Do you want to tell me about them?'

Suspicion and mistrust flashed across Carter's face as he shifted a brief, accusing glare over toward Kyra and Milton Sanderson before he dropped his chin toward his chest and shook his head no.

In an effort to give Cord the space and time to make the children as comfortable as possible, Kyra, Alyssa, Liz, and Rosemary stood at the edge of the living room. 'Even if it's only because he's mad that my husband told you about his bad dreams, that's the first bit of real animation the little guy has shown all morning, so I'll take it,' Kyra whispered. 'I'll be honest; his lack of emotional reactions have had me worried since he arrived. When CYFD contacted us and detailed the circumstances surrounding their need for care, I expected questions, hysterical tears, or even confused defiance.' She paused to shake her head before continuing.

'But he does exactly as he's asked, unless it pertains to leaving his sister's side. He even refused to stay outside the restroom while Abigail used the potty this morning. Afterwards, he declined breakfast – he didn't fuss or cry; he simply acted as if it wasn't there. But bless his caring little soul, he made certain I knew his sister preferred cheese on her scrambled eggs and then made certain she ate every morsel, as well as her toast, and drank every drop of her chocolate milk.' Kyra placed her palm over her heart and sighed. 'As far as protecting little sisters go, that's undoubtedly the most determined little boy I've ever seen.' A ghost of a sad smile flitted across her face, there and gone in seconds. 'And if he's still this protective when she's a teenager, that little girl will never get a date. And I happened to be raised with six very protective older brothers, so I would know a little something about that.'

While Kyra spoke to the others, Cord continued trying to earn back Carter and Abigail's trust. 'Even though you've been very brave, I know you're really scared. I would be, too, if I were you. But I need you to trust me, okay?'

Carter's nod came more quickly this time, proof that Cord was gaining strides.

'Now, my friend here' – Cord twisted just enough to point to Liz, who smiled gently and lifted her hand to wave – 'needs to ask you some questions about last night. Her name is—'

A loud plop interrupted Cord as Abigail's thumb left her mouth so she could shake a finger in the CYFD investigator's direction. 'She made me and Cawter goed to the hospital. I want my mommy.' The little girl's chin quivered as her thumb returned to her mouth.

Carter pulled it back out. 'Don't suck your thumb,' he scolded. 'It'll give you a buck's teeth, remember?' When he looked to Cord to confirm this statement, Alyssa wasn't sure which took center stage, the urge to laugh, cry, or hug the two kids, but of course, what she really wanted was to do all of the above.

Cord showed off his one crooked tooth that she knew had resulted from an early childhood accident when a swing had caught him in the mouth. 'That one right there.'

'I want to go home. I don't want to goed back to that hospital.' Not willing to forgive the CYFD investigator, Abigail aimed her frightened little-girl daggers straight at Rosemary. 'I don't like it there. They made me let go of my brudder, but he said, "No, No." I want my mommy,' she repeated, sniffling.

Cord shook his head. 'No one's taking you back to the hospital, I promise. Last night we just needed to make sure you weren't hurt really bad, remember? That's why the doctors and nurses had to look you over real good. But they said they didn't find any injuries on you, so you won't need to go back there right now, okay?'

Instead of being appeased, Abigail glared at Cord, affronted by his comment. Lifting the leg of her pajamas, she pointed to a scab on one of her knees, and Alyssa found herself biting back a laugh at the little girl's indignation. 'I do, too, have a 'jury! I falled in the rocks and Mommy gave me a popsicle and *two* Band-Aids so I could get more better more faster.' By the end of her explanation, she sounded less like a newly turned three-year-old and more like a teacher lecturing her classroom.

To his credit, Cord kept himself from grinning and instead nodded his understanding. 'Well, that's true, and I can see there you really do have an injury that's surely getting better already.' He motioned for Liz to join them on the floor. As she knelt on her knees beside him, he said, 'My friend Liz here has an injury just like that on her elbow. Would you like to see it?'

Last week, Liz had been knocked into a tree when a dog eluding its owner had bowled her over in the park. Now, she raised her sleeve to show Abigail, but the little girl simply shook her head and said, 'No. I don't want to see, thank you.'

Alyssa had to cough to cover up her escaped choke of laughter. With each tick of the clock, these two brave little children stole a little more of her heart.

Cord, too, did his best to cover his chuckle. 'All right. Well, maybe another time. But you know, Liz still needs to ask you some very important questions, okay? Now, some of them might seem scary and hard, but I'll be right here with you.' When he added, 'And nothing you tell us will get you in any trouble,' Alyssa knew he was thinking about last night when he'd mentioned being concerned that Carter hadn't been entirely honest about what he might've witnessed. She also guessed that the slight tremor suddenly shaking Carter's body likely meant her partner had read the situation accurately.

'We just need you to think really hard, be honest, and tell us what you remember. You can do that, right?' Cord finished.

A fine film of moisture coated Carter's eyes, and his little body stiffened, but to no one's surprise, he kept his tears from spilling over. 'You promise you'll stay here?' Even in the face of his forced bravery, his voice came out a little less sure and a lot wobblier.

Cord stretched his arm across the opening and offered his pinky. 'Tell you what, I'll do you one better. I *pinky* promise.' As far as Abigail was concerned, that was all it took to earn the rest of her trust because she reached over and gripped Cord's pinky with her entire tiny little hand. Whether it was his sister's acceptance or the pinky promise, Carter also seemed satisfied.

'Okay,' he said. 'Can we sit here, though?'

'You can sit anywhere you want,' Liz assured him as she pulled her satchel over her shoulder and extracted a sketch pad and pencils.

–

Less than twenty minutes into the interview, a haunted look shadowed Cord's face as Carter, lower lip quivering like a hummingbird's wings, tears slipping down his cheeks, whispered in all his six-year-old bravery, 'You can go find Auntie London now. She needs your help, so I won't be mad at you for breaking your promise.'

Torn between keeping his word and performing his job, Cord leaned in and made a new promise. 'I'll be back later to check on you and Abigail, okay?' He reached into his pocket and pulled out a business card, handing it to Carter. 'If you get scared or want to talk or remember something else – even if you just need to hear my voice' – he winked and ruffled Carter's hair – 'then you just pick up the phone and call me, got it?'

Kyra Sanderson, throat thick with emotion, spoke quietly. 'I'll make sure he has access to a phone for as long as they stay with us.'

Heart pounding, Alyssa moved to leave, but before Cord could push to his full height, Carter threw off the blanket still wrapped around him and his sister and leaped forward into Cord's arms, soaking the collar of his shirt. And all Alyssa could think in that moment was, 'Finally, someone's protecting him.'

Cord squeezed Carter tight, kissed the top of his head, and then handed him over to Kyra Sanderson before heading out. With every step, Alyssa could see the struggle her partner had in not turning back around. Before they even moved off the porch, Alyssa was dialing Hal back.

After one ring, impatience already gnawed at her. 'Come on, come on,' she muttered as she reached the Tahoe, slid into the driver's seat, and jammed the key into the ignition.

'Lys? I thought you—'

Alyssa cut him off. 'I need you to put out an APB on London Brecken immediately. We're not looking for one, but two killers.'

Hal's momentary silence disappeared with a loud expulsion of air. 'She killed her friends, and the children actually witnessed the crime?'

It took a second for Alyssa to realize why Hal would think that. 'No. Brecken is a third victim, so list her as missing and in grave danger. Listen, Cord and I are on our way to the precinct now, so we'll explain everything when we get there. Right now, though, get that APB issued and then see what you can do about getting access to any cameras in the area of Greenwood Avenue. In short, London *was* at the house last night, only she managed to hide in the closet with the children until... Like I said, I'll explain that as soon as we get to the precinct. Once you get access to that camera, we're searching for a light-colored cargo van that might've traveled through that main intersection between the hours of six and shortly after ten.'

Disgusted with herself, Alyssa thumped her steering wheel, honking her horn when her hand slipped, and startling the car in front of her. She prayed the delay in the APB hadn't been the signature on London Brecken's death certificate. She should've listened to her gut when that third glass insisted she was overlooking something. But that wasn't the only critical mistake mocking her inability to see deeper into the crime scene. No, she'd also assumed the bloody drag marks near Elena's body had come from her as she'd been dragged away from the door. Now she had every reason to suspect they'd come from London Brecken.

'Why would the perpetrators take London instead of killing her along with the others?' Hal asked.

'And there's the million-dollar question, isn't it?' Cord's growled response, Alyssa knew, was directed not at Hal, but himself. Like her, he was punishing himself for missing what they now both felt were obvious clues.

In his intuitive way, Hal went straight to the heart of the matter. 'All right. Deep breaths everyone. Let's focus on what we have and how to go forward from here. Now, were you able to get any kind of description that I can put out? Maybe what she was wearing? Or a ballpark figure comparison for height and weight?'

Alyssa appreciated Hal's matter-of-fact attitude because it helped her focus. 'Shoulder-length brown hair, Liz's height, so probably around five-five, five-six, wearing blue jeans and a blue blouse with white clouds and sheep.'

No matter the circumstances of a case, Alyssa always forced herself and her team to remain positive because deciding the worst had already occurred affected their urgency, even if only psychologically. But in this instance, after what Carter confessed he'd witnessed, she struggled to see how it was possible for Brecken to still be alive.

'Got it. I'm going to hang up so I can get that APB issued. I'll see you two when you arrive, and since Joe and Tony just walked in, I'll fill them in on where we are. See you when you get here.'

As soon as Hal ended the call, Cord shifted toward her. 'She's not dead. London Brecken's out there right now, still alive, and waiting for us to find her. We've worked against worse odds. We're not too late.'

Unsure whether her partner was trying to convince himself or her, Alyssa's nerves remained balled into tight little explosive devices. The statistical likelihood of London still being alive was less than slim, yet somehow they *had* to believe in a miracle. Picturing the image Carter had painted of the three of them hiding in the closet, she whispered, 'God, I hope you're right.'

Chapter Nine

Uncertain if she'd actually been sleeping or if she'd been unconscious, and for how long, London blinked against the fog in her brain and the pain burning along every millimeter of skin. Grogginess did its best to lull her back under with the promise of oblivion, of the ability to pretend what had happened to her friends had been nothing more than the absolute worst of nightmares. And she desperately wanted to go on believing that if she just rolled over a tad bit, she'd encounter Abigail's soft little form lying next to her in the guest room, where she almost always ended up whenever she stayed over at Skye's. She wanted to convince herself that Carter, at this moment, stood on a chair in the kitchen melting a mound of butter all over the burnt toast he'd present to her like she was a queen receiving a gift of gold.

No matter how badly London wanted her fantasy to be real, the throbbing pain coming from her stab wounds assured her it wasn't. In an effort to keep them from closing again, she forced her eyes wide open. When light failed to penetrate the darkness, her heart pummeled the inside of her ribcage.

Why couldn't she see anything?

Sweat beaded on her lip at the memory of the slow descent of a needle sinking into her flesh. Almost immediately afterwards, a heavy cloud of confusion had settled inside her brain. Shortly after that, both her pain and fear had faded away into nothingness. The distant rumblings of excited chatter had barely penetrated the thick fog of drowsiness as it dragged her under.

Now, a relentless, building pressure inside her chest had her digging her fingernails into her palms as more of her memories returned in bursts and flashes.

Receding footsteps, the high-pitched screech of a warped wooden door scraping against a rough floor.

Two more doors clanging shut.

The firing of an engine.

Tires spitting out rocks as they traveled away from the church.

No, not the church. *The Devil's Playground*.

That quickly, her trickle of memories became a flood of unending hellish scenes. After injecting her with some kind of narcotic, the woman had raked the tip of her blade down London's cheek, not deeply, just enough to burn like a hundred forest fires.

'Better rest while you can. We won't be gone too long. Just long enough for you to imagine all the things we plan on doing to you,' she whispered in a chilling voice. Then she'd gripped the bindings at London's wrists and pulled tightly until the fabric cut into her circulation. She'd repeated the process with the gag in London's mouth, making it feel like the back of her head was being split in half from the force of securing it.

And then the final act... sealing London in darkness as she lowered the lid of the coffin.

The reason no light penetrated the dark, even with her eyes wide open. Behind her gag, London screamed, refusing to stop even when her throat swelled from the effort.

With panic and claustrophobia hammering away at her, London tried to combat the sensation of being buried alive, tried to breathe through the burning in her lungs, convinced she was running out of oxygen. Sobbing into the rag slicing into the corners of her mouth and shivering violently, she raised her bound arms to push against the lid. With every failed attempt to dislodge the top, her struggles to breathe labored against her desire to escape this closed box.

Despite the fever caused by her festering wounds stealing her energy, she continued fighting against the lid with all she had left, ignoring every bit of the pain as her hands scraped against the splintered wood. Just when she thought her body would refuse to give a second's worth more effort, the lid budged. Not much, but enough to allow the frightening shadows of the basement to shift along the walls and into the prison of her coffin. Enough for the words *The Devil's Playground* to mock her with their letters dripping like spilled blood.

Sweat from terror and anxiety as much as from exertion drowned London's body in moisture as she allowed her hands to collapse back to her stomach, sending screaming waves of agony shooting through her when they landed on her stab wound.

Razor blades of pain robbed her of breath even as she struggled to listen for sounds that her attackers had returned. With images of Skye and Elena's murdered bodies flashing rapidly through her mind, London alternated between praying for a way to escape and praying for a quick death.

Chapter Ten

Friday, April 23

By the time Alyssa and Cord arrived at the precinct fifteen minutes later, the APB for London Brecken had gone out and Hal had already posted scores of graphic images from last night's crime scene around the incident room. At one end, Tony jotted down the beginnings of a timeline. At the other, Joe compiled a list of possible preliminary suspects, persons of interest, or individuals the team wanted to speak to. Roman Cordova's name sat at the top, scrawled in red and underlined twice. Below it was written *Carter and Abigail's Father*, followed by a question mark, and August Holt who, for the moment, was merely someone Alyssa felt the team needed to talk to. Even if he offered nothing else to assist with their case, at least they would have covered all their bases. She didn't recognize the final name on the list, Victor Reynolds.

'Who's that?' she asked, pretending not to notice how the occupants of the room suddenly stopped moving and stared as they tried to gauge her temper. She recognized that her team understood her well enough to know her anger wasn't directed at them but at herself for failing to recognize last night that they did indeed have a third victim, as her gut had tried to tell her. They also knew her well enough not to offer her empty platitudes, not because they didn't care, not because they weren't equally frustrated with themselves, but because they knew nothing short of finding London and bringing her safely home would help.

Hal wheeled his chair to a spot where he wouldn't have to crane his neck to see what she was referring to. 'Victor Reynolds. Luckily for us, London Brecken, aged twenty-six, appears to be fairly active on social media. And from what I've been able to discern so far, Reynolds was her last boyfriend – or at least the last she shared about. They were together about two years and appear to have broken things off just over a year ago. No drama. Just a status update on both accounts. They're still friends who comment on each other's posts, which supports the no drama assertion. And even though we all know everything on social is one percent honest, accurate, and never embellished, you'll probably want to verify that for yourselves. I can also tell you that Reynolds currently resides up in the Four Corners area, and according to his "About" section, is a nurse at San Juan Regional Center in Farmington.'

'So, what, basically a four-hour drive?' Cord asked.

'Yep. And I've already got a call in for the nurse of staffing to call me back, so if he was at work, that should be a quick alibi check.'

'You managed all that in the fifteen minutes it took for us to get here?' Alyssa couldn't hide her astonishment. Even for Hal, that was supersonic speed.

'I'd already been dredging her social media accounts from earlier, so after I got the APB taken care of, I got to work on this because, as Brecken's ex, I figured you'd want to establish his whereabouts fairly quickly, seeing as how London was kidnapped, not murdered like our other two victims.'

'Not murdered yet, we hope,' Alyssa mumbled.

'We'll find her in time, Lys. There's a reason she wasn't slaughtered along with Fleming and Garcia. And no matter what the reason, we have to concentrate on the fact that it gives us time. Anyway, the second I hear back from San Juan, you'll be my first call.'

Despite being confined to a wheelchair for the rest of his life after being shot in the line of duty years earlier, Hal remained one of the most optimistic players on the entire team, a trait Alyssa often admired and appreciated, even during those rare times it annoyed her, usually when she was berating herself for overlooking something crucial. She jerked her chin up toward the whiteboard. 'What can you tell us about Roman Cordova?'

'Right now, I can tell you the guy is twenty-eight, started hearing the music of those metal bars at the age of sixteen, and has a list of previous addresses that's longer than I am tall – or at least taller than I was when I was still standing.'

Knowing Hal's comment was his own weak attempt at humor, Alyssa forced what she hoped looked like a legitimate smile.

'Current address is near Tingley Beach. I'll text it to you when you and Cord go talk to him. Anyway, when he was sixteen, he bypassed all the petty theft and misdemeanor charges and went all in for domestic abuse for punching his own mother in the face after she tried taking his car keys when she caught him drinking. Did a short stint in juvie, and within hours of being released, he got picked up for drunk and disorderly, public intoxication, resisting arrest, assaulting an officer, and underage drinking.'

'Clearly, juvie set him straight,' Cord mumbled drily.

'Yeah, well, you're not wrong,' Hal said. 'Which is probably why the next judge ordered him to take anger management classes. Unfortunately, leniency in that regard didn't seem to help either since his record continues to show a series of domestic disturbance calls, mostly involving family members, but he either got his act together, or he got better at not getting caught because he stopped showing up in the system a couple of years ago. Well, until a few weeks ago, that is.'

'Skye Fleming's police reports?' Alyssa guessed.

'Yep. March eighth and April first. The first report states Skye insisted on making a police report because it made her uncomfortable that Cordova had accelerated from merely observing her from across the street to actually approaching her home. The second incident, the officer, Mel Rhodes, drove over to Cordova's and gave him a verbal warning to steer clear of the Fleming residence or she'd haul him in on whatever charges she could find.'

'Okay. Can you get me the names and contact info for Cordova's mother? I'd like to see if she'll talk to us.'

'Sure thing.'

'I have an obvious question,' Joe said. 'If Cordova was so hung up on Skye, why would he kill her but kidnap her friend? Doesn't make sense.'

Alyssa nodded because the same logical thought had passed through her mind. 'It's a good question, obvious or not. Speaking of London, let's get back to her. You said you tracked down an ex. But what about family members? Parents, brothers, sisters?' She remembered that Ashlee Garcia had mentioned something about London's grandparents raising her. 'Grandparents?' she tacked on.

Immediately shifting gears, Hal clicked on an open tab that flashed London's Facebook page onto the wall. 'So far, all I can tell you is that it appears her grandparents live on a farm in Indiana. No mention of parents or siblings, at least that I've been able to find.' He glanced over his shoulder. 'Which could mean they aren't close, or they're deceased, or they don't like their info out there. I'll see what I can do about reaching the grandparents and hopefully get some of those questions answered.' He scrolled through pages of London's Facebook photos. 'You can see for yourselves that almost all her photos consist of our two victims and snapshots of food, a trend I still don't understand. Why does anyone care what someone else ate?'

Unrealistic or not, Alyssa had been hoping to walk into the incident room and get a clear direction on who had London and where. Some people viewed her impatience as a negative trait; she viewed it as something that drove her to get results fast, which made her good at her job. 'What about Elena Garcia or Skye Fleming?' Feeling like she was standing still, every muscle in Alyssa's body tensed, as if she'd spent two hours too long in the gym.

One side of Hal's mouth tipped down into a frown. 'Fleming, thirty years old, isn't nearly as active on social media as her two friends. Her last post was on Instagram about eight months ago, first day of first grade for Carter. Elena Garcia's pretty static on both Facebook and Twitter, and her Instagram is filled primarily with inspirational quotes, interspersed with the occasional selfie, so active but not much to go on, I'm afraid.'

In an effort to alleviate some of the throbbing pressure behind her eyes, Alyssa rubbed her temples while she studied the crime scene photos and the rudimentary timeline they had constructed. 'Okay, here's what Cord and I learned.' Though she still didn't sit, she pulled a chair back from the table, absently rocking it back and forth on two legs.

'You've already heard we're looking for two assailants, not one. Carter Fleming gave us just enough to be able to piece together some of the events that transpired last night. Around eight thirty, shortly after Elena arrived, Skye tucked him and his sister into bed, and London Brecken went back to read them a story that turned into several. They were listening to *Winnie-the-Pooh* when he said someone knocked at the door. Understandably, he became agitated and a little confused about the sequence of events that followed.' Alyssa's gaze drifted to the photo of Skye Fleming's mutilated body before shifting back to her team.

'Apparently, as soon as London realized that something was wrong, she ushered the children into the closet with her, where the three of them hid. Her plan was to call the police, but according to Carter, she'd left her phone in the living room. He told us he thought he could hear his mother crying and making noises, and he tried to go to her, but London caught him before he made it all the way to the door.'

The guilt that had flashed in Carter's eyes, Alyssa knew, would haunt her for years to come. 'Only after the house fell silent – Carter couldn't say for how long – London told them to stay put and stay quiet while she went and retrieved her phone. He said he was scared that when she returned, he wouldn't know if it was her, so she told him she'd say the password his mother had taught him.'

The lines in Joe's forehead deepened. 'Is that what he meant when he asked Cord for the code word?'

Alyssa nodded. 'Actually, in this instance it's more of a code or pass phrase that Skye Fleming gave him in case anyone other than her, London, or Elena tried to pick him up from school. If the person didn't know the correct password, he was supposed to go tell a trusted adult right away.'

Hal, still tapping away at his computer, glanced up long enough to say, 'Kind of like you and Brock did with Holly and Isaac when they were little.'

'Exactly. Of course, my reasoning stemmed from being in law enforcement and being a little paranoid about someone I'd arrested trying to get to me through my kids.' She fell silent as the memory of that very thing happening flashed in her mind. Only it had been far worse than a pissed off criminal from her past. She shook the memory away and continued. 'In our case, Brock and I created a game where every week we'd come up with a new password. In Skye Fleming's case, they came up with one code and stuck with it.'

Tony removed the ballpoint pen cap he'd been chewing on. 'Maybe Fleming felt like she needed to do it, since she had her own personal stalker? It wouldn't be the first time a stalker took the kids as a way to get to his – or her – interest.'

'It could also have something to do with the kids' father,' Cord added. 'I suppose it could also have to do with her work for Intel, but I doubt it. I mean, they're a semiconductor chip manufacturer, but she, Elena, and London worked in Sales and Marketing. According to Intel's website, their job consisted of matching potential clients to the proper technology needed for that business. Not exactly high profile, if you know what I mean.'

'Speaking of the bio dad, any ideas on how to run him down?' Tony asked.

'As long as Carter and Abigail remain wards of the state, we can request DNA swabs. If their father's in the system, we might be able to track him down that way,' Alyssa said.

'Well, then hopefully, Baby Daddy'll be in the system somewhere,' Joe said. 'That would be helpful.'

While Alyssa agreed, her gut insisted the children's father was a long shot. 'Though, similar to our question about Cordova, it doesn't make sense that the bio dad would murder Skye and Elena, kidnap London, and then leave the kids behind. It doesn't add up. Still, we'll explore that avenue until we know for sure.'

Tony cleared his throat, drawing everyone's attention. 'I know we're past this point already, but I just have to say how royally screwed up our world is when we have to teach our little ones something like a password so they know not to go with a stranger. That's all I'm saying.'

'Yeah, well, Carter didn't exactly do as London instructed anyway.' Cord's comment had the effect of a huge vacuum sucking the air out of the room.

Hal's face paled under the artificial lights. 'Don't tell me he actually followed her!' Not even he could mask the horror in his voice.

'Not exactly,' Cord said. 'He decided that while London went to grab her phone, he'd go check on his mother.'

Like it had when Carter told them, goosebumps raised the downy soft hairs on Alyssa's arms.

'Jesus,' Tony breathed out.

'Yeah, Jesus,' Alyssa agreed. 'He said he whispered to Abigail that he was going to go get their mommy, but she had to stay hidden. He tucked her beneath the blanket, made sure the closet door closed, and then snuck out into the hallway. He checked to make sure London wasn't watching and that's when he, and I quote here, "saw two people dressed like Batman." One of them had a hold of London from behind, stabbing her. He got scared and snuck back into the bedroom with Abigail, where the two of them remained until we found them.'

'Holy shit. Just… holy shit. I'm sorry, but that's all I've got.' Joe's tone portrayed the same horror they all felt. 'How the hell did two cold-blooded killers *not* spot him?'

'We don't know for sure that they didn't, but if that's the case, then it was nothing short of a pure miracle' – Cord propped his forehead into the palm of his hands – 'because absolutely nothing else makes sense.'

'I can't believe what I'm hearing, man.' Tony wiped perspiration from his face. 'How did a six-year-old kid manage to keep his cool like that? Hell, I don't think *I* could've.'

'I agree a thousand percent,' Alyssa said, 'but his disobedience has given us a heads-up that we're searching for a pair of killers, not just one.' She had to swallow the nausea that bubbled up as she wondered how long it would've taken her team to realize that fact if it hadn't been for Carter doing what he'd done.

The sudden peal of Alyssa's ringing phone caused everyone to jump. Seeing that it was Liz, she swiped to answer. 'You're on speaker. What else did you learn?'

Liz sighed. 'In short, and I'll be honest, I don't know whether it's good news or bad, but as far as an actual person's description, we've still got nothing. It took a lot of time to draw out his memories, so I'll give you what I can, and we'll have to go from there.'

'It's a place to start.' Alyssa swallowed and asked the question they hadn't yet received an answer to before they'd left the Sandersons'. 'Did Carter say if he'd seen his mother's body before closing himself back into his bedroom with his sister?'

'I broached that topic very carefully, and from what I can gather, no, he didn't. After seeing what was happening to London, his focus was to protect Abigail.'

'Do you believe him?' Tony's voice conveyed his doubt.

'Actually, yes, I do. Unlike last night, he knew he was in a safe place and could tell us the truth,' Liz said. 'Which is how, as I'm sure you've all been informed now, we know we're searching for two individuals "dressed like Batman." I showed him some pictures and drew some sketches from that, and from what I can deduce, I'm fairly certain the assailants wore hooded cloaks, black in color with a red lightning bolt design on the back. It was a little more difficult to get a height estimation from him, but he used Cord and Mr. Sanderson as his base comparison. Cord, you're what, six-two?'

'Correct.'

'Okay, and Mr. Sanderson said he's five-eleven. At least one of the assailants was between that height range. Carter caught a glimpse of the second person before he closed himself back in the bedroom and told me they were possibly about as tall as me, or a little taller, so similar in height to London Brecken.'

'Did he mention anything about his father?' Joe asked.

'Rosemary did ask him about that, but he seemed confused by the question and said he doesn't have a father. No big surprise there since I don't think any of us really expected him to give a name anyway.

'One more thing before I go,' Liz continued. 'Despite what I said a moment ago, Carter clammed up tight when I asked if he heard either assailant speak, so it's possible he recognized the voice, but his brain is protecting him from remembering because he's afraid of what will happen if he admits he might be able to possibly identify one of the killers. That, by the way, was Kyra Sanderson's take. Apparently, she had a psychology practice before quitting to become a full-time treatment foster care parent. And while I'm no psych doctor, I have to agree with her assessment. So, throwing that info out there in case it helps something else stick.'

A vehicle blasting its horn burst through the speakers, drowning out most of Liz's next few words, so all Alyssa caught was that their teammate should be back at the precinct soon before dead air told them she'd already ended the call.

While Liz had still been speaking, Hal had suddenly started rolling his chair back and forth in jerky movements like a hot wheel about to race, so Alyssa's attention riveted on him. 'What's on your mind, Hal?'

Instead of answering right away, Hal divided his own attention between studying the crime scene photos and whatever he'd typed into his computer while they'd had Liz on the phone. 'You're not going to like what I'm thinking,' he finally said.

Alyssa hadn't needed him to tell her that. His agitated reaction had pretty much all but carved that guarantee into stone. She waved her hand for him to continue.

'Twenty-five years ago, before I was shot, a rash of very gruesome murders in a truly short amount of time plagued the city. We're talking decapitations, victims burned alive, literally found chained to stakes' – Hal cleared his throat before pushing out the last word – 'and quartered.'

'Christ. How many is a rash?' Tony wanted to know.

'Five. Victims varied in age from a girl just turned thirteen all the way to a sixty-three-year-old grandfather of four. There were mutilations, hearts carved out post-mortem, symbols etched into skin, and the list goes on.

But before that even, there was an influx of neighbor-hood pets going missing, mostly cats and small dogs.' As he mentally dropped back in time, Hal's face became an unreadable mask. 'The department looked into the reports, of course, but they weren't priorities. Until people started finding their pets disemboweled. I don't think I need to paint a more graphic pic for you.' This time, when he glanced around the room, he made sure to make eye contact with every member of the team. 'At the time, the perpetrators wore cloaks.'

'You can't be thinking the crimes are related,' Tony said, confused. 'I mean, it's not really unusual for perpetrators of a violent crime to wear something to help disguise their identities or even just to intimidate their victims.'

Hal rotated his neck on his shoulders before adding the rest. 'You're right. But the culprits back then turned out to be a practicing Satanic cult. One of their most prominent signatures was a lightning bolt carved into the stomachs of some of their victims.'

The room fell so silent, Alyssa could've heard a feather floating in the air.

Chapter Eleven

Snippets of words like *sacrifice* and *desecration* that London understood but that her mind refused to accept drifted into her awareness, joined by the scent of burning incense coiling into the stale air before disappearing into the dark shadows of the basement's ceiling. With the cold chilling her very bones contrasting with the warmth of the high sun peeking in through the broken window, she tried in vain not to listen to what the kidnappers were doing. Despite the effort, tiny whimpers rasped past the cloth in her lips as each of their vulgar and heavily excited breaths sawed through what little remained of her sanity.

Still, it wasn't until the two moved to stand over her, holding clear chalices filled with a red liquid that she truly wanted to pretend was not what she knew it was, that a staggering wave of nausea slammed into her. Bile, swift and urgent, raced up her throat, cutting off her airway when they hooked their arms together and tipped the viscous drink into each other's mouths, draining the glasses. Unable to breathe with the rag still shoved between her lips, London jerked back and forth, kicking at the sides of the coffin until the gag was suddenly ripped from her mouth. At the same time, someone roughly shoved her onto her side. After the violent expulsion of what little remained in her stomach, much needed oxygen finally filled her exploding lungs.

Beyond the thundering pulse of blood roaring through her ears, London heard the woman's cold promise. 'You didn't really think we'd let you die that easily, did you? No. See, we have so many plans for you.'

As she spoke, the male, his face still mostly hidden in the shadow of his cloak, revealed his glistening dagger. Placing the tip of the blade at a spot just below London's chin, he pressed, sending a fine line of wetness trickling down her neck. Her mouth opened on a scream, but before more than a low screech could escape, the woman's hand cracked down on her mouth hard enough for London's lips to grind into her teeth.

The woman's palm remained where it was as the man glided the tip of his knife down the center of London's body until he could lift her shirt. With his partner's excited encouragement, he continued dragging the blade in circles around her wounds, leaving shallow cuts and a trail of flames in its path.

With her brain entirely focused on the pain, London didn't realize the woman's hand no longer covered her mouth until she suddenly seized London's chin and jerked her head toward her. The last thing London saw before her left eye erupted in fire was liquid falling from an eyedropper. Her bound hands flew to cover her face, but the woman gripped the cloth, stopping the movement.

Screaming through the gag now being shoved back into her mouth, London watched the two push to their feet. As the man moved away and further into the light, the tiniest glimpse of his features flashed across her blurry vision. In that split second, she realized something about him seemed familiar, but her head was too consumed with the inferno licking at her nerve-endings to try to recall from where she might know him.

For several long minutes, her tormentors remained where they were, their heads cocked to the side, observing her with a glaze of excitement that depicted an evil darker than the gates of hell.

Chapter Twelve

Blood beaded where Draven's dagger traced their prisoner's skin. Swiping a finger across the flat part of the blade, Mara closed her eyes and wiped the blood across her lips, relishing the electric buzz of exhilaration flowing through her, knowing Draven was experiencing the same thrill.

A thrill far more intense than when she used to sit in her room and listen to the stories of sacrifice and resultant supreme power. Stories that, as a young girl, she'd believed to be nothing more than tales told by her father to elicit that spine-tingling zing of fear of God's wrath. Until years later when she'd attended her first 'real' worship and learned the stories had been fact not fiction.

At the front of a clearing in a hidden pasture, a severed animal's head mounted on a post soared high enough for all the members to see. By then, Mara had done enough research and learned enough to know the goat's head represented Satan, the power of darkness. An excited energy rippled through the air like a downed electric pole. Intrigued, she'd pushed her way past the friend she'd come with and through the small crowd of twelve, fifteen individuals, all garbed in black, hooded robes.

She'd reached the front of the clearing in time to witness two members standing behind an altar, drinking greedily from the chalices clutched in their hands, a light line of red fluid trickling from the corner of the man's mouth. Mara's pulse had raced, her breathing had quickened, and she'd felt *warm* inside, like someone had wrapped a toasty blanket around her shoulders on a cold day. She'd looked around, and the sense of power, of being alive, of being *seen* permeated the very air around her.

Afterwards, the group had sat inside a large circle around an inverted cross and taken turns talking about shedding their cloaks of guilt and weakness and donning their armors of darkness, boasting of personal sacrifices and mutilations and the mental gratification that fed their power. With each new testimony, Mara knew the stories her father had thundered about were at least partly true. The devil *did* prey on the weak; he also empowered the strong. And in that moment, she'd known she had every intention of being stronger and more powerful than even her father.

With each new service, the intoxication of the free atmosphere where anyone could behave in any way, living out their darkest, most twisted fantasies without fear of judgement, grew more intense. With each animal sacrifice, her sense of supremacy began to truly awaken and flourish. And then the night had come when she'd realized she needed more. Much more. Even then, she had recognized that her cravings extended beyond the dark into the forbidden, even within their circle.

For years, she'd been able to keep that part of herself buried, until the day she met the one she called Draven. He'd been angry, bitter, and disillusioned about life and family and the world. She'd lent a sympathetic ear, made herself available, offered him whiskey and drugs, and filled his head with promises of power and supremacy. And then, after almost a year had gone by, she'd invited him to a secret meeting, terrified that she'd read him wrong, that he wouldn't be enlightened.

He'd watched with fascination but also with what she considered his critical eye. And then, to her surprise, he'd thrown himself in with absolute, unadulterated abandonment. Then one night, after leaving the service, the two of them found themselves driving aimlessly through the mountains, taking random trails, discussing the thrill of using her new dagger for that night's animal sacrifice. The verbal replay acted as the most intense foreplay she'd ever experienced, so at a switchback, Mara cut to the right and killed the engine. Seconds later, they were having frantic sex in the back seat of her car.

Afterwards, she'd known she'd found her one true partner. With every meeting they attended, the clawing hunger grew. Like a junkie, the desperate urge to feel more of that adrenaline-fueled, invigorating act of domination took over her every thought. But she only knew of one way to accomplish that ultimate pinnacle of a high.

Now, standing here next to Draven, Mara's eyes danced in the light of the flickering candles. She cast her gaze in his direction as he stared down in fascination at the woman lying wide-eyed in the coffin they'd built and held together with twine and rusted nails. Together, they watched the terror gripping the woman's face as the hallucinogen Mara had dripped into her eye began to take effect.

Chapter Thirteen

Friday, April 23

Even though Alyssa had guessed the direction of Hal's thoughts the second he'd mentioned the missing pets, the revelation still managed to jar her, along with the rest of the team.

'Just to be clear,' Cord said, 'exactly what are you suggesting here?'

His expression grave, Hal wheeled his chair back around so he faced the crime scene photos. 'I'm not suggesting anything other than a possible occult angle.' He paused to rub his palm over his jaw. 'Though, in the spirit of full disclosure, I should probably inform all of you that, back at the time this all went down, we arrested about a dozen members of the occult. Of those, we failed to definitively link two individuals to any of the crimes, so we had no choice but to cut them loose. Long story short, of the dozen we busted, two were not charged with anything, two coasted with little more than a slap on the wrist, and five were convicted of extreme animal cruelty, served their too-short sentences, and have stayed out of trouble since.'

'How do you know?' Joe asked.

'Because for a while there, law enforcement kept track of their whereabouts in case similar killings cropped up again. Most of them scattered after doing their time, and before long, we no longer had the resources to keep up with, quote unquote, law-abiding citizens, so the ones who remained in the immediate area back then dropped off our radar.'

Alyssa held up her palm to interrupt. 'What about the other three? You mentioned busting a dozen people, but only listed nine.'

A hard mask fell across Hal's face. 'Was gonna get to that next. The remaining three had a long list of convictions, but the ones carrying the heaviest penalties were first-degree murder, abuse of a corpse, and extreme animal cruelty.'

With pictures of Skye's mutilated body surrounding her, and knowing Carter and Abigail had heard their mother's pain-filled, terrified cries, Alyssa's stomach took a nosedive.

'Do you happen to know if any of those three have been released back into the public?' Joe asked.

'As a matter of fact...' Hal's fingers flew over his keyboard. 'Ezekiel Henry, born Harrison Henry before legally changing his name, took a shiv in the prison shower and ended up dying less than two years into his sentence.' He glanced up. 'Which was too bad because his was the only one that came with no chance of parole. Though we had several conflicting stories, we always believed he was the head honcho or whatever it is that occults call their ringleaders.

'In 2016, Julian Lincoln was released, but died last year from complications brought on by his throat cancer.' Hal cast an image on the wall of a man who eerily resembled a younger Charles Manson. 'You might recall seeing his face and hearing about him on the news.'

Tony nodded. 'Now that you mention it, I do, because I remember thinking the dude made Richard Ramirez look like an angel.'

Hal tipped his head in agreement. 'And finally, Ewan Moore, the youngest of the three at age twenty-two when he was arrested, was released on parole in 2017. Due to the charge and conviction of extreme animal cruelty resulting in death, the conditions of his release included that Moore may not have or be around any pets or animals, including those in his own household. Nor can he come within one hundred yards of any of his victims' families.'

'Maybe he shouldn't be allowed around people in general,' Joe muttered under his breath.

'Can't disagree there. Anyway, since his release, he's been living in a little rural community off I-40, near the Route 66 casino.'

Alyssa tilted her head toward Hal's laptop. 'You got all that from that one article?'

'Nope.' Hal tapped the side of his head. 'I got that from making sure I knew where he ended up as soon as I heard about his release. He may have been young in age, but I'm not ashamed to tell you the crimes he committed or participated in gave me nightmares for a long time. Might be that he really changed and, if the rumors hold true, "found religion." It's probably still worth having a chat with him, I think. If nothing else, if he's willing to talk to you, maybe he can give some insight into what – or who – we might be looking at. And if he really is a changed man, he should jump at the chance to help. Could be part of his *redemption*.' The way Hal's lips curled in disgust made clear his true feelings on that topic.

Cord stopped pacing and leaned his back against the wall, arms crossed over his chest in a way that told Alyssa his mind was spinning a mile a minute. 'What about children, wives, or significant others? Either of the convicted three or the ones who scattered? Any of them still live in the area?'

'That's a good question.' Alyssa turned to Hal.

'Well, conditions for release for both Lincoln and Moore also included bans from social media – fear of luring in recruits since, in Lincoln's case anyway, he was still an active Satan worshiper before his death.' Hal suddenly shivered as if a frigid breeze only he could feel had blown in and clutched him in its arms. 'But I think I remember at least one of them having a daughter. I'll have to do a little research to see if I can dig up some answers, but if I had to guess, I'd say the likelihood of family or even old friends being in the area is better than fair.'

Alyssa moved closer to the crime scene images. 'Okay, since we've been bandying about a possible occult connection, and you've got the most experience, Hal, why don't you walk us through what we have here.'

Hal grabbed a yardstick leaning against the wall and began tapping images. 'The black rose stuck in Skye's mouth, the symbols on the wall smeared in blood, black robes with a red lightning bolt down the back all have both general and specific meanings within the occult. The rose could represent death or vengeance, or even a deep hatred for someone. One look at Skye Fleming's body, and it could be any or all three of those things.' As if a puppeteer had pulled their strings, everyone's eyes momentarily shifted toward Roman Cordova's name before reverting their attention back to the symbolism Hal mentioned.

'The dagger carved into her cheek,' Hal continued, '*could* represent a show of power. Again' – he waved at the images of the two victims – 'that massacre was definitely a show of power. The three Fs, well, if this is a Satanic or demonic-type following we're looking at, then it stands to reason that the letter F is the sixth letter of the alphabet, so three Fs mean...'

'Six-six-six,' Joe finished, his face losing two shades of color as he performed the sign of the cross.

Tony's Adam's apple pressed against the skin of his throat as he swallowed. 'Man, I can't remember a time when I've wanted you to be more wrong, friend. But going along with this theory of symbolism, then the lightning bolt on the cloaks could represent Satan? Like, I don't know this for sure, but didn't Lucifer, what, fall from heaven as a lightning bolt or something?'

Joe nodded. 'I admit it's been a minute since I took in a service, but I think I remember something like that, yeah.'

'The destroyer, right?' Cord's jaw tightened, and Alyssa suspected he was thinking of the destruction in Carter and Abigail's lives.

'That's what we learned more than two decades ago,' Hal confirmed.

Studying the photos, listening to Hal's explanations, it all clicked. The only excuse Alyssa could think of, and she admitted it was just that, an excuse, for overlooking something that should've been obvious was that she'd been distracted by the discovery of Carter and Abigail. And because of that, they'd lost a precious amount of time that could've been spent searching for London Brecken.

Tony reached out and touched her arm, forcing her to look down at him. 'None of us made the connection last night, Lys.'

Her team knew her well enough to know where her thoughts had slipped, and the fact that they were allowing her any amount of grace only managed to frustrate her more.

'Tony's right,' Joe added. 'So, we just need to focus on moving forward.'

Alyssa bit back the retort sitting on the tip of her tongue because it wasn't her team's fault that she'd failed to connect all the dots that led to an occult angle. 'If we're really dealing with an occult link, then I don't need to tell you what that might mean in terms of Carter and Abigail being in even bigger danger than we already feared. Especially once word gets out that they were possible witnesses. We'll need to talk to the captain about approving round-the-clock surveillance for them and the Sandersons until we track down the persons responsible.'

Cord cleared his throat, and everyone turned from Alyssa to him. 'I hate to be the one to point this out, but if we're on the right track, then whoever we're after probably isn't planning on killing Brecken right away, otherwise they would've murdered her alongside Fleming and Garcia.' His eyes swept the room, landing on the crime scene photo of Skye Fleming's mutilated body. 'They're planning on torturing her first.'

Chapter Fourteen

Something akin to an electric jolt burned through Alyssa, as if an invisible phantom had raked its talons across her exposed nerves. Cord was right. And unless they located London fast, the kidnapped woman would likely prefer, even pray for, death. With every lost second counting against them, Alyssa began barking orders.

'Hal, start researching what kinds of occult activity might have been reported in the state in the past year. Start in the metro and fan out from there. While you're at it, see if you can link any similarities between our current case and the one you worked. Flag anything you think could even be a questionable connection.'

Aside from being an eternal optimist and great listener, Hal was the epitome of a research god, as far as Alyssa was concerned, so she knew his research would go deep and be thorough. The man could unearth a gnat hidden in the dirt under a rock as long as he possessed the tiniest bit of information.

'Also, see if you can reach Moore's parole officer, find out if he's been checking in regularly or if he's missed any assigned dates. Then let's see if he'll talk to us. Like you said earlier, if the rumors are right about him finding religion, then he should jump at the chance of helping us shut down Satanic activity in the area, especially considering he's gonna be one of the first people we look to.'

'What do you want us to do first, Lys?' Tony's thumb swung back and forth between himself and Joe.

'Head over to Intel where our victims worked. No, wait. First, drop by London's neighborhood, question her neighbors, see if any of them can recall seeing anything or anyone out of the norm, find out if London might've mentioned any creepers watching her lately. If Cordova's involved, he had help. If you finish with all that, then see about getting us access to the victims' financials so we can track their credit cards in case the killers were stupid enough to take and use them. Also, let's get access to call logs and text messages. If we can get into the phones we have in our custody, great. Run down anything that looks even remotely suspicious.'

Liz walked in as Alyssa finished. She'd been with the team long enough to recognize Alyssa's persistent sense of urgency. 'I can help with the phone records and financials,' she offered.

'That would be great. Hal will fill you in on the rest. Let me know what any of you find. Oh, and Hal, would you mind updating Captain Hammond? In the meantime, Cord and I are heading out to speak with Roman Cordova as well as August Holt. I'm hesitant to name him as a person of interest right now, especially since his mother claims he didn't really know Skye. But, by her own admission, he's on drugs and approached her for money that she declined to give him. We've all been involved with cases where drugs and money lead to murder, so I'd still like to question him, find out his whereabouts last night, if for no other reason than to clear him.' At the door, Alyssa stopped and looked over her shoulder at Hal. 'I don't suppose Cordova's records say he was involved in devil-worshiping, do they?'

'Not that I've found, but I've already made a note to look into it, including checking his online profile and cross-checking anyone on his friends list that may have been around during my past case.'

'Good thinking,' Cord said.

A few minutes later, Alyssa and Cord were back in her Tahoe. As Cord buckled up, he said, 'I wonder if Cordova or Holt *is* involved in these murders, if Carter would recognize either of their voices. If he could, it stands to reason he'd be afraid of what might happen to him or Abigail if he remembered or admitted that. Even for a six-year-old, he seems perceptive enough to have picked up on his mother's fear, at least in Cordova's case, even if she attempted to keep it hidden from him.'

Alyssa nodded her agreement and pressed down harder on the accelerator as she shot down the interstate toward Cordova's house.

–

With a serious case of bedhead, green, gooey gunk in the corners of his eyes, and wearing an oil-stained tank top with holes speckled throughout, Roman Cordova opened his door with a growl. 'You have any idea what the hell time…' His words trailed off as Alyssa and Cord flashed their badges and barreled right over his complaint.

'Roman Cordova?' As soon as she saw him in person, the reason his name had scratched at her memory the first time she'd heard it suddenly clicked. Two years ago, he'd been hauled in for an interrogation regarding the rape and beating of an elderly lady. For several days, his face had been splashed all over the news, morning, afternoon, and evening. Until the sensational Evan Bishop serial killer case, one that became quite personal for Alyssa in more ways than one, broke and diverted all the attention away from Cordova. In the end, he'd been in no way involved in the assault on the woman, which had come out when the real perpetrator was captured. It was possible Hal hadn't gotten that far in his research because it wasn't actually a part of Cordova's record.

Now, Roman Cordova stood in the doorway, lips curled in a way that caused the white, jagged scar across his cheek to stand out even more, and Alyssa couldn't help but think that Skye Fleming had been right to be concerned about this man showing up randomly at her house. Even now, an air of danger practically vibrated off of him.

'Why do you want to know?'

'We have some questions we'd like to ask.'

Cordova straightened so that he was no longer leaning on his door frame. 'What kind of questions?'

'Such as where were you last night? Let's start there.' Cord's tone brooked no argument, and neither did the expression on his face, which didn't alter when Cordova thrust his chest out, crossed his arms over his torso, and spread his stance.

Alyssa almost laughed. If Roman Cordova had been hoping his 'macho' move would be intimidating, he'd first need platform shoes or to grow another four or five inches to even come close to matching Cord's height. He might also want to consider packing on a few muscles. And even then, her money remained steadfastly on her partner. Regardless, since Carter recalled that one of the assailants had been shorter than Cord, Cordova's height kept him squarely in the range of the suspects they were searching for.

After a few seconds of a silent pissing match, Cord cocked his head ever so slightly to the side. 'Is the question confusing you?' His tone rarely portrayed the type of condescension he now exhibited unless someone rubbed him the wrong way, which clearly, the arrogant Cordova did.

Another couple of seconds stretched out before Skye Fleming's stalker decided he had nothing to lose by answering. 'What time last night?'

'Why don't you start with around six?' Cord suggested.

'Six? I guess I was having dinner. Here. Tacos, in case you want to know.' Sarcasm and irritation dripped from every word. 'You can sniff my trash can if you don't believe me.'

Cord ignored the smirk on Cordova's face. 'And then what?'

'And then I hit the club around ten. Didn't get home until around three this morning.'

Alyssa arched her brows into a vee. 'Clubbing on a Thursday? Any receipts to back that up?'

Through clenched teeth, Cordova practically growled. 'Yes, clubbing on a Thursday. I didn't have anywhere to be early this morning. And no. I used cash. But I'm sure you can get witnesses or whatever to back me up. I'm sure O'Sullivan's has plenty of security cameras that will prove my whereabouts.'

Alyssa already knew the popular bar did, and she had every intention of having someone on her team check those cameras immediately. 'What about after you ate dinner and before you left to hit the clubs?'

'I don't know. I didn't write a damn journal about my day. Didn't know I was going to need to. And since this is sounding a hell of a lot like an interrogation for something I'm being accused of, I think you damn well better tell me what it is that you're accusing me of because if you don't, I'll lawyer up faster than you can spit.'

He followed the words with the action, and Alyssa resisted the urge to roll her eyes. Why was it that so many of the defensive men she interviewed always did that? If it was supposed to make her squeamish, it always failed to do its job. It was disgusting, and little more. In her line of work, it would take a hell of a lot more than expelling some smelly saliva, especially since she dealt with far worse on a regular basis.

Case in point, the Fleming massacre and the reason she and Cord were here now. At least she could be thankful Cordova hadn't spat *at* them. That would've been a little harder to ignore.

'Skye Fleming and Elena Garcia were murdered last night.' Alyssa kept her attention focused on the man's face as she explained the reason for their visit.

In the space of a heartbeat, Cordova's face morphed from arrogant to raging anger – all wrapped up in hatred. 'No. No way. If something went down at that bi—Skye's, you're not pinning it on me.'

Something about Cordova's reaction tripped Alyssa's internal alarm. Beside her, almost as if he hadn't witnessed the same thing, Cord leaned his hip into the rickety porch railing. To anyone else, it might appear to be a casual, relaxed pose, but she knew better. Still, if his intent was to come off as less intimidating, he was only marginally successful. 'Mr. Cordova, we're not trying to pin anything on anyone. We're just trying to get a timeline of events so we can determine what happened.'

'Uh-uh. I know how this goes down. If you need someone to take the fall, it'll only be a matter of time before "evidence" starts popping up, implicating me. So, I'm just going to say this, and then you can talk to me through my attorney. The last time I talked to Skye was April first. That's like three weeks ago.'

'You mean when you showed up uninvited to her house, and she had to call the police because you wouldn't leave?' Cord asked.

'Hey, I left. You can even ask the cop who came to my house later.'

'How did it make you feel when you found out Skye called the cops on you?'

'Pissed me off. I didn't do anything wrong. If I'd known the bitch was so uppity, I never would've asked her out in the first place.' Again, Cordova spat.

'But she'd already told you no, hadn't she?' Alyssa asked.

Cordova's angry gaze swept down to her. 'Yeah? So? Against the law to try to get a girl to change her mind?'

Alyssa raised her brows and cocked her head. 'Well, yeah, if it makes the girl feel threatened or becomes harassment. How many times did you ask her out?'

'I don't know. A few.'

'And you thought watching her house and delivering her roses when she'd already asked you to leave her alone would... what? Woo her?'

'Happens all the time, lady.'

'Yeah, in Hollywood movies, maybe. In real life, we call that stalking, and yep, it's illegal. And for the record, not at all romantic.' Alyssa rolled over Cordova's words. 'Where did you meet Skye anyway?'

'Delivery for Intel. Look, no matter what that police report says, I didn't threaten anyone with violence. Did I get mad? Yeah, and I'm sure her neighbors would attest to that. Especially that punk-ass kid next door, coming at me with a damn bat, like he could take me. Whatever. My pride was a little stung, and I reacted by yelling, calling her a few names, but that's where it ended. Like I said, it was the last time I saw her or tried talking to her.' As he spoke, Cordova's hands balled up tight, kind of like he'd relish throwing a punch right that minute. It didn't take Kyra Sanderson's degree in psychology to recognize Cordova's personality was exactly the type that would take being publicly turned down as a blow to his sexist ego.

'Listen, I don't even do deliveries at Intel anymore. Someone else does.'

'Who?' Cord asked.

'Who? How the hell should I know? I don't keep track of everyone's schedules. All I know is it ain't me. Look, I already admitted I probably said a few things I shouldn't have, but I had nothing to do with whatever went down over there. I'm sure you cops'll pull my cell records and try to ping my location, so go right ahead. Because all you're going to find is that I'm telling the truth.'

Cordova stretched his neck left and right, popping it, bringing to mind all the macho movies Isaac enjoyed, the kind where the actors cracked their thick, oversized necks and then their knuckles just before storming into a fistfight.

'What kind of vehicle do you drive, Mr. Cordova?' Alyssa asked.

He leveled his narrowed gaze on her. 'Are you hearing me, lady? I had nothing to do with it. I drive an '07 Pathfinder. Now, anything else you need to ask me, you can go through my attorney. Name's Edwin Mercer.'

With that, he jerked his foot away from the torn screen and slammed the warped front door in their face.

'Something tells me he didn't appreciate your last question there.' Cord glanced once over his shoulder as he followed Alyssa back to the car.

'You think?'

'Seriously, though, all kidding aside, I'll flat out say it: Roman Cordova's arrogant, obnoxious—'

'Assholish?' Alyssa finished.

'A little,' Cord agreed. 'Can't imagine why Skye Fleming didn't swoon over his stalking.'

'Well, being an ass doesn't make the guy guilty, and like he said, proving his whereabouts shouldn't be too difficult. And, since he's got a record, his fingerprints and DNA will already be on file, so if Lynn comes back with anything useful in that department, we'll be one step closer to ruling him in or out. Speaking of which, hopefully, our medical examiner will be able to provide some much-needed answers sooner than later.'

Chapter Fifteen

Friday, April 23

The fire burning in London's left eye, along with the sharp, shooting pains in her side and stomach held her cemented in this merry-go-round of terror instead of allowing her to sink into the blessed oblivion of unconsciousness. Her energy depleted from the effort it took just to concentrate on breathing, she shivered violently against the damp air and the chilly breeze coming in through the missing window where a well-fed mouse scampered across the ledge and over the desiccated carcasses of two rats, their scaly tails the only evidence of what they'd once been. Elena had always harbored the most insane phobia of rodents – she hadn't even liked Mickey Mouse.

The final, graphic image of her friend's slit throat seared itself into her mind, and London felt the muscles in her jaw clench, but not from the memory. The involuntary tension accompanied a creeping sensation of hyper awareness sizzling along every single one of her skin cells. What was happening to her? Acid blistered the back of her throat as movement from the corner of her eye stole her attention, and her neck snapped in that direction.

The scream building from the bottoms of her toes erupted, only to be captured against the gag. Disbelief and terror had London whipping her head back and forth in denial, even as she blinked rapidly against the impossibility of what had clearly appeared in front of her face. The scampering mouse had abruptly swollen to the size of a small housecat and had its red, beady eyes trained on her as it nibbled the meat from the skeletal remains of a dead – something. When it finished, it dropped back to all fours and prepared to jump in her direction. Her bound legs kicked against the coffin whose sides suddenly seemed to be bending and moving as they closed in on her.

Intuitively, she knew she'd been drugged with some mind-altering substance, but the more she tried to blink away the insanity, the larger the mouse grew, until squeaking floorboards and scuffling feet on the basement stairs had it scurrying off to safety through the broken window.

The bones in London's chest tightened, crushing her organs together, when she spotted a man carting a crucifix past her coffin before flipping it upside-down behind the blood-spattered altar. When he turned around, she squeezed her eyes closed against the face of the grotesque, red-horned monster that had taken the place of her captor. *It's in your mind, London. It's all in your mind. It isn't real.*

She *knew* it, but she still couldn't convince her head to stop seeing the impossible. Outside, the wind picked up, its shrill whistle resembling the eerie sounds of conjured spirits, and London's eyes snapped back open in time to watch a loose tree branch whip through the window like a mini missile aimed straight for the man's face before landing with a thud at his feet. It was then that she spotted the old, faded and cracked painting of Jesus that the man had removed from the, now breathing, wall.

London's heart thumped erratically, and even though she could hear her own keening cries, she couldn't keep them bottled up, not even when the man, his dark hair falling across his forehead and sweeping his eyes, dropped the painting, shattering the frame, as he turned to stare at her, a vampirish grin stretching across his face.

A chilling witch's cackle on the steps preceded the woman's reappearance, and London, in a flash of lucidity, realized that for the first time since she'd been taken, their features weren't at least partially shrouded by hooded cloaks, shadows, or her agonizing pain. Again, she thought she should *know* the man, but the woman with her scraggly brown hair, crimson lips, and cold, dilated, black-lined eyes reminded her of no one except pure evil. But trying to focus on *how* she could possibly know either of them proved impossible with the drug taunting her with hallucinations she tried to convince herself weren't real.

The woman pointed to the inverted cross and winked at her with an eye that undulated under her skin, as if it were trying to break loose of its socket. 'Adds a nice touch, don't you think?' She craned her neck up toward her partner and giggled. 'Though it looks like' – she lowered her voice to a demonic whisper – 'the '*Big Man*' upstairs doesn't like you messing with His boy's picture.'

The man's eyes drifted lazily behind him before he faced his partner again and grinned. 'Or maybe He doesn't like us making a mess of His house.'

Then, in a whirlwind of speed, the woman was suddenly in her face, leaning over the coffin, and as desperately as London tried, she couldn't make her mind unsee a demon crawling from the jagged streak of dried blood stretching from the corner of the woman's lip and upward, staining her cheek before reaching its demon's hand down to stroke her own face with a clawed talon. Squeaking whimpers escaped through the spaces of her bound mouth. *It's not real, it's not real, it's not real.* But no matter how many times she repeated the mantra, her brain refused to believe her.

For just a moment, the man dropped out of sight only to return with the lid of the coffin held suspended in the air. Their intention clear, London pleaded with her eyes, splinters burrowing into her head as she scraped it back and forth. *Please, no. Please.* She couldn't be closed in.

'What?' The woman shifted her attention from London's face to the coffin lid and back. 'Does that scare you?' The dagger, seemingly appearing out of nowhere, dragged along London's cheek and down her throat, trailing between her breasts and circling her stab wounds.

Muscle spasms rocked London's body as the woman goaded her. 'You see, as much fun as it would be to stay and watch you enjoy your acid trip, we need to go for just a little while.' She leaned in closer, lowering her voice to an eerie whisper. 'But don't worry. We're not leaving you alone. Not really. We've left the devil and a few of his demons with you.'

And then the lid lowered, locking her into the darkness while tears fell, and panic clawed at her from every side. Moments later, the crunch of tires announced the duo's departure. Within seconds, her concentration on the sounds outside the coffin snapped when the wetness trickling down her face suddenly became a raging body of water rising to drown her.

Desperate, London tried to convince herself that the walls of the coffin weren't shrinking, she wasn't drowning, there were no demons nipping at her feet while the devil watched. *Focus, London. Focus on anything else.* She tried; she really did. She pictured her surroundings, the church she was in, even if she didn't know where.

But then a foul stench wafted upward, burning her nose. And while the tiny part of her brain still capable of separating reality from the fake shadow monsters insisted the odor was nothing more than the infections from her stab wounds ravishing her body, the irrational, drugged part insisted on telling her evil spirits and ghouls were both invading and escaping her body, crowding into the coffin with her so they could suffocate her as she lay there, helpless to defend herself.

Not realizing her bound hands had been shoving against the lid of the coffin until they suddenly collapsed against her stomach, London gurgled against the fire burning through the sensitive flesh. But when one of her fingernails scraped across the seeping pus of one of her wounds, her mind convinced her it was the devil's horns, and ignoring the way the fabric pulled at her punctures, ripping apart the dried skin, she resumed kicking and punching against the coffin lid, desperate to dislodge it.

Chapter Sixteen

After their interview with Cordova, Alyssa played her messages when she noticed she'd missed a call from Hal.

'Ran down an address for August Holt; you should have a text. He works for Waste Management, and in an effort to save you some time, I took the liberty of contacting them to see if he was working today. According to his supervisor, he's called in sick the last three days, so per their policy, he'll need a doctor's note before he's allowed to return. Second, I was able to verify Brecken's grandparents, Dale and Greta Manning, live in Indiana. Again, took it upon myself to call but ended up leaving a message. Left your number as a primary callback, Cord's as a second, and mine as a third. Finally, reached out to Ewan Moore's probation officer, but he had someone in his office. And that's all I've got for now. Talk to you later.'

While Cord punched the address for August Holt into the navigation system, Alyssa decided to give the medical examiner a call in the hopes that she'd have something for them to go on. She listened to Lynn's line ring four times before Dr. Sharp, out of breath and panting, snatched up her phone. 'Don't. Hang up. I'm. Here.'

'Lynn, this is Alyssa. I was hoping you'd have something for us on the Fleming case but sounds like now might not be a good time.'

'No, no. You're good. Saves me a call later this afternoon since I was going to reach out to you anyway.'

'Good. Just so you know, I'm driving, so you're on speaker. Cord's with me.'

'Thought I heard traffic. Hi, Cord. All right...'

Alyssa listened to the shuffling of papers while Lynn mumbled to herself.

'A-ha. Here it is. Well, as usual, there's no real easy place to start, so I'll just start by saying that Elena Garcia, in my professional opinion, died immediately as I saw zero evidence of defense wounds on her arms or hands. It's likely a blunt object blow to the head rendered her defenseless before she had her throat cut. It was a clean slice, so the weapon used was brutally sharp.'

'Like maybe a dagger or sword?' Cord asked.

'I suppose it would depend on the blade for the dagger. Though, I'd lean away from the idea of a sword since the slice wasn't conducive to that large a blade.

'Now, with regard to both victims, my initial exam found no signs of a sexual assault. With Garcia, this should come as no surprise for the reason I just stated.' Here, Lynn paused, and Alyssa heard her gulping back a drink before she came back on the line. 'When it comes to Skye Fleming, I want to be clear that I'm still in the primary stages of the autopsy. Nevertheless, I'm afraid there's quite a bit I have to share with you, so bear with me while I go through this.'

Deep lines wrinkled Alyssa's forehead as she shot Cord a puzzled look. Something about Dr. Sharp's delivery, more than her words, hinted at something more troubling than the state of Fleming's body. 'Okay. Go on.'

'As I just said, there was no visible bruising on the victim's inner thighs, nor any obvious traces of semen on the body, despite the fact that Fleming was found on the bed with her skirt removed. Hence my stance of no sexual assault. Still, I extracted several short, black hairs from the victim's body near her eye as well as from the skirt. I've already got them marked to be sent to the lab today, so hopefully, we'll be able to obtain a DNA profile soon. In addition to the hairs, there were slivers of a black substance of an unfamiliar material. I placed it under a microscope and determined that it was some type of synthetic rubber, such as nitrile, which is consistent with your run-of-the-mill variety garden glove, the type you can purchase pretty much anywhere, including the grocery store.'

'In other words, not going to be much help unless we locate the guilty party holding onto a pair of garden gloves with a matching tear?' Cord asked. 'What about fingerprints?'

'Yes, to the first part of your question. And samples are much too small to obtain a usable print for your second. Sorry. Unfortunately, because I had to finish up another autopsy before beginning my initial exams of Fleming and Garcia, I've yet to examine the gastric contents of either.'

Though both Alyssa and Cord already understood the importance of examining the victims' stomachs, Lynn explained anyway.

'As you've heard me say dozens of times in the past, the stomach stops working almost immediately upon death, so what's in the stomach is pretty much preserved. Ergo, if we can determine their last meal, that could possibly get you in the ballpark for a timeline.'

When Lynn paused to sigh deeply, Alyssa's fingers tightened on the steering wheel because she knew the medical examiner well enough to realize that her sigh indicated that whatever she was about to reveal would extend well beyond disturbing.

Several seconds ticked by before Lynn confirmed Alyssa's suspicions. 'Over the years, I've seen more than my share of vicious acts of mutilation done to victims, as have the both of you. Even so, what humans are capable of doing to each other never ceases to appall me.

'In addition to the damage done to Skye Fleming's face and chest, the symbol for anarchy was carved into her right hip while an inverted pentagram was carved into her inner thigh. But that wasn't what appalled me. The number forty-seven was carved into her tongue.'

Alyssa shot Cord a baffled look, but the expression on his face showed he was just as confused. 'Excuse me?'

'Yeah, I have no idea what that might mean. Since Garcia's tongue shows nothing similar, I doubt it has anything to do with the number of victims, which I admit, was the first place my head went. Now, I can say with a fair amount of certainty, based on the lack of blood filling the victim's mouth, she was already deceased when this occurred.'

The medical examiner's bombshell managed to make it one of those rare times Alyssa was rendered speechless, leaving her only with, 'Thanks, Lynn.'

'Not a problem. I'll keep you posted on what I find. Hopefully, the information I just shared will help.'

'What do you think the number stands for?' Cord asked as soon as Lynn ended the call.

Already dialing, Alyssa said, 'I have no idea. But we know someone who might.'

Hal answered before the first ring completed. 'Hello.'

Alyssa skipped the pleasantries, eager to fill him in on what Lynn had told them. When she finished, Hal's breathing silenced, and she knew immediately that he recognized a connection between their current case and his past one. 'Talk to us, Hal. What can you tell us about this?'

'One of the things that helped us tie the victims to the occult twenty-five years ago was the fact that all the victims, both human and animal, had various symbols carved into their skin or hide, some post-mortem, some not. The symbol for anarchy together with the inverted pentagram are fairly common amongst occult followers, so those don't surprise me.'

'But?'

'But both Ewan Moore and Ezekiel Henry used to also carve the digits six-six-six into their victims' tongues, sometimes even slaying open the cheek and carving it there.'

Like Joe had earlier, Cord performed the sign of the cross. 'Does the number forty-seven have any significance in the occult that we don't know about?'

'Not that I've heard. Let me do some research.'

The coffee in Alyssa's stomach roiled like an erupting volcano. 'Before you do that, get me Moore's address. If you can't reach his parole officer, bypass him. I want to talk to Moore today, if we can.' A thought occurred to her. 'How many years was Moore sentenced to?'

'Forty, but with model behavior, was paroled early. And I have to say that this is one case where I think our justice system got it wrong. Moore may have possibly found religion, but anyone capable of committing the acts he and his buddies did doesn't deserve an early release. But you didn't ask me my opinion on that. Why did you want to know?'

'Had you said forty-seven, I would've demanded an immediate warrant for Moore's arrest.'

'Ah. Got it. Good thought, but I don't think that's it. I'm going to go now. I'll call you the second I have something, whether it's information or an address.'

Alyssa stopped Hal before he could hang up. 'One more thing before you go. I need you to reach out to O'Sullivan's bar and ask to review their security cameras from last night. If the manager or owner agrees, send Joe and Tony. Cordova claims he arrived there after six and remained there until the time he returned home around three this morning.'

'O'Sullivan's. You got it.'

A few minutes after hanging up, Alyssa pulled up to a less than stellar apartment complex and parked between a beat-up Buick and a reconditioned El Camino and climbed out. Quickly scanning the large numbers that were spray painted onto the building in an alternating pattern of black and red that hurt her eyes and offended her obsessive-compulsive preference for synchronicity, Alyssa located number four and headed in that direction.

When she knocked on the door, a dark-haired, young girl somewhere between eighteen and her mid-twenties cracked it open, leaving the safety chain in place. 'Yes?'

'Detectives Wyatt and Roberts with APD. Is August home?'

The cautious look in the girl's black-lined eyes shifted into disdain. 'No.'

'Are you sure? According to his boss, he's called in sick the last three days.'

'Yeah, well, if he's sick, he's not sick here. I haven't seen him since last Saturday.'

'Are you his girlfriend?'

The one eye still peeking through the gap in the door darted in Cord's direction. 'I'm not sure what business that is of yours, but I *was* his girlfriend, heavy emphasis on *was*.'

'You said you haven't seen him since last Saturday. Have you talked to him?'

This time the girl scoffed. 'No. He doesn't answer my calls. A few days ago, either his phone died, or he just started sending my calls to voicemail. It's starting to piss me off. He owes me his half of the rent money still. And next week, he'll owe me another half.'

'I'm sorry. I didn't catch your name,' Alyssa said.

Even though only a portion of her face was visible, Alyssa couldn't miss the girl's smirk. 'Huh.'

The girl's lack of cooperation rubbed Alyssa the wrong way. 'You know we can just go to the complex manager and get your name, so giving it to us just saves us a step.'

Rolling her eyes, August's *ex*-girlfriend shrugged. 'Ginny Gaynor. And no, Ginny's not short for anything, not Virginia or Jennifer or whatever else people ask me. It's plain and simple Ginny. My mom liked her gin. A lot.'

'Thank you, Ginny.'

'Look. I have to get ready for work, so if all you're after is August, I can't help you. If he's in trouble with the police, I don't know what to tell you. Like I said, I haven't seen or talked to him in a week. But if you find him, tell him he's not skipping out on his rent. Have you tried his mom's house, by the way? I didn't see his car when I drove by, but it's not like I stopped and peeked in the garage or anything.'

'When did you drive by?'

'I don't know. Wednesday after work, I think.'

Though she expected it to find the nearest trash can, if it made it even that far, Alyssa produced her card and passed it beneath the safety chain. 'If you see or hear from August, would you mind giving us a call, or better yet, telling *him* to call us? It really is important that we speak to him.'

Ginny snatched the card. 'Sure thing.'

The way she said it promised she had no intention whatsoever of doing any such thing. Before she could close the door, Alyssa had a few more questions. 'Do you know if August has any interest in witchcraft or anything like that?' She hesitated using the word 'occult.'

Ginny's eyes rolled all the way up to her forehead. 'August doesn't have an interest in anything but getting high, which is probably where his half of the rent money went. Again. The jerk.'

Though Alyssa hadn't really expected her to say, 'Why, yes, August is totally involved in black magic and mutilations,' she'd hoped for something more. 'You said you drove over to August's mom's house Wednesday after work. What time would that have been?'

'Nine. Why?'

'Just asking. Did you ever happen to meet any of Mrs. Holt's neighbors?'

'No. I haven't even met his mom, so why the hell would he introduce me to his neighbors? Jesus, lady, can I go now? Seriously. I'm going to be late.'

'One more question. Where do you work?'

'Are you serious? Why? You know what, never mind. Whatever. I work at Crafts and Costumes by the university. Now, I've really gotta go. Good luck finding that asshole.'

With that, the door shut in their faces. While the interview hadn't gone as she'd hoped, they may have unwittingly gotten something. Moving toward her vehicle, Alyssa jabbed the key fob to unlock the doors. 'I don't know much about Crafts and Costumes since I've never been in there, but doesn't that sound like a place where cloaks could be sold?'

'Thought the same thing the second she said it. It's not far from here, so we might as well check it out while we're in the area. Ish.'

—

While Alyssa wouldn't classify their visit to Crafts and Costumes as a total waste of time, it was still a bust. Not only were there no cloaks that resembled the 'Batman' ones Carter had described, there were no cloaks at all. The closest they'd found was a short, sexy witch's costume that had Alyssa shaking her head. Still, she'd asked the manager on duty if they were out or if they simply didn't carry them. To the manager's knowledge, they hadn't carried the type of cloaks Alyssa described in the five years she'd worked there.

Since Hal had still not called with an update on Ewan Moore's address, they headed toward the precinct.

Chapter Seventeen

Friday, April 23

Mara and Draven – she'd heard them refer to each other by name – had returned. Again. In lucid patches between bouts of panic-riddled hallucinations, she'd realized those weren't *really* their names. While Draven lit candles whose flames, in London's drug-addled brain, grew to blazing infernos, she tried to make herself focus on something else.

Like that time, about a century ago, when she was thirteen or fourteen, and she'd gobbled up every bit of gothic and folklore reading she could get her hands on. Not because she'd been particularly engrossed in the topics herself, but because one of the guys she'd been crushing on had been. Though she couldn't recall much, she remembered reading about someone named Draven, a person of the shadows. But the entity Mara had been far worse. She'd been an evil wraith who'd wreaked havoc and caused nightmares – a most fitting name, if ever there was one.

In a twisted bit of irony, London couldn't help but remember her grandmother teaching Sunday school and learning about Naomi, the mother-in-law to Ruth. One day, filled with grief after losing her husband and sons, Naomi changed her name to Mara, a name that meant bitter or strength.

London's trip down memory lane was fleeting as she found herself drawn to Draven's elastic movements and the way his hands left tracers in the air as if he were made of electricity. As she watched, it occurred to her to wonder, again, where she was. For as often as her abusers came and went, she knew she couldn't be far from civilization.

Against her will, her eyes strayed to the wall where she swore a heavy black presence with shadowy black eyes that stalked her hovered over the words *The Devil's Playground*. Shivers rocked her body, but when she tried to force her attention away from the new threat, she found she couldn't – until Mara suddenly reappeared.

In her hand, a small see-through container revealed what London recognized as a black rat snake coiled into the corner. As a child, the slithery creatures had caused her no small number of nightmares. Hoping that knowledge might somehow help her combat her crippling fear, her grandfather had taken it upon himself one summer to educate her on the dreaded reptiles. And while her phobia had stubbornly remained, she now remembered that the rat snake, while not poisonous, was far from not dangerous. Not only a great climber, if cornered or handled carelessly by humans, it was known to attack. Without venom, they killed their prey by constriction. Already, she felt her bones being crushed together, robbing her lungs of oxygen and breaking her ribs.

In a coarse, high-pitched, and altogether unpleasant voice, Mara spoke as she set the container inside the coffin. 'I thought you might enjoy some company, so meet your new coffin-mate, Satan.' A chilling giggle accompanied her words.

Despite her mental demands to remain still, violent spasms overtook London's muscles and rattled the snake. Why were they doing this to her? Tears and flakes of day-old mascara scratched at her eyes as she desperately tried to calm herself into lying still.

And then Mara kicked the coffin – hard. The container the serpent was coiled in fell to the side, and the snake slithered out onto London's legs.

Even her vocal cords froze around the scream clawing at her throat.

Chapter Eighteen

Friday, April 23

Less than a mile away from the precinct, Liz sent Alyssa a text with Cordelia Cordova's contact information. Immediately, she'd pulled over and called, surprised when Roman's mother not only answered but agreed to meet them as soon as school let out. So, just after three that afternoon, Alyssa parked and waited outside the duplex where Cordelia lived. 'She said she'd leave as soon as the buses pulled away, so she should be arriving any second now.'

Even as she said the words, a candy-red Ford rounded the corner and pulled into the driveway. A woman with shoulder-length brown and gray hair tied back in a low ponytail climbed out after reaching over to the passenger seat and grabbing a massive tote bag ripping at the seams. Weariness and wariness etched lines into her face as she nodded to the detectives before making her way up to the front door.

Alyssa and Cord climbed out of the Tahoe and reached Cordelia just as one of the tote's shoulder straps snapped. Because of Cord's quick reflexes, the loosely bound pile of papers shoved into the top didn't scatter into the wind. Cordova's mother peeked over her shoulder. 'Thank you.' Her voice was quiet but not quite timid. More resigned. 'I don't think my students would've bought my story if I'd told them their essay papers blew away. Probably because I wouldn't have believed them, either.'

Using her hip, Cordelia nudged the door the rest of the way open. 'Please come in. Let me just set these things down, and then you'll have my full attention, or at least whatever's left of it.' Alyssa chalked up the woman's weak attempt at humor to nerves and wondering what it was that her son had done to warrant a personal visit from two detectives. After placing her bag on a nearby table, Mrs. Cordova said, 'Excuse me while I grab something to drink.' She'd only taken a few steps when she stopped and swung around. 'I'm so sorry. I didn't even think to offer you something. I'm afraid all I have is water for the moment. Tap, not bottled.'

Partly to help ease the woman's uneasiness, Alyssa smiled as she declined the offer. 'I'm good. Thank you, though.'

Cord shook his head when Mrs. Cordova glanced up at him. 'None for me, either. Thanks.'

'Then, please excuse me while I get some for myself.'

Alyssa's gaze wandered around the room until Cordelia returned with a glass of water and nodded to an area that boasted two mismatched recliners and a futon all crammed into a minuscule space. With barely enough room to maneuver between them when no one had been sitting in there, the tight area became nearly claustrophobic once the three adults were settled.

Cordelia waved her arm in a small circle, laughing nervously. 'As you can probably guess, I don't really do much entertaining. Besides, most of these surfaces are usually covered in piles of papers waiting to be graded or that I just finished grading, so you're actually in luck.'

Cord smiled the million-watt smile that put most women at ease while also making them swoon. 'Thank you for agreeing to meet with us on such short notice, Mrs. Cordova.'

'You're welcome. And it's Ms. not Mrs. I never reverted back to my maiden name after I divorced my husband, but

I also don't necessarily want to be reminded that we were married.'

With a little more digging, Hal had discovered that Cordelia Cordova had filed for divorce immediately after her husband's arrest following a year-long investigation into kiting checks and money laundering. At the time of his father's incarceration, Roman Cordova had been twelve. His sister had been fourteen. Losing his father to prison at such a pivotal time in a boy's life might explain what triggered his anger issues a few years later.

'Ms. Cordova, can you tell us the last time you spoke with Roman?' Alyssa asked.

'Yes, I can tell you exactly the last time. It was two days before Christmas in 2019. He showed up at the house, drunk and pissed at the world. As per usual, he began spewing hatred and planting blame for his string of bad luck on me and my decisions. When I told him to leave before I called the police, he ripped my phone from my hand and shattered it against the wall. Then he grabbed me around my throat and shoved me back inside.'

To demonstrate, Ms. Cordova placed her hands where Roman had grabbed her before shifting in her chair in a way that angled her body away from Alyssa and Cord and placed her profile in shadow. When she spoke again, her words were barely audible. 'He asked if I had any idea how easy it would be to snap my "scrawny, miserable neck," and then he choked me until I was gasping for breath.'

'How did you get him to stop?' Cord asked.

'I didn't. My daughter, Olivia, showed up. She'd just obtained her license to carry a concealed weapon, and when she saw Roman pinning me against the wall, she pulled out her gun and threatened to shoot him, uh, between the legs if he didn't leave immediately. I don't think he believed her until she flicked the safety off. I remember it was close to noon. I was on break, and so was she. We'd planned on picking up a bite to eat and then shopping some Christmas sales.'

'Did you make a police report?'

'No, ma'am. I've learned over the years that neither they nor the restraining orders against my son do a damn bit of good. All they do is waste my time and offer him proof that he's invincible and untouchable.' Ms. Cordova took a long drink of her water, draining the glass before setting it on the water-stained end table.

Alyssa glanced over at Cord only to find him already looking at her. They'd both heard the same thing. She looked back to Ms. Cordova. 'How many restraining orders have you filed against your son?'

'Only one. When Roman was twenty. Instead of peace of mind, I managed to obtain three broken windows, four slashed tires, my rosebushes poisoned, and endless nights of lost sleep wondering what he'd do next.' Ms. Cordova divided her attention between Alyssa and Cord. 'You didn't tell me on the phone why you needed to speak to me, aside from it being in regard to Roman, but if he's done something, I won't know anything about it since he hasn't come back around since that 2019 incident. The only other thing I can tell you is that Olivia saw him eating lunch with a woman at Chester's a while back; I'm not sure how long ago. But according to her, the two were cozy in the booth together, and so she assumed they were dating. When Roman got up – presumably to use the restroom – Olivia approached the woman and warned her off. She didn't tell the woman who she was, just suggested the lady Google the man she was dining with and find out for herself what kind of person he was. Afraid of what he'd do if he spotted her, Olivia left the restaurant before Roman returned. Whether or not he actually saw her is anyone's guess.'

Cord's pen had stopped moving the second Ms. Cordova mentioned the lady in the booth with Roman. 'I don't suppose your daughter caught the woman's name?'

'No, like I said, according to Olivia, she dropped her warning and hightailed it out of there. Not that it's very helpful, I know, but I do remember her describing the woman as a brunette.'

That described half the population of Albuquerque, along with the greater metropolitan area, so as Ms. Cordova had suggested, that information might, at some point, eventually mean slightly more than nothing. Still, it wouldn't hurt for Alyssa and Cord to speak to Olivia herself. 'Do you think she'd be willing to speak to us?'

'Sure. But she's out of town and out of cell service this weekend with her friends. I'm sure she told me a month ago where they were headed, but to be honest, I have so much other information to keep track of in my head, that if I don't write it down, I'll forget. And I didn't write it down. I can, however, give you her cell number, and also leave her a message to let her know you're trying to reach her. But again, the chances of her receiving it before the weekend is over aren't good.' As she spoke, Ms. Cordova jotted the information down on a sheet of paper she tore from a mini notebook resting next to her glass.

'Ms. Cordova, I know you said you can't help us with regard to what your son might've been up to in the last year and a half, but I wonder if you could answer a few questions about his younger years,' Alyssa said.

'I can certainly try. There's not much to tell before he hit teenager status. At that point, he was still a mama's boy and thought I could heal any hurt or wrong.' Her laugh hinted at both sorrow and loving memories.

Alyssa took in a deep breath and asked the question most burning a hole in her brain. 'Do you happen to know if Roman was involved or interested in black magic or occultism at any point?'

As if the very mention of the topic had drained her of her blood, the color faded from Ms. Cordova's cheeks. 'I'm sorry. Please, give me a moment.' She lifted her empty glass to take a drink before remembering she'd already finished it and setting it back down.

Finally, after taking several deep breaths, she said, 'When he was a teenager, there was a period of time where he was into spells and magic and whatnot. However, I believe he outgrew that stage even before he moved out.'

Blood pounded in Alyssa's ears. 'What do you mean, he was into spells and magic?'

Ms. Cordova's hands clasped and unclasped on her lap, and she settled her gaze on a spot somewhere behind Alyssa. 'It was after his first stint in juvenile detention. He was sixteen at the time. Someone he met there was into voodoo and hocus-pocus, and a slew of other things that fall far outside my comfort zone. Anyway, he purchased a grimoire, a book of spells, off the internet, which is how I initially found out.'

'Did he try to keep it a secret?' Cord asked.

The lines in Ms. Cordova's forehead added five years to her age. 'No, I don't think so. Not really, anyway. Otherwise, he wouldn't have left it lying out in the open in his room. But before that, he'd also purchased a Ouija board, which he definitely didn't try to hide because he got quite insulted with his sister when she laughed at him and asked him why he thought a mass-produced board game would actually summon demons and spirits.'

'What did he say to that?' Alyssa asked.

Ms. Cordova's mirthless laugh sounded hollow. 'He looked her square in the eye and said, "I guess you'll find out soon enough, won't you?" Later that night, I caught him burning some candles to conjure up some spirits. I ordered him to stop. He ignored me, and so I blew out the candles, and he threw the board at my head.' Roman's mother paused to take a breath and try to control the trembling in her hands before continuing.

'Things calmed down after that, but one day – I don't really remember how long afterwards – I was picking up his laundry and happened to catch sight of something on his laptop that he'd left open. It was a message board which

I first assumed was attached to a gaming chat. But then my eye caught the words "incapacitating a victim" and I investigated a little closer. I don't know if the question was posed by my son, or if he'd even been participating at all in the chat, but someone had responded with something along the lines of' – Ms. Cordova's quavering hands flitted in front of her face – 'attacking the eyes and throat if the person wanted to torture someone before killing them.'

Alyssa stiffened. 'What did you do?'

'I screamed for Olivia to come look. I both wanted to have a witness to it as well as gauge her reaction to see if I was overreacting, even if I knew I wasn't. Afterwards, I finished gathering his clothes, waited a couple weeks, and then delivered an ultimatum – find a new hobby or get his own place.'

Cord beat Alyssa to the obvious question. 'How did he take that?'

'He asked me why, and I simply told him I wasn't comfortable with his fascination. The understatement of that decade, I'll admit. Much to my surprise, and Olivia's as well, he claimed to be bored with it anyway. And I never saw any evidence to the contrary after that conversation. Everything just kind of disappeared. Whether he tossed it or gave it away, I'll never know.'

'Did you ever consider going to the authorities after discovering that chat?' Alyssa asked.

Ms. Cordova actually rolled her eyes. 'No, and I'll tell you why. Because I was dating a cop at the time, and when I confided in him about Roman's interests and asked if I should report it just for a matter of record, he informed me no crime had been committed, nor could I prove potential for one.'

'That's true,' Alyssa agreed begrudgingly. 'Being interested in the macabre, witchcraft, and demon-summoning might be filed under the category of creepy as hell, but it's definitely not illegal.'

'Detectives, I've answered your questions, so now may I ask what you clearly think my son has done?'

For what felt like the dozenth time already, Alyssa found herself explaining. 'Two women were murdered last night. One of them was a woman Roman had allegedly been stalking.'

'Oh dear God, no.' Ms. Cordova's body rocked back and forth as she shook her head in denial. 'Look, if Roman *is* involved, I don't know what I can possibly do to help because he certainly wouldn't heed my advice if I suggested he turn himself in.'

Sensing there was little else they could get that might be helpful, at least for the moment, Alyssa stood while Cord closed his notebook and followed suit. 'Thank you for taking the time to meet with us. We really do appreciate it. If you could please let your daughter know we'd like to speak to her when she returns, that would be great. And it probably goes without saying, but if Roman *does* happen to come around, please be careful, and feel free to contact either of us anytime.'

Back in the car and armed with this new and possibly damning information, Alyssa turned to Cord. 'I think we have enough to request warrants to pull Roman's cell and financial records. I want to know who he's been in contact with, and I want to run down his credit card numbers, find out if he's purchased any books on the occult recently. Unfortunately, all we have is hearsay, which isn't quite enough to bring him in on an arrest warrant.' Even so, Alyssa's gut insisted they were getting closer to solving Skye and Elena's murders and hopefully locating London before the same thing could happen to her.

Chapter Nineteen

Friday, April 23

In the center of the circle, Apate and Eli wiped their daggers off on the cloth draped over the altar, the wet blood darkening the red lightning bolt design. Another member vanquished all the candle flames, save the ones surrounding the circle itself. To Mara, the circle, drawn to protect the participants from disruptive demons, seemed pointless.

Being too eager to begin with the woman they'd taken, she and Draven had foregone that ritualistic step at the church that this group knew nothing about. When no Harry Potter Dementors had whipped through the windows in search of their souls, they'd made the determination that the requirement to make their sacrifices within the circle for the purposes of protection was an unnecessary measure. By virtue of the power vested in them through Satan, they were already protected.

An unrestrained smile stretched her mouth at the memory of dropping the rat snake into the coffin and kicking it. Satan's word, the girl's terror had been tangible! Tilting her head back, swaying from side to side, Mara relished in the tingling warmth that started in her chest and spread outward to touch every part of her body. Moments later, she caught Draven's eye, and together, they shared a grin while the heat invading her body lowered. Her pupils dilated, and her breathing grew heavy, and from the desire burning in his own eyes, she knew, as usual, they were on the same page. She bet they wouldn't even make it back to the church before tearing each other's clothes off.

Mara threw her head back and let the laughter take hold, ignoring everyone's stares. Before beginning tonight, almost everyone here had taken a hit of acid. She and Draven probably should have refrained so soon after the last one wearing off, but declining when they never had before might've raised questions neither of them was willing to answer. Regardless, the group probably attributed her amusement to that.

Earlier that day, when they'd gone to pick up the snake she'd immediately named Satan – Draven knew a guy who asked no questions – they'd happened to catch a news broadcast announcing updates on the double homicide where two women were brutally slain. Engrossed in the report, Mara had nearly given the two of them away when she'd eagerly turned to Draven to tell him she wished she could be a fly on the wall of the incident room where, according to the reporter, police were struggling to find viable leads.

A sense of power at stymying the police had her craving to be back at the church with their prisoner whose head had to be drowning in a psychedelic nightmare of hallucinations and amplified sights. Before they'd left, Draven had wanted to close the coffin so the snake couldn't slither out and away, but Mara figured it would become too agitated and constrict around the girl, suffocating her before they'd finished having their fun. With an escape route, she'd explained, it would most likely glide into a corner and snatch up one of the dozens of rodents burrowed into various nests throughout the church.

She'd seriously considered not attending the service tonight but, as with refusing the drugs, it might've raised eyebrows if they hadn't come.

A new member, as yet without a cloak, stood back, watching Mara. He was disheveled, wearing torn jeans and a tattered flannel jacket over a hole-speckled T-shirt. His dyed copper hair stuck in every direction but down, and when his hands flew up to tame it, the Italian horn he wore around his neck slipped out of the neck of his shirt. She wondered if he wore it for luck or if he'd made what was known as a Faustian bargain, like she and Draven had done years ago. In their case, they'd bartered for the Lord of Darkness to take care of their financial needs.

With the way the newcomer's stare bored into her, Mara expected him to approach her, but when the chanting began, her attention was drawn back to the other members of their group, and when she thought of him again, he'd already slipped away.

Chapter Twenty

Finally home after nearly sixteen hours of sifting through evidence and dissecting interviews that chiseled away at her earlier confidence that they were gaining ground, Alyssa pulled out a chair and flopped down at her kitchen table, working up a smile and a little bit of energy to pet Ghost, Isaac's Black German Shepherd who'd become her shadow from the moment he was brought home two years ago.

Even though she sat in her kitchen, her head remained steadfastly at work, zipping through all the information they had – and all the information still missing. After interviewing Cordelia Cordova, Alyssa had called Hal immediately to start working on their warrant requests. By the time she and Cord had arrived back at the precinct, Joe and Tony had also returned from their interviews, as well as completed the trudging task of combing through the video footage at O'Sullivan's. Because the cameras were old with grime-coated lenses, pinpointing specific individuals within the bar proved to be a difficult and nearly impossible task. Still, based on the driver's license photo Hal had texted to them, both Joe and Tony believed, though with less than fifty percent certainty, that they could make out a person they believed *could* be Roman.

Pinging Cordova's phone hadn't been much more helpful because the towers tracked his phone to one location all night – his home. Instead of ruling him out as a suspect, however, it begged the question as to why a man in his twenties would go clubbing and leave his phone behind. It made sense if he'd planned on committing a crime, such as slaughtering the woman who'd reported him for stalking her, as well as her friend, and was savvy enough to know law enforcement could track his movements through cell towers.

The disappointing lack of leads continued with London's neighbors, none of whom reported seeing her since Thursday morning when they'd spotted her carrying an overnight bag and climbing into a friend's vehicle before driving off to work, even waving to a young lady out for her morning jog. Based on the descriptions they'd received, Joe placed his money on the friend being Skye Fleming. Yet another neighbor confirmed London had been having car troubles again, and that her vehicle had been at the mechanic's for a better part of the week.

Intel, where the women worked, proved almost as fruitless. Everyone in Sales and Marketing had been distraught after learning the identities of the murdered women through the news earlier in the day. To the last, each one stated that Skye, Elena, and London were jokingly referred to as the Three Musketeerettes. When Tony asked the supervisor if anyone might've felt slighted by the women's close relationship, she insisted no one had, though she also admitted no one tried to 'get in' with the trio either. As for the other departments within the semiconductor chip company, the supervisor claimed that while each department was friendly, most didn't commingle. And while a couple of the women's co-workers had known who Roman was and had suspected he liked Skye, none could recall a time or incident when he'd seemed over the line or intimidating, thereby running Alyssa's case into another brick wall.

Her frustration mounting, the pressure in Alyssa's chest only amplified when Hal confirmed that Victor Reynolds, London's last boyfriend, had indeed been working a twelve-hour shift Thursday night. So, unless Reynolds was Superman or wore his own flying cape, it was impossible for him to have committed the crime himself, though Alyssa didn't take him off her radar entirely.

Much later, Joe, Tony, and Hal had headed home in the hopes of catching a few hours' sleep. The only reason Alyssa finally allowed herself to leave nearly an hour after that was because Cord had finally checked his watch, swearing at the time because he'd promised Carter he'd stop by the Sandersons' to check on him and Abigail.

Distracted from her thoughts when Ghost, no longer satisfied with her absent-minded scratching behind his ears, laid his head down on her lap, Alyssa briskly rubbed the spot on his back that she knew he loved. When she stopped, he placed one paw on her thigh and stared up at her with his soulful, knowing black eyes, inviting her to unwrap all her problems so he could help solve them.

'If only you could give me the answers, Ghost, I'd spill all. But right now, I'm too exhausted. And also too worked up, if you get what I mean.'

As if he understood exactly what she'd said and knew exactly what she needed, Ghost swung his head toward the counter and back to her. Alyssa followed his gaze and chuckled. 'See, unlike my partner and my traitorous children, *you* get it. And I'd consider brewing a pot of coffee, but you know what might be better?' Ghost cocked his head at a funny angle. 'Yes, yes, I know that doesn't sound right coming from me, but work with me here. What would be better *right now* would be a glass of wine.' She tipped her head in the direction of the bottle. 'While I bet you would certainly pour me one if you could, you can't. And while I would never kill for a glass, right this second, I might be willing to maim something.'

Ghost whined before growling once deep in his throat.

'Oh no, silly. I don't mean it. Of course, not. Just ignore me. After all, I'm sitting here talking to a dog and expecting him to answer back, so clearly, I'm too mentally wiped out to even bother getting my own glass. But thanks for keeping me company, buddy. What are you doing down here anyway? Did Isaac's idea of music drive you away? Believe me, I get it.'

Thumping and obnoxiously loud, grating noises drifted through a bedroom door and down the stairs, adding emphasis to her statement. Her sixteen-year-old son and his best friend, Trevor Lewis, both newly licensed, had called her half an hour before she'd gotten home to ask if they could hang out and watch a late movie with a group of their soccer buddies. Her immediate response had been a hard no because Isaac's curfew was eleven. He'd mentioned the possibility of sleeping there at his friend's house, but Alyssa sensed the mild tension in her son's voice, the result of being kidnapped two years earlier.

With Ghost keeping vigil at the foot of Isaac's bed every night, the nightmares that had once plagued him regularly had almost completely stopped. On that rare occasion when one would hit, he might wake to find himself covered in sweat, trembling, and afraid to move. But the worst ones were when his screams for help woke him and everyone else in the house. The mere possibility of being around anyone other than his family or Trevor when it happened mortified him. So, Alyssa had reluctantly bent her curfew rule and relented.

Now, she checked the clock. They would be heading out any minute, so she expected a last-minute raid on the kitchen before they left. Where her son and his best friend stored all the food they consumed in a day remained one of the mystic wonders of the world. And if it wasn't, it certainly needed to be.

Two minutes later, as predicted, the discordant sound – er, music – cut off, and Isaac and Trevor flew down the stairs as if the hounds of hell were nipping at their heels. If she hadn't been so fatigued, it would've been comical how both boys skidded to a halt, their laughter at whatever they'd been discussing dying off when they saw her sitting there.

'Hey, Mom. When did you get home?' Isaac's eyes darted to the digital display on the microwave. 'Thought you were working late?'

'What? Ten p.m. isn't late enough for you?'

Her youngest child, the one whose sugar addiction rivaled only her caffeine one, rolled his eyes in his typical, good-natured response to her these days, and opened the pantry where he proceeded to drag out three party-size bags of chips and one half-demolished container of peanut-butter-filled pretzels. Then he zipped around the corner before returning with a couple of two-liter bottles of Pepsi.

'Um, what are you doing?' Observing her son and Trevor, Alyssa couldn't tell if she was more curious or annoyed. She'd wait for his answer to decide.

Barely slowing, Isaac shot a *duh* look over his shoulder at her. 'Didn't I tell you I'm in charge of chips?'

'Uh, no, you didn't.'

'Oh, well, my bad. I'm in charge of chips.' He nodded to the bags on the counter. 'And it's BYOS, so I'm bringing soda.' He held up one of the bottles as evidence, as if she hadn't already clearly seen it.

'Exactly when did I start grocery shopping for parties at your *friends*' houses?' It was bad enough that her teenaged son and his best friend packed food away like squirrels and then dove back in for more an hour or two later. In the past two years, she'd come to completely understand what some of her co-workers meant when they'd complained their children were eating them out of house and home. At this rate, she and Brock would be forced to take out a second mortgage just to support the grocery bill.

While Trevor froze with his head half in the opened fridge, clearly rummaging for something to take as well, Isaac grinned the cheeky smile that he knew full well his mother, sister, and grandma were all a sucker for, and probably half the girls at his school.

Defeated, Alyssa shook her head. 'Fine. Grab whatever you're after. Wouldn't want either of you to show up empty-handed. But don't blame me when there's no money left in your college fund.'

'No worries. Grandma will help.' Isaac laughed as she shook her head.

In the meantime, Trevor simply ignored her sarcasm as he continued retrieving a package of string cheese. 'Thanks, Detective Mom.' He held up the mozzarella. 'Man, you know how much I love this stuff?'

This time it was Alyssa's turn to roll her eyes, even as she erupted in laughter. 'Yes, I do know. That's why I keep it on hand. Barely,' she amended. Then turning serious, she focused her attention back on her son. 'What time will you be home again?'

'If we start the movie at eleven, probably about one thirty or a little after.'

'Not "a little after." Be home by one thirty. The only reason I'm letting you break curfew at all is because – except for driving there and back, *with no stops in-between* – you'll be at someone's home. And because Trevor's mom already agreed.'

'Mom—'

Alyssa cut him off. 'I wasn't opening the floor to negotiations. Be home by one thirty.' After his mumbled *fine*, she continued. 'And I assume parents will be present and no drinking or other stuff will be taking place?' Though she trusted both boys, she wasn't oblivious to the pitfalls stemming from peer pressure. If anything, in her line of work, she was hyper aware of them.

Not at all embarrassed – after all, it wasn't anything Trevor hadn't heard from her or Brock thousands of times before – Isaac leaned back against the counter as he answered. 'TBH, I don't know if Derek's parents will be home. But he didn't say they *wouldn't*, so, my guess is yeah, they'll be there. Especially since Derek swears they're like, total homebodies. Either way, there won't be drinking. Or other stuff. Pinky promise. Besides, no one wants to risk getting kicked off the team.'

Why did kids have to use acronyms for everything these days? 'You know, it takes just as much effort and air to actually say the words, "to be honest," as it does to—'

Isaac pushed off the counter and bent down to kiss her cheek. 'Mom, Mom, Mom. *I've* gotta stop you right there, and *you've* gotta catch up with the times. Your age is showing.' He tweaked the hair near her ear. 'All gray before you know it.' He winked and jumped out of her way as she swatted at him. 'We'll catch you later.'

'You boys have fun. And remember, straight there, text me, movie, and straight home. Period. Love you.'

'Yep, and same,' Isaac said at the same time Trevor offered his 'Love you, too, Detective Mom. Thanks for the donation.' He held up the mozzarella sticks, including the one he pulled from his mouth. A few seconds later, the front door slammed. But no sooner had the boys left than her son returned. 'Forgot to tell you. Holly and Nick came by just before I called you earlier. Said to tell you she was dropping Nick off and then was going to swing back by to see if you were home yet. Guess she wants to bend your ear about something but didn't want to bother you at work.' He wrinkled his nose. 'Probably girly stuff. So, yeah. Gotta skip now. Bye again.'

Alyssa lifted her hand, but Isaac was already gone, and she was alone in her suddenly too quiet house – well, except for Ghost, who watched from the front window as Isaac drove away. The noise of the silence weighed uncomfortably and hinted at what her life might be like two years from now when she and Brock became empty nesters. Sighing, she pushed back from the table just as Ghost rejoined her in the kitchen. 'I guess I decided on that glass of wine, after all. If I only drink half, it might help me sleep without making it more difficult to get back up in just a few hours.' Her eyes drifted to the time. 'Too few hours.'

The silence plaguing her moments earlier lasted all of five minutes before a car door slammed, the front door opened, and Holly strode in. 'Hey, Mom. Why isn't the alarm set? I'll have one of those.' She pointed to the bottle in Alyssa's hand.

Smiling as her daughter leaned in and gave her a side hug, Alyssa said, 'Hi, sweetie. Because your brother and Trevor just left, and he probably figured you'd be here any minute. And no, you won't.' Her eyebrows arched upward. 'Unless they've lowered the legal drinking age to twenty and I missed it?'

Holly smirked. 'You law enforcement types are no fun. Can I at least have some grape juice in a wineglass so I can pretend?'

Chuckling, Alyssa grabbed a matching glass, what was left of the grape juice from the fridge, and carried them, along with her wine, to the table. 'Isaac said you and Nick came by earlier, that you wanted to talk. What's up?'

In what Alyssa recognized as her daughter's avoidance of the question, as well as her interest in following in Alyssa's tracks of majoring in criminal justice, Holly pointed to the files Alyssa had set on the corner of the table. 'Want to bounce ideas for your current case off me? I caught a little of the news this afternoon. A double murder and a kidnapping – that sounds horrendous.'

'No.'

'Yeah, didn't think so.' Wrinkling her nose and glaring at the juice as if all her problems came from the purple stuff, Holly gripped the stem of the glass as she twirled it slowly around and around. 'Nick wants to take these weird couples' dance lessons,' she finally muttered. Her cheeks suddenly took on the hue of someone who'd been sitting in the sun for twelve hours without sunblock.

Not really knowing what she expected her daughter to say, Alyssa was certain it wasn't that. 'Okay?' She turned the word into a question.

Holly gulped down half the drink and set the glass back on the table with a thud. When she looked back at Alyssa, her mouth dropped open, and she shook her head like she used to do when she was convinced her mother knew nothing. 'Um, have you forgotten?'

Baffled, Alyssa searched the tired recesses of her mind. She came up with squat. 'Apparently. Forgotten what?'

'Mom.' She drew the word out. 'I resemble a puppet with a broken string when I dance. I can't *dance* in front of Nick, much less a bunch of people I don't even know.' Holly's tone implied her mother was not firing on all cylinders, which was actually pretty accurate at that moment.

Laughter bubbled out at her daughter's self-assessment of her dancing skills because it couldn't have been more accurate. Holly's intelligence may have earned her a scholarship to Cornell University – though she'd opted to remain in Albuquerque, closer to friends and family – but the simple fact remained that her talent by no means extended to the dance floor. 'Sweetheart, they're dance *lessons*. So, learn to dance and you won't look like a puppet dangling with a broken string.'

Holly's response to Alyssa's comment came in the form of a scowling, petulant glare.

Alyssa could understand Holly's mortified embarrassment, but what she didn't quite get was why her daughter was so afraid. It wasn't like her headstrong oldest child to back down from any type of challenge, even those including dancing and looking like a fool in front of strangers. There was definitely more that Holly wasn't saying. 'Sweetie, why does Nick wanting to take dance lessons with you, his *girlfriend*, really bother you so much?'

Holly drained her glass and moved over to the dishwasher to set it inside. 'The class says, "We can get you wedding-ready. Impress all your guests with your stunning moves." Wedding. Ready.'

Alyssa, having just taken a sip of her own drink, spewed it back out all over the place as she choked. Instantly, Ghost loped back to her side to check on her. With tears filling her eyes, she tried to catch her breath, all the while patting him on the head to reassure him that she was fine.

Startled, Holly scooted across the room and clapped her on the back. 'Mom? Are you okay?'

Alyssa waved her away as she reached for a napkin and wiped her eyes and mouth. 'What?' she finally managed to wheeze out.

Holly dropped back down into the chair she'd just vacated. 'Yeah. You heard me.' Assured Alyssa was going to live, Ghost shifted his attention to Holly who rewarded him by feeding him a snack she'd snagged off the counter and then rubbing his ears before leaning down to talk to him. 'It's nuts, right? You agree, don't you, boy?' Ghost licked her cheek. 'That's what I thought.'

'Have you two been discussing marriage?' Alyssa didn't know why it shocked her so much, but it did. Nick and Holly had been together ever since they met during one of Alyssa's cases eighteen months earlier. And it wasn't as if she hadn't thought about the idea of the two of them getting married; it was just something she envisioned occurring far off in the future, after Holly finished college.

'Me and Ghost?' At least Holly's funny bone remained firmly intact. 'Naw, we're strictly in a sister–slash–dog-brother zone.'

Alyssa didn't even bother rolling her eyes, choosing instead to stare her daughter down.

'Lose your sense of humor much?' Holly muttered without really trying to muffle her words. 'Fine. Yes, but not, like, seriously or anything. Like, it comes up in conversations, and, like, we love each other, but—' Holly's eyes strayed toward the stairs, the expression on her face one of longing to revert to simpler times when she lived at home.

Three *likes* in two sentences. Yeah, her daughter's anxiety had soared to the summit. Trying to gather her wits and wisdom, Alyssa struggled to find the right thing to say. If Holly was right about Nick potentially seeing marriage as much closer in their future, how did she, as the mother, feel about that? She honestly didn't know. And she'd do her daughter no good if she joined her at the pinnacle of angst.

Mabel, Alyssa's mother-in-law and Holly's grandma, on the other hand, would be over the moon ecstatic if she knew the possibility of an engagement might be pending. Unlike her reaction to Brock's proposal to Alyssa all those years ago. Her disappointment then had been tangible – she'd even worn black to their wedding – and had taken more than a couple of decades to dissolve, and that was only after the Evan Bishop case had impacted all their lives a couple years earlier.

Still trying to figure out how to navigate how she felt while also helping to ease her daughter's fears, Alyssa finally asked, 'Well, what does Rachel think?' Not only Nick's twin, Rachel was one of Holly's three roommates. Her best friend, Sophie, and Sophie's cousin, Jersey, made up the other two.

Holly shrugged. 'I've been too afraid to ask.'

And then all thoughts of a wedding were wiped away when headlights flashed across the front window seconds before the rumbling garage door rattled up. Both women stared at each other, recognizing the sound of Brock's vehicle.

He was home early. Since he'd said nothing about the possibility when he'd called her today or texted her this afternoon, apparently he'd decided to surprise her. Beside her, Holly gazed desperately at her mother's wineglass then the bottle on the counter, as if debating whether or not she should risk her mother's wrath by imbibing the alcohol, despite her age.

It didn't take much for Alyssa to recognize that Holly's nervousness stemmed from worry over Brock's attitude toward Nick. Not that he still harbored a strong dislike toward Holly's boyfriend. It had taken a bit of time, for sure, but her husband had finally warmed up to him. But even so, he still had moments when he had trouble accepting the idea that he'd been replaced as the number one man in his little girl's life. Her husband might've looked like a solid wall of muscle on the outside, but he'd always been a marshmallow whenever it came to his 'daddy's girl.'

Therefore, neither Alyssa nor Holly held any illusions as to what Brock's reaction would be to the dance lessons and their logo. The mere mention of the word 'wedding' would send his head into the stratosphere, possibly forever. When he finally walked through the door, luggage in hand, his smile outshone everything. 'My two favorite girls.' Setting his things on the floor, he kissed Alyssa on the lips, then pulled Holly up for a hug. When he stepped back, he glanced at the time and said, 'Isaac's not home? Cutting it close to curfew, isn't he?'

'I agreed to a curfew exception, so he and Trevor took half the groceries and went over to watch a movie with some of the soccer team. They'll be back by one thirty.'

The only hint at the discomfort Brock tried to keep hidden came in the slight lift and drop to his shoulders before he nodded and picked up Alyssa's glass. After taking a quick sip, he refilled it before placing it back in front of her. To Holly, he said, 'Not that I wasn't thrilled to see your car out front and you sitting in the kitchen with Mom, but what brings you over so late on a Friday night?' His head swiveled left and right and up and down in a not-so-subtle search. 'And where's Nick?'

Better than he used to be, there was only a slight tinge of jealousy in his voice. Normally, whenever Holly heard it, she had to bite back a smile. Tonight, her tanned face lost color.

Brock noticed. His gaze swung over to Alyssa and then back to Holly. 'What's wrong? What happened?'

It was Alyssa's turn to gulp down some of her drink as, instead of answering, she glanced longingly at the file sitting on the corner of the table, suddenly feeling the urge to drive back to work.

Chapter Twenty-One

Saturday, April 24

The sun was still at least an hour away from peeking over the Sandia mountains when Alyssa parked between Cord's car and Hal's specialized van, not at all surprised to see either already there, and headed inside the precinct. She'd bet a week's supply of her favorite java that Joe and Tony would be striding in any minute now, and if she knew Liz as well as she thought she did, she wouldn't be too far behind that.

The first thing she noticed when she walked in wasn't the quiet bustle of the place; it was Hal. His elbows were propped on Ruby's desk, which wasn't uncommon since, for the past several years, the department's all-around go-to guy regarding anything from baking a cake to mentoring both veteran and rookie officers alike had been doggedly determined to make the grumpy precinct secretary laugh. Rumor had it that it had never been seen, so bets had been placed. In the two-plus decades Alyssa had been with the APD, she'd never witnessed anything remotely close to a smiling Ruby, much less a laughing one. Which was why she'd tossed money into the second pot, the one that staked a claim that Ruby would tire of Hal's game and simply clobber him. Because there was no way she hadn't heard of the wager by now. The woman had a way of knowing *everything* going on within the department. It could be extremely helpful at times, as well as a little creepy.

But today, much to Alyssa's shock, Ruby wasn't shooing Hal away with her withering glare. She seemed to be genuinely listening to him. Granted, she wasn't smiling, but neither was she wearing the pinched expression that never boded well for its recipient. Alyssa couldn't help herself; she peeked over her shoulder and back outside at the sky. No horsemen, no plague, no whatever else the Book of Revelation claimed would occur during the end times.

She didn't feel so silly when she spotted Cord leaning up against the incident room, observing over the cubicles. When she reached his side, he nodded his head toward Hal and Ruby. 'Think the apocalypse is around the corner? Because I kind of think the apocalypse is right around the corner. Or do you think the pot will go today?'

She couldn't decide if the expression on her partner's face represented fear or scandalized shock. It made her want to laugh.

'I'm not sure of anything anymore, my friend.' She glanced back one more time and shrugged. 'Maybe we've just stumbled into an alternate universe.' Then she moved past him and over to the conference table where she set her coffee and files down. Just as she started to suggest he quit gawking so she could clue him in about Holly's late-night visit, Cord turned serious.

'So, you know I went to see Carter and Abigail last night.'

Alyssa nodded. 'How'd that go?'

'To be honest, I didn't expect they'd still be awake, but Mr. Sanderson told me Carter insisted on waiting up because he knew I'd keep my word.'

'And you did,' Alyssa said softly.

'They wanted me to read them a bedtime story, but every few pages, Abigail would stop me to ask about her mom. About the third or fourth time, Carter patted my cheek and promised he'd explain it to her later, that it would be better coming from him.' Cord reached for a tissue and wiped the moisture from his eyes. 'Apparently, Mrs. Sanderson didn't notice the time when she turned on the television earlier that day so they could watch Disney. Her timing happened to coincide with the noon news report; it flashed a picture of the Fleming house, and Carter heard just enough before Mrs. Sanderson changed the channel. I guess as soon as he knew Abigail was glued to *Frozen*, Carter went to the kitchen and said, I quote, "My mom's dead, isn't she?" Mrs. Sanderson didn't lie to him, but neither did she go into detail. She said afterwards that he dropped his head and told her he already knew but asked if they could keep it from Abigail just a bit longer – until he could figure out the best way to tell her.' Now talking around an obvious lump in his throat, Cord added, 'Kid's got more gumption than most adults I know.'

Alyssa felt like her heart had been jerked out of place, but before she could figure out the words that might help comfort her partner, Hal rolled in. From the way he darted his gaze between her and Cord, she knew he sensed something was wrong. 'Morning, mates. Everything okay in here?'

His emotions firmly back under control, Cord closed the door, but not before sticking his head out once to make sure Ruby wasn't headed their way. 'I was just talking to Alyssa about my visit with Carter and Abigail.' He hitched his thumb over his shoulder. 'So, what's the word? What's going on?'

Recognizing Cord's clear attempt to change the subject, Hal grinned. 'Well, my fellow friends and teamies, as it turns out, our dear Ruby is in a more joyful state of mind these days because her niece has just moved back to Albuquerque.'

Cord cocked one eyebrow in question, but Alyssa simply shook her head. Nope, she hadn't been aware that Ruby had any siblings or in-laws that would make her an aunt. Her life remained as mysterious as the Loch Ness monster or Sasquatch.

'Which means it won't be long now before I'll be collecting on that sweet pot. What's it up to these days? A couple hundred?' Hal waved his hand in the air as he turned serious. 'But let's save that for later, after we bring London Brecken home and find the Greenwood Avenue killers.' As he spoke, he rolled over to his laptop, clicked a few keys, and just as a city camera appeared on the wall, Joe and Tony joined the group.

'What's going on?' Tony's voice was comically low. 'Ruby didn't scowl at us. I think, I mean, I swear, she might've actually smiled, at least a smile for her? Why does that scare me so much?'

'Seriously,' Cord agreed, giving himself whiplash as he snapped his neck around when the door opened, afraid Ruby had somehow overheard them talking all the way from across the room. The comical look of relief on his face when he saw it was only Liz made Alyssa laugh.

Liz tilted her head to the side and glanced around the room. 'Should I ask what I missed?'

'Nothing important,' Alyssa assured her before waving for Hal to explain what he'd just pulled up on his laptop and projected onto the wall for the team to see.

'Early this morning,' he began, 'I finally got access to the cameras in the Greenwood area. Well, at least the main intersections there. This is the closest one to Fleming's neighborhood. I took a look before I drove in. This is from Thursday night. Watch the far-left corner of the screen just above the time stamp.'

Grainy footage of cars moving through the intersection passed at regular intervals. Until five minutes after ten when a light-colored van stopped at the red light. Alyssa's heart jackhammered as she leaped from her chair. 'Please tell me you can zoom in on the individuals inside that vehicle.'

'I can.' With a few keystrokes, an extremely blurry image of what appeared to be a male individual became visible. If Alyssa squinted, she thought she could make out the long, drooping sleeves of what could be a cloak, but aside from that, she couldn't discern any other distinguishing features of the person behind the wheel.

'Wait. There's no one in the passenger seat,' Joe said. 'Could Carter have been wrong about what he saw?'

'He wasn't wrong,' Liz snapped, as if she took Joe's doubt personally.

'Don't be aiming any weapons at each other. Just watch,' Hal said.

Then they saw it. The driver of the van continuously twisted to see something or someone in the back of the van. 'Could be his partner stayed in the back with Brecken,' Alyssa said.

'To keep her quiet, maybe?' Tony suggested.

'Possibly. I wish the footage wasn't so grainy. I can't make out any definitive features.'

On the video, the driver wiped his right hand down his face, and Cord asked Hal to pause a second. When the screen stilled, Cord tipped his head to the side and studied the individual staring up at the traffic light. 'Nope, never mind. I was hoping I could make out something in the face, but aside from swearing it looks like a male, I can't tell a thing.' Hal hit play again.

When the light changed, the driver glanced back one last time before pulling into the intersection and waiting for a passing car before turning left. Hal hit pause again and zoomed in.

'Damn it,' Alyssa swore. The license plate had a dark cover over it. When the city had put in red light cameras several years back, it was one of the public's answers to receiving a ticket for running a red light. 'Can you do anything to bring that into better focus, Hal?'

The corners of Hal's mouth turned down into a frown. 'Some things are beyond even my ability. Still, I already toyed with it some, and the best I could come up with is the letter P in the second position, and maybe a C or B in the third. Last number, I'm quite sure, is a four with second to last possibly being a one.' He glanced over to Alyssa. 'I'll keep working at it, but at least we have something.'

'I hate to be the one to piss on everyone's fire' – Tony shifted a little in his seat when everyone turned to stare at him – 'but how do we know that's the van we're even looking for? And let's just say it is; aside from south, we have zero idea where it's headed. It could be all the way to Texas or beyond by now.'

'It's still something,' Joe countered.

Hal was already pulling up the software and entering what data he had. 'I'll run a registration search to see what I can come up with. Keep briefing. I'll multitask.'

Liz, who up to that point had been quietly staring at the video, tapped her fingernail on the indistinct sketches she'd drawn while interviewing the children. 'I don't want to get anyone's hopes up here, but maybe I can try to come up with a composite using that image from the city's cameras along with what little Carter gave us. Maybe, between the two, we can get something more useful.' For just a second, her lips pressed together to form a tight line. 'Though, I feel like I should warn you' – she pointed to the paused footage – 'that might be just a bit too pixelated for me to use. But I can try.'

Since Carter hadn't actually seen either perpetrator's face, the sketches Liz had done showed little more than hooded figures in black. 'We appreciate anything you can do,' Alyssa said before turning to Joe. 'Where are we on obtaining cell and financial records for Fleming, Garcia, and Brecken?'

'Should have them sometime today. As usual, financials are proving a little more difficult to get our hands on, even with a warrant.'

While movie cops rarely ran into dead ends or hit delays, it happened more than any real-life law enforcement liked to admit. 'I'll be curious to see if any of their financials show any recent purchases that might connect to an interest in the occult.' When Joe shook his head in disbelief, Alyssa explained, 'Just because they're victims doesn't mean we can ignore that one of them might've been interested in a darker side of life, such as occult activity. Today, one way or another, I'm going to talk to Ewan Moore, especially as we now have a direct similarity to crimes he was convicted of.'

Yesterday, the team had been sickened at the news that the number forty-seven had been carved into Skye's tongue, though none of them had an inkling of what that number represented.

'Later, I plan on talking to Lillian Holt again, and Kenny, too, if he's home, since we couldn't track down August. That he's suddenly disappeared after his former neighbor was murdered makes my neck itchy.'

Hal interrupted. 'Speaking of the Holts, before everyone got in this morning—' At Alyssa's incredulous look since they'd all arrived early, he shrugged. 'What? I couldn't sleep. Anyway, I ran some background checks. August Holt has a prior for underage drinking at the age of nineteen. Record shows the judge ordered him to take DWI classes. Kenneth Holt works at Dion's, plays football in the fall, and volunteers at the West Side animal shelter twice a week. Lillian Holt, nee Brooksfeld, has two priors in the last sixteen years. One DWI when she was twenty-six, and more recently, driving with expired tags. Nothing big or checkered there. Finally, I was able to confirm her ex-husband does indeed live in Oregon.'

'Thanks, Hal. I still want to talk to Lillian and see what she can tell us about her son. When she mentioned him Thursday night, I definitely sensed some tension. Could be nothing more than normal mother/son disagreements, but either way, I want to get to the bottom of it. Yesterday, I was hesitant to name him as a person of interest, but like I just said, something about the timing of his sudden disappearing act makes my gut insist he might have gone into hiding *because* he has something to hide. Maybe I'm way off base here, but we won't know for sure until we locate him.'

A brief tap-tap on the conference room door was the only warning the team got before it was pushed open. Captain Guthrie Hammond's chest could've doubled for an old whiskey barrel, which was why Alyssa didn't immediately spot Ruby until the secretary stepped from behind him, leveling her glare upward because the man had had the unmitigated audacity to block her way. No, not even the captain himself was exempt from Ruby's wrath. And since, like everyone else in the room, he winced at the idea of being on the receiving end of even a mildly disgruntled Ruby, he immediately stepped to the side, ushering her in with what passed for a grin that she didn't return.

Alyssa barely managed to suppress her own grin. Though he'd mellowed a smidge in the last couple of years, the captain had earned his nickname Captain Hothead fair and square. Even so, an irritated Ruby could give him a solid run for his money, and Alyssa would place odds on Ruby every single time.

Shifting her scowl from Hammond, Ruby turned to Alyssa and the team. 'You might want to turn on Channel Twelve. They have breaking news.'

Hal used the remote on his cell to flip on the television mounted in the corner, and everyone swiveled around to face it.

Anchorman Monty Cannon's practiced sad face was aimed toward the camera. 'We have breaking news out of APD that two children ages six and three may have been witnesses to the Thursday night massacre we brought to your attention yesterday. One of the children described two assailants "dressed like Batman." According to a source who wished to remain anonymous, the children of one of the victims were discovered hiding in a closet and are now being held in an undisclosed foster home under the care of CYFD. Tune in at noon for any updates.'

Everything after that became a grating buzz in Alyssa's ears. She didn't know who in the hell had leaked sensitive, possibly life-threatening information to the media, but she was going to find out. But first, she had something else to do.

Chapter Twenty-Two

London couldn't remember who'd written about the various planes of purgatory, but she didn't need to in order to know she'd entered the seventh level of hell. Last night, as the moon had inched its way higher in the dark sky until it disappeared altogether, Mara and Draven had returned, giddy and full of lust as they continuously and ravenously pawed at each other after—London locked down the memory of what they'd done as she lay there, helpless to do more than listen and fight against all the things she knew were not there but saw anyway.

Blowing branches that became flying demons; the whistling breeze that became screeching spirits scraping against her skin; the inverted crucifix that transformed itself into a gargoyle. But none of that had matched the horror of watching red race up Draven's dagger like a reverse cascade before spilling over his hands, up his neck, and across his face until Draven himself had turned into the devil. A thousand tiny spiders had skittered across her arms at the sight.

And even when she'd squeezed her eyes closed, she couldn't dislodge the images.

Her eyes had snapped open when Mara, her teeth morphing into claws reaching straight for London's face, stroked her own dagger up London's cheek and over her nose before kissing it along her lips. The roiling in her stomach exploded into painful spasms when the words

Mara taunted her with finally penetrated the drugged haze in her brain. Even as her head denied the truth, she listened as Mara described in blistering detail how Draven had tortured Skye. The tip of her dagger pricked into the soft flesh beneath London's eye to demonstrate. Gagging against the velvet cloth in her mouth, she whimpered, trying to shut out Mara's demented voice.

'I always *knew* it would be intense, but I didn't really *know*… Such a sense of power in taking someone else's life. But not nearly as powerful as holding someone else's life in the palm of your hand.' She cradled her dagger as if weighing it before once again tracing it along London's cheek, down her jaw, and along the shell of her ear.

Mara had leaned in close then and whispered, 'I bet you wish you could kill me right now, don't you? I wonder if you'd take your time or just stab me through the heart, hmm?' She huffed out a derisive snort. 'With your friends, it all ended far too soon. We didn't really get to *savor* the act.' The dagger danced between London's breasts. 'But don't worry. Your end is coming. April twenty-seventh, during the supermoon when everything is heightened, including emotions and thrills. I can practically *taste* it already.'

Draven's voice came from the direction of the stairs, and London realized she'd been so focused on trying to stay sane she hadn't even noticed him leave the basement. 'Do you believe in God?'

Her head feeling three times its normal size and not knowing if it was the right or wrong answer, London nodded weakly. Her grandmother's words, like a psychological angel perched on her shoulders, echoed in her mind, reminding her even then to always *pray for her enemies*. Would she want her to pray for them, these devil-worshiping deviants, even now, she wondered?

Later, when Mara and Draven abandoned her to the church once again, there'd been no discussion between them, just a sudden absence, as if only they'd been able to hear the clock strike the magic hour.

It wasn't until much, much later that London realized they'd left off the lid of her coffin. But whether it had been done intentionally or by chance, she found she didn't care. Between pain, fear, crushing exhaustion, hunger, thirst, and fever–induced delirium that was just as hallucinogenic as the drug that had finally, blessedly left her body sometime during the dark hours of the frigid night, London found it increasingly difficult to care about anything, including dredging up the ability to wonder where Satan, the name Mara had dubbed the snake, had gone after slithering away in search of food or warmth or something else. Forewarned of what lay ahead for her, she half hoped the snake would suffocate her first.

Regardless, whether death came at the hands of her deranged tormentors or by the snake, whatever came next would just have to come because she had nothing left inside her, no will or energy whatsoever to fight or beg, even if she could. Her two best friends were dead. And she had no idea what had happened to Carter and Abigail.

Everything that had happened since lying in their bedroom reading to them was too much for London to bear, and she allowed the pressing weight of unconsciousness to drag her back into the sweet escape of oblivion. But just before the world disappeared, a huge wolf appeared in the window, its beautiful, curious eyes staring down at her. Maybe the drug-fueled hallucinations weren't gone, after all, as she'd thought. If the wolf was a trick of her mind, at least it hadn't come in the form of another demon promising torment and torture.

Chapter Twenty-Three

A starved mountain lion hovering over its prey would've cowered under a bush to avoid getting in Alyssa's path as she bolted through the newsroom doors at Channel Twelve. Since no one would patch her through when she'd called, and the manager's receptionist had placed her on hold for ten agonizing minutes, Alyssa had hurled instructions at the team and raced past Ruby, the captain, and everyone else to her car. She'd only known Cord was behind her when he'd hopped into the passenger seat and buckled up. Since she still had the phone pressed to her ear, just in case, she simply started the car and peeled out of the parking lot in a burning rubber of fury.

And now, overconfidence mixed with a bag of big-city arrogance was about to experience a head-on collision with a five-foot-three-inch pissed off detective. The new, fresh out of sunny California, investigative journalist from Channel Twelve had no idea what bear he had just poked. If he wasn't in the practice of locking every door and window in his house already, he would be after Alyssa was finished with him. Because no matter what, she would make damn sure Monty Cannon never made the same mistake again. At least not in Albuquerque.

The media did not topple her cases, and they especially didn't shove two small children onto center stage, putting their lives indelibly at stake.

'Monty Cannon?' Barely suppressed rage made it seem like Alyssa was cursing at the poor receptionist who had the unpleasant misfortune of being the first person she saw.

'He's on air.' The girl's wickedly long, mauve-tipped fingernails twitched as she pointed.

'Well, I suggest you pull him from behind that desk before I do it for your audience's viewing pleasure. And I will not be gentle or kind about it. Claim an illness, claim a death, claim a freaking lottery ticket win for all I care, but somebody *will be* answering my questions. Now.'

It wasn't the receptionist's fault, and Alyssa knew it. The young girl was probably just an intern, but her temper had slipped past the boiling point and soared to incineration the moment she'd breached the station's doorway. Through the tempered glass, the person responsible for her dangerous mood relaxed lazily in his chair, telling Alyssa they must be on a commercial break.

Alyssa's glare did its best to drill holes through the glass, and just as she was considering whether or not to crash her way onto the sound stage, the platinum-blond, surfer-looks man happened to glance up and in her direction. Cannon snagged the attention of his co-anchor and jerked his head toward the lobby area. Cameramen and the rest of the crew all swiveled around to see what the new man on campus was staring at.

Monty's co-anchor, Mandy Diaz, arched her perfect brows before presumably answering whatever he'd asked, which Alyssa imagined was something along the lines of, 'Who the hell is that, and why does she look like she eats alligators for a snack? And why is she glowering at me like I'm her next tasty morsel?' The man's cocky smile instantly morphed from 'I'm smooth and sexy and charming' to 'Oh shit, I might've misjudged this one.' He had no idea, but he was about to.

'Excuse me. Detective?' The intern with hair dyed as black as wet tar did her best to appear less than intimidated, and Alyssa took pity on her. Again, it wasn't her fault she happened to be the station's first line of defense against an infuriated detective displaying a beltful of weapons.

'Yes?'

'Um, the morning newscast will be finishing up in just a few minutes at seven, if you'd like to wait. Our manager is still in a meeting, so she can't get away right now. I'm *really* sorry.'

Alyssa's nose flared in irritability, but she forced herself to exhale slowly so she wouldn't terrify the intern. 'Thank you,' – she checked the girl's name tag – 'Miranda. We'll wait.' *Not patiently*, she mentally tacked on.

Behind her, Cord whispered only loud enough for Alyssa to hear. 'You should probably take a few deep breaths right now before you confront Mr. Cannon.'

'You should probably—' She stopped when Cord threw his hands up in the air and backed up a step.

'Hey, I'm on your side, remember?'

Alyssa didn't have time to respond because Monty Cannon came waltzing through the soundproofed doors, right hand extended in greeting. 'Detective Alyssa Wyatt from the Albuquerque Police Department. My colleagues shared—'

'I don't care who shared what about *me*. I don't know *where* or from *whom* you received your "breaking news"' – angry air quotes punctuated her every sneered word – 'but did it ever occur to that overblown, sun-fried brain of yours to *follow up*, maybe *speak* to the law enforcement officials involved in the case before delivering your news to the public?'

'Are you saying—'

'I'm sorry. Did you think that was an invitation for you to start asking me questions? Let me rephrase. Your stupid, ill-timed, ill-advised news report not only jeopardized my case, but you and your unprofessional, idiotic shenanigans may very well have placed innocent lives in danger.'

Either the man wasn't operating on all cylinders, he was a great actor, or he was stupidly more arrogant than Alyssa gave him credit for because Monty Cannon took that moment to lean back casually against the receptionist's counter and cross both his arms and his legs. A superior smirk settled onto his face. 'So, my source was accurate, then?'

'Are you hard of hearing? You. Endangered. Lives.' *And not just yours*, she added silently. 'I want to know who's feeding you information.'

'I honestly can't tell you.'

'Can't or won't?'

'Detective, if you can't keep your own squad under control, that's not really my problem, now, is it?'

At Cannon's smug leer, Alyssa's head exploded, and surfer boy might've finally gotten a clue because he took a healthy step backwards. Finally, the man was starting to comprehend that he might've just pulled the pin in this grenade.

She wasn't even aware she'd shuffled forward until Cord stilled her by touching her upper arm. 'Still illegal to maim people who piss you off, Lys.' He glowered down at the reporter. 'Despite how well-deserved it might be.'

Seething, Alyssa shook Cord's hand off and invaded Monty Cannon's space. 'You. Arrogant. Mule. Let me just spell it out for you. First, I know for an absolute *fact* that no one on *my* team slipped you that information. And second, as I've already pointed out, *your* arrogance just endangered the lives of two small children, and I promise you this. If anything – and I do mean anything – happens to them, I will arrest you for impeding my investigation, obstruction of justice, and any other charge I can come up with, even if it includes spitting in public. Furthermore, if you *ever* compromise one of my cases again, I will make damn certain you are the absolute last person anyone speaks to in this city. And I'm talking the mayor, firefighters, and street cleaners. By the time I'm finished, you'll be lucky if a tick sucking off a coyote will be seen in your company.'

'I don't really think—'

'See, that's where your lack of intelligence obviously stems from. You don't think. And just in case you really don't get it – because you seem like the kind who might need it beat into your brain more than once – if you get any more "anonymous" tips, you'd better have someone run it by me or someone else on my team before airing your story. I meant every single word about having you locked up. And when I find out who leaked you that info, and I will find out, there will be hell to pay.'

'You can't just come in blazing and hurling threats, Detective. I'm merely doing my job. Besides, the public has a right to know.'

'Yes, they do. But not when it puts people's lives in direct danger. You, Mr. Cannon, had better pray to God or whatever higher power you believe in that nothing bad happens to those children because of your "breaking news." And by the way, I can absolutely assure you, I'm not hurling any threats; I'm making promises. If I have to come here to confront you again, my next visit won't be nearly as friendly.' Peering around the man, she addressed the receptionist once more. 'Miranda, please have the station manager contact me as soon as she's finished with her meeting.' She slapped her card down and scooted it over the desk. 'I'm sure she'll be interested to hear about her newest *investigative* reporter's antics.'

'Yes, ma'am.'

On her way out of the news station, Alyssa realized Cannon's co-anchor had opted to watch from a safe distance rather than join or defend her partner. She was wondering what that might mean when her phone rang, displaying an out-of-state number with an area code belonging to Indiana. She flashed her screen in Cord's direction. 'London's grandparents, you think?'

'My guess.'

Though her insides could still boil pasta, she kept her voice level and calm as she answered. 'Detective Alyssa Wyatt speaking.'

The gravelly timbre of an old man's voice on the other end of the line spoke softly but with authority. 'Detective Wyatt. This is Dale Manning, London Brecken's grandfather. My wife is also on this call—'

A soft, flowery voice full of warmth and as sweet as her husband's was gruff greeted Alyssa. 'Hello, Detective.'

'Greta and I received an urgent message from someone within your department, Hal Callum, who left us your number.' His crackling tone hinted that he already knew something was wrong. 'When I heard detectives were calling me from Albuquerque, I knew it could only mean one thing. Something happened to our London, and when I tried calling and she didn't answer, I knew I was right. So I did one of those Google searches…' His words broke up. 'Have you found her? Is she okay? What—why did this happen?'

Crushing sadness for the elderly couple instantly replaced Alyssa's anger of moments earlier. 'We're still trying to find those answers for you and everyone else.' Quickly, and as gently as she could, Alyssa relayed what they knew. 'And while we haven't located London yet, we're doing everything we can.'

'Thank you for that. London's all we've got left. And we're all she's got.'

'Well, that's not quite accurate.' Her voice clogged with emotion, Mrs. Manning explained. 'London's parents are still alive, but we haven't seen or spoken to our daughter, her mother, since the day London turned eighteen and legally became an adult. They didn't even attend her graduation or bother sending her a card. I've tried calling my daughter over the years but finally stopped when she never returned a single one. London, bless her broken heart, never bothered trying and shredded every one of her parents' checks that would've helped her with college expenses. She refused to even allow us to tell them which university she attended back when I was still trying to keep the lines of communication open.'

Alyssa and Cord exchanged looks. 'Did London have a falling-out with her parents?'

The sigh that Mr. Manning expelled carried the weight of decades of pain and hurt. 'Detective, my daughter never wanted children, and apparently neither did her husband. Frankly, the only reason she didn't terminate the pregnancy was because she was too far along when she realized she was pregnant, something my daughter cruelly made sure London knew. Every summer, school break, and holiday, from the time she turned one, our grand-daughter spent with us, not that we complained. When she was old enough, my daughter sent her to some fancy boarding school. Greta and I begged to let London live here with us fulltime. We even offered to adopt her, but they wouldn't even consider it. My guess is they thought it sounded swankier to their newfound friends to have a child in boarding school. See, my daughter has always been ashamed of being a small-town farmer's daughter, so when her husband hit it big off some stock boom, she wrote us off and never looked back. Last I heard, they were living somewhere in Greece. Still, I'll be calling her as soon as I hang up with you, though I doubt she'll care even if she does bother to answer.'

Alyssa shook her head in amazement, unable to comprehend how parents could turn their backs on their children. But Mr. and Mrs. Manning very much reminded her of Holly and Isaac's own grandmother who would turn the world upside-down and inside out for her grand-children.

'Mr. and Mrs. Manning, did London happen to share with either of you any concerns about someone who might've wanted to harm her or her friends?'

'No, I'm afraid not,' Mr. Manning said.

Immediately, Mrs. Manning jumped in to contradict her husband. 'Now, wait up, dear. Remember London mentioned something about a boy stalking her friend, Skye? I believe that might've been a month or so ago. But she didn't sound like any of them were really frightened of the fellow. Maybe just a tad bit uncomfortable at his attention.'

Alyssa shot a look in Cord's direction. 'Is there anything else you can remember about that conversation?'

'No, I'm afraid not. All she really said was that even though Skye wasn't interested, she still tried to be kind to the young man when she told him.'

'And did London mention this alleged stalker's name?' Even though Alyssa assumed the Mannings were referring to Roman Cordova, she thought she'd ask anyway.

'No, I don't believe she did. I'm sorry.'

Alyssa hadn't really expected any other response. 'That's okay,' she said. 'I'm sorry we don't have better news for you yet, but I promise you now that you'll be the first to know once we locate her.' She had to bite her tongue before she added 'and bring her safely home' because she didn't want to make a promise she may already be too late in keeping.

Mr. Manning cleared his throat, and when he spoke again, his fear for his granddaughter leaked through. 'A few years ago, my wife and I would've hopped right onto a plane and flown out there to help you search, but we're just unable to travel like that anymore. But if you think it'll help, why, we'll find a way.'

'We appreciate the offer, but that won't be necessary. Just lean on each other and try to stay strong.'

'Greta and I know this is all in God's hands, but we'll be praying He'll find the mercy to bring her safely home.'

'Us, too,' Alyssa said. After a few more assurances that she would be in touch as soon as they had anything, she ended the call and dropped her head against the headrest. 'We have to find her alive. Please don't let it be too late already.' Then she kicked herself in the pants. 'Saying it isn't going to get the job done.' She turned the key in the ignition. 'Let's go speak to Lillian Holt about August. On the way, we'll call Hammond to see what he dropped by for and to get him to approve a cop's presence in front of the Sandersons' at all times.' A resurgence of anger seeped into her voice, and her hands tightened on the steering wheel. 'What was that overly tanned buffoon thinking?'

'He was thinking he got a scoop. And he did. The question is, who gave it to him? Like you said, it wasn't anyone on our team. But somebody got their hands on that information. Media hadn't arrived when the kids were taken away in the ambulance, so it could be loose lips within the department or someone watching.'

'It wasn't someone watching because they wouldn't have remained anonymous. It was someone who was either on scene or knew someone who was. And I will find out who.'

'Wouldn't want to be in that person's shoes,' Cord half-joked.

Not even seven thirty in the morning, and Alyssa's head already throbbed at level three on a scale of one to five. Absently, she reached up one hand to rub her temple. They hadn't been working this case for a full forty-eight hours yet, and already it felt like it had been a week.

–

The captain had just gotten off a call with the mayor when Alyssa reached him, so to call him a little cranky didn't even come close, but since that was his general resting demeanor as well, Alyssa didn't let it faze her.

'Did you find out who gave Cannon that information?' As usual, Hammond's greeting consisted of a barked order or question.

'Not yet.'

'I've already got a squad car heading over to the Sandersons' right now, so if that's why you're calling, it's done. And since I've got you on the phone, I'll tell you what I dropped by to tell you before Ruby... came in.' Neither Alyssa nor Cord could hold back their grins at the way the captain hesitated. 'I was delivering a message from Hedge.'

Bill Hedge was one of the department's top technicians. 'Good news, I hope?'

'Yes and no. That print on the blinds outside the victim's bedroom was pretty smeared, but he thinks he may have been able to obtain at least a partial print. He was going to run it through the system and get back to you as soon as he had an answer. Tread from shoe drag prints on the carpet appear to have come from a woman's size seven or eight Fila sneaker.'

It wasn't what Alyssa wanted to hear, but at least it was something, so she'd take it. After giving him an update on where they were headed, she ended the call. 'You know, I'm fairly certain that's the greatest number of words that man has ever strung together in one sitting since I've met him.'

Because they were still waiting for Hal to contact her with Ewan Moore's current location, and they were already nearby, Alyssa drove to Lillian Holt's place. Yellow crime scene tape still surrounded Skye Fleming's property, though half of it was blowing in the brisk spring wind. Before they'd even climbed out of the vehicle, Lillian Holt appeared on the porch, the lines around her mouth tightening as her eyes shifted toward her neighbor's house before she averted her gaze to watch Alyssa and Cord's approach.

Chapter Twenty-Four

Immediately after speaking with Lillian Holt, Alyssa reached for her phone to call Hal again, but thinking about him seemed to have conjured him up because he was calling her at the same time. 'Just the man I need.'

'Don't think Brock or Helena would appreciate that much. But just between you and me, you're just the gal *I* need. But I need Cord, too. No offense.' The tone of Hal's voice turned from lighthearted to serious. 'Just got off the phone with Ewan Moore's parole officer. You're not going to believe this, but he's started up a small church, congregation of only about twelve, fifteen people, but that's twelve or fifteen people too many, if you ask my opinion.'

'Where do we find him?' Alyssa asked.

'As luck would have it, he holds Saturday services beginning at three, and according to his parole officer, Moore usually arrives at the church around eight in the morning to begin prepping and rehearsing for the sermon.' Hal rattled off the address.

Alyssa performed a U-turn and headed for the interstate. 'We're on our way now. I'll call you when we leave and let you know what we found out. Now, as for why I needed to speak to you. We talked to Lillian Holt again, and she shared some disturbing news about August with us.

172

'Beginning in his junior year and continuing into his senior year, August gained something of a reputation for his hot temper, especially as he suddenly began getting into more fights than classrooms. His mom's words, not ours. Anyway, she thought he might be getting into drugs. Fast forward to after his third suspension, he decided he might as well drop out since he spent more time at home than in school anyway.

'Lillian and her husband were divorced by then, but they planned to get together to confront August about his behavior. While they were waiting on him to return home, they decided to go through his room to search for any drugs he might have had. What they found instead was what they thought at first was a bible until Lillian picked it up for a closer look.'

Like she'd had earlier when Lillian had described what she and her ex had discovered, goosebumps prickled Alyssa's skin. 'It was a book on blood sorcery.'

'What the hell is blood sorcery?' Hal asked.

Cord couldn't hide the revulsion that spilled over into his voice. 'In a nutshell, it refers to magic practiced in occultism. And vampirism.'

'The hell!' Hal's shock rivaled Alyssa's own reaction. The implication behind that news had curdled the contents in her stomach.

'That, along with the fact that we've been unable to locate August Holt since he's quite conveniently dropped from sight, now officially moves him from my list of persons to question and over to a possible person of interest. Which now makes two individuals on our radar who have potential ties to, or an interest in, occult practices. Not including Ewan Moore, who may or may not be up to his old practices.'

Hal swore under his breath. 'And unfortunately, we don't have probable cause to request pulling either of their phone records.'

'True,' Cord agreed. 'But on the upside, Lillian Holt happened to mention that she still pays for her son's phone, and while she didn't openly grant us access to his records, I think she will if condemning evidence implicates his involvement in a double homicide.'

Alyssa's heart lodged in her throat when a dog, still on its leash, darted into the road before his owner managed to yank him back just as Alyssa tapped her brakes. She took one hand off the steering wheel and pressed it against her chest, taking a deep breath so her voice wouldn't squeak. 'Well, I happen to believe we have reasonable grounds to fear August Holt *may* be involved, and since London Brecken's life remains in imminent danger, I think we *do* have grounds for a ping warrant to see if his number bounces off any of the cell towers in his mother's neighborhood the night of the murders.'

'Well, that tops the second bit of news I had for you,' Hal said, 'but not necessarily the third.'

Alyssa and Cord exchanged similar puzzled looks. 'What bit of news?'

'Joe got access to Skye Fleming's and Elena Garcia's phone logs, but as of right now, nothing stands out. Also, we had a look at the women's financial records, but there's nothing there.'

'And the third bit of news?' Cord prompted.

'We got a ping off London Brecken's phone already. Until five-thirty Thursday evening, her phone pings off the cell towers near Intel. Same with Skye and Elena's. Elena's pings off towers that show her driving home and then back over to Skye's. London and Skye's ping off the same towers and end at Fleming's home Thursday around six-thirty with two stops in between. One at Teeter-Tot Daycare and then Albertson's grocery store. From there, London's phone doesn't ping again until ten-seventeen on Central near the Rio Grande.'

'They tossed her phone.' When they hadn't located a third phone, Alyssa had suspected that to be the case, but she still swore.

'Seems to be what happened,' Hal agreed.

'All right. Well, we knew the likelihood of using her GPS tracker to pinpoint her current location was slim, but at least we now have a general direction our suspects were traveling, which is more than we had. So for now, let's see if we can get a ping warrant for August Holt's phone. If we could have that by yesterday, that would be grand.'

'I've already got a call into Judge Rosario. She'll be pissed that I'm calling her on a Saturday, but she loves me, so I'm sure we'll have that warrant in no time.'

Alyssa shook her head, only half kidding when she said, 'How the hell do you manage to do things so damn fast? We *just* now told you about it, and you've been on the phone with us for the past fifteen minutes. Do you have Flash Gordon genes?'

'Flash Gordon doesn't wear jeans. He wears really tight tank tops or a superhero suit.'

Alyssa groaned even as laughter erupted from the passenger seat. 'That's the worst one yet, my friend.'

'Oh, it was funny, and you know it.'

'Keep telling yourself that if it helps you sleep at night.' Only Cord could see her shake her head in mock disappointment, but it didn't matter because everyone knew she believed Hal Callum to be a walking – or wheeling – miracle. Plus, his sense of humor frequently managed to defuse tense situations so everyone could clear their minds and stay on track. Current situation case in point.

'We're getting close to some answers,' Cord said. 'I can feel it. Our dead ends are starting to open up into some alleyways. Before you know it, we'll have our killers.'

'And London Brecken,' Hal added.

'From your lips to God's ears,' Alyssa whispered.

On the southern outskirts of the city, Alyssa's Tahoe rumbled and bounced down the washboard dirt road, making her teeth rattle. 'Who the hell wants to drive all the way out here for church services?' she grumbled.

'Maybe they're not coming for church.'

Off in the distance, Alyssa could just make out a single-wide trailer that had clearly seen better days at least two or three decades before the turn of the century. The part of the roof visible beneath the blue tarp secured with old tires was patchwork style. Barbed-wire fencing surrounded the property full of… stuff. Alyssa couldn't decide if the place was nothing more than a cluttered piece of land or a purposeful junkyard.

As she drew closer, two grease-covered rottweilers tore around the corner of the home, their muscular bodies vibrating with the threat of latching onto the strangers daring to drive by their padlocked property. A man of indeterminate age and equally covered in grease swaggered around the front to see what had caused the commotion.

'Well, they look friendly,' Cord muttered.

Something Hal had told them earlier teased the back of her memory. As the church – if the dilapidated building could be called that – came into view, it clicked. 'Don't the conditions of Moore's parole state he isn't allowed within one hundred yards of any animals? That property may not belong to him, but his church still places him in dangerous proximity of crossing that line.'

'Technically, what Hal said, or at least the way I understood it, was that Moore isn't allowed to be around animals or have them as pets. The one hundred yards was in reference to his victims and his victims' families. That trailer is outside those bounds, so not breaking any rules that I can see.'

Unsatisfied by her partner's response, Alyssa didn't let it deter her. 'We need to get that clarified because if we need a reason to haul him in for questioning, that'll be our legal purpose.' With a cloud of yellow dust from the dirt road raining down on her recently washed vehicle, she came to a stop outside the church. So she wouldn't inhale a mouthful of dirt, she waited for it to settle before she climbed out and glanced inside the rust bucket of a truck whose side windows were covered with such a heavy film of grime, she couldn't see anything past the torn vinyl of the seat and the trash strewn along the floorboard.

Torn garbage bags littered the ground around the crumbling structure of the church, their contents spilling out rancid milk cartons, moldy fruit, and God knew what else. 'So, he's a neat freak,' Alyssa deadpanned.

Together, she and Cord climbed the rickety steps, doing their best to avoid the obstacle course of trash. When they reached the door, they were both surprised to see it open. Something she decided to be grateful for because she didn't relish touching the oily doorknob that probably hadn't been cleaned in the last half-century.

Stepping inside, she swung her head left and right, mentally noting the condition of the interior wasn't any better than the exterior. Unlike other churches she'd been in, this centrum felt icky and far from welcoming. Maybe because nearly every visible surface played host to what had to be millions of black mold spores – the floor, the ceiling, the ancient counter holding ancient brochures, everything. The urge to cover her nose and mouth to avoid breathing any of it in hit her hard, but she ignored the impulse. Somehow.

'Don't know about you, but I don't think what I'm feeling is the Holy Spirit,' Cord mumbled.

'Do you think it's because of the cobwebs hanging from the windows, the layers of dirt covering the broken tiled floor, or the I-don't-even-want-to-know-what-germs-are-swimming-in-it carpet, hmm?'

'Let's just go find this guy and try and get some answers so we can get out of here. And take a shower.' Cord pointed to the only other doorway in the church where, above it, the letters *F**CE were barely still visible through the graffiti.

They didn't bother knocking.

Prison hadn't done Ewan Moore any favors. The man reclined with his filthy boots propped up on the fake, peeling wooden desk. When he heard them enter, his feet dropped to the ground with an echoing thud, and he rose to his feet, his eyes narrowed in suspicion even as he offered a grin that showed two missing teeth and several broken and chipped ones.

As Alyssa flashed her badge, she noticed the man's teardrop tattoo near his eye twitch. 'Ewan Moore?'

'Police.' The way he said it made it sound like a curse word. 'What do you want? I haven't violated any rules of my parole. Those dogs are well outside the boundaries, and I don't know the man who lives in the trailer, though I've left flyers inviting him to services.'

'We have a few questions for you.'

'Whatever you want to know, I don't have the answers.' Moore crossed his powerful arms over his chest and glared.

'Not very pastorly of you, is it?' Alyssa asked.

'I've got a sermon to prepare for, so I'll ask you again before I insist you leave, what do you want?'

In his own form of intimidation, Cord stepped in closer, not quite crowding the man but definitely invading his space. 'Where were you Thursday?'

'Home. Why?'

'Anybody who can verify that?'

He shrugged. 'I guess you could ask my daughter or her husband since I live with them. I'd tell you their names, but I'm sure you cops already have that information, along with their dates of birth, their cell phone numbers, the kinds of cars they drive, and the first time they had sex.'

'Well, what if we told you we found a couple of bodies who, incidentally enough, have the markings of *your* past crimes?' Though only Skye had any markings on her or had the number forty-seven carved into her tongue, Alyssa wanted to watch Moore's reaction. He didn't blink, didn't even drop his gaze in her direction as he continued to stare Cord down.

'And? You want to know if I'm up to my old practices? My parole officer knows I found religion. I'm a changed man.' Moore thumped on a dusty, tattered copy of the Bible sitting on the edge of his desk.

Some consider Satanic rituals a religion of sorts. Alyssa thought it but kept the words inside.

'Do you have a cell phone?' Cord asked.

'No. See no need for anyone to be able to reach me any time I'm sitting on the toilet, out for a walk, or meditating. My daughter doesn't own a home phone either. Things changed during my time in prison. Time I've done, I'll remind you.'

Not all of it. Again, Alyssa kept the thought to herself. She nodded to the only clean object in the room, a picture frame with a photo of a young woman, probably in her twenties and a young man of approximately the same age or maybe a little older. Aside from Moore's life-beaten looks, the female looked remarkably like him. 'Is that your daughter?'

Without turning around, Moore nodded. 'Yep.'

'How does she feel about your past?'

The lines around Moore's face stretched tight. That question finally earned Alyssa his attention as he sneered at her. 'She lets me live with her, and she trusts me not to drive a dagger through her heart or carve up her tongue while she's sleeping. My daughter, *Detective*, is proud of the man her father has become.'

Both Alyssa and Cord stiffened, and Moore laughed, the sound one of the evilest she'd ever heard.

'Well, isn't that what you meant by "my markings"? After all, that is what I was known for. I never got my own media moniker, but the boys in the house liked to call me The Carver.'

'For a supposedly repentant man, I've got to say you don't particularly seem like you're sorry or that you regret your crimes,' Alyssa said.

'Regret? Sorry? Jesus forgave me, so my sins have been absolved. If He can let it go, who am I not to let the past stay in the past? Now, listen, I don't know anything about your crime, so I'm going to suggest you go ahead and get your arrest warrant and your search warrants to flip my place. And I'll go ahead and contact my attorney, so you know, we're all on the same page. And now I'll allow you two to see yourselves out while I prepare to bring my congregation to see the light of eternal salvation.'

With that, Moore turned his back and plopped back down in the chair that sent up a plume of old dust.

Without a warrant, they couldn't legally search the place, but they could check things out that were out in the open, so Alyssa and Cord did just that, finding nothing that raised any red flags. As they climbed back inside the Tahoe, neither spotted the face peering back at them from a window in the corner of the church.

Chapter Twenty-Five

Saturday, April 24

Flames licked at London's face, reawakening the scream that cried to be released but was forced to stay lodged in her throat. If the blistering heat of the high sun blazing in and scorching her skin was trying to prepare her for hell, it needn't bother. She was already there.

All the ball of fire did now was remind her that her mouth was drier than a desert, made worse by the bloodied cloth still shoved inside it and that now stuck to the cracks in her lips and the multiple sores forming between her teeth and her bottom lip. Wincing from the pain, she tried to push her swollen tongue against the cloth to dislodge it, but even something as minor as wiggling her tender jaw depleted her energy.

Drained from straddling the edges of sanity, London closed her eyes for another moment. When she reopened them, they immediately landed on the familiar, demonic words painted on the wall. In the sunlight, things she hadn't noticed before now screamed out their existence. The 'T' in *The* was actually an inverted cross, the apostrophe and 'S' in *Devil's* were actually a vampiric tooth and a lightning bolt such as the band KISS used, the 'A' in *Playground* a symbol of an anarchist, and the 'O' a pentagram. And in between all the letters were not merely black dots as she'd first thought but the numbers six-six-six. Acid from her stomach surged up her esophagus, burning her throat. What cosmic folly had occurred that had caused her and her friends to cross paths with these sadistic savages who worshipped all things evil?

Pray for your enemies, London, that they may be forgiven and brought to the light. Of all the voices she continued to hear, her grandmother's daily wisdom was the one that lingered. Knowing her grandparents had to be frantic with worry, despite the fact that they were, in all likelihood, part of a growing prayer chain pleading with God to bring her safely home, London endured yet another round of emotional tug-of-war with a twisted rope made up of hope and crushing despair.

It took no effort at all for her to picture her grand-father's strong countenance and her grandmother's steely resolve as they rallied their pastor and all their friends together. As a teenager, she'd often rolled her eyes, albeit never in front of them, whenever someone initiated one of the small-town prayer chains, wondering why they bothered.

One day, right after a friend of hers had succumbed to injuries caused by a drunk driver who'd broadsided her car, London had cried on her grandma's shoulders. Inconsolable, she'd demanded to know why God had allowed it to happen, despite all of their urgent prayers to see her friend through, screaming that it wasn't fair, especially since the drunk driver had walked away with little more than a gash across his cheek. Grandma had wept with her and explained it was all part of God's plan.

Instead of bolstering her courage, the memory managed to suffocate any inkling of faith she may've been trying to cling to. What if all this, Skye's and Elena's murders, as well as everything happening to her, was also part of the 'plan'? A plan she hadn't understood then and didn't understand now. How could an all-loving omni-scient being be okay with any of this – or even allow it to happen at all? A rush of anger sent a different kind of heat radiating throughout her body. For a few precious moments, London welcomed an emotion not filled with terror and pain.

For long moments, she held onto that rage, letting it fuel her. Until movement caught her eye, and she jerked her head to the side in time to watch the black rat snake slithering across the windowsill where the same wolf or dog she'd seen before unconsciousness stole her away sat on the ground staring inside at her. Her stomach tightened at the sight of the snake inching its way closer to the animal. Begging her muscles to cooperate, she lifted her bound hands and tried to warn the wolfdog away with a shooing motion, but it remained where it stood, its beautiful, knowing eyes observing her.

Just as her arms collapsed from the effort of holding them up, she heard the rattle of an engine. The animal glanced once over its shoulders in the direction of the approaching vehicle before rising from its haunches. Then, with one final look at London, it turned and trotted away, leaving her to face her tormentors on her own.

Chapter Twenty-Six

Saturday, April 24

Later that afternoon, and five minutes after Cord walked into the incident room laden down with a Styrofoam container holding a green-chile smothered enchilada and calabacitas for Alyssa, three bags of handheld burritos, sopapillas, chips, salsa, two two-liter bottles of soda and chai tea for himself, Alyssa ended her call. The way Joe and Tony attacked the bags made it seem like they hadn't eaten for days. Which, come to think of it, they might not have.

Seconds after setting her phone to the side, she received a text notification. She peeked down to see Isaac's name. Again. He'd already sent her four texts earlier to beat Holly's three.

> Whtevr Holly did to Dad, she needs to fix stat. He's grumpy n snarly. Also r u com'g home? Don't tell her, but don't really want G-ma's lasagna.

Alyssa shook her head and shot back a message followed by a monkey covering both eyes.

> Here's a thought: if you don't want what Grandma is kind enough to come over and cook for you, brat, try cooking for her and Dad for a change.

Almost immediately, her phone dinged again.

> Sorry. Wrong number. Pls go about yer evening. Peace out.

> P.S. U shouldn't call yer kid names. It'll scar me.

Alyssa laughed.

> Good thing I didn't call my kid a brat, just the person who texted me by mistake.

Isaac sent a bunch of cry-laughing emojis followed by a:

> luv u. Seriously, come home soon, k?

Even if it was only because she provided the groceries he bulldozed through, it was nice to know her teenage son still liked having her home once in a while.

Pushing food, napkins, and a coffee cup now filled with soda in her direction, Cord nodded to the phone still in her hand. 'Who were you talking to when I walked in? Sounded important.'

'Olivia Cordova, Roman's sister. One of her friends caught a bug or ate something bad, so they decided to end their camping trip early. As soon as she got her mother's message, she called.'

Cord popped a chip dipped in salsa into his mouth. 'What'd she have to say?'

Alyssa eyed the chip and gave a derisive snort. 'Why bother putting salsa on it at all? How can you not understand that the chip is merely the vessel used to get the salsa to your mouth? You embarrass me with your lack of respect for the chips and salsa dining etiquette. But to answer your question, she mostly corroborated what her mother already told us. That just before Christmas two years ago, she walked in on Roman choking their mother, pulled her gun and threatened to shoot him. What she added was that a couple of weeks later, he blew up her phone with apology texts and messages. She said she finally called him up and told him he needed help, and until he got it, she had no desire to speak to him or listen to his pleas about trying to mend things. She told him the ball was in his court, and whatever choice he made was fine with her.' Alyssa paused to take a bite out of her enchilada and wash it down with her drink.

'I take it he didn't really follow through with getting help?'

'Doesn't sound like it. She said she really couldn't say for sure, but that one day he showed up at *her* house, agitated, frustrated, and otherwise infuriated over some girl. Anyway, she asked if he'd talked to his therapist about it. She said he took her question as subtext that implied that this girl should dump him, and after calling her the daughter of a whore, he stormed out, and she hasn't talked to or seen him since.'

Cord leaned back in his chair and steepled his hands behind his head. 'Did you happen to ask her if he ever found out that she spotted him in the restaurant the day she warned the girl off?'

'What? Is this my first day on the job? Yes, of course, I asked. And she said she didn't think so just by the sheer fact that she hadn't seen him since that last incident at her house. But that doesn't really give us any answers, either. As for the occult, she said she didn't think Roman was still into it, and she didn't really think he was "*into it* into it" when he was a teenager, but she'd been wrong about her brother before.'

Eyeing the crime scene photos while quietly processing the information, Cord finally nodded before he turned to Liz. 'Any luck so far on creating a sketch for the driver of the van?'

Liz shook her head while swallowing the chip – which held a respectable amount of salsa – that she'd just stuck into her mouth. After swiping a napkin across her chin where her food dribbled, she answered Cord's question.

'No, I'm afraid not. I was afraid that the camera images were too pixelated when I made the suggestion, and it's actually worse than I thought. I haven't given up yet, but I'm also not holding my breath that I'll be able to get you anything usable.'

While Alyssa hadn't allowed herself to count on the sketches, she'd been hopeful that Liz's skills would be able to provide them at least a little more something than they already had. Just as she opened her mouth to thank the forensic artist for not giving up, they were interrupted by Lynn Sharp poking her head in the door.

'Oh good, you're in. I figured I'd have to give you another call. Do you have a few minutes? Looks like I've interrupted your mealtime, such as it is.'

'Come on in. Would you like a burrito?' Cord held one out, but the medical examiner shook her head and took a step back like she was afraid it might bite her.

Wrinkling her nose, she offered an apology. 'Sorry. I know I'm in the minority here in this state, but I'm definitely not a fan of those burritos.' She shuddered for emphasis while Tony stared at her like she'd grown a second head.

'These' – he held his food up – 'gross you out, but you cut up on dead people for a living? There's something disturbingly not right about that.'

Dr. Sharp laughed. 'I suppose you have a point. Speaking of.' She turned her attention back to Alyssa. 'I got DNA results back on those blood samples I sent in, but I'm afraid they're not going to be overly helpful. The blood in the hallway belongs to Brecken, the blood in the entryway belongs to Garcia, and—'

'Let me guess,' Joe interrupted. 'The blood in the bedroom belongs to Fleming?'

Lynn grimaced. 'Sorry. I warned you it wouldn't help.'

Cord pushed his chair back. 'What about the hairs you mentioned finding on Skye near her eye and on the clothes?'

'Goat DNA.'

'Excuse me. Did you say, "goat DNA," as in the animal?' Tony asked.

'Yes, I'm afraid that's exactly what I said.'

Hal, who had rolled in as Lynn made the announcement, ripped the paper off a burrito and responded to Tony's shock. 'That makes sense and is also one more confirmation that we're looking at a serious cult here and not just some wannabe kids messing around for fun and attention.'

The lines in Tony's forehead deepened. 'Two murders and a kidnapping told me that. So, explain to me how goat DNA translates into confirming the occult angle? What am I missing?'

Hal looked to Lynn, but Dr. Sharp waved her hand for him to continue. 'The goat head represents Satan. I'm not sure how or why, but I do remember that from working my past case.'

'Well, I'll never look at goats the same, that's for sure,' Tony mumbled.

'Anything else?' Alyssa asked the medical examiner.

'Not yet. But I had to be in this area anyway, so thought I'd take my chances to see if you were in or not. Sorry I couldn't have offered more that would've led you to some real answers.'

As Lynn was walking out, Captain Hammond rushed in, a pinched yet excited expression on his face. 'We might have a lead on the van. An off-duty cop was hiking up north near that old apple orchard when both his dogs started whining and tugging him toward the tree line. Didn't take him long before he spotted a lot of broken brush, trampled saplings, and tire tracks that he followed until he spotted the van. Took some photos, hiked until he got a signal, shot the pics off to his captain, who then called me.'

Food forgotten, Alyssa shoved to her feet. 'How would they have gotten the van in there at all? For the past ten years, those trails and roads have been completely closed or barricaded from the public because of the fires and subsequent flooding.'

'I asked the same thing. Captain Rodriguez said on the way down to find a signal, his man decided to follow the tire tracks that he'd just assumed came from an ATV. There was just enough space to squeeze that van past one of the concrete barricades, as long as no one worried about scratching it up. According to his off-duty guy, there were several significant and, based on the lack of rust, recent scratches down the side of the van. And from the deep grooves in the dirt and rocks, someone was pretty determined to get that vehicle past that barricade.'

Hammond handed Alyssa his phone with the images Rodriguez had messaged him already on display. With Cord peeking over her shoulder, she thumbed through them quickly before passing the phone to Hal.

'That definitely looks like the same vehicle caught on camera in the vicinity of Fleming's house Thursday night. But how are we going to get our own vehicles up there, and more importantly, how are we going to get the van out?' Hope that this discovery might lead them to London's whereabouts kicked Alyssa's pulse into high gear.

'Captain Rodriguez reached out to one of his contacts. Someone with keys will meet you at the mouth of the canyon and unlock that gate for you. It's not the same entrance the van used, but he thinks it'll get you there a little more quickly since the trail in isn't quite as bad. And Jackson Matthews, the off-duty cop, will lead you to the van. It'll be a rough trail, but your Tahoe should be able to handle it, I think. Since it gets dark up there quick, you'd better head out now.'

Nerves keyed up and vibrating like she'd just downed three espressos, Alyssa asked the question forefront in her mind. 'Any signs of London Brecken?'

'Matthews peeked inside but saw no evidence of a person.'

'Then that means we still have a fighting chance that she's still alive. Otherwise, why abandon the van without the body?' Alyssa pointed to Tony. 'Did you drive your truck today?'

'Sure did.'

'Good. You and Joe can follow us in that. Let's go.' She turned to Hammond. 'We'll call as soon as we have confirmation.'

–

With traffic lighter than she'd expected, they made it to the interstate in no time. Soon after, Alyssa's phone dinged. With her mind still racing with the hope of getting some answers that would lead them to London, she spared it a quick glance. Holly. Again.

She cleared the notification without reading the message, and Cord arched his brows. 'Holly or Isaac?'

Alyssa scowled. 'Holly.'

'So, you going to tell me what's going on or are you going to make me guess? And before you tell me nothing, I'll tell you that I know for a fact that it's completely out of character for *one* of your kids to hound you when you're working a case, much less both of them blowing up your phone. More importantly, I don't know that I've ever seen you scowl when one of your children calls or sends a message. So, spill. What gives?'

Alyssa blew out a long-suffering sigh. 'After I got home last night, Holly dropped by to tell me Nick wants the two of them to take dance lessons.'

A wide grin flashed across Cord's face because even he was aware of the legendary non-dancer that Holly was. 'Felt sorry for her, did he?'

Alyssa grimaced. 'It's a place that advertises that their specialty is getting couples "wedding ready."'

Cord, having just popped a few peanuts into his mouth, choked until his eyes turned red and watery and his hand groped blindly for the tea he'd snatched up on his way out of the incident room. With one hand still on the steering wheel, Alyssa reached over with the other and clapped him on the back until he pushed her hand away. 'Wh— what?' he finally managed.

'Yeah? See? Bad enough that was my reaction, too, but then Brock got back into town early.'

'Oh man.' Cord shook his head. 'Oh man,' he repeated.

'Yep, that about sums it up.'

'What does Mabel say?'

Out of a long-ingrained habit, Alyssa winced at her mother-in-law's name. 'I don't think she knows yet. And I imagine her reaction will be to pull out the wedding planning book she started preparing the minute she learned she had a granddaughter.'

Cord started laughing, and Alyssa risked a quick glance so she could glare at him. 'I'm glad you find this so amusing. Can we concentrate on what we might find when we arrive at the orchard?'

Instantly, Cord sobered. 'What do you think we're going to find?'

Alyssa didn't even have to think about it. 'Answers,' she said definitively.

–

Just over an hour later, Alyssa spotted a red Jeep Gladiator and a yellow Hummer parked nose to nose at the canyon blocking off the entrance to the rocky trail leading up to the old, abandoned apple orchard.

In its heyday, the site had hosted thousands of visitors every year when families from all over made the trek to pick bushels of the sweetest apples ever grown. And the cider tasted like nothing short of manna sent from heaven. Now, overgrown natural vegetation stretching as far as the eye could see, along with the deteriorated land and collapsed outbuildings, painted a drastically different picture than the one of a decade ago.

Centering the Tahoe between the Gladiator and the Hummer, Alyssa rolled down her window while two men approached. An older, gray-haired man with a tired, weathered face that hinted at a lifetime of stories greeted her first.

'Detective Wyatt from Albuquerque, I presume?'

'Yes, sir. This is my partner, Detective Roberts. The vehicle behind me is with us. And you are?'

The man reached out a hand crisscrossed with white scars. 'Damon Sawyer. Captain Rodriguez called me up and explained the situation, asked me to unlock the gate for you. Now, just to be clear, I'm gonna have to lock it back up after your team heads up because I can't risk someone going in behind you. Trails aren't the safest.' He pulled out a piece of paper from his shirt pocket and handed it to Alyssa. 'That's got my number on it, so you call me whenever you all finish up there, and I'll come back and unlock the gate for you to get out. Don't worry about the time. It won't take me long to get here.'

Sawyer stepped aside so the off-duty officer who'd come across the van could speak to Alyssa. He shook her hand and nodded to Cord. 'Jackson Matthews. Before we head in, have you ever visited the orchard?'

'Yes, but of course, a bit of time has passed since then.'

'Well, then, you're at least somewhat familiar with the area. We're going to be heading up that way' – he pointed off to the right – 'into those trees. It's a pretty steep, rocky incline, and I could lead you up in my Hummer, but it might be easier if I hop in the back and direct you that way.'

Alyssa unlocked the rear doors. 'Hop on in and let's roll. We're losing daylight fast.'

Matthews climbed into the back seat. 'If you want, when we finish up, I can show you how the van got past the barricade. For all the trouble this guy went through, it's clear someone sure as hell didn't want that vehicle found. And to be honest, if my dogs hadn't been going nuts, I wouldn't have investigated far enough to find it.'

Alyssa glanced in her rearview mirror. 'Speaking of, where are they, your dogs?'

'Oh, my brother lives about twenty minutes from here, and I asked him to come get them.'

'Got it.' Within minutes, they'd reached the steep, rocky incline, and Cord grimaced as he white-knuckled the seat and the 'Oh shit' handle as they bounced along.

Matthews noticed. 'Not a fan of the rough ride, huh?'

He had no idea. Ever since being a passenger in a nail-biting trip through the Pecos a couple years earlier while searching for two kidnapped girls, Cord had hated the very idea of being close to ridges or cliffs.

'No,' he bit out.

'You okay?' Alyssa's concern was genuine. But before her partner could answer, a concealed rut sent the three of them airborne with only their seatbelts to keep them from hitting the roof of the cab. Not the worst bump she'd ever hit, but it jarred enough to jostle the brain and snap her teeth together.

A tinge of green in Cord's already ashen face made her afraid he might hurl. Through gritted teeth, he growled at her. 'Would you, for the love of God, keep your ever-loving eyes on the damn road and pay attention to where you're going, please!'

For the next twenty-five rough, bouncy minutes, all she heard from the passenger seat were mumbled 'oomphs,' 'aahs,' and 'oh, hells' until Matthews directed her to stop and pointed.

'The van is just through that trampled brush and past those bent and broken saplings.'

Alyssa shut off the ignition, and the three of them climbed out and waited for Joe and Tony to join them. After making introductions, Matthews led the way to the light-colored van Kenny Holt had seen leaving Skye Fleming's house the night of the murders. Before she did anything else, Alyssa moved to the back of the vehicle to check the license plate. WPC414.

An electric jolt zipped up her spine. 'This is it. Anyone have a signal? We're going to need a tow truck to haul this van out so our technicians can go over it.'

'Not here, but I've hunted and hiked this area a fair share of times, so I know just up over that hill' – Tony pointed to somewhere off in the distance – 'my phone gets a couple bars. It's weak, but I can still make a call to set that up.' He turned in a slow circle. 'Though turning a tow truck around and getting back down might be a little trickier.'

'We'll figure it out when the truck gets here. Go ahead and make that call.' Alyssa handed him Damon Sawyer's number. 'Have the driver call him when he arrives so he can unlock the gate.'

While Tony headed further up the ridge, Matthews said, 'Well, the clouds are building, which means we've only got a few more daylight hours at best, so let me show you a few things I noticed.' He directed their attention to the shredded tire strips strewn along the grooved path to the van. 'My guess is that they'd planned on hiding the van further in, but their tires weren't built for this type of terrain, so they were forced to leave it here instead.'

While Tony secured a tow truck driver, Alyssa, Cord, and Joe navigated around the van, placing numbered markers before snapping pictures of a soggy cigarette butt, a piece of chewing gum, and what looked like a piece of velvet cloth before stowing them into evidence bags.

Cord came up to stand beside her, and she cast a quick glance his way, relieved to see the color had returned to his face. At least until the drive back down. 'Notice anything strange about the ground?'

Without looking, she knew exactly what her partner meant. 'You mean the way it looks like someone tried to brush away their footprints as they moved away from the vehicle? Yeah, I noticed and snapped pictures.'

Matthews walked over in time to hear Alyssa's explanation, and he cocked his head toward a shrub with several snapped, heavily leaved branches tossed almost haphazardly on top. 'I think you're right, and that's likely what your guy used.'

A clap of thunder stole her reply. Tilting her neck back so she could study the sky, she grimaced at the storm clouds hovering overhead and threatening to rain on her possible evidence. 'We'll record and note everything we can tonight, secure it the best we can, and then get an evidence collection team up here first thing tomorrow.' She hated to wait, but she had to work with what they had.

'Hey, Lys,' Joe yelled out. 'You might want to check this out.'

On the side of the van, past the door panel, a smudged handprint stood out in stark relief against the light-colored paint. 'You've got a dusting kit?'

'Yep. I'll grab it and be right back.'

He finished just as Tony finally rejoined them. 'Tow truck will be here in about forty-five minutes to haul this baby down. I gave him Sawyer's number like you said, then I contacted Sawyer to let him know to be expecting the call.' He tipped his head toward the van. 'Anyone take a gander inside yet?'

Alyssa's gloved hand was already reaching for the door handle. 'Thanks for taking care of that, and we were just about to take a look.'

–

Ninety minutes later, just as Alyssa and the others, including Matthews, returned from canvassing a quarter mile in each direction to be certain London Brecken hadn't been abandoned along with the van, a light sprinkle threatened the promise of a heavier downpour, and the tow truck driver arrived, apologizing profusely. He'd been caught in a traffic jam from a wreck on the highway.

With the light fading fast, Alyssa tried to calm her nerves as the driver slowly and tirelessly shifted forward and back as he tried to maneuver his truck in order to load the van onto the flatbed. It took a grueling thirty minutes of swearing, teeth-gnashing, and white-knuckling – and that was just from Alyssa – but the driver finally managed to get his truck into position.

They'd already decided it would be best to sandwich the tow truck between the Tahoe and Tony's vehicle with Alyssa, Cord, and Matthews leading the way down and waiting for Damon Sawyer to close off the gates. While Tony, Joe, and the tow truck continued into Albuquerque, Alyssa and Cord would follow Matthews to the spot where the van had forced its entry. With one final peek up at the building rain clouds, Alyssa issued a prayer that the downpour would hold off until they were off the ridge, and not just for Cord's sake.

As if he'd read her mind, Cord paused with one foot planted on the floorboard and stared up at the sky before staring back down at his feet as if actually considering whether or not he'd rather hike back down than ride.

Alyssa snapped her seatbelt into place. 'Climb in and close your eyes. I haven't killed us yet, have I?'

Cord winced. 'Don't say, "yet," and it's not you I'm worried about.'

'The longer you stand there' – she pointed up at the clouds and then down to the blowing trees – 'the harder it'll be to navigate around those ruts. *Especially* if we get caught in that rainstorm.'

Apparently, those were the magic words because Cord climbed in and buckled up, tugging twice on the belt to ensure it was 'I can't breathe' snug. Halfway down, Alyssa couldn't help but poke at him. 'You stare down hardened criminals every day of your life, and this is what's gonna cause you to grow gray hairs?'

He didn't even bother glancing in her direction as he bit out his tense reply. 'Just shut up and get us the hell on pavement.'

Behind her, Jackson Matthews coughed to cover the chuckle Alyssa knew her partner heard but chose to ignore anyway.

Chapter Twenty-Seven

Saturday, April 24

Just over two hours later, Alyssa and Cord ignored the barrage of insults Clarence Whipple hurled their way as she and her team executed the search warrant on his property. They'd just hit the Albuquerque city limits again when Hal had called. 'Van is registered to Clarence Whipple.'

'Sounds like the toilet paper commercial guy from the 80s,' Cord, his tense demeanor disappearing within seconds of hitting pavement, had joked. Hal's uncharacteristic silence and lack of laughter had alerted Alyssa that he had bigger news to share than tracking down the owner of the van. Even so, neither she nor Cord had been prepared for the words that fell out of his mouth.

'Clarence Whipple was one of the original occult members my team arrested.'

The air in Alyssa's lungs exploded outward in a whoosh. 'Hal, are you sure?'

'Of course.' He'd laughed, the sound neither jovial nor amused. 'As a matter of fact, when we hauled him in back then, I made a similar comment to Cord's. Still, in an effort to be thorough and positive, I ran a search. Clarence Whipple, aged fifty-one, lives out in the same direction as Ewan Moore's church, but about five miles southeast.'

'In one of those pop-up cities?' All evidence of Cord's joking had faded.

'No. But close by one. Zia Road. I'll text you the address. I've already been in contact with Rosario, and the search warrant for his property has been issued. You're good to go. Want me to send Joe and Tony back your way?'

'That'd be great. And—'

'Update Hammond. Two steps ahead of you. And Lys, Cord? Be careful out there. Just because none of the charges stuck back in the day doesn't mean Whipple wasn't every bit as dangerous as his fellow cult members.'

More than the words themselves, Hal's uncustomary warning had rocketed Alyssa's already high alert level. Mixed in with the awareness of the possible danger they often faced when executing a search warrant pulsed a healthy dose of hope that they were getting closer to locating London Brecken. Turning on her lights, she'd barreled toward Whipple's home.

Now, with its cold breeze, the night had ushered out any remaining warmth of the day, which could've accounted for part of the reason Whipple's body shook. But based on the sheer number of times the man howled about their gross invasion of his privacy as well as a negligent use of taxpayer's money, Alyssa tacked it up more to his rage than the weather.

Everywhere Alyssa looked, evidence of a man who reveled in all things dark, including Satanism, glared back at her. A bookshelf nearly collapsing under the weight of occult paraphernalia accommodated several Satanic Bibles, at least three Ouija boards – one of them homemade – melted candles, and spell books. Another shelf hosted a statue of what appeared to be a goat head inside an inverted pentagram, countless crucifixes, all hanging upside down, and several more with the arms of the cross broken and hanging limp. The entire house set her skin to crawling like an army of ants had taken up residence just beneath the top layer of her skin. Silly as it sounded, she kind of wished she had some holy water or sage in her pocket to ward off any evil.

'I already told you damn cops when you got here that I don't know a damn thing about one homicide, much less two, and there's no one I like or hate enough to want to kidnap. You have no right to be going through my personal belongings. I have every damned right to worship the Lord of Darkness. That doesn't mean I killed anyone.' The louder Whipple shouted, the more his exposed jiggly gelatin of a belly appeared to be doing The Wave.

Alyssa spared one quick glower over her shoulder. 'Well, a van registered to you and used in commission of said crime gives us that right.'

Transferring his gaze from Alyssa to Cord, Whipple snarled. 'Do you see a van anywhere on my property, man? Ain't like I got some fancy garage it's sitting in.' He reached up to scratch the doughy flesh of his cheek, showing off permanently stained fingernails that hadn't seen a good scrubbing in ages, and Alyssa barely resisted wincing in repulsion when one of those fingers went to his mouth and scraped at a crooked front tooth.

She also didn't bother telling him they already had the van in their possession with technicians going over it as they searched his property. And while it had become immediately clear there were no obvious places to conceal a kidnapped person, she remained optimistic that something in their search would reveal where London was.

'Where did you say you were Thursday night?' Cord asked.

'None of your damn business, pig. I already know you think since I'm not living in some shiny house with a white picket fence, a manicured lawn, a Range Rover, and two-point-seven kids that I must be lying, so I ain't got nothing to say to you.' For the next several minutes, he hurled a long, unending string of insults at them.

Unfazed by his belligerent attitude, Alyssa simply shook her head and muttered, 'You'd think someone, somewhere along the lines would come up with a snappier response to our search warrants, don't you think? I mean, it's the law of averages, right?'

Fifteen minutes into the search, Joe started unplugging and boxing up Whipple's laptop, sending his anger soaring to new heights. In another setting, Alyssa might have been impressed by the way the heavyset man hurdled a chair to stop him. When Tony stepped in front of him, blocking his path, Whipple growled – actually bared his teeth – and then flipped him off when Tony offered some sage advice.

'Probably don't want to do that. Assaulting an officer charges and all that.'

'Screw you, man. I need that stuff for work.' Whipple whirled around to Alyssa. 'The hell, bitch? Why are you taking my computer?' Before she could even open her mouth to have Tony escort him out of the house for the remainder of the search warrant, Whipple noticed another officer bagging up several pairs of his shoes. 'Assholes! This isn't just all kinds of messed up; it's goddamned harassment.' If his finger had been near her chest when he'd been punctuating the air, it would've drilled through skin, or at least left some serious bruises.

Minutes later, another howl erupted from him when two officers entered his bedroom and began rummaging through his closet. 'Listen. I don't know what you people think you've got on me, but whatever it is, you're dead wrong. You want to know where I was Thursday? You want an accounting of every single second? You want me to start with my morning sh—'

Cord cut him off before he could utter the expletive. 'That won't be necessary. Where's your cell phone?'

A brighter shade of red would've been hard to come by. 'What? No, no effing way! I'm not handing that over. I know my rights.'

Cord referred to the warrant. 'It's in the paperwork, so I'm afraid you don't really have a choice. Now, your phone? You can hand it over, or we can pat you down and take it from you that way. Your choice, but make it fast because time's wasting, and my patience is riding its tail.'

Whipple threw his fist into a wall but pulled his punch before leaving a hole. 'Aren't you guys breaking, like, five different civil rights laws here? Don't you have to wait for my attorney or something?'

'I don't know what cop shows you've been watching,' Alyssa said, 'but no, we don't have to wait. Furthermore, and more importantly right now, if you want your attorney, you're going to have to head outside and try to contact him because until we finish up, this place is ours.'

'Man, this is wrong. No wonder people shoot you bastards all the time.'

Like an in-flight aircraft whose door had just blown off, all the oxygen swooshed out of the room. Joe, Tony, and the other officers within hearing distance of what sounded like a veiled threat stopped in their tracks and whirled in Whipple's direction. Hands hovered over various weapons – guns, Tasers, batons, and spray – while each person's eyes bounced from each other over to Alyssa until she simply nodded for them to carry on.

Then she turned to Tony. 'Get him out of here, and make sure he stays out until we're finished.'

Whipple rammed his shoulder into Tony's as Tony attempted to latch onto his arm. Tearing across the room, Whipple managed to grab a floor lamp. Yanking the cord out of the socket, he hurled it against the wall, and then went for the granite bookends sitting on a bookshelf. His proverbial bull in the glass shop imitation was short-lived because Tony, in one lightning-fast, nearly effortless motion, fastened onto Whipple's thick wrist and wound his arms behind his back.

Bucking and swearing, Whipple threw his head back in an effort to extricate himself from Tony's manacle-tight hold.

Barely avoiding the headbutt, Tony, now infuriated himself, used his own weight to press Whipple into the wall. 'Careful there, tough guy. You're one stupid mistake away from donning some metal bracelets. Right now, all you've gotta do is stop being a dick and step outside with me while we do what we've gotta do. So, I'm asking you to get yourself together before you force me to do things the hard way.'

'The hard way, like the way I banged your mom all night long?'

Tony shook his head. 'Sure. If grave-robbing and necrophilia are part of how you get your freak on. Because that's the only way you got it on with my mom considering she's been dead a while now.'

'Whatever, man. Just finish up here and get the hell out of my house.'

Before Whipple made it all the way out the door, another officer poked his head out of the utility room. Visible through the clear trash can in his hands, a dark cloak with a red lightning bolt patch sewn onto it, sealed Whipple's fate.

Alyssa, her smile turning feral, whirled around to face Clarence Whipple. 'Tony, read Mr. Whipple his rights. Looks like he'll be heading to the station with us after all.'

Whipple glared at Alyssa, and in a voice much more chilling in its lack of rage, vowed, 'You're going to regret this, Detective. I promise.'

Chapter Twenty-Eight

Saturday, April 24

Shallow, rough, raspy breaths scratched against London's throat like sandpaper on her bare nerves. On some level, she knew her sluggish body had finally begun to decelerate in its futile fight against the infections festering from her numerous wounds. Worse, she couldn't really say if that filled her with sadness or relief. Regardless, she still struggled to keep air in her lungs, to fight off her feverish delirium for one more second, and then one more after that, so she could listen to the argument that had been brewing since the wolfdog had loped off upon Draven and Mara's return.

Darkness had long ago fallen, and in that time, the pair hadn't come down to check on her once. Instead, they'd stayed upstairs, their voices no longer cold and evil, but angry and full of panic. Most of their fighting had been difficult to make out until Mara finally screamed out in frustration.

'There were *kids* in the house, Draven. Kids. It's all over the damn news.'

Dehydrated and too weak to do more than absorb Mara's words, London blinked against the dried-up tears stinging her eyes.

'We had our cloaks on. They can't identify us, even if they did see us.' Though evidence of his stress still leaked through, Draven sounded far less panicked than his partner.

Something slammed against a wall. 'How did *two* kids escape our notice?' Something else crashed before a heavy thud hit the floor. 'In fact, where did *she* come from, huh? Where was she hiding that whole time? Did either one of us bother to ask that question? No, because we were too excited to bring her here. But think about it… how did we miss her? We were getting ready to *leave*, and *bam*, she's right there.'

'Look. We can't change any of that, all right? We've already dumped the van where no one will ever think to look. And even *if* the cops do find it eventually, we'll be long gone. In fact, we can leave now, tonight, instead of waiting until the twenty-seventh.'

'We can't risk it. We have to take care of the kids. Tonight, if we can. No later than tomorrow. Find out where they're staying. It shouldn't be too difficult. Kill them. Kill whoever they're living with. We *just got started*, Draven. I can't go to prison. I've heard… I *won't* go to prison.'

Everything, Skye and Elena's murders, the torture she'd endured, the vile acts she'd been forced to witness, the drug and fever-induced hallucinations, all of it evaporated as London realized Carter and Abigail had survived, that they were okay. A sudden lightness filled her chest, and it took her a moment to recognize it as a glimmer of returning hope that the knowledge had sparked. But just as quickly, it disappeared.

Carter and Abigail may have escaped that night, but now Mara and Draven wanted to kill them. A sense of overwhelming helplessness unlike anything she'd ever felt, even when this nightmare had begun, robbed London of breath. When a coppery, rusty flavor flooded her desert-dry mouth, she realized that in her fear, she'd bitten down on her bloated tongue.

She'd rather the sick duo got their kicks by torturing her than by going after Carter and Abigail.

As if she'd summoned him to do just that, Draven descended the stairs, holding a light that reflected the hate and anger brewing in his eyes. 'You should have told us about those kids because now, not only are *they* going to suffer before we kill them, you are, too.'

Not that she would've, but exactly when did he think she'd had the opportunity to tell them? When they were stabbing her and dragging her out of Skye's house? When they'd tossed her into the van and trussed her up like a Thanksgiving Day turkey? Or maybe the one and only time her gag had been removed to allow her to vomit because they hadn't wanted her to choke to death and rob them of their fun, torturous games?

As he lowered the coffin lid to seal her back into the darkness, Draven hissed, 'Maybe we'll bring them back here and make you watch.'

Rage and resentment boiled over, and London screamed against the rag in her mouth as Draven's footsteps carried him back up the stairs and outside where the sound of a revving engine broke the silence of the night. Despite what they'd put her through, despite the evil bred into their souls, despite the devil they worshipped turning them into monsters, underneath it all, they were really mere humans. And if any possibility of survival existed, no matter how slight or improbable, London would fight, not just for herself, but for Carter and Abigail. And then she'd find a way to send Mara and Draven straight to the hell they craved.

Chapter Twenty-Nine

Saturday, April 24

Despite obvious signs of fatigue from working nearly round the clock since Thursday night, the team stuck around as Alyssa and Cord interrogated Clarence Whipple, wondering why he hadn't actually lawyered up, considering he'd mentioned calling an attorney at his home.

Not that the man had much to say. For the past fifteen minutes, he'd done little more than bounce his knees angrily and shoot daggers across the table at them. No matter the question, each was met with stony silence with the exception of an occasional snarl that indicated they might've hit close to the truth.

Alyssa glanced down at the notes from the prior case Hal had prepared for them when he'd been informed they were bringing Whipple in. 'You and Ewan Moore grew up near each other and joined the same occult around the same time.'

'Yeah? What about it?'

Finally a response. 'Have you been in contact with your buddy since his release?'

Whipple tipped his chair onto two legs, his face twisted into a leer. 'Law doesn't say who my friends can be.'

Adopting a relaxed pose, Cord mimicked Whipple's by leaning back in his chair. 'What's the significance of the number forty-seven?'

A shadow of recognition flashed in Whipple's eyes, there and gone so fast, Alyssa would've doubted she'd seen it at all if that number hadn't been carved into Skye Fleming's tongue. 'You understand you're under arrest for two murders, a kidnapping, resisting arrest, animal abuse, and a slew of other charges, right? You're looking at a conviction that'll likely land you in a supermax cell where you'll be allowed outside your seven-by-twelve concrete slab for one hour a day. One hour. You'll have no human contact with anyone but the guards. The only sunlight you'll receive is through the one tiny window up high. You'll have plenty of *darkness* then.'

Whipple slammed his fist down on the table. 'I told you, whatever you found in my van, it has nothing to do with me.'

'Yeah, that's what you've been screaming ever since we pulled up to your property with a search warrant. I didn't think you were a stupid man who'd take the heat for someone else's crime, but maybe I'm wrong,' Alyssa goaded the man. 'Or maybe, a wise man would tell the cops who had your van since you claim it wasn't you.'

Whipple shrugged. 'Lots of people use that van for lots of reasons. I don't keep track of who's got it when and for why anymore.'

A blatant lie if Alyssa had ever heard one. 'We have technicians right this minute processing that van, and when they're finished, I predict we're going to have proof that London Brecken was being held inside there. And along with her DNA and fingerprints, I suspect it'll be your prints and DNA we find, and then you'll be going away for a long, long time.' She leaned in closer. 'My only question now is, who was working with you?'

For the first time since they'd hauled him in, Whipple seemed genuinely shocked. His chair scraped across the floor as it landed back on all fours, his face twisted in confusion before he carefully masked it.

'Tell us where London is and give up your partner. You know the DA often cuts a deal with the person who breaks first.' Alyssa wanted him to corroborate her suspicions that either Moore, August Holt, or Roman Cordova was involved, but the man remained stubbornly quiet. A knock interrupted her next question, and when she turned around, she spotted Hal in the doorway, dark shadows under his eyes, and a tightness around his lips that had Alyssa's stomach free-falling to her toes. What had he found now?

Leaving Cord with Whipple, she stepped outside and closed the door. 'What's going on?'

'Listen, as soon as that van came back registered to Whipple, I did a property search for any places he might've lived or property he might currently own.'

A parade of energy zipped through Alyssa. 'And?'

Hal's hand went down to grip the wheels of his chair, and he rolled back and forth in short, agitated bursts of movement. 'And turns out, Whipple used to own a little hunting cabin down in Montemar.'

'Montemar?'

'It's a little rural farming town about seventy miles pretty much due south of Albuquerque. Gotta know it's there or just happen to be winding your way through, exploring, to come across it. I'd wager not too many people know of it unless, of course, they're from there.'

'Go on.'

'So, I reached out to one of the deputies in the area, Jason Lopez, to ask him if he'd noticed or heard of any suspicious activities in the area that could be associated with cult activity.'

Every muscle in Alyssa's body stretched tight enough to snap while she waited for Hal to continue.

'Apparently, in the past month, a bunch of angry farmers complained of someone stealing their cattle, mainly goats.' What started as a slow tic in the lower left portion of Hal's jaw gathered speed until it looked like a tiny alien might punch its way through his skin. 'But one rancher in particular came in just a couple of days ago. Seems he was out inspecting his property and came across what he described as a killing field. Lopez drove out to inspect it, said it was like something pulled straight out of a horror flick.' Hal's eyes shifted to the closed interrogation room door, eyes narrowed in anger. 'Property line abutted land where Whipple had his cabin.'

Just like that, Alyssa's priorities shifted. 'I know it's late, but would Lopez and the rancher be willing—'

Hal didn't let her finish her question. 'He's already waiting for your call. You grab Cord, and I'll have Joe and Tony escort Whipple back to his cell.' His fist knocked against the arm of his chair. 'I knew in my gut back then that Whipple was guilty, but the DA couldn't make any of the charges stick. Everything was explained away as circumstantial. If you ask me, I think he and his good buddy Moore are back up to their old ways. Be careful out there and let me know what you find out. I don't care how late it is, you got it?'

'You'll be the first to know.'

Chapter Thirty

Consciousness trickled in a little at a time, awakening the thousand tiny cuts that burned like acid on London's hands and face where she'd been fighting to free herself from the coffin from the moment she'd heard the car drive away. A savage hatred for Draven and Mara, along with fear for Carter and Abigail's lives, had muted most of her pain. During those times it pushed through, threatening to derail her attempts, she'd force herself to picture Carter and Abigail's innocent little faces, which instantly reignited her determination. Somehow, some way, she'd escape this hell so she could warn someone.

But after what felt like hours of effort to end up getting nowhere, the voices that told her she was wasting energy on a lost cause shouted ever louder. *You'll suffocate before you can get help.* Like she had before she'd lost consciousness the first time, London ignored the voice and inhaled as much stale oxygen as she could to feed her starving lungs. And then once again, she willed her weighted eyes to lift, to stay awake, knowing if she allowed herself to black out again, not only would she not wake, but she would have failed Carter and Abigail in the worst possible way.

How will you get them help even if you do miraculously manage to escape? You have no idea where you are, and even if you did, you're so weak, you can barely lift your hands a few inches above your face.

Swallowing the sob that rubbed her raw throat, London pleaded with the voice to shut up. Even if she ended up lost in a maze of nothingness, even if wild animals attacked and killed her, then at least she'd die trying, not just lying there while vile and evil people went after two innocent children. Though convinced her stomach was being sawed in half, she lifted her arms to resume shoving against the lid, whimpering at the splinters stabbing into her bare skin. With the gag slicing into the sides of her mouth and trapping her moans inside her, she pictured Carter and Abigail curling against her sides, both with books in hands, begging her to read 'just one more.' She remembered them racing into the guest room holding cupcakes so they could be the first to wish her a happy birthday, recalled the excited way they'd gathered around her as she'd opened the handmade gift of elbow macaroni glued onto a heart with their pictures pasted into the middle. Then she pictured Mara and Draven standing in front of them, their daggers dripping – and she tripled her efforts, refusing to give her atrophied muscles even a second to recover.

Praying. Pleading. Cursing. She pushed again and again.

And then a miracle.

The slightest movement as the wood squealed in protest, and London forced every molecule of her remaining strength into removing the lid.

And then suddenly, a different kind of darkness greeted her, a familiar one. The church basement.

The agony of her whimpering muscles, the burning sting of exposed nerves and ripped skin, the wood's scream of protest, went unnoticed as she gripped the corner and slid the lid until it finally thundered to the cement floor. Her chest heaved in and out as she tried to catch her breath even as her clumsy fingers pried at the knot tying the cloth in her mouth.

A soft, shuffling noise froze her in place. Squinting into the darkness, she begged her eyes to adjust to the shimmering moonlight as she searched for the source of the sound.

In her peripheral vision, she caught a shadow of movement, and she gingerly turned her head in that direction. Her heart hammered at the sight of several rats scurrying over a pile of eviscerated animal remains in the corner below the window ledge.

Defeat wormed its way back inside London, feeding her fear, but she beat it back. That was what could be in store for Carter and Abigail if she didn't continue to fight.

Ignoring the flames licking at her insides and the infection guzzling away at her energy, she channeled her inner exercise queen, gripped the sides of the coffin, and tried to haul herself up. She couldn't manage even a centimeter before she collapsed back down. Her mind, her muscles, her entire being wept with fatigue, fever, and infection.

Do it again.

That time, she listened to the voice.

Over and over again, she tried to launch herself upward, ignoring the bruising blows to her back each time she failed and collided with the hard coffin.

As she collapsed back down for what felt like the hundredth time, something outside the window this time stole her attention, and London cautiously lifted her eyes. There, framed in the broken glass, stood the wolf she'd spotted twice now. At first it didn't move, just perched on its haunches, staring at her, unblinking.

Then, it lifted its head and howled into the sky before bringing its gaze back down to her. In her delirious state, she imagined him shouting encouragement down to her, like a coach might do.

With renewed drive, she hoisted her upper body forward, relieved when, instead of crumpling back down, she was able to angle herself so that her arms dangled over the side of the coffin, holding her upright.

Wheezing for every precious bit of air, she strangely relished the bite of splinters in her skin as she willed her body to remain where it was, to allow her just a minute or two. With her cheek pressed into the rough wood, she lifted her hands in a renewed effort to pry the vile rag from her mouth. If she could remove that, even a little, she could scream for help. But the way the rag cut into the sides of her lips, she knew she'd never loosen it enough. Instead, she scraped her underarm along the top edge of the coffin until she could flop forward to tug at the looser knots around her ankles. If she could climb out of this coffin, then… Her gaze drifted to the stairs that seemed as insurmountable and unclimbable as Mount Everest.

Outside, the wolf howled its encouragement again. *You can do this, London. You're almost there. Don't quit now.* In her weakened state, she swore she could hear the wolf giving her the pep talk.

An interminable amount of time and energy later, her ankles finally free, London took as deep a breath as she could through lungs filled with shattered glass and eased herself back up a centimeter at a time, only to find herself unable to support her own weight any longer. A crunch across her collarbone as her body collapsed back down sent a shooting arrow of agony through her, but she tamped it down, just like before. Twisting her body to the side, she slid her arms up and over the coffin. Then using her swollen feet as an anchor in the corner, she pried herself upward again, a sense of pride flooding her when she managed to keep herself from falling back.

A dizzying array of colorful fireworks exploded behind her eyes, flashing in time with the beginning rumbles of a brewing storm.

Darkness danced and played at the edge of her consciousness, but she willed it away. *Just a little longer, just a little more*, she promised herself.

The wolf howled its agreement. But this time the shadows refused to listen. Instead, they lured her back with promises of sleep and rest and no pain. Like heaven or nirvana. She tried to lift her head to apologize to the wolf, to beg it to apologize to Carter and Abigail for her, but it had moved.

Frantic that it had abandoned her, she latched onto one last burst of whatever remaining reserve she had left. Without stopping to think, to consider the consequences, London hitched her upper body over the side of the coffin. A bone snapped, and her forehead slammed against the cement floor.

She passed out to dancing demons laughing at her feeble attempt at escape.

Chapter Thirty-One

Saturday, April 24

The storm from up north failed to reach Montemar, and with the clear, nearly cloudless sky, the moon shone through, helping to illuminate the road as Jason Lopez led Alyssa and Cord to Lewis Murray's two-thousand-acre ranch. Along the way, he'd flash his lights to indicate they were passing the home of one of the residents who had reported missing animals in the past month.

Like so many of the others, Murray's sprawling ranch house boasted a wraparound front porch with a set of old rocking chairs. If it weren't for the evidence of modern technology all around them, Alyssa could almost make herself believe they'd stepped back in time and into a different era altogether. She took an instant liking to the elderly man who pushed himself to his feet and tipped his hat in greeting, taking the opportunity to wipe his forehead with a bandana he pulled from his back pocket.

'Lewis Murray. Thanks for coming all the way out at this time of night. No need to take three vehicles. Think it's probably best if we all hop in my truck so I can show you.' He hollered something through the screen door before leading them to a weathered Chevy pickup with the keys still hanging in the ignition. 'Suppose I shouldn't be doing that anymore, seeing as what I found on my property, but it's a hard habit to break since we've rarely ever had a need to lock our doors at night out in these parts.'

Alyssa didn't think it mattered how remotely off the grid she lived, she'd never feel comfortable not locking her doors. She'd seen too much depravity in all kinds of places to ever be that trusting. She bit back a smile as Murray beat Cord to opening the door for her to climb in. Apparently, her partner wasn't the only remaining male with a chivalrous bone.

The ride out to the edges of Murray's property was silent save for the elderly man pointing out different landmarks and sharing a bit of the town's history, which Alyssa found surprisingly intriguing. If she didn't have a job to focus on and a victim to locate, she would've loved to sit and listen to him all night.

Approximately two miles from his main house, he finally pulled to a stop, killed the engine, and clambered down, his knees and back protesting loudly.

Even without the four heavy-duty flashlights illuminating the area like Alaska in July, it wouldn't have taken long for Alyssa to stumble across the mutilated and rotting carcasses of animals. Due to the sheer overwhelming, rotten, musky odor that hovered somewhere between decomposing cattle and a skunk left to putrefy in a rancid mud puddle in a swamp, they would've been impossible to miss. Many of the animals had been beheaded, and all had been eviscerated. What was left of the poor, abused creatures had provided a buffet to birds and scavengers.

For several seconds, silence descended, broken when Murray issued a sigh that centered somewhere between disgust, anger, and pity. 'Hate to be the one to say it out loud, but I gotta tell you that this bears the mark of something more insidious than a bunch of kids getting a few thrills by killing animals.'

Alyssa agreed, but she was still interested in hearing Murray's explanation. 'What do you mean?'

'I mean I think this is the work of some very sick, evil people.' Murray tilted his head back and stared up at the stars before dividing his attention between Alyssa,

Cord, and Jason. 'Back about fifteen years or so ago, we had a small group of devil-worshippers try to set up shop in Montemar's backyard, but the town, especially us ranchers, wasn't having any part of it, and while we skirted the line maybe of staying on the legal side of things, we made our unhappiness with the people known loud and clear.

'Took a while, but they eventually pulled up roots and cleared out. Needless to say, we all expected some serious trouble. In fact, that was the only time I can remember ever locking my doors at night. About that same time, a bunch of us got together and took turns running security on all our properties. And I make no apologies for admitting we made sure we were armed to the teeth. When I say we expected trouble, I mean we expected the worst. But after about three, four months without a lick of trouble, we eased up a little at a time until the whole thing became nothing more than a distant memory we shared around the campfire from time to time.'

Alyssa thought back to everything she'd learned regarding Hal's case. The incident Murray referred to had occurred after that, and with Clarence Whipple's property abutting this one, she'd bet he was one of the forerunners. 'Did you ever have a chance to learn any of their names before they pulled up stakes?'

Murray scratched his head. 'No, ma'am. Never really felt the need to get to know them on a first-name basis. I don't know about the other ranchers around here, but I didn't have a strong wish to invite that kind of evil into my home. Come judgement day, maybe I'll be punished for that, but that's God's truth anyway.'

Cord swept his arms around the area. 'Did any of this type of stuff take place fifteen years ago before the devil-worshipers were run out of town?'

'No, it did not. We never gave it a chance.'

'Your neighbors started complaining of missing cattle, primarily goats, about a month back,' Alyssa said, 'but you just noticed this a couple of days ago. Did I get that right?'

'You did. I don't have more than a couple cows and a few horses anymore, so I don't inspect my property the way I used to. No need, for the most part. About once a month, maybe twice, I check for holes in the fence line or whatnot, but like I said, I don't keep a huge amount of cattle on hand anymore. Wrangling them is too hard on the arthritis. And since I don't have so many animals to feed, I don't make it into town as often and so didn't hear the buzz. As soon as I did, I decided I'd better run an inspection. Gotta admit, even hearing what I did, I never expected this.'

'Based on the animals' decay, how long would you guess this has been going on, and why abandon the animals on your property?'

'Maybe someone knew how often I checked up on things. As far as the decay, I can tell you it had to have been just about a month because the last time I inspected my property was March twenty-sixth.' Murray turned in a semi-circle and directed everyone's attention over to a charred circle in the grass where they couldn't miss the remains of yet another decapitated animal, likely a goat, based on its hooves. 'That right there, however, had to have occurred somewhere over eight hours to about a week ago.'

Alyssa glanced from the animal to Murray. 'How do you know?'

'Maggots. Larvae occurs after flies have laid their eggs, which could possibly be within a day of death.' He moved in closer, shining his light directly down on the animal. 'If you'll look real closely, there aren't too many there, and since I believe those devils can consume fifty to sixty percent of a body within seven days, I'm offering my best semi-educated guess. I know there's a science to it, and that's not my field, but in my experience with coming across cattle that's either died out in the pasture from disease or predator attack, that's my opinion. To really know, you'd have to hire one of those folks over at the university who studies that type of thing.'

Cord pointed somewhere off in the distance, where Alyssa believed Whipple's hunting cabin to be. 'Any other ranchers live over that way?'

'Nope. Other than an old cabin that's probably little more than rubble now and sits on about a quarter acre, that land's been owned by the city since way back in the early 1800s. Town council fights anyone who wants to build on it. Used to be an old mine back in the day but can't remember what they were mining for. Perlite is my guess.'

'Perlite?'

'In short, heated volcanic glass. You know those little white balls you find in your potting soil? That's perlite. It's mostly used for horticulture, helps the soil, or at least that's the extent I know it's worth. There are other uses for it, I know, but what all they are, you'd be better off asking someone else.'

Alyssa marked the location of the mutilated animals using her My Tracks app on her phone, then took photographs of their carcasses and the surrounding area, knowing, once again, she'd have to wait until daylight to get a team out there to investigate. Maybe these mutilations had nothing to do with their current case, but that beheaded goat within the charred circle shouted otherwise.

When she finished, they all hopped back into Murray's truck and headed back to the main house. After obtaining his contact information, Alyssa and Cord walked back to her Tahoe that was parked behind Lopez's patrol car. 'Thank you for meeting with us on such short notice and so late. I'll talk to my captain, but I imagine he's going to want to get a team out here probably as soon as tomorrow, but definitely no later than Monday. In the meantime, if anything else comes up, I'd appreciate you keeping in touch.'

'No problem.' Lopez shook Alyssa's hand, then Cord's. 'And I'm sure Murray will be just as accommodating, so long as you give him at least a couple hours' notice, if you can. Just because he's not actively farming as big a ranch… well, let's just say he still keeps plenty busy.'

Alyssa smiled. 'I can only imagine.'

After exchanging a few pleasantries, they all climbed into their vehicles, and Alyssa waited for Lopez to head back down the long, dirt drive first before following him. But where he turned south, Alyssa headed north, planning to circle around. She felt more than saw Cord's startled reaction.

'Where we headed?'

'I want to go check out what's over that hill you pointed out back there. Murray mentioned a cabin that I suspect might have been the one that Whipple owned, and considering everything we know and have learned in the past couple of days, especially with this Montemar development, I think it's the perfect place to search for clues. Maybe it'll give up London Brecken's whereabouts.' Slowing for a tractor that was chugging down the road slightly over a snail's pace, Alyssa glanced over. 'What do you think?'

'Well, for the most part, I think you're right. As long as what we're looking for is out in the open. But you know, without a warrant, we can't go looking for any evidence of ritualistic animal sacrifices. Are you sure you want to risk getting something tossed in a trial?'

'Of course not. But I can't shake this gut feeling that we need to go check it out.'

'All right then. Let me just send Sara a message to let her know and tell the kids goodnight.'

'Speaking of which, did you stop at the Sandersons' to check on Carter and Abigail when you went out to pick up our dinner? Which, come to think of it, seems like days ago.' On cue, Alyssa's stomach rumbled in protest, making both of them chuckle.

'Doesn't it, though? And yeah, I did.' Cord wiped his palm across his face. 'I tell you what, Lys. I'm beginning to wonder if that boy has ever been a kid in his six years of life. You know what he wanted to talk about?'

'I'm afraid to ask.'

'He wanted to know what he's supposed to do about his mother's funeral. And if he was supposed to clean their house. He didn't think the Sandersons would know these things since they're "not cops." What the hell kind of question is that for *any* kid to ask, much less a six-year-old?'

If hearts could weep, that was exactly what Alyssa's was doing at that very moment. As she couldn't hug the children to her, she wished she could pull the Tahoe over and hug Cord instead.

'I don't know if I did the right thing or not,' he continued, 'but I told him when the time came to discuss arrangements for Skye, I'd help him take care of it.'

'What are you going to do if we track down their biological father, and he doesn't want your help?' Alyssa asked softly.

'Then I guess he should've been a part of their lives starting six years ago.'

She hated to poke the bear, but she knew she needed to say it. 'You know there's a chance he never knew about them? On the flip side of things, we still don't know if the bio dad is involved.'

'He's not.' Cord's words were clipped. 'If he was, that would mean he knew about the kids, and then he would've killed them or kidnapped them, too. Bio Dad's not involved. I know it.'

'I don't disagree with anything you said. But until Lynn gets a DNA match on the swabs we obtained from Carter and Abigail, the mystery of who their father is remains exactly that.'

In no time at all, they hit the turn to the hill, and Alyssa was surprised to find the road somewhat well-traveled. At first. But then it got bumpier with far taller weeds and grass popping into view under the glare of her headlights, indicating it wasn't as often used as it appeared, though tracks hinted that someone had driven there fairly recently. Still, several times, Alyssa almost turned back. It would be an easier road to navigate in the light of day.

But then she rounded a corner where just over a small rise, she spotted what appeared to be a completely different state. Even in the dark, her headlights, along with the stars and the moon, illuminated rolling green hills and an infinite maze of boulders. That, along with granite rocks, made up most of the landscape. Far off in the distance, what was left of an old abandoned mine shaft tilted precariously to the right, ready to crumble to the ground at any second. But no cabin.

Maybe a quarter mile or less to the left of that, Cord pointed out the leaning structure of an old church, the kind one might see in old Westerns. Heart thumping, Alyssa aimed the Tahoe in that direction so she could better see it. Without giving it a second thought, she cut the ignition, unbuckled her seatbelt, and climbed out.

Mumbling another warning about not having a warrant, Cord followed suit.

The odor of rotting carcasses that had stewed a little too long in the hot sun hit her immediately, growing stronger the further away from the Tahoe she moved. Something about the church, something more than the horrific odor of animal decay, sent shudders rippling up and down Alyssa's spine. Slowing her steps, she flashed her light along the ground, noting the presence of tire tracks.

Someone had definitely been there, and though she was far from an expert in that area, she guessed from the fresh indentations in the ground, it had been rather recently.

Her hand automatically went to the weapon at her side where it hovered as she crept closer to the building. At the crumbling steps, she hesitated. Glancing back at Cord, she pointed, letting him know she was heading around to the back of the church to check out its surroundings. Then she pointed to him, the front door, and to the ground, indicating she wanted him to stay where he was and keep watch.

He nodded his understanding, and as she moved further away from her partner, she found her hand now rested on the butt of her weapon. The more she explored, the more she realized this church was in such a sad state of disrepair that one bad windstorm could send the entire thing careening down into a pile of rotten, splintered wood and cement. Everywhere her light shone showcased cracked, broken, or completely missing windows.

A crunch of leaves exploded into the silence of the night. At the same time, from the corner of her eye, Alyssa spotted a shadow moving low to the ground. Slowly unlocking her holster, she angled her body in that direction. A twig snapped, and then another. They weren't alone. Her hand closed around the grip of her gun. And then suddenly, a beautiful white, collarless dog, or perhaps a wolf appeared, moving himself directly into the path of her flashlight.

Almost as if he were willing her to follow him, he moved forward, only to stop every few feet to peer back at her, making sure she was still behind him. Feeling like she was acting out an episode of *Lassie*, she thumbed her mic and whispered into it, so as not to startle the animal. 'Um, don't laugh, but there's a wolfdog back here that I swear on all that's holy – is that sacrilegious to say outside a church? – anyway, I swear it's leading me somewhere.'

To his credit, Cord didn't laugh. 'Be careful. Do you want me to hold my place or join you?'

'Hold your place.' Alyssa thought about it for a second. 'Unless you hear me scream like a bad horror movie victim. And then you'd better come running. Don't you dare even think about leaving me behind.'

Cord chuckled. 'You're the one who chose to come this way, so I'm just going to save myself if it comes to that. But I think I'm supposed to tell you I'll never leave you first. Right? Isn't that how the scenes usually go?'

Alyssa hmphed, but other than that, said nothing because the wolfdog had stopped, and after howling up at the moon, dropped down to his belly, whining and pawing at the dirt. Down close to the ground, she spotted the hole in the frame of what was supposed to be a basement window.

Palms suddenly sweaty, pulse beating loudly in her eardrums, she dropped to her knees, screeching softly when she spotted a very long, dead, black snake. God, she hated snakes. They really were the devil. She pressed one hand against her chest and gulped in a lungful of air. *Count to ten. Exhale. Repeat.* Almost as if to show her his impatience, the wolfdog howled again and pawed at the reptile. In that moment, Alyssa swore the animal was trying to move it for her.

'Okay, okay. Give me a second here.' She sucked in one more lungful of air. Then, leaning forward, she shined her light inside the window. And recoiled. In the corner was a dead goat plus a mound of other, smaller dead animals that, at first glance, she imagined to be moving until she realized there were at least half a dozen long-tailed, mangy-looking rats scuttling around on top of and below the pile, their red-eyed glittering glares reflecting off her flashlight.

'Cord,' she yelled out in an almost embarrassing croak as she scrambled back a fraction, ignoring the wolfdog's whines.

He must've sprinted because he was there lightning fast. 'What did you find?' His eyes never strayed from the animal, who now stood, keeping his own attention glued to the newcomer. 'Is that a dog or a wolf?'

'No idea. He's not wearing a collar, and he didn't bark. Maybe he's a hybrid. But he's not the reason I yelled for you. Take a look at what's inside there.' Her voice came out in a slightly less embarrassing croak. Rats and mice were not her favorite animals, either, ranking only slightly below snakes.

Before kneeling down beside her, Cord cast a glance over both shoulders, scanning the perimeter around them, at least as far as his light would penetrate. Satisfied no one waited in the dark shadows, he finally knelt down beside Alyssa and using both his light and hers, he spotted what she'd seen. Suddenly, he grabbed her arm and hissed, 'There's someone in there. Stay here and keep a lookout, and I'll head inside.' Before her brain had fully processed his words, Cord was up and running back around to the front of the church.

As he disappeared around the corner, Alyssa shifted her light toward the far wall of the basement, opposite the mound of animals. 'Oh my God.' Dark brown droplets lined the area where a dark-haired woman lay with her body folded over a rudimentary coffin, its lid lying nearby. Her head rested at an awkward angle on the floor, as if her neck had been broken. Deep in her gut, Alyssa knew they'd located London Brecken.

Her knee-jerk reaction was to ignore Cord's demand to stay put and rush in after him. However, just as she sprang back to her feet and headed toward the front of the church, her training kicked in, and she realized she needed to think more like a criminal and less like a detective. If the person inside really was Brecken, she couldn't risk getting all three of them trapped inside if the kidnappers were nearby. Alert to any foreign noises, she wondered if they were being watched even now.

With blood pulsing loudly in her ears, she kept her attention riveted between their surroundings and the inside of the church. A few feet from her, the wolfdog, his body taut, did the same thing. For some inexplicable reason, his presence made her feel safer. Pulling her phone from her pocket, she called Hal. Even if she was wrong, and the person inside turned out to be someone other than London, the fact remained that they needed backup and emergency personnel.

After quickly filling him in and requesting that he contact Deputy Lopez, as well as put Joe and Tony on alert, she listened carefully to Cord's hollow footsteps echoing through the church as he made his way to the basement, shouting his progress along the way even while his light bounced along the shadows of the wall. At the bottom of the steps, he shined his flashlight around in search of an actual light. What he found instead was an old battery-operated lantern that he flicked on, spotlighting an inverted cross, a bloody altar, and a defiled picture of Jesus.

Stepping cautiously now, Cord inched closer to the figure draped over the coffin, speaking softly. When he was within a few inches, he lowered himself so that he was squatting in front of her, and Alyssa's stomach tied itself into tight little knots as he reached out a hand to touch the woman's neck, feeling for a pulse.

When Cord cursed loudly and shook his head back and forth, all her hopes plummeted. 'Talk to me, Cord.'

Instead, he gently cupped the woman's chin and tilted her head enough so that he could peer into her face. Glancing over his shoulder, he confirmed what she already suspected.

Chapter Thirty-Two

Sunday, April 25

Running on a toxic combination of adrenaline and sleep deprivation, Alyssa watched the creeping daylight dance cheek-to-cheek with the horizon as she and Cord finally hit the interstate after leaving the church where London Brecken had been discovered. Immediately, Cord called Hammond. Over concern for Carter and Abigail's safety since no suspects had been apprehended, he urged the captain to increase security around the foster family's home, requesting an hourly patrol on top of the surveillance team already in place. While he detailed what they knew so far – or didn't, as the case stood – Alyssa mulled over every nightmare-inducing piece of evidence they'd uncovered.

From the moment they'd discovered Brecken, her pulse barely detectable, Alyssa had struggled to maintain hope that the woman who had so fiercely protected Carter and Abigail would pull safely through to the other side. The woman lying in the basement of that church bore little resemblance to the person smiling in the social media images posted around the incident room. A bloody gag – made from the same material they'd discovered near the van – tore into the skin around her lips. Worse, her body was swathed in cuts, gouges, and stab wounds, not to mention the countless festering infections, several of which oozed and overflowed with sickly green and yellow pus. The proof and extent of the torture London had endured over the past three days lived all over her body.

As the paramedics had worked frantically to stabilize her in order to load her onto a waiting helicopter for transfer to UNMH, New Mexico's only designated level one trauma center, Alyssa had finally begun noticing London's prison outside the coffin, thanks to the ballfield full of lights the crime scene techs had erected around the place as soon as they'd arrived.

In addition to the altar, the inverted cross, the desecrated image of Jesus, incense, ritualistic candles, and what she believed to be blood-stained chalices, Alyssa found herself staring in horror at the Satanic symbols incorporated into the chilling words painted on the walls: *The Devil's Playground* and *Sacrifice Here*.

Scratched into the paint of the letters 'D' and 'P' and barely visible were the numbers forty-seven and thirteen-thirteen. Immediately, she'd called Hal back to have him see if Roman Cordova, August Holt, Clarence Whipple, or Ewan Moore had played sports, and if so, what their jersey numbers were. From the moment Dr. Sharp had informed them of the numbers carved into Skye Fleming's tongue, no amount of research that her team had uncovered hinted to the significance of those digits in the Satanic universe. Which made Alyssa wonder if they were some kind of signature.

So far, they'd been able to keep that information out of the media's hands, and she knew, if they could find the inference of those digits, they'd have their guilty parties. She flashed back to Whipple's reaction, wondering what it would take to get him to divulge the importance of those numbers.

Despite all the things they'd discovered, what Alyssa hadn't located were signs of any weapons. Neither had any daggers, swords, or knives, other than regular kitchen utensils, been located in their search of Whipple's property. Which meant someone else had to have possession of them. Ideally, she could waltz into the hospital and ask London who had killed her friends and kidnapped her, but considering she hadn't opened her eyes once since being discovered, the likelihood of that occurring skated past slim and into impossible.

What they *did* have, however, were two different types of clear shoeprints leading to and from the church and ending at a set of tire tread marks. Immediately, she'd snapped pictures and forwarded them to Hal so Bill Hedge could compare the imprints to those they'd found in the Fleming hallway.

As soon as she'd hit send, Tony, a lifetime avid hunter, had joined her, squatting down so he could study the prints. Every few seconds he'd glance around him on the ground. Of anyone on her team, he was the one Alyssa trusted most when it came to estimating a timeline based on tracks. After a few minutes, he stood up and faced her.

'I'd bet my retirement that those tire tracks came from a car and are less than a day old. Which stands to reason those shoeprints are also less than a day old. And based on size and weight imprint, I'd guess we've got a male and female pair.' Then he directed her attention to the multitude of vehicles and law enforcement that had crowded into the area so he could show her comparison treads and prints.

A lot of his scientific, outdoorsy reasoning made sense; some did not. But one of the most important facts was that both prints were less than a day old, which meant Clarence Whipple could not have been present. Which didn't mean he wasn't otherwise involved, only that he hadn't been present last night.

'Hammond's approved the extra patrol. If it weren't so early, I'd call the Sandersons myself to tell them about London so they or Carter don't hear it on the news first.'

Still distracted by trying to shift all the puzzle pieces into a clear picture, Alyssa didn't realize right away that Cord had ended his call with the captain and was now speaking to her. 'Good. That's good,' she said after he repeated himself to get her attention.

'Yeah, that's good. Now, for the bad.'

That managed to get her full attention. 'What?'

'Well, you know how you were hoping to interrogate Whipple when we got back to the precinct?'

'Yeah?'

'Well, he enacted his right to counsel while he was being escorted back to his cell last night.'

'Damn it.' Though the news hadn't been entirely unexpected, Alyssa ground her teeth together in aggravation because it meant until Whipple's attorney showed up, they couldn't speak to him.

Cord sighed. 'It gets better.'

'It's barely even six thirty in the morning. How can the hits be coming already?' Suddenly concerned that her partner was about to inform her that London had succumbed to her injuries after all, Alyssa's stomach clenched. 'Brecken?'

'No, nothing *that* bad. Well, not that Hammond mentioned, and I'm pretty sure he wouldn't forget something like that. Apparently, the media is already clamoring outside the precinct for a statement and demanding to know if it's true we've arrested someone in connection with the Fleming case, the assumption being Whipple is that someone, of course.'

Heat spread from Alyssa's face throughout the rest of her body. 'Someone's leaking information, and I'm going to find out who. And then there will be hell to pay. But right now, I'd like to know how London's doing, so I figured we'd call UNMH for an update while we're driving.'

A few minutes later, after being transferred three times and being placed on hold twice, a doctor picked up the phone. 'Detectives. Sorry I took so long to get to you. You're calling about the patient that arrived early this morning, London Brecken, correct?'

'Yes, we'd like an update on her current condition.'

The doctor's heavy and solemn exhalation prepared Alyssa for bad news. 'Critical, comatose, and on life support. Despite the intense round of antibiotics we have her on, I'm afraid there's a real possibility that the infections ravaging her body could very well finish the job her attempted killers did not.' Over the next few minutes, the doctor regaled them with an endless stream of concerns, ending with, 'I'll be honest; I'm astounded the patient's heart is still beating at all.'

In a raw moment of honesty, Alyssa admitted she was, too. But she had to believe that London hadn't fought this hard to survive only to succumb to her injuries after she'd been rescued.

'In other words, Detective, I wouldn't hinge your hopes on solving your case based on the patient's personal witness testimony. If she survives the next ten to twelve hours, *dumbfounded* won't even come close to describing what I'll be.' Sadness, frustration, and resignation ran like a current through his tired voice.

Alyssa thanked the doctor. 'I appreciate you taking our call. If anything changes, please give us a ring. We'll be stopping by later today to check on her ourselves.'

'I'll transfer you back to my nurse, and she'll take your contact information. Good luck, Detectives.'

Half an hour later, after Alyssa ran through the drive-thru of the nearest coffee shop – without a word of objection from her partner – they walked into the conference room carting several bags of bagels, muffins, lemon pound cake, and two carry-out containers of coffee for the entire team. After setting it all on the table, she ignored the chair, afraid if she sat, her exhaustion would win over, rendering her useless.

'As soon as London's awake,' Liz began, 'I'll be ready to do a sketch, see if we can get something out there to the public to be on the lookout.'

Alyssa managed a weak smile. 'Thanks, Liz. We talked to London's doctor on the way here, and the prognosis isn't good, but we have to believe she'll come through.'

Hal spoke next. 'I've got several things. First, I spoke with London's grandparents like you asked, and they said they're trying to figure out a way to get to New Mexico. Mr. Manning said he'd keep me informed of his plans and requested that we call him with any updates until they can get here. Also, I was able to reach both Lillian Holt and Cordelia Cordova. According to Lillian, August didn't participate in sports, but he enjoyed attending the football games until his junior year when everything changed.'

'I don't suppose he had a favorite player or a best friend on the team whose number was forty-seven or thirteen?' Alyssa asked.

'Mrs. Holt said August didn't particularly care about the game itself; he just enjoyed hanging out with his friends and flirting with the girls. Typical teenage stuff. As for Mrs. Cordova, she said Roman played basketball in junior high but switched to wrestling in high school until he gave up both altogether sometime around his junior year. Without offering an explanation, I asked her if she remembered what his jersey number was.' Hal shook his head. 'No help there, I'm afraid. He wore number thirty-three.'

Her mind churning as she tried to make a possible link, Alyssa finally admitted, 'My brain is too tired to mathematically figure out if there's some kind of connection between the two threes and the number thirteen–thirteen.'

'What about Whipple and Moore?' Cord asked.

'So far I've come up with nothing. No matter how far back I search, I can't find anything that answers that. I'll tap a few more resources I've got and let you know as soon as I have anything.'

'You said *several* things. What else?'

'I spoke with Hedge just before you came in. First, he wanted you to know he hasn't given up on trying to get a match on the partial print found on the blinds outside Skye's bedroom. When he ran it through the system, there were no hits. In fact, he's wondering about sending someone to the hospital to obtain London's prints because he has a feeling it'll be a match. Anyway, as soon as he can confirm or deny, he'll give you a holler.'

When Dr. Sharp had failed to note the presence of DNA that hadn't come back as their victims – and a goat – Alyssa had already suspected that the print might belong to London. In her mind, she imagined Brecken latching onto anything she could in a desperate attempt to stop herself from being kidnapped. 'Since I'd planned on making that same suggestion, I'm glad Hedge is already on top of it.'

Hal continued. 'Right. Well, that wasn't his only reason for calling. He also wanted to let us know that he'd just gotten a chance to look at the images of the shoeprints. He said he'd like to compare the actual cast from the church to the ones from the house to make it official, but yes, the prints seem to be the same. A woman's size seven to eight, Fila brand sneaker. The other, larger one doesn't have a brand symbol he could make out from the pictures, but from what he could see, he thinks it's a man's shoeprint.'

'Which is exactly what Tony said when he looked at it.'

Tony nodded. 'So, to sum it up, it looks like we're searching for a male/female pair.'

'Whipple and a partner?' Joe clarified.

Cord answered before Alyssa could. 'No, I don't think so. If those prints were less than a day old, like Tony thinks, then he couldn't have been there.'

'Even if he's not directly involved in the actual murders and kidnapping,' Hal snapped, 'he knows who is. A van he owns being used in connection with the crime, along with the cloak bearing a red lightning bolt being located on his premises proves that.'

Alyssa moved over to the crime scene photos, including those from last night, projected around the room. Behind the altar that had an inverted pentagram and a six-six-six scratched into it were a dead goat, two rabbits, and an animal Alyssa believed to be a small cat. She'd wondered about the dead snake found outside the basement window when they'd discovered London, but one of the crime techs pointed out the bite marks near the base of its head, and Alyssa found she liked the idea of believing the wolfdog had killed the snake as he watched over London.

'You know, I'm just going to come out and say it,' Tony said. 'In light of everything we discovered in a once-sacred place of worship, I once again have to ask what the hell is wrong with the human race these days. Seriously, what kind of twisted mind uses a church and calls it *The Devil's Playground*? The irony is beyond disturbing, which I'm sure was the point. I mean, how does a person even get involved with a cult, especially one on par with this level of evil?'

'Something in our water,' Joe grumbled. Even though he'd left the scene at quarter to two when his wife called to tell him that his daughter Hailee had a high fever, Joe, like the rest of them, still had gotten little to no sleep.

Hal kneaded the nape of his neck. 'Hive mind, group think. Most cults have a very charismatic leader like Ezekiel Henry who understands the art of drawing people in until they're able to influence others into doing whatever their end game is. They target outcasts and individuals with low self-esteem or anger issues. They offer a shoulder to cry on, a listening ear, maybe offer some drugs to help them relax or whatever. They perpetuate a free atmosphere around themselves, which is really attractive to self-proclaimed anarchists like Whipple and Moore, who are drawn to that lack of accountability. Over time, the already razor-thin line between reality and fantasy becomes further blurred. And then when the leader has them where they want them, they reel the individuals the rest of the way in by convincing them that their group is the person's only friend.'

'Some friend,' Alyssa mumbled.

'Right?' Tony agreed. 'And even if that's the case, when does a person's common sense kick in, shout that something's not right?'

Sighing, Hal continued rubbing his neck and rolling his shoulders, proof that his old case was weighing on him as much as the current one because he knew in some way, they were connected. 'Because,' he finally said, 'sometimes words have extreme power over people, especially where their minds are weak. And in the end, pretty much everyone wants to belong somewhere. Even if that someplace is evil.

'That being said, I don't think we're looking at an entire cult being actively involved with the murders and Brecken's kidnapping. I think we've got a couple of rogue players, if that's what you want to call them. I think we'd be dealing with several more murders or kidnappings otherwise. Plus, the fact that there were only two sets of shoeprints at the location supports that theory, I believe.'

'Ewan Moore has a daughter, right? What are the chances she picked up where her dad left off?' Liz asked.

'According to Moore, he's found religion, and his daughter's proud of him,' Cord said.

'And you believed him?' Even though Liz hadn't been there when the team had discussed Alyssa and Cord's meeting with the man, her skepticism was on full display.

'I'd say leopards can't change their spots, but that would be an insult to the leopard,' Hal mumbled.

Alyssa's phone rang, and she glanced down, surprised to see Rosemary Covington's name appear on her screen. 'Let's see if we can reach Ewan Moore's daughter, ask her a few questions,' she said before answering, automatically hitting the speaker and informing Covington the team was all listening.

As usual, there was no greeting. 'We have a DNA match for the Fleming children's bio dad. Cody Brown. Lives up in Santa Fe. CYFD was planning on reaching out to him, but I hit pause on that based on the assumption that your team will want to question him before we contact him to let him know that he has two children, if he doesn't already know.'

'You're right, we definitely want to talk to him, so I appreciate you reaching out to us first. We'll drive up to Santa Fe today.'

'Let me know what you find out.'

A few minutes later, Alyssa asked Joe and Tony to nudge Bill Hedge to see if the techs had found anything on the van that would give them some answers. Until this case was closed, she feared not only for London's life since her rescue, but also Carter and Abigail's. Especially since she no longer believed they had one of the culprits in custody, even if her gut insisted he knew more than he'd like them to believe.

Chapter Thirty-Three

Unable to see them or to communicate in any way, London listened to the medical staff discuss her chances of survival, as well as the whispered, horrified conversation about how she'd been located in the church basement, moments from death, by a couple of detectives who had decided to explore the area in search of an old hunting cabin. Their hushed, subdued voices carried the weight of knowing their patient would likely never wake from her coma, not realizing she could hear everything going on around her.

Even though the staff termed it *luck*, she rejected the idea that she'd been rescued by fate or any of those other woo-woo things, as her grandma liked to label them. It had been divine intervention, plain and simple. No other reasonable explanation could rationalize her still being alive or the wolf's presence, the animal she believed had urged her to keep fighting, whether it had been real or a figment of her imagination.

A subtle change in the air pulled London from thoughts of the wolf, and she latched onto the sounds of two new voices, a man and a woman who introduced themselves and then listened to a doctor or nurse run down her progress, or lack thereof, since being brought in.

'While her condition is still critical, her vital signs have stabilized since we've got her on a round of antibiotics and saline. Dehydration was as much a major cause for her body's distress as her infected wounds. That being said, Detectives, I'd like to warn you this patient's prognosis is still bleak, at best.'

The female interrupted. Her voice, while not unpleasant, bordered on unhappy. 'Doctor, why don't we concentrate on the positive, considering your *patient* may be able to hear us. And, if you don't mind, seeing as how she has no family here to visit, my partner and I would like to spend a few moments with her.'

The door closed, and two pairs of footsteps joined the presence of someone else – a nurse? – still beside London's bed. A soft touch settled on her hand, instantly releasing a bucket of emotion. In her mind, tears flowed steadily down her cheeks. In reality, she didn't know. She willed herself to concentrate on the woman's voice because she suddenly had the feeling that there was something urgent she was supposed to be remembering.

'Hello, London. I don't know if you can hear me, but I'd like to think you can. I'm Detective Alyssa Wyatt. My partner, Detective Cord Roberts, is here, too. You might've heard us talking to you last night when we found you.'

The detective's words pressed on London's memory, like she *had* heard and had tried to warn them about something before it was too late. But each time she tried to latch onto the reason for her sense of urgency, it slipped away, like someone was holding a pillow over her thoughts.

'We know you've been through quite the ordeal, but you're obviously quite a fighter, so we know you can overcome the trauma you've endured and beat the people who did this to you.' The detective's hand stilled on her as she addressed someone else in the room. 'Did her blood pressure just go up?'

London recognized the disbelief mixed with hope, and she wanted to beg the detective to keep speaking, to help her remember what she needed to tell them, to warn them about.

As if the nurse had climbed inside her head and plucked out her thoughts, she excitedly whispered, 'Keep talking. I think she can definitely hear you.'

Yes. Keep talking. London willed her eyes to open, but they remained stubbornly closed.

With a lighter, more enlivened tone, the detective told her about the wolfdog who'd been watching protectively over her, and again, London wished she could cry. Not a figment of her imagination, not a delirious hallucination. The wolf had been real. It had encouraged her to keep fighting, not to give up.

'He wandered off almost as soon as you were loaded onto the helicopter, but I'm pretty sure he stood just over the hill watching from afar, making sure we were doing everything right.' As she spoke, the detective's fingers stroked the top of her hand. It was the first soft touch London had experienced since her hellish nightmare began, and she didn't know how to prioritize the cascade of emotions coursing through her. For several moments, she tuned out the woman's calm voice and concentrated on touch without the promise of pain. Until she heard the detective mention her grandparents.

'I know you wish it were your grandma and grandpa standing here beside your bed, encouraging you to continue getting stronger, but they asked me to make sure I told you they're doing their very best to get to you. In fact, your grandfather told me to tell you that you'd best be fighting with all you've got because *his* London's never been a quitter.' The detective's voice thickened with emotion. 'He said to promise you they'll be here as soon as they can.'

Focusing all her energy into the movement, London struggled to wiggle her fingers or flip her wrist so that she could clasp onto the detective's hand. She needed her to know that her mind was alert, that she could hear.

She needed to beg the detective to tell her grandparents not to travel, that she understood they were both too frail right now. She wanted to tell her that what she needed most from them were prayers for healing, and if ever there was a soul to be defined as a prayer warrior, it was her grandma. But despite her efforts, her body and her words remained paralyzed behind the infections and the various drugs being pumped into her system in the hospital's desperate effort to keep her heart beating. What felt like a tear tickled the corner of her eye.

A new voice, the man's this time. What did the lady call him? Something like a rope. Cord. She'd said his name was Cord. Like the female detective's, though much deeper, his voice rumbled smoothly as he spoke.

'Like my partner said, we need you to keep fighting so you can wake up. We're going to need your help identifying the individuals who did this to you, to your friends.'

The determination behind the man's words made London feel like a bomb had exploded inside of her. Immediately, her lungs began struggling for oxygen even as her heart expanded like a balloon about to pop. Of course, they'd want her to identity the individuals responsible, but like a black-out curtain that darkened every corner of a room, her mind did the same whenever she tried to bring her tormentors' identities into focus. Whether it was a protective measure her brain had put into effect or a psychological glitch, their faces remained behind a cloud of fuzziness. *She needed to remember. Why couldn't she remember?*

'But don't worry about that right now. All your energy needs to be focused on allowing your body to heal. Okay?'

Two people murdered my friends, tortured me and poor, defenseless animals, and my psyche has blocked their physical appearances from my memories. Why? Open your eyes, London, right now. You have to warn them. Her desperation turned into a burgeoning physical pressure on her chest. Danger. Someone was in danger. Her? But she was in the hospital.

And she'd heard two of the medical staff discuss a guard outside her room. Not her. So who?

But it seemed the harder she tried to remember, the more determined her mind was to resist. The pressure in her chest increased, making it suddenly much more difficult to breathe.

Two little dark-haired children, ringlets swimming around their faces and over their foreheads swam in her vision as the fog of medicine lulled her away from the detective's voice, away from the strain of trying to remember. In no time at all, she had no idea who the hand touching hers belonged to. A meadow of yellow daisies and fragrant purple flowers welcomed her as she made her way to the children playing off in the distance, waving for her to follow them.

Their smiles traveled the wide expanse of space between them as they lured her ever closer to the brightest light she'd ever seen. Amazed at how it neither blinded her nor hurt her eyes, but instead filled her with the promise of pain-free days, she listened to the hushed murmurs all around, assuring her she had nothing of which to be afraid. 'You're safe here. No one will ever hurt you again. Come.'

What used to be blood flowing through her veins became a stream of gentle waves washing away everything and suffusing her with warmth. She reached for the tiny little hands urging her to follow. In that moment, it all came crashing back. Her reason for escaping that coffin. Carter and Abigail were in terrible, terrible danger. She had to warn the detectives. Ignoring the fire licking at her insides, she shouted in her head for the detectives to leave her so they could go protect Carter and Abigail before it was too late.

Searing pain robbed her of breath and reason seconds before the weight of an elephant settled on top of her and pushed hard enough to crack a rib, and she felt the detective's hand slip away. Someone else – a voice she didn't recognize — yelled about a flatline before sending a shock of electricity surging through her body, replacing the warmth of moments ago with a new burning sensation.

Hell. London's last coherent thought was that she'd lost the battle after all, that she'd been kicked to hell for not having as much faith as she should've, and now Carter and Abigail would die because of her inability to communicate the main reason she had fought so hard to get out of that coffin. Breathing became more difficult, more labored.

She hated herself for failing. She'd tried. She really had.

From above, she watched the crowds of people in her room frantically working on reviving her as two people stood out of the way in the corner. The woman's mouth moved, and London read her lips, 'Please, God, don't take her now. She's fought too hard.'

Clearly, not hard enough, London thought.

Chapter Thirty-Four

Sunday, April 25

After waiting on an uneven bed of nails to learn that London was once again stable but critical after having her heart restarted, Alyssa and Cord had made the drive to Santa Fe. While they had spoken to Cody Brown, Carter and Abigail's bio dad, Joe and Tony had headed out to speak to Josie Douglas, Ewan Moore's daughter, after hounding Bill Hedge about the van. And now the team, minus Hal, had all reassembled back in the incident room to compare notes.

Tony scratched his head as his brows stitched together in puzzlement. 'Sperm bank? Yeah, didn't pick that one out of the ballpark of possibilities.'

Like the others, Alyssa's head was still reeling with the news. Seven years ago, at the age of twenty-one, Cody Brown, in an effort to earn a little extra money any way he could, had heard from a buddy of an easy way to 'make a buck,' and decided to give it a go. According to him and the paperwork he'd provided, he'd only *donated* a couple of times before deciding he didn't want to run the risk of someone showing up on his doorstep one day in the future, claiming he was the father of their kids.

'Brown said he never wanted kids, and at the age of twenty-eight, still hasn't changed his mind on that.'

He'd paled so fast when they'd told him about Carter and Abigail, Alyssa had thought he might actually faint. Instead, he'd barely managed to squeak out, 'Shit. Am I going to have to like, raise them now? Not to sound like a douche, but my life is good. I'm making good money, not tied down to any one person, can come and go as I please, and answer to no one. I was told my, um, donations, wouldn't come back to bite me on the… ass.'

Alyssa had almost laughed out loud at his hesitation, knowing *ass* hadn't been the piece of anatomy Cody Brown had been thinking of.

Joe leaned back in his chair. 'What did you tell him?'

'That his parental rights and obligations were legally waived through the use of a sperm bank. Then he demanded to know how we even tracked him down since his identity was to remain anonymous. Apparently, he didn't realize that Know My Ancestral History dot com was one of the companies who sold information to third parties, so hundreds, if not thousands of databases gained almost instant access to his DNA information.'

'Not to mention the jolt he got when I pointed out the clause in his contract that stated there was a possibility his identity *might* no longer remain anonymous once the children reached age eighteen,' Cord added.

'Wasn't he the least bit curious?' Tony asked.

'I don't know. The only thing he asked just before we left was if "the kid" looked like him.'

'Kid? You didn't tell him there were two?' Tony tried and failed to hide his shock at the nondisclosure, making Cord laugh.

'Yes, we told him. But apparently, his freaked-out brain buzzed that noise out. And to answer your next question, I told him no, the children did not look like him at all. Frankly, he seemed relieved by that bit of news. And at the risk of sounding like an asshole, so am I.'

Joe held up his palm to interrupt. 'Wait. Hold up a second. I'm confused. So, how is it possible that three years separate Carter and Abigail, but they somehow still have the same biological father?'

Unfamiliar with the process, Alyssa had wondered the same thing. 'Apparently, the sperm is frozen. Once the mother has chosen her anonymous donor, the samples are reserved and used when needed.'

'Ah. Got it.'

'Moving on. We can cross Cody Brown off our list of possible suspects because we were able to verify the alibi he provided. Credit card receipts, eyewitnesses, and camera footage show he was playing in a band at The Chile Bar Thursday night. That being said, what did you two learn when you spoke to Josie Douglas?' Alyssa asked.

'Well, to be honest, neither Josie nor her husband Neal were overly thrilled to see us, and they made that abundantly clear. More than once, she accused the police of harassing her father. When I asked if he was home, she told me no, and pretty much that it was none of my damn business where he was.'

Tony grinned. 'Yeah, but while she was berating Joe, I managed to get a peek inside her house. Nothing really stood out. No crazy, dark Satanic stuff, at least not out in the open like at Whipple's place. Also, checked out her shoes. Can't really say for sure about size, but she was wearing Adidas, not Fila, which doesn't mean much since all the women I've ever dated always have half a dozen pairs of sneakers.'

Hal suddenly came rolling in, an I-just-won-the-lottery grin on his face. 'Ochocinco. He's a retired football player.' He glanced at Cord, a sports enthusiast like himself. 'Do you remember him? He legally changed his name in honor of Hispanic Heritage Month because his number was eighty-five.'

Alyssa frowned, not sure where Hal was headed. 'Eighty-five in Spanish is ochenta y cinco, not ocho cinco.'

Hal brushed her comment off. 'Not the point. What if the numbers forty-seven and thirteen-thirteen stand for a name, like initials?'

Alyssa's mind drummed like the marching band in a parade. Hal's supposition ran similar to the thought that she'd had about the numbers being a signature of sorts. She grabbed a marker and wrote it down. 'Okay, so the four would be the letter D, the seven would be G, and the thirteen-thirteen would stand for MM.' She glanced over to their list of suspects and interviewees, trying to match up the initials, but nothing stood out until Joe grabbed a red marker and drew a wavy line between the names Douglas and Moore.

Cord's phone chimed with a text, but everyone ignored it until he set his phone back down and said, 'That was Kyra Sanderson. She said someone from CYFD was planning on stopping by any minute to visit Carter and Abigail to see how they were doing and wanted to ask if she should inform the officers out front. I told her it wouldn't hurt.'

This time it was Alyssa's ringing phone that interrupted. 'It's Hedge.' Propping her cell in the whiteboard eraser-holder, she hit the speaker button so everyone could listen in. The second Bill offered his booming greeting, six sets of hands stretched outward in a race to lower the volume control. It had been said that if Hedge had been standing on the moon, it still would've sounded like he stood in the center of the room screeching into a bullhorn held far too close to his mouth. Not just a few times, people, Alyssa included, had speculated as to how the man's wife and children weren't deaf. Her own guess bordered on the belief that Hedge's family walked around with cotton balls shoved into their eardrums twenty-four hours a day.

'Good news delivery. We're not done down here, but already this van has proven to hold a treasure trove of stuff, some of it helpful, some not so much, or at least not so much yet, but once those pieces start clicking into place, well, the DA's going to have a host of evidence to nail these guys to the wall.'

Out of habit, and though he couldn't see her doing it, Alyssa's hand circled the air, motioning for the technician to get on with it, that they were all waiting, and they couldn't assemble those pieces until he handed them over.

'In the footwell of the van, we found trace amounts of something called perlite. You might not recognize the name, but you'll know what it is as soon as I tell you.'

If it hadn't been for Lewis Murray, Bill would've been right, but since he'd told them less than twelve hours ago, Alyssa said. 'Actually, Cord and I learned about it last night just before we located our kidnap victim. It's a volcanic glass heated to an extreme temperature and used in potting soil. It's those little white beads that, in my opinion, resemble spider eggs and freak my husband out a little every damn time we open a bag of Miracle Gro.'

'Oh-kay. Guess you don't need my tutoring session on that topic after all.' Alyssa winced at the high squeak of something scraping across Bill's desk. Did the man do nothing that didn't attempt to break the sound barrier? Her ears were still ringing, and she actually had to shake her head to clear the noise so she could hear the rest of what the technician had to say.

'Considering the location of your victim, that's your first bit of real proof that the vehicle was used in connection with the crime. Aside from seeing it on camera, of course. And eyewitness testimony. I mean the first bit of actual physical evidence to back those things up. Never mind, you all know what I mean.'

'We know what you mean,' Alyssa promised, not bothering to fill him in on the cloth gag from London's mouth matching the material found with the van. 'What else?'

'Well, we sent some blood samples off to the lab. That could be a day or two, maybe even longer since your victim's been rescued, but we also got lots of partial prints off the steering wheel. The only bad news is that a couple sets don't match anything in our system.

'Now, some of the prints are smudged enough to be rendered useless, but there are enough that were still usable enough to get several hits. To start with, Clarence Whipple, as you'd expect, since the van's registered to him.'

The air grew thick as stew as they waited to hear the rest. But when Hedge announced the other names, the air became top-of-Mount-Everest thin.

While Alyssa's mind was still reeling, Cord exploded out of his seat like a lit rocket, slamming open the door and barreling out without waiting to see if she was following, which was good because if he had, she would've crashed into his back.

Chapter Thirty-Five

Sunday, April 25

Heart pounding, adrenaline rushing, on high alert, and still in disbelief, Alyssa approached Mateo Garcia's and Chrissy Madison's home. With her hand hovering over her weapon, she waited as Cord took up guard on the right side of the door and Joe and Tony rushed around to the back before she pounded her fist and yelled out, 'Albuquerque Police. Open up!' On the other side of town, another team that Captain Hammond had sent out were raiding the home of Josie and Neal Douglas, Ewan Moore's daughter and son-in-law.

She pounded again, harder and louder. 'Albuquerque Police. Open up, or we're coming in!' After counting to ten, she placed her ear against the door, hearing no movement within. She shook her head and pointed, silently asking Cord if he could see anything between the broken and bent blinds covering the window.

Cautiously, he peeked inside before once more flattening his back against the side of the house. 'I can't see anything. They could be hiding or not home. What's the call?'

Alyssa thumbed her mic. 'Joe, Tony, can either of you see inside the garage?'

The seconds ticking by lasted forever before Tony answered. 'Empty save for a couple of bikes hanging on a rack.'

On the way, Hal had called to inform them that Judge Rosario had issued the telephonic search warrant, so keeping her line of communication open with the others, she said, 'I'll inform Hammond that we're going in. Joe, Tony, stay alert.'

'You got it. Watch your backs in there; we'll watch them out here.' Anger and urgency resonated through Joe's voice.

After a quick update to Hammond, Alyssa nodded to Cord, who counted to three, then kicked the door in with a thundering boom and another warning: 'Albuquerque Police. We're coming in!'

The first thing Alyssa noticed was the cloying thick scent of recently burned incense, similar to the kind they'd discovered at the church. The second thing she noticed was the nearly obsessive cleanliness of the place. Not even dust motes flew in the air, and every item on each polished surface appeared carefully, almost obsessively placed. Noticeably missing were the types of items she'd expected after their search of Whipple's property.

'Ready?' Cord asked, coming from the kitchen and moving in front of her to lead the way down the hall toward the rest of the house.

'Ready.' Systematically, the two of them checked and cleared room after room, each one as neat and tidy as the living room had been, including closets and the home's only bathroom, until the only area remaining hid behind a closed and locked door located directly across from the master bedroom.

Reaching up to the top of the door frame, Cord ran his fingers across the ledge until a metal key slid off the top and dropped to the floor. Not taking his eye off the doorway, he bent down and scooped it up, casting one quick sideways glance in Alyssa's direction before inserting the key and twisting the knob.

Like the two other bedrooms, this room had a thick, light-blocking shade covering the window. She felt like she aged a year in the second it took Cord to find the light switch. Fully illuminated, the space immediately released a thick aura of evil. Both of them stared in shock and horror. A heavy array of well-used books with spines containing words like *rituals* and *blood sacrifices*, *Reaching the Ultimate Power Through the Devil*, and *The Satanic Bible* lined a bookshelf sagging from the weight of the tomes. Inverted crosses with broken arms hung on the walls. What appeared to be a brand-new altar occupied the center of the room, a stuffed goat's head, painted red with pointed horns adhered to the top of its skull, mounted on the wall behind it. Suspended from the ceiling with a bucket beneath it was a framed family photo, minus the glass. But it was the symbolic intent that stunned Alyssa and froze her to the core, sending shivers rippling along her skin. Someone had taken a maroon-colored permanent marker and drawn a wide gash across Elena's throat.

'I guess not everyone loved her like he said,' Alyssa muttered, recalling Mateo's words upon arriving at his older sister's house Friday morning. She thumbed her mic again. 'Tony, you keep watch out front, let us know if you see anyone coming home. Joe, I need you to come in and start recording. We're going to need documentation of what we've got here. I don't want any chance of Mateo Garcia or Chrissy Madison walking on a technicality.'

Backing out of the room, Alyssa felt a driving need to shower off the evil clinging to her.

'Do you think we were wrong, that Elena was the intended target instead?' Revulsion rocked Cord's words.

While they waited for Joe, she thought about his question. 'No. If his sister was the intended target, why would he wait until she was at Skye's home and then torture Skye and not her? Also, why kidnap London?'

Cord rubbed his jaw and rotated his neck. 'Hell, I don't know. Why does anyone do *any*' – he jerked his thumb over his shoulder – 'of this? Did the guy seem like he had low self-esteem or anger issues to you when we met him at Ashlee's home? Maybe he did it to torment his sister, make her watch, know she was helpless to do anything?'

'I suppose Dr. Sharp could be wrong that Elena died immediately, but why would Elena have blunt force trauma to render her defenseless unless someone wasn't expecting her? No, my gut still insists that Skye, for whatever reason, was the initial target. And to answer your other question, neither Mateo Garcia nor Chrissy Madison, for that matter, sent any alarm bells off when we met them.'

'It's me,' Joe yelled, announcing himself just before he joined them in the hallway. The moment he caught sight of the room, he recoiled, much like Alyssa and Cord had. 'Holy Mary, mother of God. Do we need a priest to perform an exorcism before I go in there? And... shit... sorry... is that... a family photo with...?'

'Yes.'

Already recording the scene, Joe mumbled more to himself than to anyone else, 'I still don't get the forty-seven and thirteen-thirteen. Shouldn't it be, like, thirteen-seven for Mateo Garcia and three-thirteen for Chrissy Madison if they stand for a monogram?'

A fair question, which Alyssa had been pondering herself. But she knew she might have to wait for Chrissy and Mateo to explain the significance of the digits because right now, they needed to start marking evidence. But more importantly, they needed to locate the two before they slipped away or killed someone else. Because, after everything Alyssa had seen and was currently seeing, she knew for a fact the two were a long way from finished.

When Joe finally finished recording the room from floor to ceiling, he moved with Alyssa and Cord into the master bedroom, where he continued his video documentation. He tipped his head in the direction of the open laptop. 'Out of curiosity, anyone check that?'

Wordlessly, Cord moved over and ran his hand over the mousepad, waking the computer, surprised to see it hadn't requested a password to log in. 'For a couple as demented as them, they're awfully trusting, aren't they?' In the next second, his naturally tanned complexion turned ash-gray, and his eyes shifted wildly from the screen over to Alyssa.

At the same time that his horror-stricken voice croaked out, 'They've hacked into the CYFD database. They've got the Sandersons' address,' Alyssa's phone rang, making them all jump.

'What's going on, Hal?'

'When you called Hammond to say that no one was home and you were going in, I decided to ping Garcia's and Madison's phones.' The silence that seemed to drag on forever was fraught with fear and tension. 'Garcia's phone just bounced off the towers near Kyra and Milton Sanderson's home. You need to get over there, now!'

Moving swiftly back to the door, Alyssa turned to Joe. 'Get the crime scene techs out here and hold down the fort until they arrive, and then meet us at the Sandersons'. We'll take Tony with us.'

'You got it.' In an effort to reassure Cord, Joe squeezed his teammate's shoulder, adding, 'They're going to be fine.' To Alyssa's mind, he sounded far less certain than his words indicated.

Unable or unwilling to respond, Cord nodded as he raced out the front door, already dialing Kyra Sanderson while Alyssa grabbed Tony. In the back seat, Tony, using his speakerphone, called Hal back, asking him to contact the surveillance team stationed outside the foster home. Within seconds, Hal informed them neither officer was responding to either their phones or their radios. 'I'll send backup to meet you there.'

'Kyra Sanderson's not answering, either.' Alyssa could tell by Cord's white-knuckled grip on the door handle that her partner was holding on by a fine thread.

Hal's tone, while filled with tension, remained calm. 'Cord, listen to me, my friend. I know you're scared for Carter and Abigail's safety, but you can't go in there half-cocked. You're not going to do anyone, including yourself or your team, any good if you get yourself injured. Be careful out there and watch each other's backs.'

Cord's voice cracked with torment and anger. 'I promised I'd keep them safe, that no one would hurt them anymore. This' – he twisted around so that he could see Garcia and Madison's house as they pulled away – 'is not safe.'

Chapter Thirty-Six

Sunday, April 25

Knees pulled in close to his chest, Carter sat vigil in front of Abigail inside the shed where they hid. Tears clouded his vision, but he angrily wiped them away. He'd been trying to read Abigail a naptime story when he'd heard a *pop-pop* coming from outside and then a commotion in the living room with another *pop* just before Kyra screamed, 'Oh my God, what did you do?' Another *pop* made her quiet. And Carter had known the bad guys who'd killed his mom and Auntie Elena and taken Auntie London had come for them, too.

A woman's mean voice said, 'I'll check the back. You check—' He didn't hear what she said next because two loud bangs drowned out her words. When he could hear her again, her loud, angry voice crackled like sticks in a fire. 'What the—No, no, no—'

Carter's ears hurt with more of the noise, and he finally understood that what he was hearing was the sound of shooting guns. He remained frozen until Abigail tugged on his arm. 'Cawter? I'm scared.'

Wrapping his hand around hers, he whispered, 'Shh, Abigail. We have to go hide again.' Begging her not to cry when he told her she didn't have time to go grab Mr. Orange, her stuffed hippo, he tugged at her to follow him outside, remembering Kyra had left her phone by the lamp. She knew it made him feel better to have it nearby when he and Abigail weren't in the same room as the grown-ups. Without letting go of his sister's hand, he snatched the phone off the nightstand.

With his heart feeling like it was trying to escape its own scary monster, he tiptoed to the open doorway and peeked out into the hallway to make sure no one was there. Then, dragging Abigail, he ran down the hallway, around the corner, to the back door where he twisted the lock and eased the door open so it wouldn't squeak. Before closing it as quietly as he could, he twisted the lock on the door again, hoping it would fool the bad guys into not searching for them outside. As he scraped his back against the side of the house like he saw the cops do in the movies, he tried to figure out if he should go to the policemen across the street, but then he remembered the *pop-pop*, and something warned him not to try.

Before he reached the edge of the house, he stopped and ducked down so he could whisper in Abigail's ear. 'When I say go, we have to run super fast, okay?'

Her eyes were wide and shimmery, and her wobbly lower lip stuck out even while she nodded and whispered back, 'Oh—oh—okay.' Her fingers gripped his even tighter, which made him want to cry; not because she was hurting him, but because he was afraid he couldn't keep her safe another time.

A picture of his mom shouting, 'Be brave!' the first time he jumped off the low board into the pool, bounced into his head and he nodded, as if she were standing in front of them right now, offering encouragement. Like he'd done at the pool, he counted to three under his breath and then, matching his steps to his sister's, he raced them across the small expanse of the yard until they reached the shed.

Beneath the second rock beside the apple tree, Milton had hidden a key. He'd shown Carter when he and Abigail first arrived, asking if they'd like to help him work outside in the yard.

The tree wasn't far from the shed, but it was still out in the open. 'Stay here,' he told Abigail, but she shook her head no and tightened her fingers even more. Since he didn't want to take time to argue or explain, he tugged her along with him. Peeking over his shoulder so he could keep an eye on the windows, he grabbed the key and replaced the rock exactly.

Because he needed both hands to unlock the padlock and open the heavy, rickety door, he had to force Abigail to let go for just a minute. It had taken three tries, but he'd finally managed to get the door open.

It was dark inside with invisible cobwebs draped everywhere, and Carter shuddered even as he'd closed them inside and weaved the padlock through the holes on the inside of the door. After shoving the key into his pocket so he wouldn't lose it, he snapped the lock into place. Sniffling, shaking, and afraid to use the phone's light, but more afraid to knock something over and alert the bad guys to their hiding place, he pushed a random button on the phone, illuminating the inside of the shed. He pointed. 'Over there, sister.'

A big wooden workbench stood behind a toolbox, shovels, a lawn mower, and lots and lots of plastic bins. Squeezing Abigail beneath the bench, he handed her the phone and said, 'Hold this for me, okay?'

Wiping her arm under her dripping nose, she did what he asked. Then, grunting and crying, he scooted two of the bins over in front of the workbench, leaving just enough space for him to squash himself in next to his sister. He wished he could've moved more, in case someone came searching, but they were too heavy. What he'd done would have to do.

So he wouldn't cry and scare his sister even more, Carter bit down hard on his lip. He didn't understand why bad things kept happening to them. But he was all Abigail had now, so even though he'd never been more scared —

except the night his mom got killed – he had to be brave and protect his sister.

Until Cord could get here. Then he'd be able to save them from the bad guys.

He held his hand out for the phone, and Abigail handed it to him while climbing into his lap and plopping her thumb into her mouth. If sucking her thumb made her less afraid, he wouldn't say anything this time. Because he was afraid something would happen to the card Cord gave him, Carter had practiced writing and saying the phone number until he knew it by heart. It hadn't taken long because he was very good at memorizing things. That's why he always won all the spelling contests and memory games his class played every week.

Even though both Mr. and Mrs. Sanderson had told him how proud they were, they'd still programmed Cord's and the lady detective's numbers in their contact lists because they weren't as good as him at remembering things. So, with slippery fingers that felt like they had butter all over them, Carter ignored the message that told Mrs. Sanderson she had one missed call and scrolled until he found Cord's name. But when he hit the call button, nothing happened. Confused and trying really hard not to cry, he pulled the phone away to see if the battery was too low. But it wasn't the battery at all; they just had no signal.

His heart banged faster. If he couldn't call Cord, how would he know to save them or where to look? Maybe if he moved back over to the door, he'd have better luck, but when he tried, Abigail clung to his neck and cried. 'No, Cawter, pwease don't weave me by myself.'

'It'll be for just a minute, okay? Just long enough for me to call Cord.'

'No.' Her sobs made her voice go higher, and Carter was afraid the bad guys would hear her and know where they were hiding, so he rubbed her back and told her he'd stay there. But he had to think of something. Maybe if he held the phone out from beneath the workbench, he'd get a tiny signal. One bar was all he needed to place the call.

Outside, a door slammed. With Abigail still clinging to his neck, Carter pushed the button on the side of the phone, shutting them in complete and total darkness and then scooted as far back into the corner as he could, stopping only when something sharp poked him in the shoulder.

If the bad guys found them, he'd fight to keep his sister safe, but Carter knew, no matter how hard he tried, he'd never win against a grown-up. Or a gun. Just thinking about it made his lower lip wobble in frustration. It wasn't fair, these bad things happening to them. He tried so hard to be a good boy and obey the rules and clean his room even when he wanted to watch cartoons or play on his mom's computer. He didn't even get mad at Abigail for chewing the heads of his favorite action figures when she was growing her teeth.

Footsteps crunched nearby, and Carter forgot about it not being fair because he knew the bad guys were close. Someone rattled the door before moving away to the bushes lining the wall on the other side of the shed. Barely able to hear through his pounding heart, Abigail's muffled cries, and the shed walls, Carter strained to listen.

'Carter? Abigail? Where are you? I'm a police officer. I'm here to help you. I know you're scared, but the bad guys are gone now. They did a lot of really bad things, but they're dead now, and they can't hurt you anymore. Please believe me. Come out so I can protect you.' It was a woman's voice, not as mean and angry as the one he'd heard inside the house.

Carter blinked. Those were almost the same words Cord's partner had said when that guy had found them inside the closet the night his mom got killed. Were Kyra and Milton dead, too? He thought they had to be, or they, especially Kyra, would have insisted on coming to get him and Abigail themselves. But as much as he wanted to believe the lady cop was outside, he thought it had to be a trick by the bad guys, so he stayed quiet, holding a finger to his sister's lips so she would know not to speak, also.

When the voice faded away, Carter risked using the phone again. Before anything else, though, he opened up the settings and turned the phone to mute. Then dancing his fingers over the keypad, he found the call log and hit redial.

Crossing his fingers that the phone would work and that Cord would answer so he knew he needed to come get them, Carter almost cried out when he heard ringing on the other end of the line.

They were going to be okay. Cord would tell him what to do to keep Abigail safe until he could get there. Already, he felt better.

Chapter Thirty-Seven

Not wanting to alert Mateo or Chrissy to their presence, Alyssa, Cord, and Tony decided to park several houses down and walk in, even though no signs of the dark sedan Mateo had driven to Ashlee's home on Friday had been spotted on either street neighboring the Sandersons' home.

As they approached, Alyssa pointed to the surveillance team parked across from the house. Even from where she stood, she could see both men slumped over in the front seat. Cursing and crouching low, she rushed to the driver's side door and peered inside, her stomach sinking at the sight that greeted her. Reaching through the rolled down window, she felt for a pulse, stunned when it beat weakly against her fingertips. On the opposite side of the vehicle, Cord did the same while Tony kept watch for any sudden movements.

'He's alive, but barely.' Alyssa's voice bordered somewhere between a growl, anger, and amazement.

'Same here. I'll call Dispatch to send—'

'Suspects' – heavy, pained breathing pushed between the lips of the officer in the passenger seat – 'inside. Multiple—' Gasping for oxygen, the officer ignored Cord's pleas to remain silent, the promise that help was on the way. 'Shots. Fir—' The word rolling off his tongue died with the officer's final breath, and immediately, a lump formed in Alyssa's throat, not just for the loss of a comrade, but because she'd attended the man's wedding just one month earlier.

Seconds later, the death rattle of the officer behind the steering wheel came, and with his death, Alyssa felt every single bit of the weight from this case come crashing down. A fiery heat of anger temporarily consumed her, until Hal's warning to Cord echoed in her head. Going off half-cocked would only result in possibly getting her or someone else killed, and too many bodies had already piled up in this case. She wouldn't be responsible for adding to the count.

'Tell the paramedics to come in silent.' She thumbed the mic at her shoulder. 'Joe, how far out are you? The surveillance team is dead. We need backup.'

'Rounding the corner in ten seconds.'

'Park behind my Tahoe. Hurry.' Over the hood of the patrol car, Alyssa watched Cord's head swivel from her over to the house, impatient. The three of them turned as Joe, as instructed, parked his car behind the Tahoe and then climbed out, quietly closing his car door. No words or a pre-battle strategy were needed because they'd all worked together long enough to intuitively understand their roles.

With Carter and Abigail's lives at stake, as well as the Sandersons', they couldn't wait for backup to arrive, so the four of them cautiously approached with Alyssa moving to the side in the space between the door and the window. Joe and Tony took opposite sides of the house, and Cord waited until they were all in position before raising his hand to knock.

When no one answered, Alyssa leaned in slightly until she could peek through the blinds. Clearly visible were two overturned dining room chairs and Kyra Sanderson's unnaturally twisted body. 'Damn it all to hell.' Her entire body pulsed from the adrenaline dumping into her system. 'We've got a body.' She heard the audible snap of Cord's neck when he jerked his head in her direction. 'Kyra

263

Sanderson. Not Carter or Abigail.' After updating Joe and Tony, she radioed Dispatch that they were going in, then nodded for Cord to proceed. His own fear driving him, he raised his foot, and with one kick, exploded the door off its hinges.

In the living room, Alyssa realized there wasn't one body, but three. Milton Sanderson lay partway between the kitchen and living room while Kyra Sanderson lay closer to the entrance of the hallway, her arms extending out in front of her, as if reaching for something – or someone. Near Milton's feet lay Mateo Garcia with half his face shattered from a gunshot blast to the head.

The stillness of the house terrified Alyssa. Until Joe, his voice pitched high, announced that Milton Sanderson still had a pulse.

'Kyra, too.' Tony sounded as shocked as Alyssa felt.

Over the sounds of Joe and Tony offering words of encouragement for the foster parents to hold on, to keep fighting, Alyssa called Dispatch back and requested additional ambulances.

Before she could ask, Joe tilted his head in the direction of the hallway. 'We've got this. Go check out the rest of the house.'

Her attention riveted on Cord, his face paler than she'd ever seen it, she nodded, and then together they moved as quickly and quietly as they dared down the hall in search of Carter and Abigail, the entire time, praying fiercely that they were alive, forcing herself to believe they were. They had to be. The thought of them meeting the same fate as their mother crushed her from the inside out.

With each room, Alyssa's hopes rose and sank. Would the next door be the one where they discovered their lifeless bodies? Or worse, would Chrissy have taken the children like she had London, to act out some sick, twisted Satanic fantasy? A ton of rocks dropped into her stomach at the idea. Seconds later, Cord, his hand shaking in a way she'd never before witnessed, pointed to Abigail's stuffed hippo. Alyssa's heart shattered into a thousand pieces as her partner and friend reached down and grabbed Mr. Orange, clutching it tightly in his left hand.

'They're not here. I'm calling in an Amber Alert.' Every muscle in his body screamed that he was one degree away from totally snapping.

As much as she wanted to reassure him that everything could still turn out okay, Alyssa couldn't find the words because they all sounded hollow and unbelievable in her own head. A sudden, incessant buzzing caused her heart to skip a beat before she recognized the sound of Cord's cell phone vibrating in his pocket against his keys.

Cord shoved his hand in and practically tore the pocket from his pants ripping his cell out. His voice laced with fear and anger, he announced the name flashing on his screen, 'Kyra Sanderson' just before he hit his speaker button and answered.

Expecting to hear Chrissy Madison's voice telling them she had Carter and Abigail, Alyssa's heart soared from her stomach up into her throat when, instead, it was the terrified, whispered cries of Carter Fleming that filled the air around them.

'Um, Cord. We're really, really scared. Will you come get us, okay?'

How Cord managed to keep his voice level and calm went beyond impressive. 'Hey, buddy. I'd love to come get you. Can you tell me where you are?'

When Joe and Tony hit the hallway, Alyssa's eyebrows shot up in surprise even as she placed a finger to her lips, mouthing 'Carter' and then pointing back toward the front of the house, a question in her eyes.

Speaking in hushed tones, Joe explained that Milton's injury turned out to be non-life-threatening. Milton had been able to speak, and after insisting Joe help him get to his wife so he could sit with her and apply pressure, he told Joe and Tony that Alyssa and Cord needed their help more than he and his wife. Joe had only argued a moment before Milton had revealed the gun he'd used to shoot Mateo Garcia. 'I can still protect Kyra and myself. Go. Please.'

On the phone, Carter lowered his already quiet voice, and it took Alyssa a second before she understood his words were directed to Abigail, not them. Facial features tighter than a military-made bed, their bodies held stiffly, everyone waited with great restraint for the little guy to come back on the line.

'The bad guys are here, a boy and a girl, but grown-ups. When can you come?'

Every emotion Cord felt stretched across the lines of his face, aging him before Alyssa's eyes. 'Carter, can the woman who took you hear you talking to me?'

When he didn't answer immediately, Alyssa's muscles went rigid as her eyes darted from one teammate to the next before landing back on Cord. Clearly confused by Cord's question, Carter finally said, 'Nobody took us. I hid us in the shed in Mr. Sanderson's back yard.' He repeated his earlier question. 'When can you come?'

A wind of expelled *whooshes* accompanied the instant relief that pushed color back into Cord's face the second he heard the word *shed*. Even as Alyssa, Joe, and Tony swung into action, Cord's long legs were already carrying him out the back door like someone had lit it on fire.

'Good thinking, buddy. And guess what? I'm already here. Me and my whole team, and we're coming out to you right now. Are you or Abigail hurt?'

'No, sir. Just scared.'

'Okay, just a few more minutes, and we'll have you out of there. Just sit tight.'

'Yes, okay. Um, Cord, I put the phone on silent in case it rang. I didn't want the bad guys to find us.' Even with her heart pumping blood loudly through her eardrums, Alyssa heard the hint of pride in Carter's young voice.

'That was really smart thinking, buddy.' Cord paused a beat. 'Did you see the bad guys?'

'No. I just heard a loud *pop-pop* outside and then some more inside the house, and then Mrs. Sanderson screamed, and then the woman screamed, and then I grabbed Abigail and got her out of the house.' Abigail said something, and Carter shushed her before informing them of what she'd said. 'She's sad that she couldn't save Mr. Orange. But we can get her another one, huh right?'

A huge amount of respect accompanied the sad reminder that Carter was only six years old, and already, he'd had too much responsibility thrown on top of his shoulders. Out in the yard, Alyssa and the others fanned out, cautiously checking their surroundings as Cord moved forward toward the shed situated against a crumbling block wall.

'Yes, sir, we can. But you tell Abigail I already rescued Mr. Orange for her. Okay, Carter, I'm outside the shed right now, but I want you to stay put until I get inside...'

'I put one of those locker locks on it.' Carter's next words were cloaked in insecurity. 'How'm I supposed to know it's really you and not a trick? We don't have a secret word.'

Cord's shadowed eyes connected with Alyssa. 'You know what? You're right, so I tell you what I'm going to do. There's a window on the side of the shed, and I'm going to see if I can get that open. I'll only break it if I have to so that you can see it's me, all right? Are you and Abigail somewhere safe so that the glass won't cut you?'

'I don't see a window.' Carter sniffled, and Alyssa heard Abigail's soft sobs flow into the air around them.

'Then that means you're probably far enough away to be safe. Now, as soon as you see it's me out here, I want you to go to the door and unlock it for me, okay?'

'Yeah, okay.'

Weak from weather and wear, the warped frame made it much easier to remove the window than Alyssa would've thought, so it didn't take long before Cord was muscling away the huge piece of plywood propped up against the glass until he could see inside. From her vantage point, she easily picked out Carter, phone pressed against his ear, knees pulled in tight, making himself as small as possible while keeping Abigail, who peeked around her brother's shoulder, tucked safely behind him.

They could almost taste the relief in the air as Cord instructed Carter to unlock the shed. Lots of scraping and scuffling and crying occurred before the musical metallic clink of the lock hit the floor and bounced off something inside. In a matter of seconds, Cord had the door yanked open and crouched down to capture both Carter and Abigail as they propelled themselves into his arms. Forgotten, his phone, along with Mr. Orange, fell to the ground.

Just as Alyssa turned away to wipe a tear from her eye, several gunshots followed by Abigail's scream had her, along with Joe and Tony, whipping back around as Cord dropped to the ground.

Chapter Thirty-Eight

Sunday, April 25

Blinded by the rage storming through every cell of her body after Milton Sanderson shot Draven, Mara fired aimlessly before forcing herself to move on. Though it had taken every ounce of self-control not to empty her clip into the couple, she scooted past them, and only then did she feel the burning pain in her left leg. A quick peek assured her it was little more than a graze. Still, it managed to further infuriate her. Not even the cops parked out front had gotten the drop on her or Draven. She'd fired a shot into the driver, and before his partner's brain could process they were in danger and under attack, Draven had put a bullet into the other cop.

Then they'd raced to the house where, to both their surprises, they'd found the front door unlocked, allowing her and Draven to take the family by surprise when they waltzed right in. Draven calmly put a round into the foster dad when he came racing from the kitchen. The foster mom had stood frozen from shock and terror before her mind caught up, and she screamed. Mara shut her up with a bullet to the chest. Everything had been going much more smoothly than they'd anticipated, and she gave credit to the Lord of Darkness for that. But as she'd turned to Draven to tell him to search the front of the house while she searched the rest, another shot had rung out.

At first, she'd been confused because Draven's arm hung down at his side. When he crumbled to the ground, half his face missing, it took her another second before she realized Milton Sanderson wasn't dead and had a gun of his own now trained on her. Enraged, she fired her weapon, wishing she owned an automatic rifle with hundreds of rounds instead of her semiautomatic one. Instead, she checked her clip and forced herself to move on.

Nearly exploding with pent-up rage, Mara searched every room in the house, beneath the beds, and inside every closet and the tubs in all three bathrooms. Before she even finished, she'd known the kids had escaped. She'd thrown her head back and roared out her frustration before forcing herself to think things through. Logically, if they'd left the house when they'd heard shots fired, they would've had to have gone out through the back. Telling herself they were kids and couldn't have gone far, she raced to the backyard.

Immediately, she spotted the shed, but when she turned the handle, she found it locked. Rotating in a slow circle, she checked the small yard. The shed was the most obvious place for two scared kids to hide, so she tried calling to them. 'I'm a police officer. I'm here to help you. I know you're scared, but the bad guys are gone now.' No answer, and the ticking clock in her head that warned her that the numerous shots fired would've alerted the neighbors by now insisted she cut her losses and get moving.

Draven was probably right anyway. They'd been masked in their cloaks, so no one could identify them. Something she hadn't felt in a very long time that Mara recognized as guilt nudged her. What she'd kept secret, even from Draven, was that the risk of being identified hadn't been the only reason she'd wanted to kill the children. She'd read that the more innocent the life offered, the more powerful one grew, and who could be more innocent than kids? For just a moment, she'd even considered the possibility of taking them back to the church, relishing in the idea of a true sacrifice on the church altar, but ultimately decided she couldn't risk it.

Heart racing one way while self-preservation guided her in a more logical direction, Mara studied the shed, considering whether she should waste her bullets spraying into the structure in the hope of hitting the kids. Whispers and movement at the front of the house stole every other thought as Mara's head whipped in that direction. The two officers who'd delivered the news of Elena's death to Ashlee and Mateo stood on either side of the car housing the dead surveillance team. Another officer stood watch in the street between the two detectives and the house.

Without drawing attention to herself, Mara slipped around the shed until she was shielded from the street view. Heart pounding, her eyes swiveled back and forth, searching for an escape route. And then she saw it. A gap behind the shed hid a hole in the rickety fence. It would be tight, but she knew she could squeeze through. With seconds to spare, she slipped through as the detectives stormed the house, now joined by a fourth cop. Just as she drew her head through the hole, she heard the quiet sobs inside the shed and realized her gut hadn't steered her wrong at all.

Hunkering down beneath a low-hanging tree in the neighboring yard, she waited until the coast was clear before moving swiftly to the street, knowing she had minutes if not seconds before the place was swimming with reinforcements.

But the devil on her shoulder whispered 'Anarchy rules' and that she could still kill the kids and take out more cops. Reaching into her pocket for her second clip, she reloaded.

She didn't give herself time to talk herself out of the lunacy. Her neck snapped repeatedly back and forth as she kept a steady watch on the street, the houses, and anyone who might be lurking about. She had no sense of how much time passed before the four cops inside moved outside to the shed. Since they were so completely preoccupied with saving the brats, she went completely undetected. Keeping to the shadows as much as possible and using what objects she could to remain hidden, she crossed to the front of the house until she reached the side yard. Not taking time to aim, she unloaded her gun the second the kids poked their heads out and raced into the detective's arms.

Chaos erupted, and Mara dropped the weapon to the ground, using the commotion to slip away. Without looking back, she sprinted across the street, barely clambering over a fence before the boys and girls in blue surrounded the place, trapping her in. As she raced from yard to yard, no longer worrying about who might see her, she recognized the wisdom of Draven insisting they park two neighborhoods over. Stumbling over a rock, she righted herself as she made it to the car and yanked the door open, barely getting it closed before cranking the engine.

By the time all the cops speeding past the one person they sought realized she'd slipped through, she'd hopefully be almost to Mexico. She only had one more stop to make. With every block she placed between her and the chaos she left behind, her exhilaration rose, muted only by the loss of Draven by her side.

A heavy sensation that her one true partner wouldn't be joining her on the rest of her journey filled her chest with the unfamiliar ache of sadness. As the miles stretched out behind her, she wondered if she'd ever find another Draven to plug that hole.

Chapter Thirty-Nine

Sunday, April 25

Adrenaline and fear sent Alyssa's heart to pumping wildly as Cord, his arms drawing Carter and Abigail in tight to shield them from flying bullets, collapsed on top of them. Beside and slightly behind the house, Joe hunkered down while Tony took shelter behind a far too narrow tree trunk. A chorus of sirens, both ambulance and law enforcement, pierced the air, letting her know reinforcements were on the way. When the gunfire ceased, she shouted out, 'Are you hit?'

'Negative,' Joe hollered back while waving his arm in Cord's direction.

Tony's wide-eyed gaze remained glued on Cord's prone body as he yelled out, 'I'm good. Go, go. We'll cover you.' His voice vibrated with the fear and anger billowing through him.

Keeping low to the ground, her eyes sweeping all around her, Alyssa scurried toward her partner, not allowing herself to think of anything but getting the three of them to safety. Just as she reached his side, he twisted his head to look at her. 'I don't think we're hit.'

Her pulse thundered inside her ears as her critical and disbelieving gaze fell to his neck. 'There's blood, Cord. Hold still. Carter and Abigail?'

Their terrified screams nearly drowned out his answer. 'Scared. Where's the blood coming from?' Beneath the pitch of fury underscoring his words, Alyssa heard Cord's struggle to remain calm for the kids' sake.

Likewise, she did her best to control her own shaking voice. 'Looks like something ricocheted off the shed, splintering the wood, and it gouged a chunk out of your neck. It's gonna sting like a bitch – sorry, kids – but you'll live.' A witch's brew of emotions clogged her throat. That number of gunshots, and no one hit – that had to be more than luck and the shooter's lack of skill. Later, when she had more time to dissect it, when they played back their lapel cameras, when her mind forced her to relive it over and over during the day and especially at night, she'd pick out the tiny details that eluded her in the moment.

But for now, her main priority was to get everyone out of the open where they remained sitting ducks. Because chilling, cold, narcissistic personalities were the opposite of stupid, she suspected the shooter – it had to be Chrissy Madison – had disappeared with the chaos of sirens, bullhorns, and flashing red and blue lights. Still, Alyssa couldn't and wouldn't take the risk of being horribly, deadly wrong.

In the street, a swarm of officers approached, shouting out questions that all blurred together in a cacophony of confusion, fear, and rage. While Tony yelled something about getting paramedics inside to check on Milton and Kyra Sanderson, Joe hollered out instructions to set up the perimeter before Madison slipped through their net. Other officers automatically took over the task of keeping the gathering crowd of neighbors and onlookers at bay as one pair of paramedics was guided inside the house. After directing another team to Cord, Carter, and Abigail, now on the back porch, Tony watched helplessly as his teammate gathered the children in his arms and tried to calm Abigail's hysterical sobs. When one of the paramedics tried to extricate her from Cord, she pressed her face into his chest and wound her tiny arms around his neck, squeezing tightly, despite the blood flowing from it.

In the meantime, Alyssa kept a careful eye on Carter whose sudden silence terrified her in a whole new way. No longer trembling or crying, he stood frozen as madness continued to erupt around him. The only thing that reassured her was the way he, too, adhered himself to Cord's side, his little hand gripped tightly around Cord's bicep, as if he knew, despite all that had happened in the past few days, this man would protect him and his sister. Tears stung at Alyssa's eyes before she blinked them away and focused.

If Chrissy Madison listened to the breaking news, it wouldn't be long before she learned that her efforts to take everyone out had failed. Wherever Mateo's girlfriend thought she was heading, Alyssa knew it wouldn't be far enough because what Madison didn't know or had gravely miscalculated was Alyssa's drive. Never mind the saying 'hell hath no fury like a woman scorned,' hell had no fury like an infuriated Alyssa, especially when people she loved and cared about became personal targets.

'Detective Wyatt?' A young deputy approached, his eyes darting between her and the children.

'Yes?'

'The perimeter is secure, but the suspect slipped through before we could catch her. However, I noticed a dark blue or black four-door Kia pass us heading south. I was focused on getting to the scene, so I didn't latch onto the entire license plate when I glanced in the rearview, but they were New Mexico plates and began with a W and ended with twenty-six.'

Because Alyssa had had no need of checking the license plate when Mateo had arrived at his sister's house Friday morning, the plate number was unfamiliar to her. Still, she recognized the deputy's description as the same vehicle that had nearly rear-ended her Tahoe when they'd delivered the news of Elena's murder to Ashlee Garcia. She thanked the deputy and called Hal who answered with a frantic, 'What the hell's going on over there, Alyssa? Who's been hit? Wh—'

Alyssa had to cut him off, and probably for the first time in her two decades of working with him, she truly understood what the impact of always waiting to hear from his team had on him. Especially at a time like this, when he sat in his wheelchair at the precinct, knowing that shots had been fired in the place where two officers had already been gunned down.

'Hal, we're all okay. Cord was hit in the neck by some shrapnel and will need medical attention.' Her comment earned her a scowling glower from Cord's corner, but she ignored it. 'But aside from an adrenaline surge and a piss-your-pants scare, we're all okay.'

Hal's loud sigh of relief sounded as shaky as his voice, sending a new wave of guilt through her for not thinking of contacting him immediately. At the same time, she also knew he understood why she hadn't and couldn't.

On the heels of that thought came the realization that at any second, if it hadn't happened already, there would be a breaking news report of shots fired and two dead cops, and her family, as well as Cord's and Joe's, would be climbing the walls until they heard they were safe.

'I've got to call Brock to let him know I'm okay. I'll get in touch with you again as soon as I can. But before I go, extremely abbreviated version of a long story, Milton Sanderson shot and killed Mateo Garcia, and Chrissy Madison managed to get away. One of the deputies spotted her vehicle heading south on Westmore, so let's get on top of that before she gets too far. And Hal? Deep breath. We really are okay. No getting rid of us yet.'

'Good. I need you all around so I can boast and brag when I win the pot.'

It took a second for Alyssa to realize he was referring to the bet regarding Ruby, and she barked out a laugh as she hung up. By the time she turned to suggest Joe and Cord contact their wives, they were both already on their phones. In Cord's case, the paramedic patiently waiting to clean his wound held the phone to Cord's ear because both her partner's hands were still occupied by Carter and Abigail.

Off in the corner, Tony was just hanging up, and by the haunted look in his eye, she knew he'd just gotten off the phone with his father's caretaker. In the past two years, his dad's dementia had gotten progressively worse, but the hardest part for Tony had been the violent outbursts his father had displayed, forcing Tony to put him into a specialized care home. At the time, he'd felt like he'd let his deceased mother down, but Alyssa assured him that he'd done exactly what he'd promised – that he'd taken care of his father.

A few minutes later, Brock reluctantly let her get back to work after promising to call Holly and Isaac, who was hanging out with Trevor, before they heard about the shooting from someone else.

'Be careful out there, babe. Love you.' Voice thick with a mix of emotions that ran the gamut from relief to anger and fear, he hung up before Alyssa could reciprocate. Putting her phone back in her pocket, she whispered, 'I love you, too,' and then moved over to help distract Carter and Abigail while the paramedic cleaned Cord's wound.

–

Hours later, evidence technicians and what appeared to be more than half of Albuquerque's entire police force occupied the Sanderson house as well as the street, and Alyssa was finally heading back to the precinct. Joe and Tony had already gone, and Cord had been taken to the hospital, far from willingly, where he'd required eleven stitches to close the wound in his neck. If it hadn't been for the supremely angry phone call from his wife, a registered nurse, demanding he quit being so stupid and stubborn and get his ass to the hospital, Alyssa had her doubts as to whether or not he would've gone at all. Primarily because when Rosemary Covington had arrived, both Carter and Abigail had to be tearfully and forcefully pried away from him. Everyone's composure had been shaken, and more than one person turned away with glassy eyes.

In fact, the only person seemingly unaffected was Covington. Though not a normal part of CYFD procedure, she relented when Cord demanded two cops remain with her and the children until he could personally get back to them. Perhaps it was because she sensed she'd be wasting breath and energy because she knew no way in hell would Cord risk those children being removed from his sight any other way.

Now, as Alyssa rolled to a stop outside the precinct and shut off her engine, her phone rang, interrupting her looping replay of the entire day's events. She snapped it up as soon as she saw Cord's name flash on her screen. 'How're you feeling?'

'I'm good. They wanted to give me morphine or something, but I refused. And don't ask if that was wise because I'm not going to be doped out of my mind when some lunatic wanting to kill a six and three-year-old is on the run.'

Relieved to hear the fight still in his voice, Alyssa's stomach high-fived her heart. 'I wouldn't expect anything else. By the way, thought you'd like to know that Holly, *my* daughter, called asking if *you* were okay. I'll have you know she inquired about you before she asked about me.' She spoke the truth; Holly had, but only because she'd already known her mom was fine since her dad wouldn't have lied to either her or Isaac about something that serious, not after all their family had gone through in the last couple of years.

Still, that wasn't Alyssa's reason for telling Cord. As a teenager, when Cord had first become Alyssa's partner, Holly had harbored a not-so-secret crush on him. Well aware of it himself, Alyssa knew her words would make him chuckle, and they did. When his pained laughter slowed, she asked, 'Have you been sprung? I can swing by and whisk you out of there if you need an escape vehicle. Or is Sara there?'

'Sara was here up until about half an hour ago when I sent her on her way since the squirrely monkeys, referred to by some as Shelley and Shane, oscillated between 'I just broke a major bone' crying because Sara gave them the wrong-colored cup and straight-up monster tantrums because she woke them from their nap in the first place to come here, which I told her she didn't need to do because I was fine.'

'First of all, my friend, you are her husband and the father of her children, so nothing short of seeing you with her own two eyes would allow her any sense of peace. Secondly, your wife is a damn good nurse, so of course she'd want to see for herself that you weren't lying about the seriousness of your injury. You would've done the same, and so would've Brock. But I digress. I take it from your explanation that you need to hitch a ride.'

'As long as it's not out of your way.'

Staring up at the precinct, she said. 'Of course it's not out of the way. I'll see you in ten, fifteen minutes.' She glanced around at the increasing traffic. 'Better make that twenty, just in case. Hang tight, though, I'll be there as soon as I can.'

'Not going anywhere. But don't take your time.'

Alyssa laughed as she hung up and then immediately called Hal to let him know why she was running behind.

Chapter Forty

Monday morning arrived far too quickly, but it didn't stop Alyssa and the team from once again assembling pre-sunrise to go over the evidence the crime scene techs had collected at Garcia and Madison's home, some of it being the verification that the shoes Mateo Garcia had been wearing matched the shoeprints located outside the church. Between that and what they'd learned from Josie and Neal Douglas last night as well as Clarence Whipple, they were hoping to determine where Chrissy Madison was hiding out.

Joe, the shadows under his eyes making it look like he'd gone a few rounds with a boxing champ, held up two large, clear plastic bags. On the left, the red lightning bolt visible, was a black cloak similar to the one Alyssa's team had confiscated during the search on Whipple's property. This one, however, showed a dark and dried substance resembling blood on the part of the sleeve visible through the plastic. In addition to that, a pair of torn nitrile gloves had been found deep inside one of the cloak's pockets. From their size, Alyssa guessed they'd been worn by Mateo Garcia.

The bag in Joe's right hand he placed on the table in front of Alyssa. Then, keeping both eyes trained on it as if afraid it might catch fire or strike at him, he lifted his hands into the air and shuffled backwards. Considering the strong emphasis on the dark, supernatural leanings of this case, she couldn't help but be a little unnerved herself, so she didn't blame her teammate for his overly cautious retreat.

Donning a pair of gloves, she pulled the book on the occult from the bag, carefully flipping through the book-marked pages. The first one described the proper type of garment one should garb himself in during sacrificial slayings or victim mutilations. Various pictures similar to the cloaks worn by Whipple, Mateo, and Chrissy were depicted as one example. Another page highlighted the most powerful incantations, chants, and spine-tingling spells to conjure up or summon demons. Alyssa fought the impulse to check over her shoulder.

But all that paled in comparison to the hair-raising paragraph, highlighted and underlined, detailing the supremacy one could achieve, almost to the level of the devil himself, if a person were daring and willing enough to take the life of an innocent. It argued that moral values were nothing more than rules set by an ignorant society and should, at all costs, be ignored in order to reach the ultimate spiritual power. Alyssa blinked as her brain tried to accept what she'd read. The incident room suddenly felt suffocating and too small, as if the dark subject matter contained within the book had physically manifested itself from the pages to permeate the very air around them.

'We need to find her before she kills someone else,' Cord finally said, cracking the fault-line of tension. 'And we need to do it before she decides to go after Carter and Abigail again.' Wincing at the stitches pulling in his neck, he made eye contact with everyone. 'I can't fail them again.'

No one bothered to tell him he hadn't failed them at all because they knew their words would only fall on deaf ears.

Alyssa shook her head to clear away the disturbing passage. 'Okay, here's what we were able to get out of Josie and Neal Douglas last night before they stopped talking.

Though they attended the same schools from middle on, Josie and Chrissy did not become friends until their sophomore year, about twelve years ago. That's when Josie introduced Chrissy to, for lack of a better description, the act of Satan-worship. According to her, she wasn't in the habit of recruiting followers, but Chrissy approached her, said she'd heard some "rumors," and asked how it worked. Because she knew who Chrissy's father was, Josie claims she vetted her over the course of several weeks before actually inviting her to one of their gatherings.'

'Chrissy's father?' Joe asked.

Hal stopped clicking on his keyboard and swung his screen around for the team to see. 'Abel Madison.'

Tony set his coffee mug down with a thud. 'The evangelical Bible-thumping preacher who spouted hellfire and brimstone for everything from females exposing their ankles to boys piercing their ears? That Abel Madison?' His biting tone expressed the true nature of his opinion regarding the man.

'One and the same. On a completely different level, the man made a frequent nuisance of himself before his death. Couldn't walk outside the courthouse without him shouting all the ways people were going to hell.'

'Didn't he die of a heart attack or stroke or something back in 2005?' Joe asked.

'2009, stroke,' Hal clarified.

'Can't imagine why he'd have a stroke,' Tony muttered.

'That would've been about the time Chrissy was a sophomore in high school, then,' Alyssa added. 'After he died, Chrissy's grandmother on her mom's side moved in to help, but according to what Hal learned, that didn't last long.'

The team turned to Hal for an explanation. 'Chrissy Madison's only living relative is her grandmother, Dorothy Rhymes, who lives in San Diego. When I contacted Mrs. Rhymes to see if Chrissy might try to hide out with her, Mrs. Rhymes hung up. No goodbye, no dramatic monologue, simply ended the call. I tried two more times, but it went straight to voicemail. I waited about an hour and tried again. She answered that time, but she made clear her reluctance to discuss her grand-daughter.

'In short, as soon as Abel died, Chrissy started behaving badly, getting into trouble at school, staying out late, et cetera. Dorothy stuck it out as long as she could, but when Chrissy started playing what she called literal devil-worship music, she told her daughter that Chrissy needed help, apologized, and headed back to California. From telephone conversations she had with Chrissy's mother, Mrs. Rhymes knew things continued going steadily downhill after she'd left. And then two days after Chrissy graduated high school, Rhea Madison committed suicide. Dorothy blamed Chrissy for driving her daughter to her death and hasn't spoken to her since. Before she hung up, she insisted Chrissy would never come to her for help, but if she did, Dorothy vowed she'd call the police the second she laid eyes on the girl. Then she wished me luck and hung up again.' Hal took a deep breath and pushed his wheelchair back from the table.

Alyssa rolled her thoughts around in her head before finally telling the others what she was thinking. 'Not that I'm making excuses for any of this, so everyone hold onto your tempers and hear me out. But living with Abel Madison had to be a difficult household to grow up in. Just having to hear him once in a while made me want to stab my own ears, so I can't even imagine what living with him day in and day out would've been like. So, strictly playing amateur psychologist here, her father's authoritarian and controlling nature could very well be the reason Chrissy Madison rebelled and turned to Satanism. Her father's tyrannical rule suddenly disappears with his death, and what better way for a teenage girl to show her hatred for such oppression than by turning to the one thing her oppressor despised?'

Tony cocked his head to the side. 'I don't disagree, but that's a bit of an extreme sway, isn't it?'

'Guess it's not a matter of like father, like daughter in this case,' Joe said.

Hal's lips curled into a sneer. 'No, that attribute goes to Josie Douglas and Ewan Moore.'

'Theoretically speaking,' Cord said, 'you're probably right on some level, even though Josie was only three when Ewan Moore was convicted. Growing up, we know she heard the murmurings of rumors and stories, but according to her, no one, including her mother, would ever answer any of her questions regarding her father. It bothered her because she had very vague but happy memories of him. It only makes sense that, the older she got, the more she'd want answers, right?'

Scowling now, Hal nodded.

'Josie's mother legally changed their names after Moore went to prison, and so it was only after she overheard her mother and an aunt talking about an upcoming parole hearing that she learned her father's identity. Her aunt said the name Ewan, and Josie ran a search with just that. From there, it was just a matter of time and research. At the age of sixteen, she visited her dad for the first time in prison, much to his delight. On the fourth visit, she broached the subject of Satanism. That's when Moore told her about Clarence Whipple, told her he was still in the area and would answer her questions, but that she had to keep it on the down-low because Whipple had managed to maintain a fairly discreet profile since he'd skated on Hal's case.'

'If Josie was sixteen, then she couldn't have been dabbling in the practice for long when Madison approached her,' Tony threw in.

'You're right,' Alyssa agreed. 'It had only been a matter of a few months, actually. And Josie went to Moore about it before she even entertained the idea of introducing Madison to anyone. In fact, it was Moore who suggested vetting Chrissy because he'd once had an encounter with

Abel Madison, and so he warned Josie to practice caution until she knew for certain Chrissy could be trusted. Ironically, the words he used were to "make sure the apple falls far from the tree."'

'All right, so how do all the players tie together, then?' Tony asked.

'Josie met Neal, who was already heavily involved in the practice, through Whipple. Chrissy is brought into the fold, and neither Josie nor Neal could say how long it was before Mateo joined the group. All they knew was that Whipple no longer attended any of the *services* by the time Mateo came along.'

'So then, how did Garcia and Madison get ahold of his van?' Joe asked.

'We asked him the same question,' Alyssa said, 'and he claimed he didn't know either of them, but Whipple's poker face is in sad need of work.'

Cord chimed in. 'Didn't matter, though, because that's where Whipple's attorney shut us down. So we posed the same question to Josie, expecting the same result. Needless to say, we were clearly surprised when she freely offered the information. According to her, even though Whipple no longer participated in any of the rituals, he still loaned out his van whenever a member needed to transport an animal for sacrifice. He never asked who needed it or why, and Josie never offered the information. Plausible deniability, she called it.'

Joe rolled his eyes. 'Yet she continued answering your questions. Not that I'm complaining,' he hurried to add.

Tony ran his hands over his face and through his hair, shaking his head. 'Nothing like being a little nonchalant about animal sacrifices.'

'About that, I asked if it was normal for the van to be borrowed over several days, and she said no, that they usually used it for the one night and returned it. So, I asked if Whipple was at all concerned when the van wasn't returned right away, and she said, nope, that she'd called to tell him Chrissy and Mateo had used it last but hadn't yet returned it to her. According to her, all Whipple said was that if the vehicle was "hot," to dump it and set it on fire. So, at their next gathering, this past Friday night, Josie simply passed on the instructions to burn the van if it was hot. She hadn't expected Chrissy to dump it and leave it swimming with DNA and evidence. Luckily for us, neither Garcia nor Madison heeded that advice. Or maybe they had still planned to but got interrupted. We can ask when we track her down. Either way, we caught a break.'

Tony leaned back in his chair. 'I'm kind of curious. Why was Josie even cooperating?'

'Because facing charges of animal cruelty, theft, and property destruction, just to name a few, appealed more to her than charges of a double murder and a kidnapping she had no part in.'

'Do we know for sure she — and Neal and Whipple — weren't involved?' Joe asked.

'No. But I'm hoping London will wake up and be able to answer that question for us,' Alyssa admitted. 'Regardless, none of this gives us a peek into *who* Chrissy Madison is outside of the occult or gives us insight into where else or who else she might go to in order to hide out for a few days.'

Cord checked the time. 'What we're also still trying to figure out is how and why it ended up being Skye Fleming's house that Mateo and Chrissy targeted. Hammond already dispatched a couple of officers yesterday to break the news about her brother to Ashlee Garcia, but Lys and I are heading over to speak to her again. We're hoping she and her parents will be able to clear up some of those questions for us.'

'While we're doing that,' Alyssa said, 'why don't you guys try to track down Chrissy Madison's financials, see if we can track her credit card usage? Maybe she slipped and gassed up using a card instead of cash. Hal's already pinged her phone at the house she shared with Mateo, so we know it was likely her cell that evidence techs collected yesterday.'

A few minutes later, Alyssa and Cord were on their way to Ashlee Garcia's home. But this time, even though the bad news had already been delivered, she knew this visit wouldn't be any less difficult than the first one.

Chapter Forty-One

Monday, April 26

The sleek black Denali parked in the driveway of Ashlee Garcia's home looked conspicuous and completely out of place for the neighborhood. As Alyssa and Cord walked up the sidewalk, Ashlee, like she had the first time, peeked out her front window. Even from outside, it was obvious she'd been crying.

Taking a deep breath, Alyssa raised her fist to knock, but Ashlee had already opened the door. 'Detectives, please come in.' The thick air of denial surrounding Ashlee and her parents hit Alyssa like a rough, physical touch.

Seated on the sofa, an older, male version of Elena's sister sat beside the smaller, feminine version of Mateo. Dressed less than formally but more than casually, neither looked comfortable in their daughter's home. Yet their puffy faces, red eyes, and Mrs. Garcia's smudged makeup told a much deeper story of grief, shock, disbelief, and betrayal.

'Please, have a seat,' Ashlee said as she took an empty spot next to her mother, clasping the woman's wrinkled hand between both of hers.

For the entire drive over, Alyssa had struggled to come up with the best way to begin this interview, and she still didn't know how. But Mr. Garcia jumpstarted it for them.

'You're certain that Mateo is responsible for Elena's death?'

The hope in his voice cut Alyssa deep. 'Yes, sir. He and Chrissy Madison both. That's why we're here this morning. We need to ask your family a few questions because, as you've already heard, after opening fire on our officers, Chrissy disappeared, and we're hoping you'll know something that could lead us to her.'

'And London? She'll be okay?' Like her daughter had Friday morning, Mrs. Garcia strangled a handful of tissues.

'We're hoping she'll pull through,' Cord said. 'But to be completely honest with you, right now, the prognosis isn't good.'

'We wanted to go visit her, of course. But after... after... we thought maybe it was perhaps best if we stayed away.'

Alyssa directed her next question to Ashlee. 'Did you notice any out-of-character behaviors from either your brother or Chrissy after we left your house Friday morning?' Whether Ashlee's face colored from embarrassment or something else, Alyssa couldn't tell.

'Not at the time, no. I mean, at first I was just numb with grief, and then anger and denial. But looking back now and putting things into a different perspective, maybe I did notice that Mateo was acting a little strange, even for him. Of course, I attributed it to him dealing with his grief in his own way.'

'What do you mean?'

'Well, for starters, right after the two of you left, Mat and Chrissy disappeared into the kitchen for a really long time. I couldn't hear anything but whispering, and I guess I just figured she was trying to help him come to grips with Elena's murder. When they finally came back into the living room, Mateo insisted on being the one to call Mom and Dad.' She paused to grip her mother's hand. 'Selfishly, because I couldn't bear to hear the pain it would cause, I let him. Looking back and knowing now what he's being accused of, it makes sense why I thought it sounded so cold, to the point of almost being cruel, when he broke the news to my parents. But again, I granted him grace because Mateo has always dealt with things differently than the rest of us.

'And then I kind of forgot about that part because as soon as he hung up, he and Chrissy said they had to leave. I assumed he just needed his space, and I wanted to give it to him. I managed to get ahold of him twice over the next couple of days to try to talk to him about funeral arrangements, but he always blew me off. Most of the time, his phone went to voicemail, and I didn't bother leaving any messages after the first one.'

Ashlee made eye contact with both Alyssa and Cord. This time, there was no mistaking the anger brewing inside her.

'Even though I admit I was a bit upset and even a little jealous that Mateo chose to be with Chrissy instead of his own family after learning of our sister's murder, I tried to be understanding. Of course, now, his and Chrissy's disappearance makes more sense as I'm sure they were… doing horrible things to London.' Ashlee choked on a sob. 'I swear if I had known—'

Alyssa nodded her understanding. 'You would've called us immediately. We know that. You said a moment ago that you tried to be understanding that Mateo would want to be with his girlfriend to process his grief, so Chrissy must've been in the picture for a while. Can you tell us how long they'd been dating?'

Mr. and Mrs. Garcia both looked to Ashlee for an answer. 'I don't know. At least a couple of years.' She turned to her mother. 'When did Mateo stop celebrating Christmas with us?'

'Yes, I'd say that was at least two years ago. Maybe three.' Mrs. Garcia's hands squeezed her daughter's.

'So at least two, three years,' Ashlee continued. 'But he and Chrissy were friends for a really, really long time before he ever introduced her to the family as his girlfriend. Before that, he would just mention her name.

Since Mom and Dad live in Maine, they really never got to know her. Not that Elena or I did much more.'

Alyssa really hated to ask the next question, but she needed to know. 'Did you begin to notice any signs of change in his behavior, or did he exhibit any signs of anger before meeting Chrissy? Or maybe even after?'

Mrs. Garcia clutched her stomach and doubled over, her sobs ringing loudly in the room. Next to her, Mr. Garcia's face was akin to watching a whiteboard being erased as all evidence of any prior happiness just melted sway.

Frantically rubbing her mother's back while her father wrapped his arm around the woman's tiny shoulders, Ashlee answered. 'It's not as easy as that.' She took the time to blow her nose and gather her obviously waning emotional strength. 'I'm the oldest at thirty-three. Mateo is... was... three years younger, so thirty. Elena came along four years later.'

Alyssa guessed that, as the baby of the family, Mateo didn't appreciate being usurped. She'd seen that story time and time again. But that wasn't what Ashlee said.

'At first, he absolutely adored her, even introduced her to strangers in the supermarket as his baby. But all that kind of changed when he entered school. Right away, we knew something was wrong. Eventually, he was diagnosed with dyslexia and other learning disabilities that always made him feel stupid. In a way, I could relate because I'm also dyslexic, but not to the extent Mat was. And while I didn't have learning disabilities, I certainly had to study my ass off to get passing grades. In the meantime, Elena just seemed to be gifted with a natural talent for everything. Even science, which she loathed. She aced it with little more than absorbing the lectures.'

'And Mateo began to resent her?' Cord asked.

Ashlee nodded. 'But not right away. It happened over time, I think. He started getting into trouble, and Elena just kept getting heaped with awards and praise for everything she was involved in, academics, choir, sports. You name it, if she touched it, it turned golden. It got to the point that Mat's jealousy turned to him destroying his own homework and then blaming it on Elena. It worked the first couple times, and she was punished, despite her denials. Both times, Mat became a different person; he became the Mat we knew before he'd started school – happy, cracking jokes, just being *normal*. Anyway, the third time he tried it, I actually witnessed him sabotaging his own reading project and then blaming Elena. I told Mom and Dad.'

'Did he treat you the same as Elena?' Alyssa asked.

'No. I guess I had to work hard enough that he never felt intimidated or threatened or belittled by me. And Lord knows, aside from the one and only award I received in eighth grade for "Most Improved" in my English class, I certainly wasn't getting noticed for my achievements like Elena was.'

'Did Elena belittle him?'

'No. Never. She would spend hours in my room crying, asking why he hated her so much. Even then he resented how much everyone just naturally took to her. When we told you Friday that everyone who met my sister loved her, it was the truth.'

Not everyone, Alyssa thought.

'And she always held so much empathy for *everyone*. Like, I swear she could feel everything anyone else was feeling. If someone or something hurt, she hurt, too. And she always wanted to make things better. Including her relationship with our brother.'

'Did you all attend school here in Albuquerque or in Maine?' Alyssa asked, trying to connect the dots on when and where Chrissy and Mateo met.

'We all three graduated here. Mom and Dad moved back to Maine six years ago after Elena graduated college and started her job at Intel.'

'And that's where your sister met London and Skye?'

'Yep. Like I told you on Friday, three inseparable peas in a pod.' Despite the crushing weight of her emotions, Ashlee still managed a small smile.

'How well did you know them, Elena's friends?' Cord asked.

The lines in Ashlee's forehead crinkled as she thought about the question. 'I mean, I guess well enough to talk with them at Elena's birthday parties and such.'

'Did Mateo attend your sister's parties?' Alyssa asked.

'Once. Even before he and Chrissy became a couple, he very much stayed out of family gatherings. But Elena never stopped trying, never stopped inviting him. Much to our surprise, he agreed to come to her twenty-sixth birthday in March, though he and Chrissy didn't stay long at all.'

Alyssa straightened. 'I assume Skye and London were also there?'

'Of course. No, wait. I mean, yes, they were. At least Skye was, but London's car broke down again, and I remember she arrived late. Mat and Chrissy had already left, and I remember she was so disappointed not to be able to meet our brother.'

'Did Mateo or Chrissy speak to Skye?'

Closing her eyes, the color in her face fading, Ashlee barely managed a weakly whispered, 'Yes.'

Alyssa hated seeing the struggle going on with the Garcia family because she had a personal inkling of what they must be feeling. 'Tell us what you remember about that,' she said softly.

'We'd rented a space in the convention center for Elena's party. Skye, Elena, and I were sitting at a table laughing about…' She swallowed audibly. 'We were joking about London always tempting fate with her car, like she was just one bad movie scene away from a serial killer being the one to come to her rescue.'

Her eyes still closed, her voice clogged with tears, Ashlee grew harder to understand, and Alyssa had to lean in closer while Cord stopped the sound of his pen scratching across the paper.

'Elena or Skye said something, I remember, and we all started laughing hysterically, and Elena cried because she was laughing so hard she was afraid she'd pee her pants. And that's when Mat and Chrissy walked up to the table.'

Ashlee opened her eyes, though they were still blurry with moisture. 'Elena jumped up immediately and hugged Mat. She tried to hug Chrissy, but Chrissy kind of took a step back, so Elena just patted her on the shoulder and thanked her for coming. Then she introduced the two of them to Skye.' Her eyes closed again, and this time, Mr. Garcia reached past his wife to place a comforting hand on his only remaining child's shoulder. 'Skye got this huge smile on her face, and she stood up and asked if she could hug him, too, since she'd heard so much about him and couldn't wait to meet him.'

'And how did he respond?' Alyssa asked.

'He smiled and said he'd love a hug. I remember thinking there was something off about the way he smiled, like we were missing a private joke or something. But then we all started laughing about something else. Sometime later, before London finally arrived, Mat and Chrissy left.'

'I know this is difficult for you. Do you need a minute before we continue?' Cord asked.

'No. Nothing will make this any easier. Not time or— just nothing.'

'Did Skye have her children with her there that night at Elena's party?'

'No. It was one of those very rare occasions when she got a babysitter. Her neighbor... I don't remember her name.'

'Lillian Holt?'

'Yes, that sounds right.'

While Alyssa processed the information, Cord continued with their questions. 'We really hate to ask you this, but was your family aware that Mateo was involved with the occult?'

Absolute and awkward silence followed his question. With trembling hands, Ashlee grabbed for a cup beside her and swallowed the last bit of water in it. 'His senior year in high school, his girlfriend broke it off, and he spiraled into a severe depression. We tried to get him to see a therapist or take meds or something, but he refused. Then he started coming home later, missing curfew, listening to some seriously disturbing bands, like way worse than death metal stuff. Every lyric was about making someone pay or paying tribute to the devil or whatever. He started growing his fingernails out and filing them into sharp points and painting them black and just really weird stuff. One day, Mom caught him trying to file his teeth into points. Anyway, his behavior got bad enough that I remember Elena admitted she'd started locking her bedroom door at night.'

'Were you still living at home then?'

'More or less. I mean, I lived there, yes, but I was in college, so I wasn't really around too much.'

'How long did this go on?' Alyssa finally felt like they were on the edge of some answers.

This time, Ashlee looked to her parents for direction. 'I don't really know,' Mr. Garcia said. 'All I can say is he'd mellowed, or he seemed to have, before he moved out. He chose not to go to college, and so we told him if he wasn't attending school, he needed to get a job, and he took that as he needed to move out. We told him that wasn't what we meant, and he said he preferred his own space anyway. But he didn't seem angry, like we expected.'

Mrs. Garcia stared at her hands clutched in her lap as she whispered. 'Even though he wasn't as angry all the time, the house was so much more peaceful after he moved out. And I remember crying because I felt that way.'

Alyssa had no idea how to comfort or console the woman. Neither could she imagine what that type of guilt felt like, and she prayed she never would.

'Um, Detectives, I don't know if this will mean anything to you or not, but… we heard on the news about all the… *things*… found at Mat and Chrissy's place' – the way Chrissy's name rolled off Ashlee's tongue made it sound more like a four-letter word – 'and I honestly don't understand the significance of it, but at Elena's party, after he'd approached us at the table, I was walking past them, heading to the bathroom, and I heard Chrissy refer to Mat as Draven, which I thought was a weird nickname, but whatever.'

Just like that, the number forty-seven clicked into place in Alyssa's mind, and when she turned to Cord, she could see in his eyes that he'd come to the same conclusion. DG, Draven Garcia. Which meant… 'Did you happen to overhear what your brother's nickname for Chrissy was?'

'Mary? No, that wasn't it. Mare. Mara. Again, strange, but aside from telling Elena about it, I didn't give it much thought.'

And there was the connection to thirteen-thirteen. MM, Mara Madison. She'd have Hal look into the symbolic meaning of those names. Maybe that would be their clue in tracking her down.

After several more minutes and offering their sincerest condolences, Alyssa and Cord walked to the door, turning to thank Ashlee and the Garcias once again.

Ashlee held up her hand. 'You can thank me by finding Chrissy and bringing her to justice. I'm not going to be naïve enough to claim she's the root of all my brother's issues because clearly he had them long before her. But right now, from the bottom of my heart, I hate him as much as I hate her because, aside from doing what they did to London, they murdered Skye and Elena. They robbed the world of a kindhearted soul who would've done *anything* to see her brother happy again. And since he's no longer alive to take the punishment he deserves, my parents and I will have to settle for watching her pay for it.'

She closed the door before Alyssa or Cord could respond.

On the way to the car, Alyssa said, 'Well, so much for the theory that middle children are the peacekeepers in the family. Let's call Hal and see what he can tell us about the names Draven and Mara and see if that'll help us pinpoint her location.'

Hal answered the phone with a question of his own. 'Did you find out where Madison might be?'

'No. We were hoping to put your mad research skills to the test to see if you could tell us the significance of the names Draven and Mara, or see if you'd come across them in your old case. Why?' Alyssa asked.

'Don't know anything about the names. Though I remember a lot of the cult members we arrested back in the day had so-called cult names for anonymity reasons or simply because an alternate alias appealed to them. And I asked because I think I know where you can find Madison.'

Chapter Forty-Two

If Hal had announced he was a purple dinosaur masquerading as a human, Alyssa couldn't have been more stunned. Her pulse took off like a horse at the Kentucky Derby. 'Well, don't hold the information hostage, Hal. Spill it.'

'That's not really the thanks I expected.' Hal's teasing tone deserted him. 'Well, we discovered Madison's phone at their place yesterday, but what was noticeably missing was Mateo Garcia's phone, which we knew he had to have had on him at some point because that's how we knew they were at the Sandersons'. So it occurred to me to ping Garcia's phone again in case Madison had taken it. Didn't seem likely, but thought it was worth a shot. And guess what?'

'You've got a location on Mateo's phone?' Even if Madison was already across state lines or halfway across the country, Alyssa knew they were closing in.

'And unless Mateo's body is currently being transported south as we speak, his phone is bouncing off the towers leading in the direction of Montemar. Now, Madison could well be heading toward Mexico… or she could be heading back to the church where you found London.'

'Why would she risk that?' Cord asked after Alyssa's phone switched to the Bluetooth in her car. 'Evidence collected everything they could. I highly doubt she'd risk capture for nostalgia's sake.'

'I don't speak Satanic brain,' Hal said, 'but I do understand fluent criminal activity, and my guess is the evidence team didn't find everything. *If* she's going there at all. Like I said, those are the towers the phone's bouncing off of. Could be she's just driving through. But isn't it worth checking out?'

'It is,' Alyssa said. 'But I've got to side with Cord on this one because not only does it not make sense that she'd return to the scene of the crime when there's nothing there for her to gain, but why would she be using her dead boyfriend's phone at all? I cannot believe she'd be dumb enough to snatch his phone, especially when she left hers at home when they went after the Sandersons and Carter and Abigail. It doesn't make any sense.'

'Maybe she doesn't realize it's with her? I don't know. All I'm doing is giving you the information so you can decide what to do with it. Besides, aren't you the one who always tells us not to look a gift horse in the mouth? Same advice here.'

Maybe she'd seen too many movies or television shows herself, but Alyssa couldn't help but be suspicious. By virtue of her career choice and life experiences, it was in her nature. It helped make her a better detective. It took her head just a few seconds to discredit the idea that Chrissy Madison would risk hijacking her freedom by grabbing the phone just so she could toss it into a vehicle heading in the opposite direction she intended to travel for the mere sake of throwing the authorities off her trail. Not only did it not fit her narcissistic personality, but like she'd said to Hal, it also made no sense for her to take Mateo's phone at all.

But Hal was right; it didn't matter. They had a possible location, which wasn't as great as a possible sighting, but it was more than they had five minutes ago. 'All right. I'll call Hammond and let him know we're heading that way.'

'No need. He's standing right here.'

Hammond's voice came on the line. 'Keep me posted along the way. Hal's going to reach out to Deputy Lopez to put him on alert. I want you to give him a call when you get closer for some backup. You two be careful out there. I don't need you being shot at again.' Though the captain did his best to cover the gruff emotion in his tone, it still came through, and Alyssa and Cord shared a smile. It wasn't often he wore any part of his heart on his sleeve.

'You got it. Thanks, Captain.'

'Before you go, what are the chances we can get a chopper in the air in case Madison really is dumb enough to head back to the church?' Alyssa asked.

'We're already on it. Here's Hal back.'

'All right, like the Captain said, be careful out there. And hey, Cord, try not to catch any more shrapnel in your body. You're not Superman, my friend.'

Cord chuckled. 'Are you sure about that? I'm pretty sure that shit bounced right off me.'

The three enjoyed a quick chuckle before Alyssa said, 'Keep us up to date on Madison's movements, if she changes directions, or anything else.'

'You'll be the first.'

—

The closer Alyssa and Cord got to Montemar, the more hopeful she became. Hal had sent one text to update them on Madison's movements, and from what he could tell, the phone was tracking her straight to the church. Hal said he'd call back only if Mateo's phone bounced off any towers further south than the turn-off to the abandoned church. And so far, they'd heard nothing.

'What could she possibly want or have left behind?' Though she spoke out loud, Alyssa directed the question to herself.

Cord, his hand absently tapping around the bandage covering his neck, answered anyway. 'I have no clue.'

'Getting itchy now that the local anesthetic's finally worn all the way off?' When Cord shot her a puzzled look, she nodded to the way his fingers were dancing around his stitches.

His cheeks turning pink, he immediately dropped his hand. 'Yeah, I suppose so. But I'm not in pain, so nothing that's going to impede my thinking if that's what you're worried about.'

Alyssa darted a narrow-eyed, scathing glare his direction. 'Right, because I can't just be concerned about you.'

Realizing he'd taken his own embarrassment out on her, Cord joked. 'Did I just hear your eyes roll at me?'

'No. You heard my eyes doing a new acrobatic routine at your insulting comment.'

'Well then, I give it a solid ten, gold medal.' Cord let a couple of seconds tick by before adding, 'All joking aside, you're right, and I apologize. I'm just tense because I was thinking of everything Chrissy Madison – and Mateo Garcia – have put Carter and Abigail through.'

Like a pricked balloon, Alyssa's irritation deflated. 'Apology accepted. But speaking of Madison and Garcia, do you know what I can't make sense of?'

'Any of it?'

'Well, yeah, but if Mateo had such an issue with Elena, why attack Skye?'

'I've been giving that some thought, and I think I've got an answer. Not to bring up bad memories, especially since it was just two years ago this month, but when Isaac was kidnapped, that was aimed at making *you* suffer. So, maybe he saw how much fun Elena was having with her friend and decided to take it from her in the worst possible way.'

'Makes sense, but if the purpose was to make Elena pay, why kill her, too?'

'Again, been playing this through in my head. According to Dr. Sharp, Elena was rendered defenseless with a blow to the head before her throat was cut. Maybe, like you suggested earlier on, she took Madison and Mateo by surprise, kind of like London did?'

Alyssa let that theory marinate in her mind for a minute. 'That makes as much sense as anything else in this case. I say let's track her down, bring her in, and see if we can get some real answers.'

'Sounds like a fairly solid plan to me,' Cord said.

Approximately ten miles from the turn-off, Alyssa cut her sirens but not her speed; two miles from the turn-off, Cord contacted Jason Lopez to get ready. A mile out, the tension in the car grew more tangible. Especially after Hal sent one final text fifteen minutes earlier that simply read,

Lost tower location in area consistent with turn-off to church.

Another text chimed through, this time on Cord's phone. Grabbing it from the center console, he read it and summarized. 'Lopez has his guys assembled nearby out of sight. If Madison is at the church, we should be able to box her in.'

The moment Alyssa had the turn-off in her sights, she flashed her lights, the predetermined signal alerting the officer partially concealed between some shrubs.

Because of the brief but heavy rainstorm in Montemar earlier this morning, Alyssa could easily see recent tire tracks. The massive butterflies flitting through her stomach took flight and spread outward until her left foot jittered against the floorboard near the brake pedal.

Slowing down, she and Cord exchanged looks. Nostrils flaring, pulse throbbing wildly in his temple, Cord clenched his jaw and made a promise she knew he had every intention of keeping. 'No matter what, If Chrissy Madison's here, her reign of terror ends today.'

Alyssa nodded. 'We'll make sure of it.'

Chapter Forty-Three

Monday, April 26

Though it had been quite some time since Mara had actually thought of herself as Chrissy, the 'Christ follower' name given to her by her deranged father, she now shed it like a snake sheds its skin, reemerging new and fresh. After her father's death, she'd shed lots of things, including the beliefs forced upon her by his tyrannical fist. By the time she turned ten, she figured she was already going to hell anyway, according to her father's reasoning, so she'd quit repenting. If no hope for redemption existed, she saw no point in bothering to try.

She hadn't actually set out to go in the completely opposite direction of her father's rantings, but one night she was given a particularly harsh beating for drawing what she later learned was a pentagram onto her hand. At the time, however, she'd had no idea what it was or what it represented. She'd simply seen an illustration of it, thought it was cool, and sketched it onto her hand during class. She'd meant to scrub it off before she arrived home, but she'd forgotten. By the time she'd remembered, it was too late; her father had already seen it.

Very rarely did her mother ever try to stand up for her against her husband, but that night she had intervened when Chrissy's bottom began bleeding and her back was striped from the belt strap. She remembered her mother screaming for Abel to stop, that Chrissy didn't understand what the symbol meant. After he backhanded her mother hard enough to send her reeling across the room and practically into the fire burning in the fireplace, he'd sent Chrissy to her room. Suffocating her own cries into her pillow, she'd heard her father's Old Testament, archaic rantings interspersed with things she definitely didn't understand. For days, he'd raged about some group of people now in prison for murder and animal mutilations and worshipping the devil and… As usual, she discounted his rants as just another fear tactic he employed.

But she listened in earnest when she heard him mention the supposed power these people thought they gained. Though frightened of what her father would do if he caught her, she snuck out one night so she could carve six-six-six into the tree outside his office. A week later, she tied two branches together to make a cross and planted it upside down on the hood of his car. It was enough to send him off on another of his tangents. He became paranoid that the *Devil Worshippers* had come for him, even going so far as to blame Chrissy for inviting the darkness into their home by 'staining her skin' with the pentagram. Apparently, that had been all it had taken to alert Satan himself as well as his demons.

That was the moment Chrissy learned she had power. In the library she began to research what she could, based on her limited knowledge. And one day, she came across the name Mara, a female wraith in Scandinavian myths that caused nightmares. She liked the sound of it, but when she remembered the story of Naomi from the Bible who became Mara, she loved it. Even if he couldn't know it, the slap to her father's face had been too perfect.

After his death, she finally got the courage to approach Josie Douglas, though she'd had a different last name then. And the rest was fate.

Subconsciously, her right hand rubbed the serpent tattoo circling high on her bicep where it was easily hidden. Interwoven in the snake's skin were the numbers thirteen-thirteen. Draven had a similar tattoo on his back with the number forty-seven.

She'd been the one to relay the story about Josie's father carving six-six-six onto the tongues of his victims. Draven had wanted to taunt the police, knowing they'd have no idea what the forty-seven meant. The simplicity of the taunt had appealed to her as well.

Thoughts of Draven brought a return of that strange, fluttery feeling of sadness as it crept through her veins and wound around her organs. It took her a second to realize she was actually crying at the loss. She couldn't recall the last time she'd cried, much less cried over a person.

But Draven was gone, and she had to accept that. She'd allow herself to mourn him her own way when she made it to Mexico. And as much as she hated to take the risk of returning to the church, she had no choice. She'd wanted to come last night, but the graze to her leg had needed tending, and so, not knowing where else to go, she'd hidden out in Ewan Moore's church until this morning.

From one church to another. For the past three years, long before they'd ever discussed killing a person, they'd planned for the hypothetical need to leave town in a hurry, specifically, if any of their group got busted for the animal killings, like the ones in Montemar. She and Draven weren't responsible for them, but their organization was.

In a drug-induced rage one night long ago, Clarence Whipple had ranted to the others about the cabin he'd once owned out in a place called Montemar. He'd railed on about how the ranchers had run them off, how he'd wished he could've made them pay before he abandoned the place. But having escaped jail time when Ewan Moore and the others had been convicted, he didn't want to risk doing something so close to his own property, knowing it wouldn't take much for the authorities to put two and two together.

Since they knew Whipple no longer owned the cabin, the new leaders relished the idea of getting back at the ranchers and took it upon themselves to start mutilating the ranchers' herds. Mara and Draven had been out casing the ranches with the largest number of cattle when they'd happened upon the church.

Maybe it had been the all-day acid trip talking, but they'd eagerly explored the building before deciding it would be perfect for them. They discussed telling the others but wanted to keep it their own little hideaway, so never did. Not trusting banks or the government, they'd begun squirreling their money away. After rent and their other bills were paid, the remainder of their paychecks went into a giant duffle bag they kept hidden in the rafters of the church. Each week, they added to their stash. After the first six months, they'd stopped counting, trusting that by following Satan, their riches would grow. It was why she refused to ever remove the Italian horn around her neck. However, it also meant that she had no idea how much they'd accumulated over the years.

Tomorrow would've been the day she and Draven counted it together. Their plan was to kill the kids yesterday, sacrifice London tomorrow during the super-moon, and then leave town with the money. They didn't worry about what Mateo's family would think because they didn't care. But that damn cop and her curiosity had ruined everything. Except for one thing. Mara knew the likelihood of the police coming across the cash was less than slim to none, simply because of where they'd stashed it. So now, all she had to do was grab it and be on her way.

She wasn't concerned about the authorities tracking her because she and Draven had purposely left their phones behind when they'd gone after the Sandersons. In preparation, they'd replaced the car's license plates with ones they'd stolen off another car. She expected her disappearance would become one of those cold cases she and

Draven used to watch on television, marveling at the stupidity that got people caught.

Inching her car into the soft grass so it wouldn't sink into the mud and get stuck, she threw it into park and left the engine running as she headed inside. As she stepped foot through the door, she admitted she'd miss the symbolic message of this place.

Without a ladder or Draven's help, reaching the money proved a little more difficult than she'd initially anticipated, but after dragging the old podium to the wall, she was finally able to get her hands on it. Tugging carefully to avoid ripping the duffel bag on any exposed nails, Mara was finally able to free it. Carefully, she hefted it onto her back and secured it with one arm hooked through the straps before maneuvering herself back down to the floor.

She considered making one last trip to the basement but decided there was no need. Lugging the heavy bag to the door, she stepped through. And stopped at the sight that greeted her.

Chapter Forty-Four

Monday, April 26

Alyssa, Cord, Jason Lopez, and three of his men parked a quarter mile away from the church and walked in on foot, not wanting to alert Chrissy to their presence. With Alyssa and Cord in the lead, they moved quickly and quietly until the church and Madison's car, door open, engine still running, were in sight. Alyssa waited for Lopez and his men to fan out, blocking every possible avenue of escape, before she and Cord moved into place. But just as she waved Cord to the right, she held her arm out to stop his movement instead.

There, his body low to the ground as he moved up the steps, stopping just outside the door, stood the same wolfdog that had led her to check the broken window of the basement. The hair on his neck bristled against the tautness of his body while his ears stood straight up, and his teeth bared in an obvious sign of aggression.

As Alyssa tried to come up with a plan to get the wolfdog out of harm's way, Chrissy appeared in the doorway, stomping and hissing at the dog – and completely oblivious to the fact that Alyssa and Cord stood in front of her vehicle, blocking her path. Instead of retreating, the animal bared more of its teeth and shifted as if to pounce. While the idea of an animal, especially this one, taking Madison down appealed to Alyssa on a completely 'that's what she deserves' level of irony and justice, she needed to get it to back off. Placing her fingers into her mouth, she prepared to whistle, knowing, at the very least, her action would distract Chrissy long enough for Cord to take her down, something she wanted for him as much as he did.

But Chrissy had other plans that made the next few seconds move forward at an ultra-slow speed while also occurring far too quickly for her mind to process all at once. Chrissy dropped the duffel bag she was holding, the booming thud as it hit the ground hinting at its weight, before withdrawing a wicked long dagger from the sheath strapped to her side. Without aim, she hurled it at the animal blocking her from reaching her waiting car.

At the same time, Alyssa went for her Taser. Across from her, Cord had the same idea, and together, they hit Chrissy Madison with thousands of volts of electricity, sending the sick, twisted killer to the ground in a writhing agony of misery that allowed Cord to move in quickly, wrenching her over so he could cuff her.

The entire thing felt almost anticlimactic, but Alyssa sent a prayer of thanks that it hadn't ended in another dramatic shootout. While Cord read Madison her rights, the wolfdog turned in Alyssa's direction, staring so unwaveringly into her eyes, it felt like he was trying to see into her soul, and then, just before it loped off, determining the threat to be over, she swore it smiled at her, as though congratulating a teammate on a job well done.

She wanted to call him back, but she had a job to do.

But tomorrow, she vowed to find out if he was a stray, or if he had a home and a wandering heart. If it was the former, she'd hang out and see if he wanted a forever home with her. Something told her the wolfdog would get along great with Ghost.

Chapter Forty-Five

Monday, April 26

As Alyssa and Cord escorted Chrissy Madison, aka Mara, to an open interrogation room, she watched Joe, Tony, and Hal exchange high-fives before offering a thumbs-up. Until Madison filled in some holes, Alyssa wouldn't feel like celebrating.

After escorting a still-fuming Chrissy to a seat, Alyssa took the chair across from her while Cord stood near the door. Alyssa wasn't sure if it was because he felt the need to block Chrissy in case she stupidly bolted for it, or if he simply didn't trust himself to be that close to her yet, especially as neither of them knew what to expect from her in the way of answers.

Before they began, for the sake of the digital recording, Alyssa reminded Chrissy of her right to counsel. She didn't want any possibility of Chrissy walking on some technicality or lie, and so she would carefully dot every 'i' and cross every 't'.

Something Alyssa recognized as superiority brewed in Chrissy's eyes as she waived her rights, much to Alyssa's surprise and glee.

'Please state your name for the record.'

'Why? You already know it.' Chrissy sat back with her arms crossed, doing her best to stare Alyssa down.

Alyssa smiled and repeated the request. 'Please state your name for the record.'

Chrissy rolled her eyes, turned to the red blinking light, and sneered, 'Mara Madison.'

'Is that your alias or birth name?'

'It's my name.'

'What name were you given at birth?'

Chrissy threw her head back and laughed, a sound so evil, it actually sent chills skating up Alyssa's spine, making the hair on the back of her neck prickle with unease.

'Christ Follower. My father – you've heard of him, right? Abel Madison? He insisted on naming me Chrissy because it translated into *Christ Follower*. I guess he got that one wrong, didn't he?'

With effort, Alyssa softened her voice. 'Tell us about your relationship with your father.'

Clearly not expecting that, Chrissy's grin fell, and her eyes narrowed, trying to predict Alyssa's head game. 'He was an asshole who used the Bible as a weapon, both religiously and physically.' Her smile returned. 'I bet you when I die, I'll actually meet him in Hell. Where I will spend an *eternity* rubbing it in his burnt face that he's the reason I worship the Devil and not his cruel, vindictive, *unforgiving* God.'

Careful not to show too much interest, Alyssa asked, 'How do you mean, he was the reason?'

'Just that.' For the next several minutes, Chrissy detailed the many beatings she'd received during her childhood for seemingly small infractions. Yet, it was the beating that occurred after innocently drawing what she later learned to be a pentagram on herself that perpetuated the murderous direction her life would take. As a mother, Alyssa couldn't help but cry out for the innocent girl Chrissy had once been before her father's tyranny had destroyed her. Even though the justice-seeking part of her mind remained immune to the reasons Chrissy had murdered innocent people, Alyssa envisioned the rest of Chrissy's story through the eyes of that lost little girl.

'Later that night, I heard him talking about a Devil Worshipping case from years back. Like most of his rantings, it meant nothing to me. Not even when he mentioned the mutilations that had taken place. I only started to really pay attention and actually care when he fumed about the power those people thought they'd obtained. Even though he never knew it, he'd piqued my interest. And so I began sneaking off to the library so I could research because I didn't want to risk using my own computer.

'Of course, I'd heard rumors about Josie and her father, but I also read he was in prison. Then after my father died – there was a glorious day – I no longer had to fear his wrath or punishments, and I approached Josie.' Chrissy shrugged. 'Took her a while to trust me, but after I showed her a few YouTube videos of my father and a few news clips of him outside the courthouse, boom, I was in. My first congregation' – she grinned at the term – 'I learned I could choose an alias if I wanted to keep my anonymity a little. Like Josie called herself Apate. I think she was like a specialist in blinding humans to the truth and making them believe whatever lie she chose. Pretty clever, if you ask me.'

'And did Neal also have an alias?'

'Eli. It humored him to be known as a prophet of God.'

'And when did you meet Mateo Garcia?' Alyssa asked.

A flash of pain crossed Chrissy's face, there and gone in an instant, but it was enough for Alyssa to fear Madison wouldn't answer the question.

'I met him after I graduated high school. He was a couple years older than me. When we looked at each other, we clicked immediately, like kindred spirits. We were together a long time before he ever told his family I was his girlfriend. But that was more my doing because he hated them so much, I didn't think they really needed to know about me.'

'Why did he hate them?'

Again, Chrissy rolled her eyes, suggesting she knew exactly what Alyssa was trying to trap her into. Still, she answered. 'You know, when I met *Draven*, he was already so full of anger and hate that, really, it didn't take much to draw him into our own church.' She grinned, showing off one sharpened tooth that Alyssa hadn't noticed before.

'All I had to do was offer a shoulder to cry on, a sympathetic, understanding ear, righteous outrage at the way he was being treated so unfairly, ply him with some drugs, and he was more than willing to hear how I'd overcome such treatment. The skeleton of his descent into the darkness was already there when we met. I just helped him move it along a little faster.'

The next part of her questioning would be tricky, especially with a narcissistic personality like Chrissy's. But Alyssa was counting on the woman's superiority complex to keep her speaking. She adopted an expression of doubt as she leaned back in her chair, casually matching her posture to Chrissy's. 'I don't know. If he hated his family so much, why did he only target his sister Elena?'

Shaking her head as if Alyssa was clearly far stupider than she thought, Chrissy said, 'He didn't target Elena. *I* targeted her *friend*. The second I saw Skye at Elena's party, I knew I wanted her to be our first human sacrifice. It was the way she looked right past me before she even knew who I was, like I was invisible or not good enough to smile at or greet. And when we *were* finally introduced, everything about her shouted that she thought she was so superior to us. I wanted to be the one to wipe that smug, haughty smile off her face. The fact that she was one of Elena's best friends was simply icing on the cake. Draven knew Skye's death would have a huge impact on his sister, that her friend's murder would torment Elena for the rest of her life. That's why he *relished* the idea of torturing Skye, of making it so bad, Elena wouldn't be able to close her eyes without picturing it.'

Chrissy laughed, reminding Alyssa that the woman in front of her no longer bore any resemblance to the innocent girl she'd once been. 'Not that Elena would understand what it meant, but the forty-seven Draven carved into Skye's tongue was his way of reminding himself that he'd stolen something from his perfect sister.' Her laughter stopped as she stared blankly past Alyssa's shoulder, almost as if she'd forgotten where she was and to whom she was speaking. 'We planned it out, took a hit of acid to heighten the excitement, and went in. We didn't actually expect anyone else to be at the house that night. I mean, we didn't target *all* of Elena's friends, just Skye. Anyway, I was supposed to knock on the door to distract Skye while Draven snuck in the back. Then I'd force her into the bedroom.' Her eyes closed, and the smile that stretched across her face chilled the room. When she reopened her eyes, she continued, 'Imagine my surprise when I saw Elena open the door instead.

'I didn't even think. I just hit her with the rock I was holding in my hand – in case Skye screamed, we didn't want to kill her too quickly, you know. Then I slit her throat. Draven didn't even know his sister was there until we'd finished with Skye. When I told him, he didn't so much as bat an eye. At all. He just shrugged and said, "Good." He figured it was the perfect way to get back at his parents and Ashlee for always making him feel like a failure, like no matter what he did, he'd never live up to the precious and perfect Elena.'

'Whose idea was it to take London? Yours or…' Alyssa hesitated… 'Draven's?'

'Mine. I mean, they weren't even supposed to be there, so it was like a personal sign, right from my ruler, right? I mean, take another one of Elena's friends – too bad she wouldn't be alive to freak out about it, but we can't always have everything we want – and really take our time, you know?'

'And which one of you decided to kill two innocent children?' Cord asked from his spot near the door.

Alyssa knew even before the cold mask replaced the cruel smile on Chrissy's face that it was the wrong question at the wrong time. But she couldn't blame Cord. Frankly, she was shocked Chrissy had answered as much as she had.

Cocking her head to the side and sneering first at Alyssa then Cord, she recrossed her arms and said, 'I would like to exercise my right to an attorney and state for the record that I felt coerced into answering for fear of my life after what you two did to me at the church.' Turning her face to the red blinking light, she even managed to produce a few tears.

Alyssa pushed back her chair and moved to the door. 'Someone will come and get you soon to escort you to your cell.'

Chrissy's head tilted to the side, and just as Cord's hand closed around the doorknob, she stopped them. 'Why were you at the church today?'

Puzzled by the question, Alyssa turned back. 'To arrest you.'

Chrissy shook her head. 'No. I mean, why did you even go there? Didn't the police already collect all the "evidence" they thought they'd need?'

It finally dawned on Alyssa what Chrissy actually meant. 'We pinged your location and followed you there.'

Chrissy's smirk returned. 'Not possible. I don't have a phone or GPS. Try again, copper.'

Alyssa matched Chrissy's smug look with one of her own. 'No, you're right about one thing. You didn't have *your* phone. We found that at the house you and Mateo shared.' She watched as Chrissy worked the explanation around in her head. When understanding finally slapped her in the face, it flushed through a rainbow of different reds.

Alyssa shook her head in mock sympathy and clucked her tongue. 'Yeah, I guess you didn't see that one coming,

Mateo leaving his phone in the car. Too bad, huh? Was it an accident, or do you think Satan told him to do it?' And then she and Cord stepped out and closed the door behind them.

As they headed down the hall to the incident room to brief the team, Alyssa spotted Lillian Holt standing up front near Ruby's desk. With her was a young man with hair sprouting in every direction but down. His eyes darted left, right, up, down, and behind him as he bounced on the balls of his feet. Alyssa guessed she was looking at August Holt.

Together, she and Cord approached them. 'Mrs. Holt, are you here to speak to us?'

Lillian Holt placed either a comforting or restraining hand on her eldest son's arm. It was difficult to tell, but if Alyssa had to guess based solely on the way the kid looked ready to dart into traffic to avoid speaking to them, it was likely more restraint. 'Yes. This is my son, August. He came to me this morning with some news, and even though he's quite frightened, he knows this is the right thing to do.'

'Why don't you follow us?' Alyssa and Cord turned around and walked back the way they'd just come. Just before they reached the room where they'd interrogated Chrissy Madison, two officers stepped out with her between them. Her expression gave new meaning to the phrase, 'if looks could kill,' but it was the way August Holt suddenly stopped in his tracks and turned away that put Alyssa on alert. If Lillian Holt hadn't been walking just behind him, Alyssa was positive he'd be out the door faster than the Tasmanian Devil. Automatically, she winced at the description her mind had conjured up.

After Chrissy passed, Alyssa decided to go down a few more rooms. Inside, she asked if she could get August something to drink.

His wide-eyed gaze glued to the door, his head wobbled back and forth as he shook his head no.

'Okay. What brings you and your mother here?'

'Before he tells you, I want to make sure you realize that he's very nervous because what he's about to share doesn't exactly paint him in the best light. However, he's here willingly because he didn't actually do anything wrong.'

Alyssa didn't say she'd make that determination herself. 'Of course. Go ahead.'

'I saw what happened to Skye Thursday night.'

Of all the things she'd expected, that had not been anywhere on the spectrum. She pulled out a chair, as did Cord. 'What *exactly* do you mean, you *saw* what happened to Skye Thursday night?'

August Holt's leg bounced hard enough to scrape his chair along the floor. 'I didn't have my share of the rent money, and since I knew my mom wouldn't loan me any, I was going to sneak into the house and raid the stash of cash she keeps in her jewelry box. But Mom and Kenny were both home, so my plans changed, and I decided, what the hell, I'd rob Skye instead.'

His eyes shot from Alyssa to the blinking red light to his mother to the doorway. 'I was planning on going in through her bedroom, but when I got there, I heard some weird noises, and I noticed the door was already kind of open, and so I peeked in. And I saw... I saw... someone sitting on top of her, stabbing her. Then someone else came in the room.' He pointed toward the door. 'That woman. Her hood had fallen, but I got a good look at her before she put it back up. I got scared, and I think I kicked something, and then I freaked out and ran.'

Alyssa recalled the way she'd noticed the trampled grass outside of Skye's bedroom, the way it hadn't seemed to go toward the alley, and realized it was likely from August running away.

'Why didn't you call the police?' Cord asked.

'Because I was afraid I'd go down for the murder.'

Cord's lips formed a straight line as he considered August's answer. Finally, he asked, 'Why would you think that?'

August swiveled his head back and forth several times before blowing out a heavy breath of air. 'I was high as shit, and I didn't think the police would believe me if I told them I'd just stumbled across a murder in action. I figured I'd already turned my phone off a few days earlier so my girlfriend wouldn't be calling me every five minutes, demanding money I didn't have, and so I kept it off and just kind of hung out at a buddy's house for a few days until I could figure out what I should do. And in case you're interested, no, I didn't tell my buddy what I saw for the same reason I didn't call the cops.' His fingernails, already chewed to the quick, returned to his mouth. Once again, Lillian placed her calming hand on her son's arm. 'Tell them the rest, sweetheart. That's the only way you're going to be able to deal with this.'

In a move that reminded Alyssa of his brother, Kenny, August removed his fingers from his mouth and ran them over his head, pulling the ends of his hair before dropping his hands to the table. 'Ah shit. I don't... man... I don't know.'

'Why don't you just try us?' Alyssa coaxed gently. 'If it gets to be too much, you can always stop.'

August placed his head into the palms of his hands before finally sitting back in his chair, his spine stiff as a board. 'Okay, look, I know my mom already told you I was into blood sorcery and stuff. And someone I know recently told me about this group who...' His hands returned to his hair. 'Ah, hell... okay, this group who worships, like, the devil, you know. And so I got an invite...'

Alyssa suddenly knew where this was going.

'And when I went, I saw the same woman I saw at Skye's house, the same one that just passed us in the hallway. She was with some dude. I didn't recognize him because I never actually got a look at his face, but his build was about right, you know? Anyway, I kept, like, staring at her, and then she saw me staring at her, and then I just—I freaked out, okay? Like, in no way cool about it, I just waited until she wasn't looking, grabbed my friend and told him I had to split. After everything I heard that group talking about that night, I was convinced they *knew* I knew. I swear to God I'm not high right now. That's what happened.'

'You mean the group was talking about the murders?' Cord couldn't mask the shock in his voice.

August's eyebrows slammed together in confusion. 'What? No. They were talking about sacrificing animals and shit. And, like, drinking each other's blood and *getting off* on it. It was enough for me to know that wasn't my scene after all.'

Slightly disappointed that both she and Cord had misunderstood what August meant when he'd mentioned "everything" Chrissy's group had discussed, she recognized that an actual eyewitness that could – and had – identified Madison was far more than they could've hoped for. While they still prayed for London Brecken's recovery, they no longer had to rely only on her testimony.

'August, thank you for coming in. Your mom is right. You're doing the right thing. Also, you didn't actually commit the crime you considered. I'd like you to put everything you just told us into writing, but before you do that, I have some advice. Coming from a member of law enforcement, as well as being a mother myself, I suggest you get yourself into treatment. Talk to someone about whatever anger issues you've got. Get some help for your drug addiction. Let your mother and father help, your brother, too. You got lucky this time. Another tragedy stopped you from actually committing the crime you fully intended to commit, but you have to ask yourself what would've happened if you hadn't seen what you did?'

Alyssa didn't miss the shame burning from August's eyes just before he hung his head low. 'Yes, ma'am.'

Later, after thanking Lillian and August again, Alyssa and Cord finally made it to the conference room where the team erupted in a chorus of cheers. But what made her smile was the huge cup of coffee Joe held out to her and which she grabbed gratefully and greedily.

It took the better part of an hour to break down everything that had happened.

When they finished, Joe said, 'Well, Holt's phone being powered down explains why we were only able to ping his last known location as being at his apartment on the Saturday prior to the murders. His girlfriend did say she hadn't been able to reach him since that day. Now, we know why. Hell, I didn't even know someone that young was capable of going without a phone that long.'

Tony nodded his agreement. 'Hedge was really on top of things, so we now know for sure that the fingerprint on the blinds in Skye's bedroom definitively match London's. And while we haven't yet heard back on whether or not DNA from the gum or cigarette located near the van matches Madison or Garcia's, the district attorney is thrilled that all the pieces are coming together for a solid case when it goes to trial.'

Hal sighed. 'That's true, and I'm glad for it, but I've gotta admit I'm a little surprised that, aside from Moore's daughter's involvement, nothing up to this point ties him to our current case, not that I don't still think that something will pop up. But if I'm going to be completely honest, I'm mostly disappointed to hear that the only charges Whipple will be facing, at least for now, are animal cruelty and accessory to a crime after the fact. That being said, I do have some more good news to share.'

Everyone looked at him expectantly.

'You know how we always joke that Ruby somehow always knows everything?'

'Yeah?'

'Well, once again, she's proven that she does.' Hal slid a piece of paper over to Alyssa. On it was a name she didn't recognize, and she raised a quizzical look his way. 'That would be the name of your leak to Monty Cannon. Ruby was grabbing her lunch from the break room, and when she walked out, she overheard that gal' – he nodded his head to the paper – 'chatting about going out on several dates with Cannon. And I quote Ruby's quote, they "talked about everything from surfing to sun to crime in Albuquerque." I'd say go easy on her because Cannon was, and maybe still is, clearly using her, but she definitely needs to be warned.'

'Oh, I'll definitely be warning her and Cannon both,' Alyssa promised.

Chapter Forty-Six

Before dawn on Tuesday morning, Alyssa's phone rang, and Brock groaned louder than she did. 'No, babe. It's not even five yet.'

'Well, clearly, someone didn't get the memo that crimes should only occur between the hours of nine to five.' She kissed his forehead, checked her caller ID, vaguely realizing she should recognize the number, and crawled out of bed to take the call, moving out into the hallway where she wouldn't disturb her husband any more than she had to. 'Hello.' She did her best to stifle the yawn escaping around her greeting.

'Detective Alyssa Wyatt?'

'Yes.'

'This is Dale Manning, London's grandfather. I'm sorry to have woken you, but I thought you'd want to be made aware. London woke from her coma almost an hour ago.'

Better than three cups of espresso, that news jolted Alyssa from half asleep to brutally alert.

'The doctor's been in, and Greta and I know she's nowhere out of the woods yet, but this is a positive first step. She's asking for you. And we know it's early, but we didn't want to wait, and I suspected you wouldn't want us to. I hope I read you right.'

'You absolutely did. Thank you. Detective Roberts and I will be there as soon as we can.'

Back in the bedroom, Alyssa forgot about being quiet for Brock's sake as she threw on a pair of jeans and randomly grabbed a shirt from the closet, ripping it back off and tossing it to the floor after slipping it over her head only to realize it wasn't hers. How did her husband's clothes always manage to make their way over to her side of the closet? She'd growl at him if she wasn't otherwise distracted.

Instead, she dropped another hasty kiss on his forehead, ran to the kitchen, grabbed her keys, and raced out the door. As she was backing out of the garage, she called Cord. 'Do you want to meet me there or should I just fill you in later today?' she asked after announcing London was awake and asking for them.

'Hold on a second.' Cord covered the mouthpiece, but Alyssa could still hear the muffled conversation, so she knew his answer before he told her. 'I'll meet you there. Sara's right. I won't go back to sleep anyway.'

'Sounds good. See you in a few.' Her next call went to Captain Hammond, his voice bleeding through the grogginess of a man who'd been roused from deep into his z's. She almost felt bad. 'London Brecken is awake. Cord and I are headed to the hospital. We'll keep you updated.'

'Call me the second you're out of there.' This time Hammond's voice sounded more like himself, gruff and to the point.

—

As soon as Alyssa and Cord reached the nurse's station, a doctor approached. 'Are you Detectives Wyatt and Roberts?'

Alyssa's heart leaped into her throat, afraid of a sudden turn for the worse in London's condition. 'Yes.'

'I'd like a minute if you don't mind before you go in. It won't take long.'

'Of course.'

'I know we're all excited, none more than her grand-parents, but I want to be very clear that Ms. Brecken still has a long recovery in front of her, and I'd anticipate many setbacks, both physical and mental, before she's fully on the mend. I'm only telling you this because I don't want anyone offering false hope, but we also don't want her to have no hope. We'd like to remain positive while keeping it real, if you know what I'm trying to say here, not very well, I might add. Saving lives is my strong suit, not communication.'

A light laugh of relief escaped Alyssa. 'On the contrary. You're doing fine, Doctor, and we understand perfectly.'

'Then I'll show you to her room. Follow me.'

It wasn't that Alyssa hadn't seen what she deemed as miracles over the years, but she couldn't quite get her head wrapped around London Brecken's alertness. If it weren't for the labyrinth of bruises covering her body, or the way the young woman kept a tight grip on her grandmother's tiny wrist, or how her eyes constantly shifted to the door whenever someone passed by her room, Alyssa wouldn't believe anything had happened to her at all.

Perched on the edge of an uncomfortable, plastic hospital chair, tremors either from old age or nerves causing him to shake was London's grandfather. As soon as he spotted the detectives, he rose to his feet and, moving slowly, met them halfway, giving both their hands a firm pump. Frail in appearance he may have been, but the man still had quite an impressive grip. 'Thank you for calling us, Mr. Manning.'

'It's a pleasure to meet the heroes responsible for saving my granddaughter and...' The rest of his words disap-peared in a cough as he choked up. Wiping his eyes with the sleeve of his shirt, he motioned them over to London's bedside, introducing them to both London and his wife.

London managed a weak smile before her eyes drifted shut again.

'She's merely closed her eyes,' her grandmother whispered. 'Give her a moment. That seems to be all she needs for the time being. I think she's just making sure we're still here, that she didn't imagine or hallucinate us. Poor dear.' Like her husband earlier, tears filled her eyes and spilled over, the drops tapping London's hands where she held them.

'I'm awake.' London's scratchy voice sounded like she had to speak around a mouthful of gravel. Her eyes drifted open and over to Alyssa and Cord. 'I heard you when you came to visit me. I don't remember when that was.' She had to pause to take several deep breaths, wincing with each inhale. 'You told me my grandparents were trying to get to me.' She squeezed her grandma's wrist. 'And you told me the wolf was real.'

The machine monitoring London's vitals began flashing, and afraid she was overexerting herself already, Alyssa placed a palm over London's free hand. 'London, I'm going to need you to take a deep breath with me, okay? Let's get your heart rate back under control. Can you do that for me?' For a full minute, Alyssa concentrated on London's breathing. Only when her pulse returned to somewhat normal did she take a relieved breath herself.

This time, London offered a grateful smile. 'Did you know there was a time I thought I'd make a great nurse? It took me less than a month working in a hospital to know I'm not cut out for the medical field, not at all like my childhood friend, Tracy, who was a born natural at it.' London lifted her eyes to her grandma. 'Do you remember her?'

Greta Manning patted her granddaughter's cheek. 'Of course, dear. The two of you used to line up your dolls for triage when you were younger. And when you were a little older, Tracy would chase the dogs, cats, and chickens around so she could listen to their heartbeats. I imagine that's why she's quite the nurse practitioner now.' Mrs. Manning bent down to kiss the top of London's head.

London smiled up at both her grandparents before facing Alyssa and Cord again. 'My grandparents told me who did this. I never met Elena's brother, but I know now why he seemed so familiar to me. There was just enough of a resemblance. You know, she never said a bad word about him. Not once. She only ever talked about how much she wished he could see how much she loved and missed the brother she'd once had.' Her voice cracked, and again, her machines started flashing.

Her grandfather interrupted. 'Are you sure you're up for this, sweet girl? You don't have to do this now.'

'Yes, Grandpa, I do.'

'Okay, but remember, we're right here with you. You're safe, and we won't be letting any more harm come to you.'

Tears trickled down London's cheek. 'Do you know Elena and Skye used to tease me about my car breaking down all the time—'

London's grandfather interrupted again. 'We're replacing that car immediately when you leave the hospital.' His hand shot in the air, stopping London's protest before it could start. 'Stop your nonsense. It will help with our peace of mind.'

It was a dirty argument, whether it was true or not, Alyssa thought, but it did the trick because London nodded. 'I was saying they used to tease me about tempting a serial killer or some other psycho.' For several seconds, Alyssa watched on helplessly as London's chest heaved in and out, sobs wracking her body as she managed to croak out more questions. 'Why? Why did they do this? To his own sister? Did he hate her so much?'

'Yes, he did.' Though Alyssa admitted it as gently as she could, she knew the impact and pain remained the same. Because it didn't matter that Mateo had been a train wreck sliding downhill on an oiled track that only derailed faster after he encountered Chrissy. The bottom line remained the same – what London had been through, the fate her friends had suffered at Mateo and Chrissy's hands was unfathomable and inexcusable.

'London,' – Cord stepped up so she wouldn't have to strain her neck to see him – 'did anyone else besides Mateo and Chrissy ever join them at the church?'

As if the reminder was too much for her body to handle, London jerked her head to the side, vomiting into the bag her grandfather had intuitively grabbed. Watching the young woman's reaction tore at Alyssa's heart, and she found she could no longer keep her own tears at bay.

A nurse stepped in. 'I'm sorry, detectives, but our patient is still in ICU, and if you're upsetting her, we're going to ask you to leave.'

'No,' London choked out in a whispered croak. 'They're… fine.' Then to Cord, she shook her head, confirming what they already suspected. 'No. No one else.'

Mrs. Manning wiped the sweat from her grand-daughter's forehead before cleaning her mouth with the cloth her husband had dampened with water. 'I know London is still willing to speak to you, but I'm afraid I'm going to have to agree with the nurse – not that you're upsetting her, but that she needs to get some more rest. I think maybe if you return later this afternoon, we can try again.' She pushed London's hair off her face. 'What do you say sweetheart? Will that be okay? Do you think we can do that?'

London nodded, and Alyssa couldn't help but smile at the sudden, if not faded, twinkle in London's eye as she added, 'But only if you and Grandpa promise to leave and go get some rest yourself.'

Both Dale and Greta chuckled. 'You drive a hard bargain, young lady, even if you're in no position to be bargaining at all,' Mr. Manning said. 'But you've got your-self a deal.'

After promising to see London later, they said their goodbyes, but at the door, Cord hesitated. Finally, he turned back. 'I'm sorry. I have one more question, if that's okay?'

Fear froze in London's eyes, but she nodded her agreement anyway.

'Please know there is absolutely no pressure whatsoever for you to say yes. However, I wonder how you'd feel if I brought Carter by to visit in the next few days. Ever since he learned you'd been found, he's asked if he could please come see you.' Cord smiled gently and shook his head. 'He did say he didn't think Abigail was old enough to come to the hospital yet, but he'd allow it if you wanted.'

London's tears drenched her pillow. One braced hand pressed against her chest. 'Yes,' she finally whispered. 'I'd love to see them. If you don't think they'll be too scared. But if you think they will, I'll wait until I get out of here.'

'Thank you. Get some rest, and we'll see you later.'

Before the door had completely closed, London's eyes clapped shut again as her grandmother sang softly to her in soothing tones.

–

Outside, the sun still hadn't even hinted at its appearance. No longer tired, Alyssa was still looking forward to returning home and crawling back into bed beside her husband, if only for a couple more hours. She missed him. As she and Cord walked together toward their cars, she said, 'London's one of the strong ones. With her grandparents by her side, she's going to pull through. It's too bad her parents, as Mr. Manning predicted, didn't care to come see her, but you know what? Maybe that's actually for the best while she's healing. I don't know.'

'I think you might be right. Too many shocks to the system can't be good. And hey, speaking of shocks, did you ever find out if Nick's dance class intentions were what Holly suspected?'

Alyssa choked out a laugh. 'No. But apparently, he came by the house Sunday night with Holly, and Brock did nothing but glare at him and make barbed comments that made everyone, including Mabel, his own mother, feel awkward and mightily uncomfortable. If it hadn't been for their fear for our safety from being shot at, I think Holly would've fed her father his own tongue for breakfast. So, if Nick's intention was to propose, he might be rethinking wanting to marry into our lunatic family.'

'Nah. He'd still be lucky, and Brock would come around. He's just that kind of guy.' Cord stopped moving, placing his arm over Alyssa's to stop her. He cleared his throat and stared up at the streetlights before taking a deep breath and looking back down at her. 'Speaking of families… I wanted you to know, Sara and I talked all of last night and into early this morning – enough to know we're doing the right thing – and I put a call in to the CYFD, specifically to Rosemary Covington.'

Alyssa's heart leaped in excitement. 'You're going to foster Carter and Abigail!' She didn't care about the embarrassing pitch in tone. This was great news.

But Cord wasn't finished. 'Yes, we're requesting we be their new foster home, but more importantly, we want to adopt them.'

Completely out of character for her, Alyssa squealed and threw her arms around her partner, nearly knocking him off his feet when she threw him off balance. 'Oh. My. God. Cord! That's the greatest news ever! What an incredible family they'll have. You'll be great for each other, and Carter will finally be allowed to be a kid, even though he's now going to be a big brother to three siblings.' Tears fell unbidden down Alyssa's face, but she didn't wipe them away or stop grinning from ear to ear. 'And Abigail will have someone closer to her age to play with, and oh my gosh, I just can't quit grinning. I look like an idiot, don't I?'

Cord threw his head back and laughed for a long time. With twinkling eyes, he finally stopped and stared down at her as he added one more little detail. 'I'm glad you feel that way because Sara and I are going to ask you and Brock to be their godparents. And Shelley and Shane's, too.'

Moved beyond words, Alyssa swallowed against the lump lodged in her throat. 'What? Really?' she finally managed to croak out through a fresh flood of tears.

'Yeah, really. We couldn't ask for two better people to be a part of our kids' lives. So, does that mean you'll say yes, even without talking to Brock about it first?'

She didn't think it was possible for her smile to stretch any wider, but the physical ache in her face assured her it had. 'Brock will be just as thrilled as I am. And oh my gosh, I can't even imagine how much Mabel will spoil them when she finds out. But if you think you and Sara are going to change your minds and back out, well, I won't let you. Just saying.'

'Not a chance, friend. We know exactly what we're doing.'

'I do have a question, though. What about London?'

'Well, we've definitely considered that, and I hope she's going to be happy about our decision. Sara and I took Carter and Abigail to the park last night, and at one point, Carter ran over to get a drink of juice and just happened to mention that he wished they could always stay with us. Since we'd already been discussing it, that was our sign. And of course, we're going to want London's blessing and for her to remain a major part of their lives. We'd never want her to feel unwelcome, especially not with all they've been through. After all, she will always be the remaining link to their mother. Eventually, whenever she's up for it, I'd like to introduce her to Sara and the twins, and I'm hoping she'll see for herself how happy Carter and Abigail are with us. No matter what, we'll do what's best for them, and from what we know of London so far, I believe she will, too.'

Overcome with emotion, Alyssa released one more delighted squeal. 'When do I get to tell people? I mean, besides Brock?'

'As soon as we hear back from Covington and get the ball rolling. And once everything's finalized, and they're ours, we'd like to get all four of them baptized together. Given the way their mother was taken from their lives, it just feels right whereas before, we never really thought much about it except as a passing idea here or there. How do you feel about that?'

'I think you and Sara are perfect for all four of them, and like you said, you'll always do what's best, no matter what. I meant it when I said they were lucky. But so are both of you.'

'You know, I don't want to say my sister's death all those years ago turned out to have a happy ending because that's not accurate, but it did lead me here to you, as your partner and your friend, and for that, I'm extremely grateful.' Cord shook his head. 'I didn't say that right, but you know what I mean, don't you?'

'I know exactly what you're saying, and I feel the same way. Also, I have some news of my own I'd like to share.'

Cord arched his brows and waited.

'Remember last night when you called, and I told you I couldn't talk?'

'Yeah, I was calling to ask your opinion about what I just told you.'

'Oh. Well, I couldn't talk because I was on the phone with Jason Lopez, and by the time I finished, it was later than I expected, so I didn't call back. Anyway, I wanted to know if London's wolfdog already had a home.'

'And?'

'And yes, he does. But his owner is an elderly gentleman who lives alone and has trouble getting around. Lately, though it pains him to do so, he's been talking about putting it up for adoption. Of course, my first thought was to bring the dog home with me, as long as his current person is okay with that. However, I plan on asking London if she'd like to keep him herself. I have a feeling she'll say yes, and I have to admit, that's where he belongs if that's what she chooses.'

'I think you're right. It's uncanny the way he seemed so determined to protect her.'

'That's what I thought, too. Anyway, Jason already set something up, so Brock and I will be heading out there this evening. With luck, Schutz – apparently, that's his name, and by the way, he is part wolf, part dog – will want to come home with us as much as we want him to, even if it's only a temporary stay until London can take him.'

Cord crinkled his nose. 'Schutz?'

'Yep. It means "protector" in German. Fitting, right?'

It was Cord's turn to smile. 'Very. Let me know what you find out.'

'I always do.'

A few minutes later, they parted ways, and Alyssa raced back home where she had to force herself not to wake her husband to share the exciting news regarding Carter and Abigail's possible adoption.

After a long, trying five days, she couldn't imagine it ending on a happier note.

A letter from Charly

I do a lot of crazy googling in the name of research for my novels, sometimes to the point where I feel like I need to add a caveat search that promises I'm researching for the books I write. As one can imagine, I've come across some head-scratching, toe-curling, stomach-curdling, nightmare-inducing stuff. As it is, I'm actually quite lucky to have several professionals who are also close family or friends that are my go-to people. For instance, anything law enforcement related, I just blow up the phones of two of my cousins, Bud and Ray Wolfenbarger. If it's a medical question, I head straight to my dear friend, FNP-C Tracy Banghart, who never blinks at the weird medical things I ask.

But this time, for once, I didn't have a go-to person, someone I could just call up and say, 'Hey, since you're the expert…' I mean, I don't *think* I had any go-to folks. But never mind. What I'm trying to say is that researching the occult, specifically the one for this book, had me, let's just say a little on edge at times. Especially when one of the sites popped up a message that said something along the lines of, 'Hey, you know what would be great is if you allow our site to pinpoint your *exact* location.' Considering the very first image on that site made me want to hide under my bed or cower in my closet, maybe burn a little sage, that was a hard and fast hell no and click away. I didn't need to have my question answered *that* badly.

So, why am I telling you wonderful readers all this? Because, while I certainly did my research (that I'm fairly certain I'll be shredding and burning), the truth is that I definitely claimed a writer's ability to take creative license based on what I learned.

Finally, I can't possibly thank you all enough for reading and sharing my books, and for all the reviews and messages you send. To keep up to date on what's coming next and when, you can subscribe to my website, Charly's Chat (www.charlycoxauthor.com/). Or you can follow me on Facebook, Instagram, Twitter (@Charlylynncox), or Goodreads.

Happy reading!

Charly Cox

Acknowledgments

As always, I have a long list of people to thank for their invaluable help, input, and insight.

First, there's someone very special I'd like to give a shout-out to, for answering my Children, Youth and Family Division questions regarding the process that occurs when fostering children, something that takes a kind, patient, giving heart. Karen Snyder, you (and Matt) are heroes in my book for all you do, and I know you've changed the lives of so many children. Thank you for being such a great friend, an amazing cheerleader, and for just everything!

Melissa Naatz, as usual, kept me from losing all my marbles as she talked and texted through hours of plot issues with me. Drew Dooley, my dear friend, pho eating partner, and co-gremlin fighter, always knows the exact right thing to say to get me back on track. My husband, Kevin, for far too many things to list. Keshini Naidoo and Jennie Ayres for their impeccable editing skills that help me hone my stories so that they come out so much stronger than that first draft. You are amazing!

A few people offered insight into the drug-driven, hallucination parts of *The Devil's Playground*. I probably shouldn't list their names, but they know who they are, and so if you're all reading this, thank you! And a giant hug for that awesome person who took all my calls, even though so many of them started with, 'So, I have kind of a strange question to ask you.' At least they weren't *all* drug related, right?

I can't forget my usual group of cheerleaders and supporters who support me every step of the way: Susan Johnson, Theresa and Kevin Rolfe, my group of Forever Friends, Mary McAfee, Hallie Tassin, my sister, Kim, and of course, my son, Timothee (from whom I borrowed the secret password, "Are you my mudder?"). And even though they don't know it, I've got to hand it to Imagine Dragons and Pink for providing the majority of the background music that helps fill my creative well.

Finally, a massive, gratitude-filled thanks to all the readers out there who continue to ask for more books. Thank you for the incredible emails, messages, shout-outs, encouragement, and reviews. You are all the best, and I wish I could hug each one of you. Without you, I couldn't do what I do. If you don't yet follow me, but would like to, please check above for the links.

Until next time,

Charly Cox